HOLLYWOOD
DREAMS

HOLLYWOOD DREAMS

A Karmic Tale of Money, Love,
and Bitchy TV Drama Queens!

L.J. DIVA

★ Royal Star Publishing ★

Love Beats is an imprint of Royal Star Publishing
www.royalstarpublishing.com.au

Originally published as *How I Won Lotto, Moved To L.A., & Married A Really Huge Tv Star!* in 2011 and 2014
Third edition paperback published in 2019
All Rights Reserved, Copyright ©L.J. Diva 2011, 2014, 2019

Trade Paperback ISBN: 978-1-925683-94-3
Large Print Paperback ISBN: 978-1-922307-43-9
Dust Jacket Hardcover ISBN: 978-1-922307-44-6
E-book ISBN: 978-1-925683-93-6
A catalogue record for this book is available from the National Library of Australia.

Cover design: Royal Star Publishing and Odyssey Books
Cover photos: legs - dmvbros/Shutterstock.com
crown - ImagineCGImages/Shutterstock.com
Typesetting in Minion Pro by Royal Star Publishing

Dedications

To the two most important people who inspired this book…

Michael Weatherly and Carmine Giovinazzo.

Need I say more?

Chapter 1

His thick luscious pink lips parted as they made their way toward mine.

My lips quivered with wild anticipation of what was to come. My heart pounded like a jackhammer in my chest.

They were closer now. Only inches of space between us.

My eyes couldn't tear themselves away. My breath came orgasmically in quick, uneven rasps as I struggled for air.

He was so right, so sure he wanted to take me into his arms and make me his.

Those lips were only centimetres away now, coming closer and closer. The world fell away...there was nothing. Nothing but his lips, my racing heart, and a body that was so ready and ripe for him and all he could do to it.

Fingers slid around my arms in vice-like grips, ready to take me to heights I'd never known.

My tongue snaked out to wet my lips, ready to mate, as his found their way home.

They were so hot, so sure, as they planted themselves and hungrily devoured mine…

Bring bringgg. Bring bringgg.

Huh!

Bring bringgg. Bring bringgg.

I came to in a daze, dragged out of my daydreaming. Away from locking lips with the gorgeous TV naval drama actor heartthrob, Michael Anthony, and being taken to heights I *so* wanted to go with him. Coming back down to earth to realise…there was something calling out to me.

Bring bringgg. Bring bringgg.

The phone rang out loud and clear in my apartment's tiny lounge room. I turned from staring out of the tiny window to run from the tiny kitchen to answer it, which wasn't far, since the place was so small. And I *mean* small. I only took five large steps!

I saw that my fave Aussie group, Human Nature, or as I call them, Australia's Singing Sexpots, were still performing some mushy love song on *The Morning Show* with Larry Emdur, so it's no wonder I'd been dreaming of Michael. I grabbed the TV remote and turned the boys down as I reached for the phone. I love Laz, as I affectionately call him. I think he and David Reyne, another morning show veteran, should get together and have their own show, calling it *'The Big Spunk Rats Show'*, with Big Dave and Big Laz. I'd definitely watch it, as would millions of other women aged 25 to 105. Anyhoo, back to reality. "Hello."

"Hello, Ms Tahlia Cameron, I'm Rose Dawson, calling from the Lottery Commission."

Well, knock me down with a goddamn feather!

"Ms Cameron, are you there?"

My heart raced a million miles a second, and I gripped the phone, almost breaking it, not sure if I'd heard correctly.

"Ms Cameron, are you there?"

I knew what it was about. There's only one reason the Lottery Commission calls you at nine a.m. It's because you won the jackpot. The prize. The division one multimillion-dollar dream. I swallowed the lump in my throat that was making my eyes water and pushed a few words past the lump. "I'm here." It came out in a squeak, my hands shaking and sweating.

"Ms Cameron, as I said, I'm Rose Dawson from the Lottery Commission. I'm ringing to tell you that you won division one in lotto last night. Congratulations."

"Oh, my, God!" I gasped in a rush, my body sliding downward, my knees bending, my butt landing on the couch. Thank God I didn't fall flat on the floor and hurt myself. Now *that* would have been a problem. I sat there stunned out of my mind. My head moved back and forth in slow motion. No! I couldn't possibly have, I, oh, my, God! All of the things I had thought about, all of the dreams I had dreamed about, were about to come true. Everything I wanted to do flew past my eyes in a delirium of joy. I would finally do everything I wanted to do. Buy everything I wanted to buy. Have everything I wanted to have...etc, etc, etc.

"Ms Cameron, are you there? I know this must be a shock for you. Everybody we call is in shock. They can't believe they've won either. But they do, and now you have too. Let me tell you a bit more."

I don't think I heard a thing she said, as her voice was this muffled sound warbling down the line. My mind was still full of things to spend my brand-new money on.

"Twenty-three million…division one winner… cheque in two weeks…"

Of course I heard the particulars, which brought me back to reality. "Ah, yes," I muttered. "Are you absolutely sure you have the right person? You have to be positive that the numbers are right, that's definitely my ticket with my name on it. You *have* to be certain." I was animated now. "I mean if you sit there and tell me I've won, and then I go on a huge spending spree and rack up debt while waiting for my money to come in then you call again and say it's been a huge mistake and you're so sorry…" I gasped for air. "Then I'll kill you!"

There was silence at the other end. Well, yeah! I'd just dramatically threatened to kill her!

"Ms Cameron," she went on, unperturbed, "it's definitely your ticket, the right numbers, the right game. I understand your reasoning. A lot of people ask the same things." She gained momentum now. "Besides, you used your lotto player's card when you bought your tickets, so your name is on them, and your details are registered. That's how I contacted you."

We have cards the size of credit cards that we apply for from the Lottery Commission. They have our details, phone, address etc. It's all registered when we buy tickets. So if we win, they can call us. And if we lose the ticket, they still know it's us, and we get our money.

"Believe me, Ms Cameron, you have won division one in lotto. Twenty-three million dollars."

"Oh, my God!" I interrupted. "Oh, my God, oh, my God, oh, my God!"

She laughed. "That's understandable, Ms Cameron. It's going to take some getting used to being Australia's newest millionaire."

"Screw Australia! I'm getting the hell out of here," I blurted out.

"Oh!" She seemed shocked. "Well, that's up to you. Remember though, you can't cash the cheque for two weeks. Do you want to be in the news? You can stay a secret if you wish."

"Ah," I said, thoughts coming in quick succession. As much as I'd love the people in my life to know I'm now filthy stinking rich, so I can brag to my heart's content and tell them where to go when they come slinking out of the woodwork scavenging for money...I decline.

"Okay, that's fine. We will need to meet so you can sign some papers and claim your cheque. When will you be in?"

"What's today?" I asked, having a mental gap. "Hell, I'll be in today!" I remembered it was a weekday. Who cares about the book I'm writing, or the dolls I want to bid on, on eBay? I've won shitloads of money, and I can buy whatever the hell I want!

"Okay, Ms Cameron, that's fine. We'll see you today. Come to the third floor of the Lotteries Commission in town, and we'll fill out all the paperwork. We'll see you then."

"Okay," I managed.

"Oh, Ms Cameron. You *have* won twenty-three million in lotto. I guarantee you."

I sat there like a stunned mullet, the phone still in my hand, my backside still plastered to the couch. Images and dreams screaming through my mind of all the things I'd do and buy. I inhaled, deep and slow, then exhaled, once, twice, three times, and then realised the phone was beeping. I put it in its cradle and sat there contemplating my future.

"What the hell am I going to do?" I kept repeating to myself as I hauled my big butt up and stumbled over to my desk in a daze, still stunned out of my brain. This hasn't? Could it? Really? No! Don't even joke with me! My bladder threatened to overflow, but I ignored it as I fell into my chair and just stared out the window at the crappy, weedy front yard, and the dead tree across the road. The suburb I'd re-named Hicksville. No more Hicksville. Hicksville will be gone forever in two weeks.

"Two weeks?" you ask.

Yes, two weeks. That's when I'll be able to cash my cheque and have all that glorious money in my bank account. Wait, it will take longer than that to get my visa and passport. Damn, I don't want to wait that long. Well, who cares! L.A., here I come!

Oh, my God! I moved around in my seat at a frantic pace as I came up with one good idea after another. *I have to get rid of my junk and have a clean out. Put in notice with the banks, the bookshop, the library, the doctors, and oh, my God...I'm a freakin' multimillionaire! A mega multimillionaire! I'm freakin' rich beyond my wildest dreams. Woohoo!*

My heart was still racing, and I was panting in shock. Oh, my God! Tears sprang to my eyes. *Oh, my God! I'm going to live the life I've always wanted.* I wiped at the teary overload. *I'm going to leave Hicksville, move overseas, start my companies, publish my novels, and with God as my witness I'll meet and marry Michael Anthony…* Okay, so I sound like Scarlett O'Hara at this time, but seriously, the moment calls for dramatic poise.

The tears flowed forth, and I sat there at my little old desk, in little old Hicksville, and thanked God for the abundant riches he had bestowed upon me in good faith.

For a few moments, I let the quiet wash over me, then I opened my gratitude diary.

Well, actually, it's a folder, full of pictures of things that I want to buy, have and do.

As I turned each page, starting with wanting to be a millionaire, I thanked God for the abundance he had given me to look after and to do much with. I thanked him for the financial freedom so I could move to L.A. and be with Michael – pages three and four – publish my first novel and make the movie – five and six – start my fashion and jewellery labels – seven and eight. I moved through the folder and scanned the pages, so thankful I could now have all that I want. Tears sprang to my eyes, and I let them fall. I was now about to have to most amazing life ever and believe me, I thank you, God.

An hour later I flew into town. I live about forty minutes out of the city, but when money's at stake, the time flies. I was now a multimillionaire. Owner of twenty-three million dollars. I arrived at the Lottery Commission, and three floors up met Rose Dawson, the woman who'd called.

"I'm so glad you could make it. Congratulations. Do you believe it yet?"

"No," I replied, shaking her hand and taking in her black hair, blue pinstripe business suit and pearls. "I guess I won't believe it until I'm told the money's in my bank account."

"Well, it is an awful lot to take in," she said, striding around her desk.

Awful? I thought with a cocked brow.

"Most people are still overwhelmed days, weeks, even months later." She sat down. "So, what do you plan on doing with your money, may I ask?"

No, you can't! It's none of your business! "Moving," I said, hoping I hadn't said the other thing out loud. "Lots of shopping. New car, etc. You know, the usual." I just wanted to snatch my cheque and run the hell outta there.

"That's what most people say," she said, signing a few forms and handing them to me. "Sign here, here and here." I read the forms first, and then with overwhelming happiness, signed my name. "And here's your cheque. Now, you can't bank this for two weeks. The money's not applicable till then. Well, you can take it to your bank, but you can't cash it."

"That's fine," I said, gingerly taking the twenty-three million dollar cheque from her, the half million was a nice extra bonus of extra money. I folded it and tucked it into my bra for safe keeping. "Should be safe in there till I can get to the bank." I saw the comical look on her face. "Do you know where the closest bank is? I haven't been here for over ten years."

"Just down the mall," she said, standing. "I'll show you out, and you can be on your way to a big, brand-new world."

I followed her to the lift, thanked her before she left, and thought about what to do next on my way down. I suppose I could have a bit of a shop while I'm here. After all, I won't be coming back. What a great idea! I headed for the first store, remembering that big fat cheque in my bra, waiting to be banked.

I arrived home six hours later, laden with bags from almost every store. Since I didn't have the money yet, I just booked it up on credit. Isn't credit wonderful! Buy now, pay later.

Feeling so damn good, and having a need to dance, I threw a cd into the player and cranked it up loud. To hell with my soon to be ex-neighbours I say! Indecent Obsession, an Aussie pop-rock group from the late eighties, early nineties, belted out of the speakers. To think, it was over twenty years ago that four young, good looking guys burst onto the Aussie scene.

Girls loved them, and I had a huge crush on the keyboardist for six years. Ironically, his name is Michael, and he's got brown hair and blue eyes! Mmm, I see a pattern forming! I still love listening to them and wish they'd reform like all the other eighties bands. It would be so cool to see and hear them again.

So, here I am in my small Hicksville bedroom, listening to good music, dancing around, and sorting out everything I'd bought, knowing I had to have an almighty clear out. After all, I wasn't going to be caught dead in L.A. in some of the crap I owned.

I suppose at this stage I should tell you a little more about myself. Well, I live in Australia, in a state I won't name as I'm being mysterious, and because I don't want you thinking you can hunt me down. As much as I don't mind living here in Aus, now, L.A. is more important.

I live alone. At my age I damn well should I suppose. A wannabe singer, author, collector, entrepreneur, businesswoman of the year, and a fashion and jewellery designer, struggling away to get my designs out to the world.

Except I'm no longer struggling, thanks to those wonderful coloured dollars of money.

Which reminds me...the time is flying by and there's a hell of a lotta stuff I gotta start doing. Let's see now. I told the girls at my local bookstore they wouldn't be enabling my Nancy Drew addiction anymore – they were sad at that. Oh, and I got to tell the girl at the lotto counter that she wouldn't be serving me anymore. I'd won the jackpot. Take that girly! She *could not* get over the shock. I need to cancel my memberships everywhere. *And* I get to quit my crap shit job. Woohoo!

My boss didn't like me quitting, although I only had the job to pay the bills while I got my designs up and going. He begged and begged me to stay and work for him.

"But, Tahlia, my sexy little minx."

What the?!

"I do not want to lose you." His fat greasy hand crept over to my leg, while his filthy black tongue licked his fat, cracked lips in anticipation. "You my most valued employee." His fingers reached me, and I slapped them away in disgust.

Considering this guy is a sleazy old sleazebag, I figured it was a definite NO to me staying and working there. "Listen, shit head," I hissed, "you think you're such hot stuff and you can hit on all the girls who work for you. Since you don't hire guys, then I'd say it's a fair assumption that you only hire girls to perve down their tops and up their skirts. Ugh, how gross."

I stood up in the store's small office, which I'd once called work, and with great delight said, "You can stick ya job up ya fat arse 'cause I've won shitloads of money in lotto and don't need you touching me up 'cause ya think ya can." I moved toward the door. Ugh, the poor girls left behind will get twice as much crap now that I'm leaving, but that's their problem. They need to stand up for themselves! My boss also seemed to think now that I had loads of money I should pay him back as a thank you for giving me the job and helping me out.

"But, Tahlia." His fat sweaty body managed to get from the desk to the door in one quick step. He spun me around and slammed me back against the door.

His gross body was against mine, his foul breath overwhelming me. I tried to quash the ever rising panic that sped around my body. I moved my head to the side, trying to get fresh air. I was unsuccessful.

"Tahlia!" His tongue licked his lips again. "You won lotto? You have money? Maybe you, no, you *should* pay me back for helping you out all these months."

What the hell?!

Oh, crap, I should've kept my big mouth shut, and my lotto win to myself. That'll teach me for opening wide and letting words spew out of my mouth before thinking about it, I thought.

Bugger!

His hands tightened around my arms, and he pressed his body closer against mine. I felt his erection eagerly trying to find its way through his pants to get some relief.

EEEWWWWWW!

"You should pay me back, Tahlia, for helping you. That would be so nice of you...wouldn't it?"

Well, you know what I told him. "GET STUFFED you fat arrogant bastard." I pulled my right knee up into his groin and shoved him back into the desk. He yowled in pain and tumbled to the floor. I shook the feeling of him off and spat at him. "I should call the cops on you, you lowlife piece of scum. GET STUFFED!" With a kick to his groin for extra good measure, I slammed the door open and ran out of the shop to my car. I almost sped all the way home, then lay panting and shaking on my couch. "Ugh, how gross. How could I have put up with that? Ugh." Once I'd showered three times, and calmed down enough, I checked my phone messages. There was one very important call waiting for me.

"Ah, Ms Cameron. This is David, from your bank. I'm just calling to let you know that your money is now deposited into your account. You can start spending it any time now."

My money was now safe and sound in my account. Snug as a twenty-three million dollar bug in one damn big rug.

Fan, freakin', tastic!

I went over my list of things. I needed statements to get a passport as I had to prove who I was and where I lived. Then a passport so I could apply for a visa to move to L.A. After all, I was going to be with my gorgeously gorgeous Michael. So, during the week I found a post office that took passport applications and the photos to go with it. I had an appointment for all of five minutes and was told my application would be sent off, and I'd get it in about two weeks. Well, I couldn't wait.

I rang the Australian branch of the American Consulate to find out which visa applications I would need and any other relevant details such as when to make appointments, get my fingerprints taken etc. There's a lot required when you apply to move to the U.S. While I was waiting for my paperwork I got to work, emailing someone who follows my blog.

See, I own and write a blog coz I love bitching about all things big and small. I started it up because I found myself sitting in front of the TV yelling abuse at everyone who said or did anything stupid. I was good at it and decided to start a blog, so I could bitch to the world. I also write about my fave actors, Michael Anthony, and Carmine Gionetti, from one of my fave crime show spin-offs. Things like what movies they're in, what functions they attend, magazines they may pop up in, or the latest entertainment show they give an interview on.

My posts attracted my first follower, Sin Mainwaring, a lawyer who lives outside of L.A. I had sent her a copy of the book I'd written, a raunchy sex novel that our fave actor had inspired so much. And believe me, he inspired most of the sex in the book. We did it all over the place, er, ah, I mean the *characters* did it all over the place.

I emailed her about me moving to L.A. and, of course, all the particulars that I had to have. Cough, Michael Anthony, cough. Our emails ran as follows:

Hey Sin,

Oh, my freakin', God I'm moving to L.A. I won lotto baby and am on my way. Just waiting on my passport and visa. I want you to be my lawyer. I need to show the U.S. Consulate I'm ready to set up or invest in a company. I need to know about registering/copyrighting /trademarking my company names. If there are any businesses I could buy out. Are you up for it?

Tahlia :)

Sin replied with...

Hey, Tahlia,

Fuck yeah! I'm so happy you want to move here. I'll be your lawyer. Okay, so I looked into it, and you need to pay to register your company name etc. But you need a place of residence. Do you want me to file on your behalf? By the way, how are you paying me?

Sin

I replied back...

Sin,

I can pay you in person, or in shopping. Go ahead and register my business. I'll put the money in your PayPal account. I need you to find a place for me to live, as close to Michael Anthony as possible. Book a couple of rooms at a hotel in the same postcode so we can look for a house nearby. Give me a number I can call you on.

Tahlia :)

I got Sin's number, and we started talking. "I want a warehouse, and since I'm thinking big, I need at least a hundred workers to make the clothes, print the clothes, and pack and ship. I want it all in the same area I'll be living in. And have you tracked down where Michael lives yet?"

"Fuck you, I'm not a miracle worker, but yeah, I have. I'm a lawyer, I have privileges."

"Of course you do. Let me know about the warehouse. I want a new one."

So, that was the first of many calls to Sin. While waiting for my passport and visa, I had many things to do, so my life was incredibly hectic. *And* I still had months to wait. Argh!

*****

Since money had been tight for so long, I had struggled to scrape together enough cash for a one hour singing lesson a week. Now, I could make it a two hour lesson a day. The teacher didn't mind the extra money, and she knew I was determined to be the best I could be. Definitely not a world-famous rock or opera singer, but one who could carry a melody, sing a song, and look and sound good while entertaining the crowd at hand.

I had also been taking free weekly self-defence classes at my local gym since I was unable to afford those either. Now, I paid for extensive classes and added martial arts to my already full schedule. But as it turned out, this body could only do so much, and twist and turn in so many ways. So the instructors found my strengths – there weren't too many of them – and worked on those while helping to fix my weaknesses, which were unbelievably far and wide.

I also got into weapons training. I was going to be living in California, and I needed to be able to keep myself safe. I trained hard, with firearms and other weapons such as bats, swords, knives etc, that may be used against me. I know, it sounds strange, but muggers, killers, and home invaders will use anything against you these days. I made sure I knew how to deal with almost any weapon. My teachers were great; they helped me figure out some quick, simple and efficient moves that my body would allow, and would get me out of any situation without being hurt, and without turning myself into Chuck Norris or Bruce Lee!

I worked out hard in the gym, and danced up a storm at the local studio, including pole dancing. I found a doctor to suck out any fat I couldn't burn off. Liposuction baby! I also found a dentist who whitened my teeth and gave me a Hollywood smile. I needed one since I was moving there, and had to look my best when I flew in to L.A.

I had my body hair permanently removed, and my face and body sucked free of all the nasty germs that were embedded in my pores. I thoroughly enjoyed my first time at the day spa. It was very relaxing and invigorating. I had some moles removed that were either sore or itchy, or just in the way of straps. 'Cause God, I've got millions of them. Really!

I had defensive driving lessons and learned how to drive on the other side of the road, succeeding in getting an international driver's licence. I donated money to the Cancer Council as a thank you to God for the abundant riches he'd given me.

I even had a Nancy Drew luggage set made in turquoise blue with black embroidered silhouettes on it. And on top of all that, I collected as many Nancy books as I could, to try and complete my collection before I left. Especially since time flew by. And believe me, you really don't need to know any more details than the above mentioned. Otherwise, you'd be bored to death if you're not already. And we're not even through the first chapter! Ha, ha, ha!

My passport arrived, and thanks to Sin, I could send in my visa applications. A week later the U.S.

Consulate rang and told me my appointment was in two weeks. Two weeks, oh, my God, oh, my God, oh, my God! I needed to get prepared...and have everything ready...I had to come up with documents...

God, where are they...I needed time, time I tells ya. 'Cause right now, I'm running around like a chook with its head cut off.

*****

The U.S. Consulate was in another state, so I flew over the day before. It's only open in the mornings, and I made sure to be there when the doors opened at eight thirty a.m., even though my appointment was for nine. After going through security and being looked over by the guards, who were *so* not good looking, I sat and waited.

"Ms Cameron," a woman called, after what seemed like a very restless eternity.

"That's me." I dove out of my chair and followed her into her tiny white office, sitting in the chair she pointed to.

She seated herself and looked at me. "So, tell me why you want to live in America."

Well, I wasn't expecting that, although I should've, since it was of great importance, and pretty much bordering on the whole, me getting a visa to move there thing. I certainly wasn't going to tell her I only wanted to move there to meet and marry Michael Anthony. No way! She'd consider me a stalker. "Well," I started. "I've lived all my life here in Australia, and now that I've won lotto, I'd like to spread my wings and experience the joy and wonder of another country." I gazed at her with great expectations. No... *not* the book!

"Nicely put," she said, reading over my application.

I twittered in my seat – no, *not* the social media website – and tried not to show my nervousness.

"I see you have plenty of money to support yourself. Congratulations on winning lotto." She looked up at me with a huge grin.

"Thanks. I still can't believe it." Her smile made me relax a little.

"I see you already have a business plan in place."

"Ah, yes. My friend who lives in L.A. is a lawyer, so she's put it all into place for me."

"That's very nice of her," the woman said, not giving me an indication of anything.

"Yes, it was," I replied before silence fell around us. I glanced at the walls and saw posters of America, advertising the many states and touristy things you could do there.

A few moments went by during which all I wanted to do was pee myself with nerves.

After what seemed like forever, she looked up. "Well, Ms Cameron, everything is in order, and your application will be looked at. We'll be in touch." She stood and extended her hand.

I almost leapt out of my seat to shake it.

That was it. A few heart wrenching, gut twisting, mind altering minutes.

"Thank you for seeing me," I said, and walked out

the door. I stood on the steps outside the Consulate, my brain slowing down long enough to understand it had happened. All I had to do was wait for my visa. But in the meantime, it was still early, and I didn't leave until later, I may as well get in a spot of shopping while I was there. After all, I'm a multimillionaire. I could buy whatever the hell I wanted.

I ended up going home with far more than I'd taken, so it was just as well I had a case that I'd only thrown a few outfits into. As if I needed any more than I already had! I wanted to look good and all, but does a person *really* need *everything* I'd bought?

Of course the answer is *yes!* When one wants to be a fashion icon, darling, *one needs EVERYTHING!*

*****

Here is another month flying by with me running out to the mailbox every day waiting for my visa. It will come, it will come. I believed! In the meantime, more lessons, more lipo, more dancing. I was going to be a new person when I flew into L.A.X. I was very determined about that. There were a million emails and phone calls to Sin about the business. She'd found a warehouse that sounded perfect, a couple of struggling businesses I could buy out, and she'd gone house hunting in the same area Michael lived in.

And, of course, I'd been scouring the internet for all things Michael. I had to keep up with his comings and goings. Find out where he was eating, where he was shopping, where he went for relaxation. I knew every little detail about Michael Anthony. Every little detail that mattered that is. And no, while you may think I am, I am *not* a stalker!

Oh, yes baby, this will happen. I was prepared. As prepared as I could be. I had all my business and legal papers ready. I knew which boxes of my stuff I wanted to be sent over to America once I found a house. I was ready. And then the parcel post van delivered a huge bulky envelope labelled – "The U.S. Consulate". I ripped it open in apprehension, and with very shaky hands I pulled out a pile of papers and read from the letter sitting on top.

Dear Ms Cameron,

Congratulations on your successful visa application.

Chapter 2

OH, MY HOLY FREAKIN' GOD!

It's happened. It's come. It's happened and it's come.

My hands were shaking so badly I dropped some papers and they fluttered to the ground. Snatching them up, I ran into the lounge room, and sitting at my desk, spread the papers out.

Dear Ms Cameron,

Congratulations on your successful visa application. Welcome to the United States of America as a new resident.

I read the letter five times. I had to make sure it was really real. There in black ink on white paper. The words swam before my eyes. I was moving to America!

Oh, my, holy, freakin', God! Yes, I do repeat myself. A lot! I sat there shaking my head. *I can't believe it's true. I can't believe it's true. But it is. It is true. I have been given permission to move to the United States of America. Oh, my God!*

Oh, my God, there's so much to do. There's, there's, there's getting my tickets, and packing my bags. All of the stuff I can and can't take. There are rules to flying, and I need flight socks – don't want to get a DVT now do I – I had so much to do.

I consulted my calendar and diary. "Okay, let's see," I said, my finger running down the week. Absolutely nothing. Well, I need to call Sin and see if she can come to L.A., book my hotel room, and sort out car hire. I slid all the papers into a folder. I'll have to see when she can meet first. That will depend on when I go. I grabbed the phone.

"Hello, so when are you coming?"

"I got my visa today," I squealed. "It just came by delivery. All my papers are inside, and I can come anytime. When can you be in L.A.? Can you hire a car and where are we staying?"

"Whoa, just a minute. I can't be there until Wednesday, and we'll use my car till you get yours. I can make some reservations at that hotel we picked out. It's not summer yet, so they won't be busy. When can you fly in?"

"Well, it's Monday now. I need a few days to pack and prepare and buy my tickets etc. So…I can see if my flight lands on Thursday."

"Fantastic. You're comin' to L.A."

"Yay," we both squealed.

"I'll make a phone call to the hotel and call you back."

"Okay," I said, ending the call.

Five minutes went by.

Ten minutes went by.

I busied myself with my list for preparing to move to America. It's a list I'd had for many months. I always added to it when I thought of something new to take or do. There's a lot of stuff in my notebook. Lists of places to go, and things to do. What I'll do, and buy. What I wanted from the coming week and year. What I wanted in my house. How I wanted my wedding…

The phone rang…twenty minutes after our call.

"We've got two rooms reserved at The Colonial Inn, right next to each other. Twenty-eight and twenty-nine. I take it you want twenty-eight."

Twenty-eight is a strange number for me. In numerology, when you add up all of your birthdate, you get a number. Mine is eleven, which is the master number. Apparently, you're not supposed to add the two ones, but if you do you're also a two. And Michael claims eight is his lucky number, so, two, eight. Twenty-eight. There's gotta be a good omen in there.

"Of course," I replied. "When do we get our rooms from?"

"I can get them on Wednesday night when I drive down. I told them a filthy rich millionairess is moving to our country and needs a nice place to stay while searching for a house and setting up her multimillion dollar clothing business. That sucked them into waiting. Besides, you're paying."

I snorted at her description of me. "I suppose their eyes bugged out of their sockets when you told them I was filthy rich?"

"Of course they would have."

"Okay. I'll track down my tickets and let you know the details. Bye."

Okay, so there it was. My hotel was booked. My chauffeur was ready. All I needed were my tickets and a ride to the airport. I called the airport.

"Hello, you've reached Main City Airport, this is Tamara speaking, how may I help you?"

"Hello, I'd like two seats, side by side, to Los Angeles this week. Qantas business class." I heard a tapping of computer keys and a message on the loudspeaker in the background. I tapped my foot, then my pen. Waiting.

"Okay, then." Some more tapping. "When did you want to go?"

"Well...I'm hoping to get to L.A. on Thursday morning. So, whatever flight lands then. On *their* Thursday morning that is," I said, having no idea about the whole dateline thing.

"Okay, you're in luck. Two seats, side by side in business class on Qantas flight 208, Thursday morning at ten. How's that?"

Flight 208 did she say? Ha, another numerology omen. Things were looking good.

"Sounds great, thank you so much." I wrote down the details in my notebook. All I had to do was pack according to the regulations, get rid of my stuff, and then...leave the country.

I called Sin. "Thursday morning I arrive. Qantas flight 208 from Oz. Yay."

"All right," she crowed. "I'll be there to pick you up and we will paar-taay."

"Let's just get to the hotel first. I'll want a shower and a lie down before we go out. We have a lot to do next week."

"We do," she agreed. "But a lie down? Seriously? This weekend we are gonna paar-taay!"

*****

My, God, it's happening. All of my dreams are about to come true. True, true, true. Yes! Woohoo.

I surveyed my bedroom. I had already packed my clothes, jewellery, and personal belongings into my new turquoise blue Nancy Drew luggage set. The amount of times I packed and repacked. Sheesh. All of my cosmetics were sealed nice and neat in a ziplock bag. A varied assortment of personal books and folders were in my carry-ons ready to go. Having thrown in a few other items I couldn't do without, I zipped shut and sealed my luggage.

God, there was so much I had to have on me. Just for a plane flight! All I needed now was a moving company to pack and ship my monstrous Nancy Drew collection, and a rubbish removalist for all the crap I had left to get rid of.

I marked off each job as I did it in my notebook. Phone calls to the removalists and the rubbish men. I also called my landlord to let him know I was moving out the next day. Yay!

*****

"Well, Miss, that's all of it."

I watched the last of my boxes being packed into

the back of the moving van. "Thank you so much," I said, signing the papers he handed me. My stuff was going to be stored in their warehouse, which I had already paid rental for until I wanted it shipped over. I watched the van drive away then turned to survey what was left; my luggage and some cleaning supplies.

My disgusting landlord walked in. "Sad to see you go, you've been a good tenant."

Yeah, right, I thought. *You lecherous old perv. I was only good for you to perve at.* Ugh! "Yeah, well, time to move on." I hadn't told too many people about winning lotto as I didn't want all of the leeches to come out of the woodwork expecting a handout. A car pulled up to the curb. "Taxi's here," I called in relief, gathering as much as I could with lightning speed.

"Here, let me help you," my lecherous landlord said, reaching for one of my flash blue suitcases with his meaty, sweaty hands.

"No," I cried, then recovered as the taxi driver came to the door. "The driver will help. You don't need to." I threw my luggage at the poor driver and hurried him back to the car. "That's all of it," I told him, stuffing my overstuffed bags into the backseat.

"All right, Miss." He shut the boot – that's trunk to some – and got into the driver's seat while I flung myself into the back and landed among my bags.

"Ah, what do you want me to do with this stuff," my ex-landlord yelled.

I realised he meant the cleaning supplies. "Keep them," I yelled back as we pulled away.

"Where to, Miss?" the driver asked.

"The airport hotel please." I leaned back and sighed in immense relief.

*****

That night, before going to bed, I laid out my flying outfit – I had to be comfy, but cool, not slobby in track pants and ugg boots – so I had chosen a nice pair of black cotton pants and a blue top. I had an extra set in my carry-on bag for changing before we'd land.

My visa, passport, and papers were in an undergarment safety belt, and I had a blow up neck pillow as well. I even had flying pills from the doctor, just in case.

Settling into bed for my last evening of Australian TV, I watched the gorgeously gorgeous Michael Anthony. Drooling as he removed his shirt, I sighed longingly, my hand snaking its way to the big furry nest upon his chest, so ready to tangle itself in the soft silkiness of his hair.

What can I say? The man is gorgeous, insatiable, sexy, amazing, blah blah blah. I want him. And I will have him. My feelings are so overwhelming that my heart dances in double time every time he comes on TV. God, I love that man. And considering I had used Michael as inspiration for one of the characters in my book, it's no wonder I fell in love.

He's suave, he's dashing, he's downright sexable.

"Sexable?" you ask.

I have no idea what that word means, but I like it. Michael is "The Sexiness". The Sexiness that is

Michael. The sexable Michael Anthony!

"Stop," you cry. "You'll make him blush."

Damn right! But I want him to do so much more than that...

Damn it...an ad break...GO AWAY!

I fell against my pillows, my hand dropping to my side, and I made a face at the TV. Four bloody minutes of idiotic crap before my Mikey came back on. I watched the rest of the show with adoration for the producer and director. *I love you for getting Michael shirtless.*

I'm dreaming big. But to get Michael, I have to be with Michael, and that means moving to L.A. America doesn't let just anyone in. Especially stalkers. Which I'm not.

I sniggered under my breath, switched off the TV, and rolled around for awhile trying to get comfortable. Finding a suitable position, I fell into a deep Michael-filled dream.

*****

I was awake at seven and eager to go, and bounding out of bed with newfound excitement, I showered and dressed. Though my flight was for ten, I needed to be there two hours early for check in and safety measures.

L.A. here I come!

Making sure I had everything, I grabbed a taxi and arrived at the airport right on time. When I'd unloaded my fancy Nancy luggage set, I rolled into the terminal and all but ran to the queue for my plane. Standing for thirty minutes was tiring, but I made small talk with a woman who inquired about my luggage.

"What lovely blue luggage," she said, her eyes taking in the black embroidered Nancy silhouettes. "I've never seen anything like it." She looked up at me. "Are you going for awhile? You seem to have so much."

I felt a little annoyed at the intrusive question. But then *we were* at an airport, where people usually fly away to somewhere else. And they did usually take luggage with them. "I'm moving to America," I said, a small smile on my lips.

"Why?" the woman asked in horror. "What have they got that Australia doesn't?"

Michael Anthony!

Oops, I hope I didn't say that out loud. I snuck a look. *Nope, no reaction. Thank God I didn't say that out loud. It's true enough. Australia doesn't have Michael Anthony. He may have visited twice, but he doesn't live here. I can start my clothing and jewellery business anywhere. Buy a house and do it up how I want. Have my two cats and two dogs, but I can't have Michael Anthony because he doesn't live in Australia. I could settle for some dickhead Aussie bloke who'd want to sit on his fat, lazy arse all day doing nothing the minute he finds out I've got loads of money.*

Hey, where did that thought come from? I silently berated myself for thinking such an idiotic thing. *What were you thinking?* I asked my brain.

Obviously, you weren't, came the reply.

Wait, what? I got a reply from my brain. Good

grief. I cocked my left brow and tried not to look crazy. Now *that* was strange.

After all, I *don't* want some dickhead Aussie bloke 'cause I think too highly of myself to stoop that low. I'm not *that* desperate. I sighed inwardly. *It's still true though. Michael isn't here and I want him more than anything in this world.*

More than your money? my brain asked.

Stop that, I snapped silently. *Well, no. I want them both equally. End of discussion.*

I made it to the front of the line, sent my bags off on the conveyor belt, made my way through security, and away from the unnerving woman who wanted to start World War three because I was moving overseas. Settling into a nice comfy chair in the business class lounge, I watched my fellow passengers, studied the detail in the carpet, watched the planes go by, and wasted time by dreaming of my wedding to Michael.

"Would the passengers of Qantas flight 208 to Los Angeles, California begin boarding."

"Oh, finally," I muttered. Gathering my carry-on bags, I made my way to the loading zone, handed my ticket to the attendant with a smile, and walked down the aisle into business class. I found my seats, stashed by bags, and sat down to watch everything going on around me. It was very nice. Business is a class of its own. Sure as hell not economy, but not first either.

Who wants first? It would be first to crash into a mountain or sea. Argh, don't think about that. Did I mention I'm scared of flying? I strapped myself in and waited, closing my eyes and breathing deeply, thinking positive thoughts about my flight.

It will be fine. The flight will be fine. Everything will be fine.

Oh, it will!

I listened carefully to the safety procedure, noted all exits, and made a mental note of which door to flee through in a panic. Soon, I was winging my way to L.A.

And Michael Anthony!

I tried to entertain myself by watching a movie – it was boring as hell – writing in my journal, thinking positive thoughts, and watching my fellow passengers.

Oh, sure, there were a few A-grade celebs and minor D-grade celebs on board who'd caught my attention. Like the ex-footy star who was on his way to Miami, with a crossover in L.A., for being arrested last year. There was the radio announcer who thinks he's shit hot and tells everybody so. The TV star who's been around so long no one seems to be able to get rid of him, and another ex-footballer who's made a ritual of running to L.A. to go on benders. Drug benders.

But this one woman, in particular, was fascinating. I didn't know who she was or where she was from, but she certainly grabbed my attention. There she was, sitting regally in her seat, wearing a high-necked frilly blouse and ankle-length skirt with a hat perched perilously upon her tight grey curls. She wore too much make-up and flung her bejewelled hands around as she talked. Everyone could not only hear her but see her jewels. She reminded me of Barbara Cartland.

Or Nancy Drew in disguise, my brain said.

No. I scowled. Nancy would never be so obvious. So loud. So...tacky! I sat there with an amused look and listened to her stories about the old days.

She was from the theatre, and a huge star in her day, in every play, every musical. Started off as an understudy at sixteen, and made lead by eighteen. She detailed her dalliances, which made more than a few people blush, and told on her husbands. Such mean men apparently, only wanted her money. I could relate to that. She had two sons and a daughter but wasn't going to leave them anything when she died, and was running away to America to prevent her kids from stealing her fortune...

Something was shaking me, and my head moved in the direction of the person speaking.

"Ms Cameron. You asked me to wake you. We'll be landing in L.A. soon. You wanted to change and freshen up."

I wiped my eyes and covered a yawn. "Yes," I mumbled. "Thank you."

"Breakfast will be served soon."

"Thank you," I mumbled again, pushing the button that made my seat rise into its upright position. I grabbed my carry-on bag and tottered my way to the bathroom. It was a tight fit, but I managed to freshen up and put on clean clothes. Making my way back, I saw other people waking up, some already drinking their morning coffee. I had a light breakfast, and pulled out my notebook, going over the list of things to do upon arriving.

"This is your captain speaking. The fasten your

seatbelt sign is on as we are approaching L.A.X. and will be landing shortly. I hope you've enjoyed your flight, and I might see you again soon."

Well, that's a strange thing to say, since he didn't see us at all! I gripped my armrests and tried to keep breathing past my tightly fastened belt. Now, we just had to wait for the landing.

And miracle of miracles, it went as smooth as a baby's bottom.

The door flung open, and we all stood at once, except for the old lady who demanded to leave first. I grabbed my bags and walked slowly toward the exit, and once free, bolted through the overcrowded terminal till I came to the luggage area. I was the first one there and positioned myself to claim my bags. After all, I was the only one with turquoise blue Nancy Drew luggage. All four pieces came out quickly, and I was on my way to Customs.

I fidgeted while waiting in line, moving from one foot to the other, and that made several workers watch me suspiciously. But they didn't know I was just so eager to get going.

"Do you have anything to declare?" the woman asked when I finally reached the counter.

"Just that I'm bloody excited to be moving here and living here and I'll start my companies and publish my books—"

"All right, all right," she said, putting her hand up to stop me. "Place your bags up here, and I'll search them."

Two suitcases, two bags and two carry-ons later, I

was free to leave.

"I hope you enjoy your stay," the woman said.

"Oh, I definitely will," I replied with the biggest grin I had. Wheeling my way back through the terminal to meet Sin, I was overwhelmed for a moment. I was here. I was in L.A.

"Oh, my God, there you are," I heard, and looked up to see this nutty woman running toward me. She dove at me, and I barely managed to release my cases before they toppled.

"All right, Sin, all right," I cried, hugging her back. Here I am, five foot eight, and she's towering over me. "Hang on, aren't you five foot six?" I pushed her away to glance down at her feet and saw four inch black stilettos. I looked up at her porcelain white face with its spattering of pale freckles and saw her fiery brown eyes, daring me to some sort of verbal duel. "How can you teeter around in them things? You didn't drive in them did you?"

"I did, but who cares, let's get you out to the car." She grabbed a case, with a bag attached, and walked off as she kept talking. "Booked us in to the best restaurant... 'Stang dealership nearby... Need to sign some papers..."

I tried to hear what she was saying as I followed her – the airport was packed and noisy to boot – and I almost had to run. It was all I could do to keep up with the size four powerhouse.

Sin's fire engine red hair swung back and forth in a long curly ponytail that had a few colourful braids wound through it. Her short black skirt and heels showed off her long, lean legs to perfection. And, of course, there was the obligatory fake California tan.

I felt so plain next to her. So boring, so short, so...white! I was also getting shoved every which way by the busy crowd around me. Kinda hard not to in such an incredibly busy place.

"Why don't you look where you're going?" someone hissed in contempt.

"Excuse me!" I turned around to find myself face to face with a famous actress. "I *know* you weren't talking to me. Especially since *you're* the one who bumped into *me*."

Her hazel eyes burned into mine, and her delicate English hand flung her dark glossy hair over one shoulder before placing itself on her hip. The dark fur coat draped around her glistened with expense, and the diamonds in her ears radiated brightly. But not as brightly as the anger in her eyes.

She stood as tall as she could, but that was only five foot six. *No one* spoke to Margaret Daly-Tomes that way. How *dare* anyone *even think* of speaking to her that way? She glanced over me, her eyes cold and critical, her rosebud mouth ready to let go of the venom it was waiting to release.

"Where are you from, dear?" She spat the last word.

Dear? Ugh, I hated being called dear. It's so patronising. I watched her husband creep up behind her like a little boy. He's a famous actor himself. And thirty years older than her.

"I'm from Australia," I said. "But that *doesn't* give

you the right to talk to me that way—"

She threw up her hand to silence me. "It's obvious Australians have no manners. After all, your country was founded by convicts."

Oh, I bristled at that. "Yes," I replied acidly, noticing the crowd standing around watching. "Convicts, that *your* ancestors couldn't be bothered dealing with because the poms are so goddamn useless that you decided shipping your criminals off would be far easier than sticking them in jail."

"Ooooh," the crowd cried.

Margaret narrowed her eyes in hateful anger and came in for the kill. "How old are you, dear? A little young to be so rude to your elders. Didn't your mother teach you manners?"

"Aaaahhh," the crowd said in unison.

Strange, that second sentence, coming from a woman so obsessed and worried about getting older that she'd use the term "elders" when referring to herself.

Now it was my turn to kill. I stepped in closer, so we were inches apart, my own eyes narrowed. "My mother *did* teach me manners. And thank you for noticing I'm so young." Here it comes. "Because regardless of how old *I* get," my left eyebrow cocked in excitement, "I will *always, be younger, than you!*" With a flick of my head and a turn of my heel, I grabbed my luggage and strode off toward the entrance with Sin while the crowd loudly cheered us on, and Ms Margaret Daly-Tomes screeching something I really couldn't repeat. We made it to the door, then Sin's car, before collapsing against each other in a fit of unbridled laughter.

"Oh, my God," she gasped, wiping away tears of laughter. "*That was so hilarious.* I caught a glimpse of her face before following you, and let me tell you, she was *seething.*"

We packed my bags into the car.

"It serves her right for thinking she could mess with an Aussie chick," I said, wiping away some tears of my own and sliding into the passenger seat. The car was a comfy blue sedan.

She drove out of the car park. "I wonder if she's had anyone speak to her that way. She's a big movie star, married to an *even bigger* movie star. Maybe no one's stood up to her before."

I wound the window down and took a deep breath, then quickly wound it up again as I gasped for air.

Sin laughed. "You do know it's smoggy here, don't you?"

"I do," I choked, and then cleared my throat. "I do, I do." I coughed. "Well, I don't care who she is, or who she thinks she is, or who she's married to for that matter. I will not let anyone get away with speaking to me like that. No one!" I emphasised with a fist.

We drove along the main highway out of L.A., heading north. To Michael. It's about half an hour out of the city, and the air seemed cleaner, sort of. The sky was bluer – not so much smog – and it's a nice rolling suburb.

"Which suburb?" you ask, fluttering your eyelashes.

Alas, I cannot tell you. That would be giving away

where Michael lives.

I marvelled along the way. The buildings, the cars, the clothes that people were wearing, or should I say, lack thereof. My God, I was really in L.A. The places to shop, the restaurants to eat at, and a million things to buy and see and do.

Sin pulled to a stop in our hotel's car park. "Here we are." She popped her belt and the boot at the same time.

I got out and looked around. It really did look like a colonial inn with the architecture, colouring with its red bricks, and tall white columns at the entrance. The gardens were nice and green, neatly manicured and spread out for as far as my eye could see on three sides of the hotel. Everything was neat and tidy and in its place.

"Wow." I pulled my bags from the car. "This is nice. Really nice."

"You have to check in at the front desk. They'll want to meet their millionaire guest."

"Ah, yes," I said with a wink. "Their filthy rich millionaire guest."

We rolled into the lobby, which was amazing. Crystal chandeliers, paintings, art. Very expensive. But then, there was no doubt guests like me paid for it.

We stopped at the chiselled oak wood front desk.

"This is my fellow guest," Sin said. "*Ms Cameron.* Whom I told you about."

The clerk became a flutter. It was obvious that the staff had been waiting for me to arrive and start spending my money, as suddenly five other people hurried up to us.

"Miss, let me take your luggage," the porter said.

"Ms Cameron, it's so nice to finally make your acquaintance," the manager added.

"If there's anything I can get you and do you," the concierge said, then corrected himself after my icy stare. "I mean *do for you*. Let me know," he hastened to add.

"And, of course, I'll make any dish you want," cried the head chef.

"And if you need security. I'm your man," the guard chimed in.

I cocked my eyebrow in amusement. "Okay, people, enough," I said, trying to get a hold on the situation. "I just want to get up to my room and unpack. If I need any of you, I'll call. But until then, please, go back to what you were doing."

Everyone seemed a little perturbed at my forcefulness. But tough! I signed in and the porter brought my luggage upstairs with us.

Room 28.

My room.

My lucky numbers 28 room.

The porter opened the door then waved us in. I stepped into a luxuriously decorated lounge room. A sofa stood against the wall to my right, a table and chairs were under the window in front of me that overlooked the manicured lawns and garden. To my left was a huge, well-endowed four-poster bed beckoning me into the bedroom. Its coverings were like the kind royalty would use. The carpet was a rich blue, the drapes matching in colour. Expensive-looking paintings adorned the walls, and statues and vases of flowers were placed artfully on the tables.

"The bathroom's through there, Miss." The porter pointed, waiting for his tip.

I rolled my eyes, and Sin dug around in her bag for a five.

"Thank you," he said, tipping his hat.

Shutting the door behind him, Sin turned to me. "You'll have to get used to tipping you know. It's a custom here."

"Yeah, I know." I sat on the bed, sank a foot and floundered a bit. "Mmm, comfy."

"I'll let you change. When you're ready, bang on my door next door," she said.

"Okay," I called as she shut the door behind her.

I sat for a moment to take it all in. It was overwhelming. Absolutely. I stepped over to the bedroom window and pushed aside the curtains. A smoggy L.A. in the distance, mountains on the side, lush green lawns below me.

It was L.A.

It was America.

A sly grin slid across my face.

Yes, it was L.A.

Yes, it was America.

And I had finally arrived!

Chapter 3

Bang. Bang. Bang.

I jumped so high I thought I'd hit the pale blue ceiling.

Bang. Bang. Bang.

"All right, already," I yelled, getting up from the sofa and opening the door.

"I said an hour," Sin stated, walking in. She'd changed into a short green dress.

I shut the door. "Yeah, yeah. Isn't it an hour?"

"No!" She turned and looked at me. "It's two!"

I looked at my watch, which I had fortunately changed to L.A. time. "Oh, it is." I tried to look sheepish. "Sorry. By the time I unpacked, showered and changed, then stared out at the view for awhile, I guess time got away. Plus, I just sat and took in the view of the room." I shrugged, sat on the sofa and glanced around. "I still can't believe I'm here. This room is really nice."

"I know." She sat beside me. "And you can afford it. Anyway, I'm here for some girly time, and a holiday from my husband. But for now, we have things to do, like shop and eat, and shop and sightsee, and shop and perve at gorgeous men, and shop and—"

"I take it you want to shop," I muttered dryly.

She pretended to look hurt. "I don't want to *just* shop..."

"Uh, huh. You want to eat, sightsee and perve in-between, or all at the same time." I was amused and so ready to go.

"If we can do it all at the same time that will be even better," she said, a huge grin on her face. "It's Thursday, we will not talk business until Monday, which means we have three and a half days to have fun."

"And shop and eat, and shop and sightsee..." I added with an amused snort and hauled myself up from the sofa. "All right, I'm dressed. Just let me get my bag." I wandered into the bedroom and got my bag. I had already picked one to go with my outfit – have to colour co-ordinate, darlings – and piled everything I would need into it. Magnifying glass, Swiss Army knife, lock picking kit, flashlight, handcuffs…

"What do you want to do, break into someone's house?" you ask in amusement.

No, not at all. They just might come in handy, especially the cuffs. They're the furry animal print kind. Michael Anthony look out 'cause here I come.

"So, where we going?" I asked as she ushered me out the door and into the lift.

"We are going to lunch at Big Willy's, drive by The Ivy to see who we can see, and then we'll go to The Grove for some easy shopping. Eat out for dinner, and maybe split a Sprinkles cupcake for dessert."

"First off, we ain't sharing no Sprinkles cupcake," I admonished her with a furious wave of my finger as we walked toward the car, "second, you seem to have my itinerary all worked out."

"Absolutely!" came the smug reply.

I sighed. "Next week's going to be bloody busy, isn't it?" We looked at each other.

"You'd better believe it."

We lunched at Big Willy's, the father of Little Willy's – joking – and it's co-owned by an actor who's on the show we talk about on my blog. We were hoping to see him since we eyed a few other celebs coming and going, but it seemed his work schedule conflicted with him appearing. What a bummer!

Over amazing food, Sin and I talked about the weekend; what she'd organised, where we'd go, what we'd do. We talked about the coming week, my new life, and what sort of plan I had in motion for getting what I wanted.

Dessert time, and I ordered a big fat slice of chocolate pie. After all, I'd been working out hard, getting thinner, and having lipo in preparation for coming here. After a long plane flight, I needed chocolate. At first, Sin refused, but when I offered her some, she happily agreed.

Who can say no to chocolate? Well, I should've 'cause she ate more than half damn it!

When we walked outside, I stopped on the sidewalk to take it all in. Here I was, in L.A., eating at an actor's restaurant, and now standing here watching my new world go by. Twenty year olds with spiked coloured hair, a wannabe D-grade actress arguing with her companion, normal everyday people driving by in their normal everyday lives.

Dang, was that Britney Spears?

Dang? *Good grief, I sound like an American already.*

"Is there a Starbucks nearby?" I asked, getting into the car.

"Down the road. Why, do you want a coffee? We just left Willy's." Sin started the car.

"No," I said, looking down the street for Ms Spears. "I don't drink coffee, but dear old Ms Britney does, and I swear I just saw her go by."

"You know you're going to see anyone who's everyone who thinks they're someone around here." She patted my knee. "You're in L.A. baby."

I threw her a sour look. "Don't pat my leg or call me baby. And yes, I know we're in Hollyweird." I saw the huge sign as we crossed an intersection. It was snuggled into its position on the hill. "Hell, I'm in Hollyweird baby, woohoo," I yelled out the window. A few people cheered at me as I pulled my head back in...the window that is. Sin and I laughed and headed for The Grove for our shopping expedition.

Six hours later, I dropped onto my bed and lay there, staring at the ceiling. "Good grief that was hectic. Store to store to store." I glanced at Sin. "You didn't stop." I leaned up on my elbows and watched her place her own million bags on the sofa.

"You didn't stop either." She came and bounced onto the bed next to me. "I think you bought more than I did."

"I didn't buy more. I have fewer bags."

"That's because every store we went into you just shoved what you bought into the bag from the store before it. You have a hell of a lot of clothes and shoes. Not to mention jewellery, hats, scarves."

"All right, all right," I said, sitting up. "My back is killing me, and my feet feel like they're about to fall off. I don't know if I want to go out."

"Oh, no you don't," Sin said, pulling me up from the bed. "We are going to get ready and go out to eat." She emptied my bags onto the bed. "Now, let's see if we can find you a decent outfit to wear."

*****

The next day I was dead tired, but so eager to get started on my car that we were there first thing. Driving into the Mustang dealership my jaw dropped and I drooled.

They...were...gorgeous!

I jumped out of the car and ran my hands over a jade coloured convertible. The chrome shone and dazzled in the spring sunshine, and I was blinded by love.

A man came out and introduced himself. "I'm Mac Steele." He shook Sin's hand.

She looked at me. I cocked my brows in amusement and stifled a grin. Mac Steele sounded like the name of a porn star. Although he sure as hell didn't look like one.

"I'm Sin Mainwaring. I rang you about getting a Mustang painted and detailed. This is the lady who wants the car." She pointed to me.

"Ah, yes," he said, shaking my hand with way too much vigour. I tried to extract it from his grasp. "Do you know which Mustang you want and how you want it?"

I took in his appearance. Tall, about five foot eleven. Brown hair, neatly combed. Well built, but a bit on the soft side. His grin seemed friendly. "I know I want a 'Stang from the sixties, and how I want it."

"Well then, little lady, why don't you come inside, take a look at some pictures and you can decide what year you want."

Little lady! I mouthed the words to Sin as we followed him into the office and looked at prints of every Mustang from every year hanging in rows on the walls.

"So, you know what colour?"

"Electric Blue metall..." I stopped. It was obvious he didn't know the colour.

"We'll have to look that one up," he said, rifling through some papers on his desk.

"I want all of the interior done with hot pink leather, including the roof. I want a blazing star painted on the bonnet, oh, that's hood to you, with three rows of stars shooting from it and going down the sides of the car. I want them done in iridescent paint and outlined in a one inch wide strip of black paint. On the black paint, you will stick Swarovskis in all shapes, sizes and colours." I watched his face carefully. His jaw was on the floor, and he looked ever so bewildered. "I want it as soon as possible." I threw my right hand up, my thumb pointing over my shoulder to a picture of a Mustang. "And I'll take that to go in a '65, thanks."

Sin looked from him to me, trying to hide her grin.

"Um, ah, um," he gulped. "You, can't, seriously…"

I didn't let him finish. "I am deadly serious." I stepped over to him and withdrew a picture from my notebook. "In fact, here's what I want it to look like."

See how prepared I am!

He took the photo and stared at it…then me.

"How soon can you have it done? Time is of the essence," I told him.

"Well, um." He stood. "I don't know about the paint and leather colour, or those Swar thingies you want, but we can get a '65 tomorrow."

"That's fine. Do you have paint and leather samples to show me?"

"Um, yeah, sure." He still seemed dazed that a woman wanted a car like I'd described. He brought me the samples and I quickly went through them.

"I'll take this blue paint. I call it Electric Blue metallic, but you call it something else." I handed him the sample and turned to the leather.

"Oh, yes," he mumbled. "We can do that."

"And this pink leather. For the seats, the roof and steering wheel."

"I guess we can get that in."

"Fantastic! I want my car ready to go by the end of next week." I gazed at him expectantly. "You *can* do that can't you?"

He mumbled something under his breath, then, "Of course, of course. But, ah." He wiped his mouth in nervousness. "It will cost to do all of this, and so quickly."

Sin and I looked at each other. With her a lawyer and me not caring to be ripped off, I think we made him nervous. Mac was certainly *not* made of steel.

"Oh, believe me, I know it's going to cost to have it done this week." I flashed a grin of friendship to relax him then went in for the kill. "But don't even *think* of ripping me off because I will *not* tolerate it." A shocked wave of emotion rolled over his face. "I want you to detail *every*thing on my receipt and don't even *think* of adding money for something I *didn't* want or ask for." I watched his face for a moment then stuck out my hand and grinned. "Do we have a deal?"

He was white all over and a little sweaty. In fact, a lot sweaty. "Um, oh, yeah, yes, of course we do," he stuttered, shaking my hand without enthusiasm.

I hung on a little longer and a little tighter. "Good," I said, knowing he saw the icy seriousness in my eyes. "Then it's a deal."

We drove out of the lot with Sin laughing her head off. "I can't believe he just stood there and took it. His face was so white, and he looked so sick I thought he was going to *be* sick." We laughed even harder, tears rolling down our cheeks.

"Well, look," I gasped. "When I came here, or should I say when I *knew* I was coming here, I made the decision to stand up for myself and not put up with crap. I know car salesmen try and rip you off. I've experienced it back home. Besides," I glanced at her, "I want my car as soon as possible."

*****

The next two days were a blur of jet lag, shopping, eating, perving, and shopping. Sin dragged me from store to store, street to street, suburb to suburb, looking for all I would need to be the style icon I knew I should be. Plus, I had a few things in mind.

In a wig store, I tried on every colour, style, length and shape. They showed me how to put them on and keep them on, and I walked out with ten coloured ones.

I like the idea of dressing up. Becoming someone a little or a lot different to the person you are. And wearing a wig is easier than dying your hair as that can ruin it.

I bought hats of all kinds, plus ankle boots, knee high boots, thigh and crotch high boots – you do need them for different occasions – leather skirts, jackets and pants, jewellery galore and about a million handbags. Okay, maybe not a million, but 999, 999. Of course, I had to make sure everything was in the styles and colours that I liked, and it all had to co-ordinate.

So now it was Sunday. I thought I'd be relaxing by the pool sipping a cool drink then later shopping for Nancy Drews on eBay, but Sin had other ideas.

"Look, your lessons start tomorrow." She'd signed me up for dancing and singing lessons plus martial arts and weapons training already. "And on top of all that, we'll be sorting out your business this week."

I sighed and sipped my icy fruit drink. My business. For a few days, I'd forgotten it and thought I was here on holiday. I knew a lot had to be done and I wanted it done quickly. I had to look at businesses in bankruptcy, businesses I could buy or take over. The warehouse needed looking at. I needed to hire designers, artists, a receptionist, jewellery makers, start my production company and hire a CO to run it when I wasn't there. Dear God, there weren't enough hours in the day with my classes. I sighed again. Life was about to get very hectic.

"God, I'm tired just thinking about it all," I told her, but she came to the rescue. She's OCD and probably ADD don't you know, so it makes her one hell of an organiser.

"Don't worry, I have the next two weeks sorted." She pulled out an A3 piece of cardboard from her bag. It had a grid on it with all my activities lined up. "Tomorrow morning we'll look at the companies and warehouses, so you can see if you want them. Then you have classes" – that would be singing and dancing – "Tuesday you go see the chiropractor I found for you" – I have a twisted spine that kills me – "then you have your weapons training, then classes. Wednesday, we'll look at the office space I found for setting up your fashion labels. It's really nice and has a nice view of the beach."

"Oooh, I love the beach," I piped up.

"Thursday," she continued. "Martial arts on top of your classes, and Friday we'll have some interviews and talk about the business some more before your classes."

"God, that's way too much," I groaned, wallowing in the agony.

"Well, you wanted it," she replied. "And then, of course, there's the week after, and the week after, and all the shopping on the weekends and everything else we have to do..."

"Stop it," I cried in mock anger. "I can't hear any more of this, I just can't." I put down my drink, flew from my seat and jumped into the pool, making sure to splash Sin.

The water waved over her making her gasp. "That's war," she cried, throwing down the A3 chart she'd so neatly prepared and diving in after me.

*****

The following week was hectic, well, duh, so I'll try and put it in a nutshell.

Monday morning Sin and I inspected two clothing factories that were going under. I spoke to the workers and watched them sew. They seemed to take pride in their work, and it was very good. I asked them if they wanted to continue working in the same job but as a part of another company. Many of them said yes, and I seriously considered buying the companies. We also looked over a new warehouse that had been built in a semi-industrial park near where we were staying. It was huge, cream coloured, and sat on a lot numbered 11-28. There's my numerology numbers again. It also happened to be on Gemstone Way. Two signs in a row. I knew I had to buy it. And I did. I now had a warehouse to call my very own.

How's that for quick business?

*****

Tuesday at nine a.m. I walked into my chiropractor's office. She asked a lot of questions, had x-rays taken of my body, and told me as a practising chiro and physio she would do a detailed fitness regime for me. I made an appointment for the week after and headed off to weapons training. Now that I was in L.A., I needed to keep up practice so I could protect myself or others. The shooting range was very accommodating and quite surprised at my level of knowledge. I told them I had taken lessons back in Aus. Then they insisted on teaching me the way Americans handled guns. And they insisted that I start from the beginning.

*****

Wednesday morning, Sin took me to see the office space for my clothing label. It was a two storey building in plain white paint; structurally sound, with one way windows, wide front doors and plenty of parking. It was two streets from the beach, but still managed to have a great view. It was in a nice part of town, but too far away.

"I don't want to travel far from home. I'd rather have an office nearby in case I need to run back and forth from home. As much as I love the beach..."

"I'll look up your way and see what there is," she said. "In the meantime, let's shop."

I rolled my eyes and followed. After all, who can say no to shopping!

*****

Thursday was martial arts class in the morning, and singing and dancing in the afternoon. It was going to be pretty boring, except when I picked up my brand-new 'Stang.

There she was. Sitting there in the bright sunshine sunbaking her little pink leather roof off. She was gorgeous! And she was also getting attention from everyone who came and went.

I stood next to her, lovingly stroking the door. "Hello, baby," I said softly, laying my head on the roof. "Mama's here."

"Good grief," Sin exclaimed, shaking her head. "You're talking to it."

"Ladies." Mac Steele came striding toward us. "How are you? As you can see, the car is done and ready to go."

"Just tell me how much and I'll be on my way," I said, running my hand over the gems.

"All right then. Come this way, little lady," he replied and led us to the office.

Five minutes later I handed over a cheque and was walking toward my baby when I saw a middle-aged, balding man standing beside her. And he didn't look happy.

"Are you the owner of this...this...monstrosity?" he

spat in anger when he saw me.

"Yes, I am," I said, opening the door.

He blustered uncontrollably. "Do...have...any idea... what...you've done?"

I was a little confused. "What do you mean?"

"How dare you do this to this car? This is a Mustang. A 1965 Mustang convertible in pristine condition, and you've...you've...wrecked it."

So, now I was pissed. How *dare* he talk to me that way! "What do you mean *wrecked it*? I haven't done *anything* to it. It's not damaged or slashed. What the hell are you going on about?" I'd had enough and threw my bag into the passenger seat.

"Young lady." His face was so red. "By doing what you have done to it, you have wrecked a perfectly good Mustang. You do not have the right to do so, and you should be arrested and locked up for doing so."

What the hell?! Who did he think I was? Some idiot woman who had no idea what I was doing obviously. I cast an icy stare over him. "*You, sir*, are dead wrong. You *do not* have the right to speak to me that way, and I will slap you down if you open your mouth once more." I swept him aside with a flourish. "I have *not* wrecked this car...I have made it *my own*." I threw myself into the driver's seat and started up that lovely grunty engine. With a slam of the door, I laid rubber out of the lot.

*****

Friday we set up in a room supplied by the hotel to

conduct interviews. Sin had placed ads in the paper and on the internet the week before. Now, it was time to find employees.

One hundred people turned up for positions in my company. I had several available since I planned on publishing my own books, then there were the clothing and jewellery labels.

Fifty interviewees were well educated and extremely efficient. Forty were qualified for other jobs. Ten were art students from the local colleges. I needed artists to design the pictures for my clothes otherwise there would be no clothes.

Four hours flew by and we got through the interviews quickly. I had picked out a few that interested me, and the art students stood out as well. I told everyone they'd get a call back next week, except for the art students whom I told to stay. Once the other applicants had left, I called four art students into the room one by one, to tell them I was letting them go as well. When they had left, I walked into the lobby and told the last six students they had the job. And, as you'd expect, they jumped and whooped for joy.

The hotel manager cast an irritated eye over us, and I gave him a cool glare in return. I was their filthy rich millionaire guest. They were getting what they wanted out of me.

I turned back to the students hand clapped my hands. "Okay, listen up. You're not going to work in a conventional office." They looked a little shocked. "Unless you want to?"

"Ah, no," they mumbled.

"Okay. The office you're going to be working in is right out that door."

They turned around and looked out the door.

A girl named Alice turned back to me. "Outside?"

"Yes. Outside. I want the six of you to go out into the big bright world and look at everything around you. Take inspiration from it. Come up with ideas, any ideas, and make a design from it." They looked impressed.

I paced back and forth in front of them, watching them realise how free they were going to be. "I want two designs every day; more if you've got it in you. At this stage, I don't want designs of people or celebrities. I want things. All things. Everything you can see, find, hear, smell, taste." I stopped in front of the three young men. I'd hired three guys and three girls to even things out. "I want you boys to concentrate on manly things for the men's label."

They gave each other huge grins and high fives.

"After all, you don't want to do hearts, flowers and rainbows do you?"

"Ah, na," they replied. Young guys don't say much, do they?

"Okay, then. Your challenge is to ask all your mates, family, friends, fellow students and anyone else in the eighteen to thirty-five or forty age group and find out what they'd wear."

"I've got a lot of cousins my age I could ask," a guy named Matt said.

"And I can ask my friends at college," Joe said.

"Great," I enthused. "That's great. Make note of the

sort of designs they'd wear. Cars, motorbikes, music, guitars, anything guys would be into. Remember, the print will be in colour, so design something clear, not too busy and overdone. Something you'd want to wear." I pointed to the t-shirts they were wearing. "Something like that, but better."

"All right," they said.

"Now, girls." I turned to them. "That pretty much leaves everything else for you to do. Stuff that your friends and family would wear. Hearts, flowers, rainbows, stars, trees, anything you can come up with." They were excited. "When we open, I want to be set up with as many designs as we can do. Okay?"

"Okay," they chimed.

"We have your details and will be having you checked out, and if you're good, you'll be on the payroll. But you have to show your stuff. Everyone agreed?"

"Agreed."

"Good, now get the hell out of here so I can have some lunch," I said, and waved them off. I watched them run out the door in excitement and tiredly turned to Sin. "God, I'm buggered and starving. I'm starving and buggered."

"At least you've got your designers," she said as we stepped into the lift.

"Damn right!"

I was so tired by the time I got home that afternoon that we had a lazy weekend. Plus, I had to go through the interviews and pick some staff. All day Saturday I read every application – besides the artists – and Sin read them too. After talking, we decided on who we thought would be the best for every job I had on offer at that time. Then we made a list of the other people that seemed perfect, and whom we may want in the future.

On Sunday, we made calls all day. Those that got a position were excited, and those that were told they were on our list weren't too happy.

"Hey," I said. "If you end up with a job let me know, but until I get the company going, I won't know how many more positions I'll need."

They grudgingly thanked me.

"They didn't seem too happy to be on the list," I told Sin after the last call. We'd split them in half. "Maybe I shouldn't give jobs to those who are ungrateful."

"Ugh," she groaned, leaning back in her chair and propping her feet on the table. "What you do is up to you. You're the one paying. If you want ungrateful people, hire ungrateful people."

Mmm, I was thoughtful, staring out the window toward the smoggy city of L.A. *I'm grateful for everything I have and everything that's to come. I can't work with people who aren't grateful.* So, with that, I crossed five names off the list.

*****

Monday morning, Sin and I checked an office building near the warehouse in our suburb. Since I was going to be buying a house there, I needed it close by. And it was. Ten minutes away. Two storey, cream brick, black roof, nice garden in front, parking on the side. It was in a nice green, leafy neighbourhood, and guess what?

"What?" you ask.

It was perfect! Except for the colour.

I spoke to the agent that was showing us the building. "How much is it?"

"Five thousand a week to rent," he said, sensing my interest.

"I meant to buy," I said, casting a glance at the building.

His brows hit his hairline they flew up so quickly. "Um, um, it's not for sale," he stuttered. "Only for rent at this time."

I looked him square in the eye. "Mr White. I've started my global production company. I want to own the building I operate in." I straightened his tie and smiled at his nervousness.

Why do men get nervous in front of strong-willed women?

"I'm sure the current owner would be grateful to know *someone* is willing to buy their office space. Why don't you call them and let them know they have a very interested buyer." I was still smiling.

"I…could…do…that," he said, taking a step back. Pulling out his cell he spoke to someone long and hard for a good five minutes.

I waited patiently by decorating my new office with my imagination. A huge sign on the front, repaint the building in pink and blue. The inside would be bright and colourful. And my office. Ha! I'll have the best one there. Even though I'll be working from home as well.

"Ah, Miss," the agent called. "The owner says he'll only sell at his asking price."

"What is it?" I asked.

He told us.

My brows shot up, and Sin and I exchanged a glance. We knew the asking price was cheap, a lot lower than what the site was worth, and how much work had gone into it. And I know that 'cause lawyer Sin does her homework.

"Tell the owner I'll take it," I said, standing there wondering why they wanted to sell so cheap. I turned to Sin. "We'll have to get the painter and decorators in this week. And notify my new employees. They can have a say in what their new offices will look like."

"We'll do that tomorrow," she said. "In the meantime, how about you sign a cheque."

I now owned a building. An office building. A building to call my own. I was still going on about it after dropping Sin off at an appointment near the beach. I was driving my 'Stang and promised to pick her up later. Driving down the coast, I found a cute little fifties style diner and pulled in for a bite to eat. My car fitted in well and drew everyone's attention.

And damn did it make me feel good!

Inside the diner, there were fifties memorabilia everywhere. Black and white tile floor, bar stools, booths, tables and chairs, a jukebox in the corner. It was so damn cute! I ordered a burger and Coke and sat at the far end next to the window. I went off into my daydreams again and didn't hear the deep grunting Harley roar into the car park.

The waitress, dressed in her fifties outfit – God it was like an episode of Happy Days – brought me back to reality when she placed my food on the table. I munched away while reading through my notes and appointment book, seeing I still had much to do, and was oblivious to all around me; especially one hunk of a man sitting three tables in front of me. I finished my burger, wiped my mouth and hands, and sat slurping my drink, making some more notes and a couple of phone calls. I had no idea I was being watched.

After what seemed like forever, Sin called. "Pick me up in twenty minutes, and can you bring some food? I'm starving."

"I'm at that fifties diner down the road. I can bring you a burger."

"Oh, God no, you know I only eat fresh and organic. Is that sushi bar nearby?"

"Nope, don't think so." I made another note.

"Well, if you can't find anything I'll grab it when you pick me up."

"All right, see you in twenty."

Little did I know it wouldn't be twenty.

I threw my diary and phone into my bag and reached for my drink. Putting it to my lips, I saw him. And blinked.

Rapidly.

He cocked his left eyebrow and smiled, then raised his cup to me in a salute.

I blinked again.

He nodded toward me and my brow furrowed. He nodded again, and thinking I had something all over my top – I had thrown on a black t-shirt and jeans along with my trusty tyre-tread boots – I looked down. Only to discover *I did* have something all over me.

I looked at him, then down at my top. There it was. In all its glory. Splashed all over the front of my shirt...

His face!

I looked up at him and blushed. The man whose face I had printed on my top was sitting three tables in front of me in the cute little fifties diner.

A huge grin spread across his face. His gorgeously tanned Italian face.

Carmine Gionetti!

His brows wiggled comically, and he nodded again, then silently clapped.

With as much grace and dignity as I could muster, and beet red to boot, I grabbed my bag and walked down the aisle with confidence, trying not to look at him. I pretended to go past then stopped as my heart beat furiously against my chest.

He looked up at me with his famous big baby blue eyes and grinned oh so sexily.

"So, Mr Gionetti. What's it like knowing that your face is plastered from left to right over my breasts? You must be so proud?" I waited, trying not to show how shaky I was.

His sexy smile never wavered, but he shyly looked down at the table then back at me. "Actually," he said, in his New York twang. "I *am* proud. Aren't you? You have great breasts."

In a split second I was red all over.

Damn that man!!!

Chapter 4

I didn't say anything. I couldn't. I just stood there staring at him. Beet red from top to toe. And hot as anything. This man was damn sexy! And he was proud of my breasts!?

Carmine spoke first. "Do you want to sit down?" He pointed to the chair opposite him, still smiling shyly.

I gathered my courage. Why the hell not! I've got his face splattered across my chest, after all. "Okay," I managed, pulling the chair out. I tried to sit delicately, since his gorgeous eyes were watching, and looked him square in those big baby blues as I studied his features.

Golden-brown hair, short and splayed all over his head – that means sticking up all over the place – tanned skin, facial hair on his chin and top lip. And damn those lips. Thick and luscious. So kissable.

I think I unconsciously, or is that subconsciously, licked my lips while looking at him. Then I noticed him watching me. I blushed again, and he smiled that damn sexy grin, showing off even white teeth. His forehead was wide and high, his nose broad. His body muscular and lean. A tattoo branded his right upper arm; an arm whose bicep bulged as he flexed it. His hands fidgeted with his plate. They were manly hands. Hands that knew how to handle a woman...

I swallowed hard. I knew I was still blushing, and inside I was panicking, desperately trying to keep it together. "You know," I pushed out. "You should know I own a blog, and, we...talk about you a lot." I glanced shyly at him.

He was still grinning and stared with those big blue eyes. "Really? I know the one you mean." Carmine nodded. "I've read a few things on there. Even got a present from one of you girls."

My face fell like a tonne of rocks. *Uh, oh. I was one of those girls.* Can you feel me going up in flames, people? "Well..." My voice cracked. "We like to show our appreciation for you, and your band, and the work you're doing."

He was still smiling at me, tapping his fork on the table. His eyes seemed to penetrate my soul, and that smile made me want to kiss him.

Wait, what?

"Well, why not?" you all ask, shaking your heads in disbelief.

No, I can't be thinking that way. God, get a grip.

"Well...I guess I'd better go back through that present an' see if you're in there."

I was mortified. He still had it and damn it he'd find me. Unfortunately, I think all of my expressions told him that's where he *would* find me. Bugger! I gave myself away. Damn it!

"Mmm, ah, well I'm sure you will," I mumbled, feeling incredibly self-conscious. That man's eyes were doing things to me. He only had to stare at me.

"Your accent," he said softly. "Is it Australian? I've never been to Australia. I've thought of visitin'. Maybe now's my chance to immerse myself in someone Australian." There was a look on his face of blatant desire, lust, passion, anything you could call it. And the sexual connotation was so evident I didn't know whether to laugh or panic. I tried not to do either. I mean puh-leeze, *him*, interested in *me?*

"I think you meant to say, immerse yourself in *all things* Australian," I said with a slight smile on my face.

He looked determined. "No. I meant someone."

Good grief, dear God, and anything else you can think of to say right now!

I swallowed again. I couldn't believe I was sitting here at a table, across from one of the sexiest actors I'd seen. And it seemed...he...wanted me?!

So not really happening. Nope, not happening at all. I must be in some kind of weirdo dream that I'll wake up from any minute and realise I'm being an absolute moron.

Yep, absolute moron!

"Well, I should go," I said, grabbing my bag. "Oh, and don't worry. I won't tell everyone on my blog what we talked about. I'll just say...I met you, and you seemed..." I wasn't sure what words to use. "Very nice."

His brows furrowed in disappointment. "Very nice? Very nice? You wanna say I'm very nice. After all the things you write about me, you wanna say I'm very nice." His New York accent came thick and fast and damn it, it just made him even sexier.

I blushed at the thought of what we'd written. "Well." I shrugged. "Yes," came out softly.

"You know," he leaned back in his seat and licked his luscious lips, "they may not believe you. That you met me, I mean. You may need to show them proof."

"Proof? Oh, you mean a photo of us." I knew I was blushing again.

"Absolutely." He nodded toward my bag. "You gotta camera?"

"Uh, yeah." I frowned, not sure I liked where this was going.

"Well...let's have our photo taken." He whistled and waved to a waitress. "Miss, could you take some photos of us?" he asked with his devilish smile.

She fell for it. "Of course, of course," she gushed, taking the camera I'd pulled out.

"And you, beautiful lady," Carmine said to me, "come sit next to me." He moved to the chair beside him.

I changed places and sat a little awkwardly. I was *so* nervous. Especially when he put his arm around my shoulders and said, "Say cheese."

He pulled me so close our faces were side by side, our cheeks touching.

The waitress snapped away.

I could feel the roughness of his facial hair, even though it was soft – kind of a weird contradiction I know – as it mooshed against my face.

He grasped my hands with his left. "Let's keep our

hands down. That'll keep 'em guessin' about what we're doin'."

I blushed and felt uncomfortable as the hot skin of his bare arm rubbed mine.

"Wait, one more," he told the waitress. He looked at me and said, "Let's give the girls at your blog somethin' to *really* talk about." Grabbing my head, he planted his lips on mine.

His hot Italian tongue pushed its way into my mouth and probed around.

I sat there in stunned silence as this amazing stud kissed me. I didn't know what to do. So I kissed him back! But only for a few seconds... I pulled back, still stunned, and just stared at him in a daze.

"Oh, my, God," someone said, and I turned toward the voice. It was the waitress. She'd been snapping pics the whole time.

"Um." I licked my lips and could taste the mango shake he'd drunk. "That was, um..."

"Very nice," he said with a cocked brow, as the waitress took a few more snaps then handed me the camera.

"Thanks." Carmine flashed his devilish grin again, and she walked away giggling.

I heard a ringing sound from somewhere. It was close, but I couldn't make it out. I was still floating in a very foggy daze.

"I think that's your phone." He motioned to my lap.

I looked at him with a furrowed brow before looking down at my bag. The fog cleared. "Oh, right. Right, I'm coming, I'm coming." I pulled it out and flipped it open.

It was Sin. "Where the fuck are you? I said twenty minutes, and I'm hungry. *WHERE. ARE. YOU?*" She was pissed, can you tell?

I glanced at the hot stud beside me, poured into ripped blue jeans, biker boots and a worn sleeveless t-shirt. "I, ah, got waylaid by someone, and, ah, sorry, I'm coming now."

"What do you mean you got waylaid by someone? The person could not be as important as me. Who the fuck is it? It would have to be Michael Anthony for you to have an excuse."

"Um, no. It's not." An idea sprang to mind. "There's someone that wants to say hello." I handed the phone to Carmine. "Say hello to Sin."

He took it, and in his thick New York accent said, "Hello, Sin. It's Carmine Gionetti. From your favourite show you talk about online. I'm sorry I've kept you from bein' picked up. Your friend'll be there shortly. I'm sure you'll have so much more to talk about."

There was silence at the other end, then the explosion.

"Fuck you, it is not. Stop playing games whoever you are, and tell me who this really is."

Carmine and I looked at each other then burst out laughing.

"No, seriously. I'm Carmine Gionetti, an' to prove it, your friend an' I are sittin' here an' we had a waitress take photos, which I'm sure she'll love showin' you when she picks you up. In the meantime, she'll be there as soon as she can." He snapped the phone shut, leaving her hanging in utter suspense I was sure. After handing it to me, I popped it into my bag.

"You know she's gonna freak out," I said, snorting in laughter.

"Then let her freak out," he replied. "Make sure you post them tonight an' see what they say." He changed tack with a one-eighty. "How long are you here in L.A.?" His right arm was resting on the back of my chair, and I felt his fingers touch me.

"Um, actually I live here," I managed. "Moved here week before last."

His smile dazzled with the brightness of laser whitening. "Great, that's great. Maybe we could uh," he licked his hot pink lips with his hot pink tongue – and I know it's hot, I felt it – "get together sometime, see L.A. I'll show you around." He seemed so eager I didn't have the heart to tell him I wanted someone else. "Can I have your number?"

"I don't know," I said with a quick look. "After all, you know I own a blog full of your fans. I might let it slip that you've offered to show me around and where you live." I glanced away in amusement, trying not to laugh.

"Please," he said softly. "May I have your number?"

I looked at him and didn't want to disappoint.

"Him, or you and his fans?" you ask.

"On one condition." I looked him in the eye.

"What's that?" He was eager again.

"You give me yours."

"All right."

Just like that! Just like that, I was about to get the

Italian Stallion's phone number!

"Wow, um, okay then." I reached into my bag and pulled out a business card for him.

"Tahlia Cameron," he read. "Nice to meet you, Tahlia."

Blushing, I pulled out my diary and flicked to a page in the address and number section. I handed him the pen. "Write here."

He scrawled his name and number across the whole page in big bold strokes.

"That had better be *your* number." I took the pen and put everything back in my bag.

"It is," he said, watching me stand. He stood too. Such a gentleman! "Are you leaving?"

Aw, he didn't want me to leave!

"You know I have to go pick up Sin," I said with a laugh. "She'll be busting to see the photos, and hear all about our meeting."

"I'm sure she will. I'll walk you out." We walked out the door and he followed me to my car. "Oh, my God." His eyes bulged out of his tanned head. "Is this yours?"

"Yup, this is my baby." I unlocked the door, jumped in, and wound down the window.

"Then maybe you can take me for a spin sometime," he suggested with his sexy grin as he leaned on the door.

I smiled half-heartedly. I didn't want to lead him on. My heart belonged to Michael, but God, I'd just given the guy my number. "Maybe," I said. "I gotta pick up Sin." I started the grunting engine. "Nice to meet you." I backed up and changed gears.

Carmine followed. "It was *definitely* nice meetin' you, baby."

Baby!?

I cocked a brow. He did say it in a very sexy way. In fact, it sounded damn good! "Bye." I drove off, seeing him standing there watching me in the rear-view. I glanced at myself in the mirror and prayed to God that I didn't regret exchanging phone numbers.

It took me seven minutes exactly to screech to a halt in front of the building I'd dropped Sin in front of. She came running out at the speed of light and dived into the passenger seat.

"Oh, my God, you have got to tell me everything, *everything*, and I mean *every...thing*. Every little detail about what happened, what you said, what he said, what you did, what he did. He said you have pictures show me the pictures. Now. Now. Now!" She was like a speeding train out of control.

"All right, all right," I said in annoyance, and pulled my camera out and turned it on.

There, for the whole world to see, was Carmine Gionetti and me.

She grabbed the camera and flicked through the pics. "Oh, my, God! Oh, my, God! Oh, my fucking, God!" She looked at me, incredulous. "He kissed you?" she squeaked.

I blushed all over.

She gripped my arm with force. "You have to tell me *every...thing*," she yelled again.

"All right, all right," I repeated myself. I told her

every little detail about seeing him looking at me, what I said to him about my t-shirt, what gets written at my website, and moving to L.A. I pulled my camera from her grasp and put it in my bag.

She leaned back in her seat in shock, shaking her head, mumbling words I didn't quite catch. "Sex... kiss...oh, my, God."

"It's no big deal, you know." I shrugged nonchalantly and looked out the window.

"No...big...deal," she managed. "Do you have any idea what this means?" She was still incredulous. "You are the *only*, and I mean *only*, person I know to kiss him." Sin had briefly met him for a few moments years before when she'd been lucky enough to have a tour of the show's set. "Oh, my, holy, freakin' God!" She shook her head again. For a married woman, she did carry on quite a bit about some guy she could never get involved with.

I glanced at my watch. "We gotta go. I've got classes, and you've got, whatever it is you do when I've got classes." I started the car and Sin slowly buckled herself in.

She looked at me. "Do you have any idea what this means?" she asked again.

How many more times did she need to go over this?

"Actually," I said tartly, "it means I have his phone number, and he has mine."

"What..." Sin shrieked, the rest of her words lost under the grunt of the 'Stang.

*****

Tuesday morning, I went back to see my chiro. She'd worked out an exercise plan for me and wanted me to start Pilates that afternoon.

"That's fine," I said. "I also want to get back to the gym as well. Three times a week. I'd been going back home and feel the need to get back to it."

"That would be good." She looked up. "I was going to suggest it."

My left brow cocked in suspicious surprise. *What did she mean by that?! Did she mean I was fat? That I needed to go on a diet? That I was going to explode from eating too much? How dare she!* I calmed down a little, and my brow slid down to its natural position. I remembered where I was. Here in Hollyweird, you *have* to be anorexic!

She showed me a schedule for the next three months. "I'll see you once a week for the next month. Once a fortnight for the following two months, then once a month after that."

"Sounds good to me."

"I'll send you to Aerofit Gym. One of the trainers works with me, and I'll write a letter letting him know what to do with you."

My eyes narrowed in cat-like style. *What did she mean by that?* "That's great. Thank you so much." A million thoughts raced through my mind about what was going on in her head as I walked outside and drove off to the shooting range.

*****

Wednesday morning, Sin and I went to my brand-new office building to meet with the painters and decorators. My new employees came along to pick out their colour schemes.

"Okay," I told the painters. "I want the outside to be blue and pink, the roof red."

"Blue and pink," I heard them mutter.

"Yes, blue and pink," I repeated with a stern look.

We walked inside. The entrance way and lobby was quite spacious, with an atrium style ceiling through to the first floor.

"I want coloured carpet, bright colours on the walls, the reception desk to our right, chairs and sofas to the left. I want pot plants, funky prints, and the company logo on that wall there." I pointed to the wall in front of us. "Now, where's the lift?"

We glided upstairs and stepped into a spacious area that overlooked the ground floor. With hallways to my left and right, I decided to check all of the offices on my left.

"I want more colour and prints up here." I opened each door and stepped into the rooms. There were three each side of the hall and a spacious one at the end. Both halls were the same. I decided I and my CO would have the end rooms.

"Richard," I said to Richard Manning, my new CO. "This will be your office. You will be running the company most of the time anyway. I'll be going back and forth between home, the warehouse and here."

"All right," he said enthusiastically, checking out his new space.

All the rooms came with personal bathrooms; they just needed freshening up. Richard conferred with the painters, and we moved on.

"Sonya, as head of my women's label this will be yours, and the one next door can be for an assistant." I pointed to the two offices on my right as I walked back down the hall.

"Woohoo," I heard. Sonya McMahon was an up and coming twenty-five-year-old graduate of fashion. Now, she was head of an up and coming label.

"To my left, the two offices will be for Matthew Ridgely and his assistant. You are head of the men's clothing line."

He beamed a big grin and chose an office. Matthew was a business exec at twenty-eight. He had already run and managed several successful businesses. Now, he was here.

"Michelle." I stopped at the last two offices in the left hallway and pointed to my left and right. "These two will be for the kids' line. Choose which one you want, and your assistant will have the other."

Michelle Michaels was a mother of two kids, and at thirty, I thought she was the obvious choice. Plus, she had degrees in business and accounting.

The rest of us walked across the landing. I pointed to the two offices to the right. "This will be the accessories line. Tina, that's you."

She ran girlishly into her new digs.

"And Ben. These two will be for you to run the

book section. Once my books come out, you'll deal with any and all publicity, calls, interviews etc."

"Thank you," he said, walking into his brand-new work area.

I stood outside the last of three offices. "Okay, now. I know the big one is mine, but I don't know what to do with the other two."

"Do you need to hire anyone else?" Sin asked.

"Not at this time," I said, wondering what to do with the rooms. Then it hit me. I blew my whistle. Yes, I had a whistle. Besides, everyone was in their office, and they wouldn't hear me yell, so I whistled. They came running. I opened the door to the two small offices. "Okay, people, listen up." I waited till they calmed down. "These two rooms," I pointed to either side of me, "will be for storage of products. And what I mean by that is there will be one of everything put in these rooms. I want them set up as storage with hangers and shelves, and we put everything we make in here so I can check it all over and we can refer back to the products. We can also store files on them in here. Richard." I turned to him.

"Yes, Ma'am."

Ma'am!? "Uh, don't call me Ma'am. Call me Tahlia."

"Ma'am. Ah, Tahlia," he stuttered, blushing. He blushed! A man blushed! Oh, my!

"As CO I need you in charge of getting this place done up and ready within the month. Sooner if possible. We'll all design our offices, and you'll make sure designs and signs for our labels and the building are ready to affix. I'll also need you to help out with the warehouse management as well until we can get everything started. Will that be a problem for you?"

"No, Ma'am. Ah, Tahlia, I thrive on challenges."

"Good. Your first challenge is to get this place done. So, let's go, everybody, make sure you know how you want your offices and that the decorators know."

Thank God I'd hired a decorator to lead the charge.

I walked into my own office with Sin and Chantelle, the decorator mentioned above. "It has to be blue and pink. Funky, like the rest of the place. Throw in some yellow, green, red and a touch of purple. A big wood desk opposite the door, the company name on the wall behind it. Comfy sofas and chairs, colourful prints on the walls, some bookcases for the knick-knacks, and throw rugs and cushions."

"You certainly know what you want," Chantelle said.

"I certainly do," I replied as Sin and I stood at the floor-to-ceiling window.

There were office buildings across and down the street. The trees on the sidewalk were lush and green, and it was close to home. When I found a home that is. Next stop. A house!

"Now we need to fix up downstairs," Sin said.

"I want each stair painted a different colour," I told Chantelle as we walked down the stairs slowly, taking it all in, watching everyone run around in a frantic panic.

Thandie, our receptionist, was telling the decorators exactly what she would need to manage her position. Thandie Newton – not the actress – was a striking

African American woman of twenty-four, and had done several courses on communications. She was perfect.

There were six rooms downstairs, one of which would be the conference room. I led Aaron Jenkins into an office. "Here's where publicity is," I said. "You'll be dealing with it and transferring it to the heads upstairs depending on what it's for."

"Nice," he said. "Bright, airy. I'll have a few computers, phones, plus I'll need a pile of filing cabinets."

"Whatever you need, tell her." I pointed to Chantelle, and we moved on. "Ms Funk," I told our new webmistress. "This will be our new web design office. I want the site funky and bright. Think you can do it?"

Leslie Funk had the perfect name to be our web designer. At twenty-two, she'd graduated at the top of her class with five degrees.

"I'll need computers and lots of power. I hope the net connection is up to standard?"

We left her to figure it out, and I turned to Sin. "Do you want an office?"

"No."

"You don't want to work here full-time? Hell, I'll even pay to move you here."

She looked interested at that. "Mmm, I'll have to think about that."

We moved on to another office. "Andrew," our accountant, "this room's for you." I stood aside to let him in.

"I can definitely get used to this," he said, with a grin.

"Good. 'Cause you'll be working hard," I replied.

That left two offices if Sin didn't want one. "Not sure what to do with those," I said. "Maybe have the jewellery designers in there."

Jewellery makers I still had to hire. Oi, there was still so much to do.

I blew my whistle. "Can everybody come downstairs please?" I waited till they all rushed into the lobby. "Okay, now look. I know you all need assistants, so I'd prefer you to choose from this list first." I handed out copies of the list of candidates from the interviews. "These are the people I was impressed with and thought of using in the future. If you need to conduct interviews with them yourselves, please do so by the end of the week. Some of you might have friends or family that you think may be perfect. But since I haven't interviewed them, and if they screw up the job, then it won't just be them I fire." I looked at everyone's faces. "You need to be competent, and you need to work together. Do you understand?"

"Yes," they chorused.

"Good. Richard, you're in charge, and I'm bloody hungry, so we're off to lunch. I'll drop by at the end of the week to check on the progress. Bye, all."

We lunched at The Ivy. Yes, we managed to get in, and chose to stay outside on the patio so we could watch for any celebrities. Sitting down at the table under a large shady white umbrella next to the white picket fence, we scanned our menus, sneaking quick peeks over the top of them at all around us. Photographers were ready to pounce, hovering, waiting for someone to turn up or leave.

It was all so fabulous! And I daydreamed a little that they were there for me!

"You know," Sin said, a twinkle in her eye as she leaned in toward me. "I'm feeling excited just 'cause the paps are here. It means a celebrity is not too far away."

I snorted with a laugh. "And here *I* was thinking they were here for *me*."

She looked at me with a deadpan expression. "One day they just very well might be."

"May I take your order?" a waitress asked.

"Ah, let's see." I perused the dishes. "Southern Chicken Caesar Salad, and a diet Pepsi."

"The organic vegetable platter with salsa, and a mineral water," Sin said.

The waitress took our menus and walked away for our drinks.

The paparazzi went nuts and surrounded someone who was trying to get into the garden. It was well-known party girl, part-time actress and singer, Monica Leeway, and a few friends.

We studied them as they sat and ordered, our gaze flitting back and forth from her to the photogs. She was looking good. Healthy. Black jeans, a white tank, and a black hoodie with simple silver jewellery. I didn't know who she was with, but we watched them sip on the sodas the waiter brought.

Sin and I glanced at each other, grins on our faces.

"I wonder if she's out of rehab again," Sin muttered

as the waitress brought our drinks.

The waitress leaned in. "I heard that she was seen drinking again," she said in a hushed tone before going over to another table.

Sin and I exchanged another look, our brows raised in amusement.

"Waitress. Waitress. Get me another drink. This one's gone," a drunken loudmouth whined.

The paps raced past us to where the man was sitting. They *had* to get a picture of the sloshed Warwick James and all the mischief he was about to make.

He staggered around the outside dining area, bumping into tables, tripping over chairs. "Hello, sweetheart," he slurred to a woman he fell over.

I don't know much about Warwick James. He was an ageing actor who still thought he was hot, that women still loved him, and that he could *still* hold his liquor.

The answer was no on all of the above.

He was at least sixty-five, but looked eighty-five thanks to the decades of drinking, and thought every leading lady he worked with had the hots for him. Rumours abound that he turned up to every audition sloshed, and when he did get a job, he drunkenly rolled onto the set every day, holding up production for hours while he stumbled around and forgot lines. Then there was the time his leading lady slapped him clear across the face after he lurched at her and managed to grab her breasts on the way down. He claimed it was an accident, that he was trying to stop himself from falling. The problem was, when he tried to pull himself up to a standing position, he grabbed at her dress and bang, off it came. So, the leading lady kicked him in the nuts as well.

Good for her!

But it didn't stop him from getting drunk!

All right, so I know a lot. I read the tabloids when I have a spare five minutes. Which isn't often these days. And here was Warwick James, slobbering all over women again.

And the strange thing was, he reminded me of George Hamilton. Poor George!

Our food arrived, but before we could dig in, he staggered towards us.

"Ladies," he was still slurring. "How 'bout a drink." He bumped into our table, knocking our drinks over. The waitress came running, as did the manager.

"I'm so sorry, Miss. Please, let me get you another drink." The waitress cleaned up while we all shot deadly poisonous daggers with our eyes at Mr James.

"How about getting me another one while you're at it," Warwick mumbled.

"Your drinks are on the house," the manager told us, before leading the drunk away.

"Thanks, that'll be nice," Sin called, straightening the table.

"No. Let me go," Warwick shouted, wrenching himself free from the manager. "I was having a drink with those lovely ladies." He lurched back toward us but tripped.

And you can guess what happened…

Arse over tit he went and landed on me from behind. His hands flew around me to steady himself.

The problem was he grabbed my breasts with one hand, while the other landed in my crotch. Just as well I was wearing pants!

Well, I wasn't going to sit there and take that. Besides, I'd been taking martial arts classes. With a flick of my wrist, I grabbed his arm, twisted it around, and spinning out of my seat, I flipped him onto his back. Another twist and I rolled him onto his stomach, stomped my foot into his back, and wrenched his arm out of its socket.

He screamed in pain.

The paparazzi went nuts.

The patrons sat quietly, watching it all unfold in wonderment.

And damn, I was enjoying myself!

I leaned in close to Mr Warwick James. "The next time," wrench of his arm, "you want to touch up a woman," another wrench, "remember what I did to you."

He screamed again. Like a girl!

"Because this lady ain't gonna take it." One final wrench and I let him go.

Sin started applauding, whistling and cheering. The crowd followed suit. I just dusted myself off while the manager helped Mr James, who was still screaming like a little girl, to his feet.

"Who the fuck do you think you are, you bitch? You bloody bitch."

The manager steered him toward the entrance.

"Get off me. Get your filthy hands off me." He turned to me. "You bitch, I'll get you, you filthy bitch. I'll sue you for all you're worth."

The paparazzi furiously snapped away as Warwick James, deranged has-been actor, stumbled like the drunken idiot he was down the street.

"Yeah, yeah," I mumbled, as we once again straightened our table. I sat down, and our waitress brought us fresh drinks and salads.

The manager came over again. "Ladies, I am *so sorry.* Your drinks, food, and anything else you want is on us. You should *not* have had to deal with that. I am so sorry."

"Look, it's fine." I waved my hand at him. "Thanks for the freebies."

"There is one thing, though," he continued in a low tone. "I hope you've got a lawyer, because Mr James is notorious for suing everyone *he* assaults."

"Don't worry," I said, looking at Sin, with a twinkle in my eye. "I have a fantastic lawyer."

He stepped back with a final brush of the tablecloth. "That's good. Enjoy your meal."

"We will," Sin and I chimed in unison.

I took a sip of my drink and laughed, then shook my head in amazement at what had just unfolded. "I guess it's just as well my lawyer saw the whole thing."

"Maybe I should sue the bastard myself. My salsa spilt into my lap and ruined my skirt," she said, swiping at it with a napkin.

I looked from Sin to the paps to Sin. "Well, it's just as well we have proof then." I pointed to the photographers.

We laughed.

They snapped away.

Chapter 5

My Southern Chicken Caesar Salad was delicious, and I was enjoying myself immensely. Sitting at the table, we watched everyone come and go. Some even came over and mentioned the incident, applauding and cheering me on with, *'you go girl'*, *'good for you'*, *'it's about time someone set that drunken bum straight'*.

I thanked them for their support and kept on munching until the paps started snapping again in a complete frenzy of shark-like behaviour.

"Let me through. Let me through, you vile animals. *Don't you know who I am?*"

Oh, we knew. In fact, that voice was still very clear in my head.

The woman barrelled through the photographers into the front garden and stood still. Her head moved slowly from left to right while her cold hazel eyes scanned the tables.

"Ms Daly-Tomes, how nice to see you again." The manager rushed up.

"Frederique, darling. How nice to see you too." They air kissed, and we nearly puked.

"We can have a table for you and your guests in a few moments if you'd like to wait."

She had still been scanning the crowd but stopped when her eyes landed on me. There was a flash of recognition. "We'd like to sit over there." She pointed in our direction.

"Uh, oh." Sin stabbed at a carrot. "We could be in for some more trouble," she sang softly, flashing a big grin at me.

I leaned in close, but watched Ms Daly-Tomes stalk toward us. "What do you mean, *we*," I muttered under my breath. "I'm the one who told her off."

She stopped behind me. "We'll take this table." She violently pulled the chair out. It hit my chair with force, and I lurched forward. "Oh," she said acidly. "I'm *soooo* sorry." Her concern was *soooo* fake. "Did you spill your drink?"

"No, not at all," I replied with tarty sweetness. "You missed."

Her eyes narrowed like a cat's, and her rosebud lips pursed together in anger. She sat down and flung her fur coat from her shoulders over the back of her chair.

God knows why she was wearing a fur coat in late spring.

The coat landed on the back of my chair, and I flicked it off in distaste like it was some kind of dead animal. Which it was. I just didn't know *which* dead animal.

Her friends eyed me then leaned in to whisper to her.

Sin and I resumed our meal only to hear Margaret Daly-Tomes speak in a loud tone.

"Oh, yes. She was the one from the airport that I

was telling you about. That nasty little Australian girl. Ever so rude. Her mother *obviously* didn't teach her any manners. Mmm, now let's see, what do I want to eat."

We sat silently and ate, eager to hear what else she'd lie about.

"Mmm, I might have the salmon, with lemon on the side," she said.

"I'll have the grilled chicken."

"I'll have the broiled trout."

"I'll have the duck breast in garlic butter."

Ew, duck breast in garlic butter. I screwed up my face and shuddered.

"Michelline," Margaret said. "How can you sit there and have garlic butter? You'll smell awful for hours."

Two women tittered.

"Because," Michelline started. "My doctor told me to have garlic twice a day in my meals."

"Oh, well." Margaret sighed. "Just don't come near me then when you're done."

More tittering.

Sin and I rolled our eyes.

"So," one woman said. "Guess what my darling Richard bought me for my birthday?"

"A diamond bracelet?"

"Pearl earrings?"

"A house in Jamaica?"

"No, no, no," she said. "The new model Mercedes convertible. Oh, I could have died when he drove up to the house in it and presented me with the keys."

"Congratulations," a woman said. "But it's not nearly as nice as the enormously expensive diamond and emerald jewellery set that my Pierre gave me for our wedding anniversary. The stones are *huge.* Earrings, necklace, bracelet, ring and a matching brooch. It's extraordinarily extravagant. You must all come over to the house and see it." A pause and some tittering. "Or better yet, why don't you wait until the big fundraiser we all have to go to next week. You'll see it then."

A waiter served their food and wine.

"Well, that's nothing, darlings. My Mathew bought me a brand-new fur, an *enormous* diamond ring, a shopping spree at Prada, and a brand-new Porché, all because of my horrible time at the airport the other week."

Sin and I perked up.

"It was *horrendous,* darlings. The humiliation alone made me die on the inside. I mean *the nerve* of that woman. Bumping into *me* and then insulting *me* for bumping into *her.* And the crowd. The crowd were on her side, clapping and cheering her on."

"Damn straight," I muttered under my breath.

"You know, I've been to Australia before, and the people have been so nice. But this one must have slipped through the cracks. Her manners were atrocious, her breath smelt, *and* she was badly dressed. No make-up, no decent hairstyle, *no nothing.* She was pitiful. Absolutely, positively pitiful."

My eyebrow cocked and my face scrunched in anger as I expelled a silent furious sigh.

"And," she took a deep breath, "She had the audacity to call *me* old."

"How dare she!"

"You're not old, darling."

"You're as young and gorgeous as ever."

I rolled my eyes.

"Thank you, darlings," Margaret said. "I just can't believe that nasty little creature treated me that way."

Underneath I was seething and Sin could tell. Thankfully, we'd finished our meals and were ready to get the hell out of there.

Sin leaned in. "She just picked up her wine glass. *Red wine,*" she stressed in a whisper.

So, that was it. As I stood, I shoved my chair back as hard and fast as I could.

"Oh," came the growl.

I turned to stare at Ms Margaret Daly-Tomes.

"How dare you," she screeched. "My new Gucci dress is ruined. Ruined. You stupid little imbecile. How dare you." She flapped her hands around, and her friends madly sopped at the red stain on her formerly pristine white dress. "You idiot. How dare you. It's because I was talking about you, wasn't it? Just because you bumped into me at the airport, you think you can keep getting back at me. You bitch! You bitch!"

By now the manager had flown to her side and was flapping around her as well.

Margaret Daly-Tomes tried to regain her composure, and then looked up at me, not even noticing the paps flashing away. "How *dare you* do that to me," she said icily. "How dare you spill a drink all over me!"

Me? Spill a drink all over her. That was it!

"*Ms Tomes.*" I left out the Daly on purpose. "It's not *my* fault that *you're* getting too *old* to hold *your* liquor. You really should be careful." I pointed to the press. "You just never know who's watching." With that, I turned on my heel and left.

Margaret Daly-Tomes sat there screeching, the paparazzi stood there flashing, and the manager ran around all over the place like a chook with its head cut off.

Sin and I just walked away.

*****

That night we ate in the hotel restaurant before going upstairs to work on some business. I opened the door to hear my phone ringing and ran to grab it while Sin booted up my flash new wireless computer.

"Hello, who's calling?"

"Um, hi. Tahlia? It's Carmine Gionetti."

My heart caught in my throat and I spun around to face Sin. She looked up to see my shocked expression and was immediately interested. I collapsed onto the bed. "Um," my voice cracked. "I'm here. It's uh, me."

"Oh, good. Hello there."

"Hello," I said, blushing.

"I, uh, thought I'd call, since we exchanged numbers an' all, an' ah, thought maybe, we could ah, go out sometime?"

I looked at Sin and panicked, shaking my head, not

knowing what to say or do.

She came over and sat beside me. "What?" she asked softly.

I covered the phone. "It's Carmine Gionetti. He wants to go out."

Her eyes widened to the size of saucers and she nodded in excitement. "Do it, do it."

"Um, Carmine," I said. "Um." I picked at the bed cover. "I think it's only fair to tell you that um, oh, God, how do I say this?"

"You don't wanna go out with me."

"Um, it's just that, there's a guy I'm interested in, and, so it wouldn't be right to date you and let you think I'm available," I gushed in a rush, and saw Sin's look of disapproval.

"Oh...okay. Ah, well, thanks for tellin' me." He paused. "Do you still wanna go out?"

I was stunned. "What do you mean *still wanna go out?* Even though I can't offer you anything more than friendship 'cause that's all it would be. I don't wanna get involved with you." I paused before adding, "No offence."

"Look, ah, I like you. You were fresh an' fun an' I really like you. Are you datin' the guy?"

Like that was any of his business! "Um, not yet, but still, I don't want to lead you on when my heart belongs to him."

"I understand. I do. So...maybe we could go out an' grab a meal somewhere?"

"Um." I felt my resistance caving in. "I suppose we could?"

"Maybe...Gino's?"

I knew that was a romantic restaurant. No way were we going there. No way, José! "Um, no. How about we go somewhere bright and light." Sin was grabbing my arm. "Maybe Sin could come along." She'd kill me if she wasn't invited. "And maybe you could invite a co-star and we'll make it a foursome. So, we're not at a loss for conversation."

Sin gave me the thumbs up.

"Oh. I, guess. If that would make you more comfortable, we could."

"Yeah, it would."

"Okay, then. I'll, um, make some calls an' get back to you. Is Friday night all right?"

"Friday night's fine."

"Okay. I'll call back. Bye."

Sin grabbed my arm with both hands and bounced up and down. "Oh, my, God! He called you. He called you. And we're going out Friday night – thanks for inviting me – we're going out Friday night. We're going out Friday night," she sang.

"All right, all right," I said, releasing my arm. "You know, he wanted to go to Gino's, even though I said I wanted someone else, he still wanted to take me to a romantic restaurant." I looked around the room in bewilderment.

"Oooh, Gino's. My husband took me there once. It's very romantic. Oooh, he wanted to take you to Gi-no's. He wanted to take you to Gi-no's," she sang.

As you can see, we have a habit of repeating ourselves.

"Oh, God, stop it already," I laughed.

A few minutes later the phone rang.

"Hello?"

"It's Carmine. I called Keith Pritchard an' he can come along Friday night. That all right?"

"Keith Pritchard's fine," I said, excitement quivering my voice. Sin's eyes widened, and she nodded vigorously, giving me two thumbs up.

"He owns a sports bar," Carmine said. "Well, he co-owns, an' he said we could go there an' it would be on the house. Have you heard of Big Willy's?"

"Uh, no. Never heard of Big Willy's." I glanced conspiratorially at Sin.

"We can go there Friday night. About seven. Is that okay?" he asked softly.

"Friday at seven is fine," I replied, getting another thumbs up from Sin.

"Okay then...can I pick you up?"

"Ah, no, that's fine. We'll find our own way there."

"Okay. See you Friday at seven."

"Friday at seven."

"Bye."

"Bye." I hung up just as Sin dragged me off the bed. "What are you doing?" I demanded, pulling my arm from her clutches...again.

"We have to get you an outfit ready." She yanked open the wardrobe doors.

"It's only Wednesday. I have till Friday."

"I know. But we're having a date with Carmine Gionetti and Keith Pritchard from our favourite crime show. We have *got* to have the right outfits."

I sat back on the bed, shaking my head in disbelief, watching Sin tear through my clothes like a tornado. Good grief!

*****

Thursday morning, I was greeted to the day with tabloid after tabloid showing my run in with Warwick James and then Margaret Daly-Tomes. The story ran the gamut of pure fiction to halfway decent truth, especially since no one knew my name. And that drove the paps nuts. Needless to say, I *really* wanted to forget both Wednesday and Thursday.

*****

Friday, the day of our celeb date, we headed back to my production company office to see how things were going. I also called a meeting of my COs and design students.

The building had been painted outside and in and was almost done. As each room was being finished, furniture was moved in, and prints were hung on the walls. And since the conference room was finished, we all trudged in there.

I waited till everyone was seated. "Okay. Now, first things first. Ben, I need you to find out if it would be cheaper to hire a self-publishing company to help publish my books, or whether we could set it up ourselves. Either way, I need to know by Monday."

"Okay. I'll check into that today and over the

weekend," he said, making notes.

"Tina, I need jewellery makers for the jewellery we'll be producing. I can do a lot from home. Once I have one. But we need original pieces to be started now. Can you find some students or whoever we'll need?"

"Sure thing."

"Oh, and I'll also need to know how much making our own accessories will be, or if it will be cheaper doing it in conjunction with other companies. Like for our sunglasses. I want to do them with the Cancer Foundation to help people protect their eyes."

"Okay, I'll ask a few companies about that."

"Andrew. I need you to look into the financials of buying the factories. They're in debt or about to sell, and I want to buy a business on the cheap. It might make it easier. I also need you to look into printing machines. Silkscreen, foil, paint etc. I want machines that will do it all, and do several at the same time. Richard, I need you looking over the factories to see what extra things we'll need to get going. Industrial sewing machines, tables, storage etc."

I looked at my list. "I also need materials, stones, heating, cooling, cutters, decorators. Oi. We still need a hell of a lot." I sat down and glanced around the table. "Until the clothes are in production you all need to pitch in. Find me suppliers, machines, material, sewers, cutters, anything and anyone we'll need to get this going. And for those of you who have business or accounting degrees, pitch in with ideas. If you know someone or something that can help, let Richard and me know." I turned to Andrew again. "I want this done cheaply, but well. No shonky deals, no bad machinery. Understood everyone?"

"Understood," they chorused.

"Ms Funk. How's our website going?"

"Nicely," she replied. "Full of colour and animation. I'm working on each page and putting in everything you wanted."

"Fantastic. Sonya, Matthew, Michelle and Tina, stay here, I want to go over the designs."

Everyone else filed out except Sin and the students.

"Okay, guys, let's see what you've got," I said.

They pulled out their laptops and design pads with at least ten designs each. We all oohed and aahed over the pics. They were fantastic.

I flicked through the girls' designs. "Michelle, would these be okay for the kids' line?"

She looked at a few. "In smaller proportions maybe."

"Good. We do need designs for the kids' line." I looked at her. "I don't really know what to do for them."

"It would have to be kiddy things," she said. "Some hearts, stars, music, things like that."

Mmm, I was looking at the heart design in my hand. "Do you guys have these at each stage of layering? Or is it just one total picture that you came up with?" I asked everyone

"I layer each separate piece to make the total picture," Alice replied.

"Do versions of these, but make them smaller and simpler for the kids' line. Otherwise, these are fantastic. Also, I want you to do designs in stages for the adult lines too. As in, say, a huge heart which we'll fill with stones, then maybe a few in a circle, then a whole front of the t-shirt in hearts. Then people have a choice of a little bling or a lot. I also want to put some on the jeans, so do designs that will wrap around a leg." I turned to Matthew and the guys. "Let's see." I looked at their designs. "Wow. These are great. Would you and your friends wear them?"

"The bike and car ones, I would," Joe said.

"Okay, good. Matthew, what do you think?"

"They're great. As long as there's not much bling. Guys don't dig that."

"I wasn't going to over-bling the men's line," I said a little tartly, feeling insulted that he assumed I wasn't on top of things. I saw his slightly shocked expression and calmed down, realising he may not have meant any disrespect or harm by it. I recovered. "Guys, these are great. As far as I know, everyone's getting a pay packet." I saw Sin nod. "Good work and keep it up. Before I go, Tina, don't forget I need jewellery designers."

"I'll start looking at the colleges and courses," she said.

"Good. Okay, bye everyone." I turned to Sin. "I really need to stop thinking the world is out to get me. Anything else?"

"Just getting ready for our date tonight," she replied with girly excitement.

Goddamnit!

*****

I took my time driving home after dance class and tiptoed through my door hoping to avoid Sin. The problem was she'd been waiting and pounced through the door after me.

"Let's get you ready."

"Oh, God, stop it. It's only Big Willy's…I don't need to get dressed up. I just need a shower, jeans and a top."

"Like hell! You need more than that. You need to impress."

"I'm *not dating* the guy," I interrupted; annoyed at the drama she was creating.

Sin sighed and looked at me like I was a child. "*I know* you want Michael Anthony," – a man we hadn't mentioned in quite a few pages – "but Carmine asked you out. You have to look good. Now, go have a shower, and I'll lay out your clothes. Then I'll get ready myself."

I ran into the bathroom and shut the door behind me. I wanted peace, quiet, and a long hot shower. After two hours of dance class, I needed one. Although pole dancing did do wonders for my body and made me feel very sexy, sexy was not what I wanted for that night. I sighed deeply and stood under the beating water which felt good on my skin. I washed my hair, towelled off, and wandered into the bedroom.

Sin had laid out an outfit I wasn't sure I wanted to wear. Skin-tight jeans and a skimpy cami. I rolled my eyes, and slipping into my underwear, grabbed a looser pair of black jeans, a top that covered my breasts – no need to give him an excuse for perving at them – and a pair of red leather cowboy boots. I tied my hair into a ponytail and slapped on some make-up. We were going to Big Willy's, a sports bar, no need to dress up. I grabbed my bag, left my room, and banged on Sin's door.

"We taking the Mustang?" I asked when the door flew open.

"What the hell are you wearing?" she cried. "I *did not* pick that out for you."

"Let's go," I said, walking toward the lift. I was *not* going to argue.

"Why didn't you—?"

"I'm not wearing a sexy revealing outfit on a date with a guy I won't end up with. End of discussion. Besides, I need jeans that will expand as I eat."

She pouted all the way to the car, then all the way to Willy's. And I mean, *all the way.*

I pulled into a space in the car park and looked at my watch. "Ten to seven. We're early."

"Not too early. Let's go." Sin was out of the car and running for the door in her skin-tight red dress, and gold five inch stiletto heels.

How she did that I just don't know. I can't wear heels. I don't want to wear heels. I'd rather keep my back in shape than screw it up by wearing idiotic shoes like that. I shook my head in amusement, and after locking the car, followed.

She was standing just inside the doorway looking around and frowning. "Doesn't look like they're here yet."

I glanced around the half crowded bar and saw Carmine walk into the room from a hallway at the back. Clad in dark blue jeans, a black shirt with the sleeves rolled up, and black biker boots with chains, he looked damn good. "There he is."

Sin's eyes bulged as he strutted over to us.

"Ladies." His accent was thick and sexy.

Sin swooned. "Oh, my God!" she squealed. "Carmine Gionetti. Oh, my God, you're so gorgeous. Even more gorgeous in person." It really didn't matter that she was married. She was living her lifelong fantasy of going on a date with a celebrity. A hot studly one at that!

I found her reaction strange since she'd met him a few years ago. I wondered if she'd acted this way then. "Calm down," I said, agitated, and wondering what her husband would think.

"Hi," he said to me softly, his eyes taking in my outfit as he gazed up and down.

"Hey." I smiled.

"Keith set up a table in back for us. It's this way." He held my elbow gently as he escorted us to a corner in the back. It was semiprivate, and a little quieter.

I slid into a chair, and Carmine sat beside me. Sin flashed me a grin and sat opposite him.

"Ladies." We turned to see Keith Pritchard, Carmine's hot African American co-star walking toward us. "We've got Willy's Wings and beer on the way. Unless you want something else?"

"I don't drink beer," I said. "Cola's fine."

"I'll take the beer," Sin offered.

Keith went off to change the drink order then came and sat down. "Ladies, wait, I know you," he said to Sin. "You're from that blog that talks about our show. Carmine showed all of us the present you gave him. How are you?"

"I'm good," Sin enthused. "Believe me, we don't mind making up presents for our guy." A very sly twinkle lit her eyes, and she stared longingly at Carmine. "We like to show our appreciation of the stallion and his *body* of work."

Oh, my God! I felt myself become insanely embarrassed.

Carmine turned bright red and pushed back on his seat, turning toward me, so he was leaning against the wall. His right arm lay on the back of his chair, his fingers gently tapping the back of mine. It made me nervous, and I shifted uncomfortably.

"Speaking of presents," he said softly. "I found you in mine."

I blushed, feeling the heat rise to my hairline then gather speed down my back. Oh, God!

"Oh, really," Keith said, interest perking him up. "What was your contribution?"

"Oh, her contribu—" Sin started.

"Don't worry about it," I cut in. "It was ages ago, and things have changed since then." I remembered only too well what I had written, and by God, it was *so* embarrassing.

Keith, sensing my embarrassment, changed tack. "Well, Carmine's glad you like sending presents. In fact, when he called and asked if I'd like to come, he mentioned you were the reason for the date. You have to be Tahlia since Carmine's sitting next to you." He leaned toward me. "And because he told me every little detail of what you looked like and what happened that day." He sat back in his seat.

I glanced uneasily at Carmine. His eyes were half closed, and he was watching me with a sexy smile. He also had the decency to look a tad embarrassed.

Good!

Keith continued. "I know both of you ladies talk about Carmine on a regular basis. That's cool. You're helping to publicise the show. I've seen some of the things you write."

Uh, oh. That could be trouble. Considering some of the stuff we talk about can be so risqué and explicit. It can also bore your brains out.

"Yeah, we do," Sin said. "We talk about him a lot. What his character does, and how he handles the situation. Whether he gets his clothes off, and what he looks like naked…" She smiled cheekily and glanced away.

Keith grinned in return. "Mmm, well it's been awhile since I've gotten *my* shirt off." He thought about it. "Have I gotten my shirt off?" His finger pointed to Carmine. "It's this guy *here* they like to undress. The head honchos get his gear off as much as possible, and we *know* all of you girls love that."

"Oh, we *definitely* do," Sin gushed as a waitress set our drinks on the table.

Even I had to hide a smile, so I took a gulp of cola and tried to calm my racing heart.

"Here comes Big Willy's Wings," Keith said, as a waiter put two platters of steamy hot wings on the table. "Everyone dig in," he added.

For a few minutes, we ate Willy's Wings and chatted about my blog. While I was starting to relax and enjoy myself, I really wanted to be somewhere else.

"Where?" you ask. "Why would you want to be somewhere else when you're sitting at a table eating wings with two hot actors?"

With Michael Anthony.

"Oh," you remember. "What happened to him? We thought you'd be with him by now."

Well, since it's been two weeks you'd think so. I know *where* he lives, but the house next door to him isn't for sale. So, I'm sitting tight for now. Besides, I have a business to run.

"Tahlia, tell us about yourself. I know you're Australian by your accent, and because Carmine told me; he also said you moved here the other week," Keith said, bringing me back to the somewhat smoky ambience of Big Willy's.

I looked up, dragged out of my dreaming, and glanced at everyone. I didn't like being asked questions like that. I always found them too personal and nobody's business. Questions like – 'what do you do?', 'do you have a boyfriend?'. Like *that* would be anybody's business. If things came up during conversations, fine, I don't mind so much. But being asked straight out was rude and disrespectful.

And since winning lotto, I had *really* stopped talking about myself. I didn't like people prying into things that were none of their business before, I sure as hell wasn't about to give them a reason to talk about me, or ask more personal questions, or even expect some of my money now. My extremely personal business was nobody's business. And neither was how much money I had and whether I could pay for their new car.

I shrugged. "I moved over a couple of weeks ago to do some stuff, and now here I am, sitting here with two gorgeous actors." I waved my Willy's Wing at him and Carmine.

"Well, that can't be all," Keith went on. "From what I know you can't just up and move here. You need a good reason or relatives."

I *really* didn't want to talk about myself. I put down my wing and took a sip of cola.

"Oh, she's just being modest," Sin piped up when she saw my mood.

I flashed her a warning look. I *really did not* want to talk about my personal details.

"Really?" Carmine asked. "Now, you've got me curious."

So! I threw him an annoyed look. "I don't particularly like talking about myself. I'm very much into my privacy." I looked at both men. "As you two know all about. Neither of you gives too much away." I took another sip of drink then wiped my hands in a serviette.

"That's very true," Keith said. "I'm definitely into my privacy. I didn't mean to pry."

"You have to tell them," Sin said. "Your story is so cool."

I shrugged again and sighed. "No, I don't. And no, it's not."

A waitress placed four plates on the table. Grilled chicken sandwiches. Open, salad on the side, guacamole, and cheese melted all over.

"Thank you, Cheree," Keith said. "This is the house speciality. It's Big Willy's Holy Guacamole Chicken Sandwich. Dig in."

We munched our way through the sandwiches, which were freakin' fantastic, to say the least, and when we finished made small talk until Keith mentioned another book he was planning on releasing.

"Are you?" Sin asked. "Tahlia's written a couple of books and is publishing them herself."

I stared at her long and hard trying to convey my anger while scrunching my serviette into a tiny ball. Did this woman *never* learn to shut the hell up?

"Really?" Keith asked and cocked a brow. "Why don't you tell me yours, and I'll tell you mine." He tried to be Groucho Marx. And he failed.

I rolled my eyes and sighed. I do that a lot. Especially when I'm annoyed. It was no use fighting. I had to give in. For the sake of my sanity, I had to just let it go. "Okay, look." I brushed some crumbs from my jeans. "I won lotto, moved here, started my production company, and am not only publishing my own books, but I have clothing lines for men, women and children, and an accessories line as well. Enough said."

"Wow," Carmine said. He'd been somewhat quiet throughout the meal but now seemed impressed. A smile spread softly across his face. "You're doin' all that? That's great. Where have you set up, an' when are you debutin'?" He seemed genuinely pleased for me.

I flashed him a soft smile. "I have a new office up north, about ten minutes from my new warehouse. We'll be making the clothes ourselves. The books, I've only just had the time to get into the publishing aspect, and they need to be edited by a professional before printing. As for the debut, it will be whenever the clothes are ready to go." I grabbed my bag. "I need to freshen up. Which way to the ladies'?"

"Down the back hall and to your right," Keith said.

"Thanks." I stood.

"I'll come too," Sin said, grabbing her bag and following me.

Standing at the basin, I washed my hands and patted my face, and looking in the mirror, I saw I was beet red. A long deep sigh left my lips. This was not going very well.

"You know, you need to loosen up a bit," Sin said, drying her hands. "It's like you don't want to be here."

"I don't. I *really don't like* talking about myself. It makes me uncomfortable."

She powdered her nose. "Then talk about something else, but for God's sake, loosen up."

I dried off and smeared some lipstick on. "I guess you're right. There must be something we can talk about besides me."

Sin snorted. "What? Like them?"

I shot her a look. "Absolutely." We laughed. "Get them talking about the show. Maybe we can get some future storylines."

One last look and we were out the door. "Not a bad idea," she said.

We walked down the hallway to the dining room and found Carmine waiting for us, provocatively leaning against the wall. "Hey, baby," he drawled sexily. "I thought I might throw you on the pool table an' we'll have some hot sex!"

Chapter 6

I blinked.

"Excuse me?" My brain focussed and I frowned. "What did you just say?"

"I thought I might throw the balls on the pool table an' we'll play some sets," he repeated, a little confused by my change of attitude, and now standing straight.

I blinked again and blushed. "Oh, sorry. I thought you said something else."

"Really?" He flashed a small smile. "What?"

"Ah, never mind, doesn't matter now," I said, catching Sin's comical expression.

We walked over to the table where Keith had set everything up, and while Carmine grabbed some cues, Sin pulled me aside to a counter against the wall. "What *did* you think he said?" she whispered quickly.

I leaned in close. "I thought he said, 'I thought I might throw you on the pool table and we'll have some hot sex'."

Sin snorted with laughter while I went a *very* deep shade of red.

"You ladies ever played pool?" Keith asked, curiously

watching us laugh.

"I know how to hit a ball into the pocket," I replied, taking a cue from Carmine.

"All right," he said. "Why don't you pair up with Carmine, and I'll take Sin. Then the team that wins will play each other." We all agreed, and I got to smack the first ball.

The game went on for some time, and Carmine and I ended up taking the lead. "How old are you?" he asked in an undertone, leaning on his cue.

"That's a rude question to ask a woman," I said. "Didn't your mother tell you to never ask a woman how old she is?" I smiled and glanced around at the people in the bar.

He looked at the ground and grinned shyly before looking at me. "Ah, yeah. My mom did teach me that. An' I'm sorry if I offended you."

I shrugged. "Nah, not really." We watched Sin try to hit a ball. "I'm almost thirty-six."

He looked interested. "Really? Then we'll both be thirty-six till my birthday in August."

"I know," I said, with a knowing grin.

The game ended with Carmine and me winning. Then we played each other and I won. But he's one hell of a vicious opponent and the game was full on. He certainly wasn't shy about trying to kill me at pool. Afterwards, Keith decided to help Sin with her style, so I sat on a bar stool and watched. Carmine sat beside me.

"I saw you in the tabloids this week. First landin' that ass Warwick James on his back, then spillin' wine all over that cow of an actress. They both deserved it. That was somethin'." His voice grew softer. "I'd like to know a bit more about you."

Oh, dear God, he'd seen it too. I just wanted to forget that day ever happened. I gazed at him and thought about telling him a bit about me. Would there be any point? I didn't want to deter him, but maybe, we could be friends. Damn, he had kissable lips. I shrugged and looked away. "Not much to tell really. It's what I said before. Won lotto, moved here, starting up my business, publishing my books."

"Did you always want to do that? Start a business I mean."

"No. It's just been the last year or so. I keep coming back to designing, and I started selling some homemade jewellery on eBay, so it kind of came up then."

"That's great," he said. "It must be a big deal though, takin' on so many clothin' lines plus a book. Ownin' a warehouse an' office. That must be a big undertakin'."

I glanced at him again. "Yeah. It's bloody overwhelming. *But* I'm incredibly determined to do it." I watched Keith and Sin having a good time. He was trying to get her to hold the cue properly, but she just rammed it back into his stomach. He doubled over in pretend pain, and she burst out laughing at his comical expression.

"When did you start designin'?" Carmine asked, watching me.

"I didn't really." I swung my legs back and forth. "I just started drawing when I was twelve. It was those Jem and the Holograms clothes, from the eighties cartoons. 'Cause I had a doll and absolutely loved the clothes." I shrugged. "It's been off and on since. What I'd really like to do is design one-off gowns and evening wear for clients. All feminine and girly. But till then, we'll put out mass-produced t-shirts and tops, jeans, jackets and accessories to get going. And once I'm known, the clients for gowns will come."

"Well, ah, maybe I could let the girls on the show know. We're always gettin' gussied up for things, maybe you can design somethin' for them."

I looked long and hard at the man beside me. He was being so sweet and nice, and he looked like a little boy sitting there with his big blue eyes and soft smile. "That'd be great." I smiled in return.

His smile turned into a big grin. "Great." He fiddled with the wide leather band around his right wrist. "What about your jewellery? You said you made it."

I looked around Big Willy's. It was getting crowded now. I glanced at my watch. 9:30 p.m. already. I turned back to Carmine. "I always loved jewellery. There's photos of me when I was young wearing plastic jewellery. Then as I got older, I made it or bought it cheap. And now that I'm older still, I can afford better stuff."

"An' how long have you been writin'?" He'd noticed my uneasiness and seemed a little uncomfortable himself.

"Ah, I've been writing since August 2006. I'd wanted to write a book for about ten years, but never had a story, and never knew how to go about it. I read a lot of how-to books and joined online groups to get help and experience. I've finished my second and have two more, plus a Nancy Drew on the way."

"Nancy Drew?" he said with a smile. He *so* didn't know who Nancy Drew was!

I stared at him and took slight offence. "Yes, Nancy Drew. I've been a collector for twenty-six years. Now, I've written one."

He could tell I was annoyed by the tone in my voice. Although I didn't mean to be.

I looked at my watch, then at the door. God, I wanted to leave.

"Is there somewhere you need to be?" he asked, miffed at my sudden disinterest.

"Not at all. I just don't want to be here." My hands were under my legs as I swung them back and forth. I didn't look at him.

Now *he* was really annoyed. "Well, I'm *so sorry* I ruined your evenin'," he said, sarcasm as clear as day in his tone. "I won't ask you out again."

I sighed. I hadn't meant to insult him. "I didn't mean to be rude. I just…" I shrugged. "Don't feel comfortable."

"Why not?"

I looked at him and decided to be honest. "Because you want to date me, but I don't want to date you. I told you my heart belongs to someone else, and I don't want to lead you on by going out with you. On top of that, I just don't like talking about myself. I'm very private about my personal life. I don't mind getting out and doing things, or mentioning what I do if it comes up in conversations and I feel like talking about it. But as for being asked straight out, or just telling people, then I don't like it, and prefer not to." I watched Sin and Keith.

"You told me you weren't datin' him," Carmine said softly. "You told me on the phone you didn't want to date an' you could only offer friendship. I get that. I do. If I'm givin' out a vibe that's pushy, I'm sorry." His tongue licked his kissable lips. "Tahlia, I *really* like you." His head shook slowly. "I've never met anyone like you. Ever. You're different, you're hot, you're not up yourself or lookin' to get on the show. You're just..." He licked his lips again. "Amazin'. Incredible. Great. An' I really like you."

Oh, God. Come on. Make me gag. I'm feeling so sick from all this crap. Ewww!!!

"Carmine, don't, please. You saying all these things makes me very uncomfortable." I desperately looked everywhere but at him.

"I'm sorry 'bout that, but that's how I feel." He leaned toward me. "But if friendship is all you can offer right now, then I'd like to take it."

I turned to look at him and found his face inches from mine. Gorgeous big blue eyes framed by long dark lashes, lips so kissable – I know I keep saying it, but they are – and close. He pouted a little, so his lips were more inviting.

I found myself starting to give in, leaning toward his pouting lips with pouting lips of my own. But then, remembering who I was in L.A. for, I recoiled and stood. Looking at my watch, I saw the time. "It's ten p.m. Sin, time to go."

"What? I don't want to go," she said, straightening up from the pool table.

"Then you can find your own way home 'cause I'm goin' now." I turned to Carmine and grabbed my bag. "Thanks for tonight. It was nice spending time with you, even though it may not have seemed it." I glanced at Keith. "Thanks for the meal, it was delicious."

He gave me a nod. "You're very welcome. Come back anytime."

Carmine stood. "I'll walk you out to your car."

"That's not necessary," I said quickly, hoping to make a quick getaway.

"Yes, it is," Sin insisted. "You're making us leave, then they can walk us out."

I sighed and didn't want to give in. But there was no point arguing. "Okay. Let's go."

The boys escorted us out to the car park where Keith marvelled at my 'Stang. "That is some car," he said, fingering pieces of bling on the bonnet.

"Thank you. I like it." I unlocked my door.

"You should have seen the salesman at the dealership when Tahlia told him what she wanted. His face went white, and we thought he was going to be sick. It was hilarious," Sin said, getting into the car.

I climbed in and wound down my window. "Thanks again for tonight. The food was great. So was the pool game."

"You're welcome," Keith said again, then stood back while Carmine leaned in.

"I want to see you again," he said softly, those damn lips wet and pouty.

I groaned on the inside. "I don't know. That may not be a good idea."

"Please." His tone was urgent but gentle. "As friends."

Oh, God help me. "Maybe," I said, gunning the engine and pulling out of the car park.

"I can't believe you—" Sin started.

"Don't," I butted in harshly. *Do not* start with me. Let's just go home."

*****

The weekend was taken up with house hunting and op shopping, or opportunity store shopping as you may know it. Goodwill, Salvation Army. You name it, we shopped long and hard. We also raided every secondhand bookstore I could find in the area. I had a Nancy Drew collection to complete, and they were the places I'd get the most bargains.

Sin pouted all weekend. She just couldn't understand why I wasn't even into the *thought* of dating Carmine. Hello! Maybe it's because I didn't want to date him, I'd told her. I wasn't being rude, I just wasn't interested. *He was,* and it made me uncomfortable. I'd never dealt with an Italian man before – although Carmine is only half Italian – but he was very sexually aware, and that radiated from every pore. The way he walked, the way he talked, even the way he wore his clothes, did his hair, and that dazzling white smile made girls weak at the knees. Whether he knew it or not was a different matter, for me, it was too much. The guy just oozed masculine sexuality. From *every pore.*

And Sin is married. She couldn't have him for herself, although he was her 'celebrity screw', where her husband said she was allowed one celebrity to sleep with, and one only. His was Angelina Jolie. Big surprise there! Carmine was hers; she also knew that he wasn't interested, but she could dream about it, and drool over him anytime. She also didn't understand why single old me didn't want him either. After all, I wasn't with Michael yet. I had the time to have some fun with a certain Italian stud who was showing his interest wholeheartedly. Sin...*GO AWAY!!!!!*

*****

Monday we were back at the office to discuss the clothing factories I was interested in buying. My lovely office building was almost complete. The paint was dry, the carpet laid, and the furniture almost set up. It was coming together. My workers and I all sat around our conference table and looked over the papers for every factory and business I could choose from. And it was decided to take on the two factories I had already looked at, and transfer all the workers to my warehouse. A lot of machinery had been bought in the hope of boosting the company, so it was still somewhat new. We'd just have it moved to the business. I did have to buy new printers, though. They were those new fandangled fabric printers that could do a variety of art in different effects. Foil, paint, silkscreen. I wanted ten.

Plus, they could do ten t-shirts/tops or five jeans at the same time. We also needed computers and storage, not to mention a lot of workers.

"Guys, listen up. I'll need you to come to the factories to check them out. You can meet the workers, so you'll know who and what you're dealing with. Ben, how's our publisher?"

Ben handed me a piece of paper with loads of facts and figures on it. "Unless you want to buy a printer and do it yourself, which may be a waste if you're not going to continue writing, it's easier to use a company. Then they can print as many as we need."

"Mmm, yeah, I thought it might be that way. Okay, I'll set that up myself. I need to get it edited anyway." I looked at Ben. "Can you start looking into promotions for the books? I'm thinking about selling them in a gift bag with posters and key rings of the actors that inspired the book. Can you find out what that would entail, besides the legalities of using the actors' photos? Other than that, everything seems to be in order. Richard, grab your car. Sonya, Matthew, Michelle and Tina go with him. We're off to buy some businesses."

We all stood and filed out the room. "Aaron, how're the designs for the ads?" I asked as we walked side by side.

"Black background and colour writing," he said. "And I'm looking into overseas magazines as well."

"Good, good. Keep up the good work. Okay people, let's go."

We arrived at the first factory and met with the manager, Sol Meyers, and the current owner, Manny

Consuelo, and after shaking hands, we all walked inside.

"Mr Meyers," I said. "Would you like to stay on as manager?"

He seemed unsure of his answer. "As much as I want and need a job, I'm not sure I want to keep doing this."

I watched him carefully. He was a big man of about six foot, but a bit overweight. He seemed nice enough. "Is it the hours?" I asked. "You can work day, night, or morning shift if you want to change the schedule."

Now he seemed interested.

"You think about it," I told him, then turned to the owner. "I want to buy the factory. I know the building's old, so I don't want it. But the workers and most of the machinery will be moving to my new warehouse. I'm willing to buy now."

Mr Consuelo was beyond excited. "Thank you, thank you, thank you. You don't know how much this makes me happy. I am so in debt and have not had a buyer yet." He pumped my hand up and down.

"Okay, okay, that's great, I'm happy to help you." I extracted my hand and turned to Sin. "Can you go over the papers with Mr Consuelo? I want to talk to the workers."

"Sure." She led the current owner over to the office.

"Can you get everyone to stop for a moment please," I asked Sol.

He rang a bell on the wall. How simple! "Everyone listen up. This is our new owner." The workers stopped sewing and listened patiently.

"Okay. Hello, everyone. You may remember me from a couple of weeks ago when I came by looking to buy the business. Well, now I have." I looked around at their faces. "And as I asked you then, did you want to keep working. You'll have to transfer to the new warehouse, but the jobs are still yours if you want them." Most of them nodded.

"Good. Now as an added incentive, I will be raising your pay." That got them excited. "I know it hasn't been what it should be, so I'm taking it to the proper pay rate and adding an extra hundred per week." That brought a round of applause.

"Thank you." I paused. "I knew that would make you happy. I need to know if you want to continue working day shift, nine to five, or if you'd like to work night shift, five till two, or the morning shift, two till nine. I want three shifts for awhile so we can stock up for the big opening. I will hire temporary extras during that time, but for those of you that want your job, it's yours permanently." More cheers.

"Okay, if you want to work day shift go to Sonya." I pointed to each of my COs as I spoke. "And tell her your name. For night shift, let Matthew know, and morning shift is Michelle. Now." I turned to Sol Meyers. "Would you still like to stay on? You can have any shift you want or stay on days."

He was impressed. "I'll stick with day shift." He flashed a big grin. "Thanks for the raise."

"You're all very welcome." I turned back to the crowd. "While the warehouse is being fitted with most of this machinery, you can all have the week off till we're ready to go." There were a few mumbles.

"Don't worry," I added. "It's paid leave." That made them happy. "Now, my assistants here will hand you a form with all the details and addresses of the business. Next Monday morning I expect you there at nine a.m. We'll go over new employment arrangements, making sure you all get your benefits, and you can see where you're working. Right now though, I need to go buy the place. Thank you, everyone."

I was applauded as I walked into the office. Five minutes later I owned a factory.

And two hours later, I owned a second. It went as smoothly as the first and everyone was happy to still have a job. With a pay increase, of course.

"Richard," I said, "I need you to make sure everything we want is transferred to the warehouse and set up exactly like in the plans."

"You got it." His new job was exciting him, and he easily got what needed to be done.

"Guys," I said to them. "You'll need to pitch in on this as well. Both managers are staying on so they can deal with their part of the factory. But then I'll need someone to manage the whole place. Can you find me, someone?"

"Absolutely," they said, raring to go.

"Okay, then," I said. "I think going to the warehouse once a week to check on progress is a good idea. So I'll either make it Monday or Friday mornings. Is that okay with you?"

"Great," Richard said. "And I'll start looking for a factory manager today."

"Great. In the meantime get the warehouse set up, and can you find out if their stocks are enough for us right now? Until we find suppliers, we'll need something."

"Actually," Sonya piped up. "I've worked with some suppliers. American material, beads and gems. I'll give them a call."

"Fantastic. Let me know the details, and I'll see you next Monday at the warehouse."

We went our separate ways, and I was feeling good...until I met my fitness instructor.

"Okay," he said, clapping his hands. "We're gonna get moving, we're gonna burn off fat and calories, we're gonna move, move, move." Bright nylon shorts full of bulging muscles that moved in a *very* inappropriate manner were making their way toward me.

I looked at him with distaste. I was standing there in my gym gear wondering who the hell my chiro had sent me to.

She *really did* think I was fat!!!

I hate her!!!

Sven Golden. Swedish gym trainer extraordinaire. His name said it all. Tall, very blond, and very, very muscular. Kinda like the sun shone right out of him. He saw the look of disdain on my face.

"Don't worry," he crooned. "I'll have you working hard and burning fat in thirty minutes."

Thirty minutes. Now I was feeling better.

*****

I dragged myself out of bed Wednesday morning. "Ugh," I groaned, flinging open the curtains. I was in pain. Pain, I tells ya. On Monday, Sven had me burning so much it was ridiculous, and yesterday I had Pilates with my chiro. I was in pain. And I had Sven again tonight. Ugghh.

I sighed. There was no point arguing, I had to stay in shape. After all, I had to look good for Michael. I was going to track him down and marry him. I just had to bide my time. Until then, I had to suck it up and get to the publisher.

It was a great company. There were editors and artists to help you create your very own book cover, and make sure it's word perfect to the point it's guaranteed to be a bestseller.

I was given an editor by the name of Amy. She was a thirty year old who'd graduated college and gone straight to an agency. Now, she was helping people to self-publish.

I plopped a box onto her desk and sat down. "This is my first book. It's four hundred pages, an erotic romantic suspense thriller and I need it ready for sale as soon as possible."

She looked at me with light green eyes. "Usually, it takes months for a book to be edited and published." Sliding the box toward her, she opened it.

"I understand that," I said. "But time is of the essence. I know what I want for my cover so I can get that going now. Plus, I can edit my ms as quickly as you tell me the changes to make. I need this to happen fast. How soon can you read it?"

She flicked through a few pages. "I can start reading it today and let you know."

"Great. I'll pop by every day or so to see what needs to be done." We shook and exchanged numbers. I was then shown to the graphics department and met the designer for my book. We sat for half an hour and discussed what I wanted. It was going to be relatively easy, and the artist knew exactly what to do.

I'm going to digress here for a few moments, since it now seems appropriate, and tell you a little something you don't know. Until 2006, I hadn't written a novel. Sure I had an idea floating around in my head, especially after reading a particular book by Jackie Collins. I'm still not sure if I ever read the whole book then, as in getting it out of my local library, or whether I just flicked through it in my local Target store. But either way, there's one scene I distinctly remember and it has stuck with me ever since. And when I mean ever since, well, it's about twenty years by now, so that's one hell of a long time to remember a scene.

Since Jackie came to Australia quite often, I still recall her visit from 2007. She came blazing into the country, flitting from TV show to TV show with flair and style, and a never-ending supply of snazzy coloured blazers and matching jewellery. She was elegantly put together, and I sat mesmerised by her appearance.

She spoke about a lot of things and eloquently answered the questions put to her. And while I was unable to catch her on every TV and radio show, I saw and heard her plenty.

The interviews were very interesting. Intriguing.

Drawing me into the world of Jackie and her novels. *Mmm,* I had thought at the time. This is inspiring me to track down her website and find out more about her writing technique to see if I can learn a thing or two. In fact, she inspired me so much, that I not only started borrowing her books from the library, but when I looked up her website, I signed on to her fan club and sent off a question. After a few weeks, a reply was posted on her site. And let me tell you, it was a morale booster to an aspiring writer like myself. I saved a copy of the web page to a folder, and every now and then I look at it, and my morale is boosted again.

Yay Jackie! Go, Jackie! Woohoo, Jackie!

And I have to say, that when my first novel is published because my book is similar in style to hers, i.e. sex and relationships, that I may very well be called the new/the next/the young, Jackie Collins. For an aspiring writer publishing a first novel that would be absolutely fantastic.

Claps hands in glee.

But to those people saying, or writing it, i.e. authors, reviewers, TV talk-show hosts, will they consider Jackie's feelings when they say or write it. After all, Jackie may not want to be referred to as the old/the before/the has-been, Jackie Collins.

For shame. Poor Jackie!

A round of applause for Jackie Collins people. Claps hands again in glee.

Jackie has paved the way for aspiring writers in this genre, style of writing, or subject matter of sex and relationships.

Go, Jackie!

Can you tell I'm still a big fan? A huge grin is plastered on my face, right now. In the meantime, since she *always* included an Aussie character in her books, I decided to repay the gesture by writing about her and what she means to me.

Thank you, Jackie!

*****

After another gruelling workout with Sven, I was trying to relax on my bed and go over my schedule when my cell rang. "Hello."

"Hey. It's, ah...Carmine."

His voice melted all thoughts away, and I blushed. Then I got annoyed. I loved and adored Carmine as an actor and seemingly great guy, but I didn't want to be involved.

"Tahlia...you there?"

"Yeah, yeah, I'm here."

"How are you?"

"Uhhh, busy, tired, worn out, determined."

He laughed a little. "Yeah. I know those feelin's...so everythin's all right then?"

"Ah, yeah. I've bought my factories, and it's all being shipped to my warehouse. We're also getting suppliers and workers." I looked around the room. "And today I met with my publisher. I'm self-publishing, but I've got an editor and cover designer. It's pretty exciting."

"That's great. I'm glad everythin's happenin' for you." There was noise on his end. "Um, look. About

128

the other night—"

"Look, I was rude, and I didn't mean to be...sorry," I butted in.

"No, you told me you only wanted to be friends. I thought havin' a meal would be okay. It obviously wasn't."

I heard him exhale. He must be smoking. Such a filthy habit. I played with my papers. "Yeah, I did. But, I just felt uncomfortable. I don't know. I guess it was from you kissing me in the diner. It just put me off, and it didn't feel right hanging out with you when I love someone else."

Another exhale. "I hope I didn't come over as pushy. I was tryin' to respect your boundaries, but I had to make small talk. No point goin' out an' not talkin'." He laughed.

I smiled. "Guess not. You were kinda pushy." I looked at the ceiling. "But not as pushy as you could've been." I studied my nails. "You weren't that bad. Like I said, I was uncomfortable. That's all. It's not every day I grab a bite to eat with the hot actor from the show I talk about online."

He laughed. Deep and guttural. It was *very* sexy. "I guess not," he said. "Have you gotten with the guy you're in love with?"

My eyes narrowed. *Now, why would that be any of his business?* "I don't want to talk about that with you." I didn't mean to sound nasty, but I think I did anyway.

"That's okay. I didn't mean to pry."

Oh, yes you did!

He exhaled. "I was wonderin' if you'd like to come

over to my place on the weekend for a barbecue. You could check out the place, meet my cat, brag about it to everyone online. How 'bout it?"

So not a good idea! "That's really not a good idea," I said. "Why would you want me telling all of your fans every detail of your bedroom? 'Cause that's all they really want to know, you know. They wanted to kill me after seeing the photos when Sin put them up. She bragged and bragged. It was sickening. And they all hated me."

He laughed, long and hard, with a coughing tilt at the end. "That's funny. Really funny."

"Glad you think so," I said dryly, playing with the bedspread.

More coughing. "It would be worth it just to get you here."

"It's not a good idea, Carmine. I'll have to say thanks, but no thanks."

A long silence, then, "Are you sure?"

"What, are you kidding? You pashed me in a diner. What the hell would you do to me in your own home? Definitely not a good idea." I crossed my arms in defiance.

"I wouldn't force you to do anythin' for a start." He sounded annoyed.

I shook my head. "It's still not a good idea. Thanks for asking, but I won't be coming over. Was there anything else you called about?" I needed to get rid of him right now.

"Ah, no. That was it."

"Okay, great. Thanks for calling. Bye." I ended the

call. Sighing, I scrunched down on my bed. God, what was he doing? Not pushing me, then inviting me around to his place. Argh! Bloody Italian Stallion. Why'd you have to be so damn sexy!

*****

Thursday I went about my business of martial arts class, and after an hour I had forgotten all about Carmine's call, until I was driving down the road and passed a billboard with his face on it, advertising his show.

"Damn you, Carmine," I said viciously. "Why are you so kissable?" The photo showed him with a slight pout, showing his lips to full advantage. His eyes were so big and blue. I half sighed, half laughed, and had to pull over to the curb, so I didn't cause an accident. "Damn it. What am I gonna do?" Resting my head in my hands, I leaned on the door.

What am I gonna do to distract you? I love Michael, and I want him. There is absolutely no point in getting involved with you. I shook my head. I might very well just have to ignore him. *I* was on a mission.

Pulling away, I headed for my hotel, but found myself on a detour, as some streets were being paved. The new route took me away from the hotel, but it didn't matter as I had time. And I got to see some more of the suburb I currently called home.

Turning onto a side street and cruising slowly along, I spied a flash looking car on the side of the road. The driver, a man, dressed in what looked like an expensive grey suit, was pacing back and forth in front of the car, waving his arms and shaking his head.

At first, I was going to drive past, but then noticed who the driver was. I did a double take and slowed down even more. Then it hit me. I needed to pull over!

I screeched to the curb, turned the car off, and yanked the key out of the ignition. I was out of my seat and walking toward the man within seconds. "Do you need help?"

The man threw his cell into the bushes at the side of the road and turned to me. His features softened, and he smiled. "Thank you for stopping, my dear. You are a God-send." He looked up to the sky then back at me.

"Um, that's okay. What can I do to help?"

"My car stopped, and I can't start it. Then my cell died. And I can't use the car phone because the car doesn't work. I'm stuck here with no way of calling for help."

We both looked around and realised there were no houses on the street.

"Well, you can use my cell to call for help," I suggested.

"That would be wonderful. Thank you so much."

I retrieved my phone from my bag and handed it to him.

"Thank you, thank you so much," he said, dialling a number.

I sat on the boot of my car and waited, trying not to listen, pretending not to look, and admiring the area. Out of the corner of my eye, I took in his appearance. He was a man of fifty-ish, grey hair neatly combed, trim build. Well-mannered and well dressed.

"Well," he said, ending the call. "I rang my secretary who's going to send a tow truck and my driver with another car. It will be about twenty minutes. Do you mind if I make another call? I need to let my friend know our meeting will be a little later than planned."

"That's fine. Go ahead." I was curious about the man. I knew who he was and what he did, and spending a little time chatting with him would not be a hardship. I looked at my watch. I had the time before my next class.

He finished his second call and handed me my phone. "Thank you so much, my dear. I appreciate it so much. If there's anything I can do for you—"

"No, no." I waved my hand. "It's fine. Doing my good deed for the day." I grinned, and he grinned back.

He noticed my car for the first time and walked around it. "Wow," he gasped. "That is some Mustang. I've never seen anything like it."

"Thank you. I love it." I patted my baby affectionately.

"Did you buy it like that or have it detailed?"

"I had it detailed. The car dealer looked like he was going to be sick when I told him what I wanted. And when I picked it up, a Mustang collector had a go at me for wrecking," – I made quotation marks with my fingers – "a perfectly good specimen of a car." I smiled happily. "But this is what I wanted, and it makes me happy."

"Well," the man said, spreading his hands. "If it makes you happy then who cares what anyone else says?" He stuck out his hand. "I should introduce myself. I'm Richard Sayer. And again, I want to thank you for stopping and helping me out."

I shook his hand. "Hey, not a problem. I'm Tahlia Cameron."

"I want to repay you for your generosity," he continued. "I'll give you my card." He reached into his jacket pocket and withdrew a business card. "Do you have a number I can contact you on?"

"Actually, I have a card of my own." I took his and went to the front seat of my car, grabbing one of my cards and handing it to him.

"Tahlia Cameron. Cell number only. Where are you staying?"

"The Colonial Inn, next suburb over," I said, pointing back over my shoulder.

"If there's anything you need, let me know."

"No. That's okay," I replied, with another wave of my hand.

"Are you sure?"

"I'm sure. Enough already," I cried, laughing a little.

We chatted for a few more minutes, and I mentioned my business. He offered to give me advice on running an empire.

"Empire? It's hardly an empire...yet!" I exclaimed with another laugh.

"I'm sure it will be one day," Richard said, as a limo came around the bend. "Ah, here's my ride." The limo pulled over, and he spoke to the driver. A tow truck came rambling past as well.

"Looks like my cue to leave," I told Richard.

"It was very nice meeting you, Tahlia. And thank

you for stopping and helping an old man out."

"Old! You're hardly old. And you're welcome. I'll let you get on with it. It was very nice meeting you too." I got into my car and started her up. Waving a hand out the window, I cruised off down the road.

Watching in my rear-view, I couldn't believe my luck. I had just helped the CEO of the biggest TV broadcasting network in the United States of America. His network played all of my favourite shows, including Michael's and Carmine's.

At that moment, little did I realise, or have absolutely any idea at all, how much of a role Richard Sayer, CEO of the biggest TV network in the world, would have on my life.

Chapter 7

I spoke to Sin when I got back to the hotel. "You will *not believe* who I ran into this morning." I threw my handbag on the bed and pulled a gym bag from the closet.

"Who?" she asked, plopping down on the bed. Her eyes widened. "Oooh, tell me you ran into Carmine Gionetti." She stuck her hands on her hips. "And don't tell me you turned him down again."

"My life is not about Carmine," I said, rolling my eyes and laughing. "Although, I nearly ran into another car when I saw that huge billboard of him on Chestnut Street. I had to pull over and fume for a moment." I shook my head at the memory.

"Oooh, I've seen that picture," she said, crossing her legs. "It's definitely droolworthy. So, who'd you meet?"

I looked at her. "Richard...Sayer." I let the name sink in.

Her eyes widened again. "Oh, my, God. You ran into the CEO of TNM. They play Carmine's show." She bounced up and down on the bed then stopped.

"Wait, you didn't *actually* run into him, did you? 'Cause he could sue you."

I snorted and zipped up my gym bag. "I didn't *actually* run my car into him. I didn't need to. You know those roads that have been shut down for paving?"

"Yeah."

"Well, I took the detour on some road that way," I pointed forty-five degrees front left of me, "I was cruising along, saw a car on the side of the road and a man pacing back and forth. When I saw him, I knew who he was and stopped to help." I pulled his card out of my bag and showed Sin. "He said he owed me, and if there was anything he could ever do, or help me with, I had mentioned starting a business, then call. He was very nice."

Sin handed the card back. "Well, I *am* impressed. Three weeks here and you've done well. Groped by a drunken has-been actor, screamed at by a queen bee bitch, and helped out the CEO of America's biggest network." She stood. "Who else are you going to run into?"

"You forgot Carmine and Keith," I said.

She waved a hand. "There you go then. Look at all the people you've met. I gotta tell you, girl, I'm *sooo* glad I'm your lawyer," she said with a laugh.

I laughed with her. "Well, hey," I shrugged and rolled my eyes in amusement, "I wanted to start with a bang when I moved here."

"Damn girl, you certainly have."

*****

The next two days were hectic, but then which days weren't. Classes, house hunting, book collecting on the weekend, and finding professional dressmakers. I was no closer to finding a house. It's not that they weren't nice, they just weren't what I wanted. I wanted a studio, a study, a huge master bedroom and a massive walk-in closet. And I wanted it next to Michael.

"Oh, so you haven't forgotten about him then?" you ask.

Oh, no, absolutely not. I don't want to appear to be a stalker. I mean I know *where* Michael lives, and that he works hard all day, five days a week. I also know he doesn't run around town flaunting himself. He's a very private person. But I need to bide my time. I have a plan you see. I've approached his neighbours and asked if they'd sell. That I love the house and its location, and it would be perfect for me. They said they were surprised that I'd want to buy, but after hearing my offer, they were definitely going to think about it.

So, here I am. Ensconced in The Colonial Inn, surrounded by boxes and boxes of books, dolls and collectables. An overflowing closet filled with wigs, dresses, tops, jeans, boots, bags, hats, accessories, and anything else you can think of. I was settling into my new life, my new world. My business, my book, which I was editing every day, and you know, it may seem great, but it's *so* overwhelming. And little did I know, things were going to become so much more complicated.

*****

On Monday, my employees and I met at my warehouse. I love my warehouse. Huge, cream coloured, right number, right street. It was lovely. I pulled my car into a car park and walked through the front door. There was a small reception area and hallway which led to the work area. My workers were waiting for me along with my managers. In the sewing section, I saw the machines were set up. Ten sewers in ten rows. So efficient.

"Okay, everyone, it's good to see you here. How do you like your new workplace?" I looked at the crowd of workers; they were very happy.

Richard came up to me looking excited and introduced the new factory manager. "Tahlia, I want you to meet Todd Ettridge. I've hired him to manage everything on this end."

We shook hands, and I looked at Richard inquiringly. "Is there anyone else *we've* hired?" I asked, pretending to be annoyed.

"Ah, yes, actually." He shifted uneasily. "We've also hired a material and gem supplier."

I raised my brows. "Really?" I studied his face as it became a deeper shade of beet red.

"Ah, yes," he continued. "We've struck a very good deal, and supplies are on the way this week. With everything set up and ready to go, we just need the material to start the lines."

"Mmm." My lips moved around a little, in and out of a pout before smiling. "Well done!"

Richard relaxed. "Thanks," came out in a huge sigh of relief.

I looked over some of my workers and spied some ladies who had to be those I'd spoken to on the phone. "Get everyone acquainted with the factory," I told Richard and then walked over to the women. "Ladies, you're my dressmakers, right?"

"Right."

We introduced ourselves, and I led them to the design tables I had set up and pulled out my pad. "Okay, ladies. You're going to be my personal dressmakers. I want to start a line of one of a kind dresses, outfits, suits, but mainly evening. I will be designing for whoever wants an original, and your job will be to take measurements and put it together." I looked at each one. "Besides making sure my lines are properly cut out. They need to be even. I don't want clothes that don't line up at the seam or have a crooked neckline. You'll see to it that the patterns are exact and the material is cut out properly. I'll also need you to inspect each article as it's finished. Is that okay with you?"

The ten women before me seemed happy.

"Okay." I laid some papers on the counter. "Until we get the supplies and it all gets going, I want you to make me some costumes. I've got the pics here and some fabric samples, so you'll need to find that as well."

We pored over the designs. I'm not sure what the women thought of me wanting to turn Jem and the Holograms clothes into outfits for myself. But what did it matter? What I wanted, I would get. Besides, I was paying. The ladies took my measurements and then I was off.

*****

I woke Thursday morning to an overcast sky. It didn't look like rain, which was a pity since I love rain, but there were fluffy grey clouds bouncing across the sky. I rolled out of bed in my new silk negligee and threw on a matching robe. I wasn't used to wearing such nightwear, but since shaping up and moving to L.A., I needed something to wear to bed. Sin had dragged me to five different underwear and lingerie stores, telling me to try on everything in the shop. I didn't want to, but as I fingered the materials, I got excited. I was going to marry Michael Anthony, so I needed something sexy to wear for him. I ended up with more undies and nighties than I'd ever had in my life.

After ordering room service of a ham, mushroom and cheese omelette, I went into the bathroom for a shower. Twenty minutes later when breakfast arrived, I was dressed and ready for the day.

With *The Morning Show* playing in the background, I read through my schedule. Except for martial arts, I was free for the morning until afternoon classes. I drank the last of my juice, grabbed my bags, and left the breakfast tray outside my door on the floor. Walking to my car, I had no idea of what was about to happen.

*****

"Thank you, Sensei," I muttered and went into the change room, and five minutes later, I walked back into the main room. Martial arts was over for another week, with people already arriving for the next class.

"Miss Tahlia. How is your weapons training going?" Sensei asked.

"Very well, thank you," I told my fifty-year-old teacher. "In conjunction with these classes, I feel I could take on the world."

Sensei smiled tightly. "Miss Tahlia. You know that is not what these classes are about. They are about control and awareness. The need to protect yourself, and stopping your opponent without force or anger."

I sighed inwardly and looked around the studio. I knew what the classes were for. I had been joking, but Sensei never got jokes. *Nooooo.* And because he didn't, he came across as patronising, treating you like a child when you weren't. I kept my temper in check.

My eyes took in the well-lit, red floor studio in the northern suburbs. It was fifteen minutes from where I lived and had a great reputation. "I know this is serious business, Sensei, I was joking, even though this is nothing to joke about." I glanced at the door. "Both of my classes are working in conjunction perfectly. Thank you for asking." I bowed. "I really must go. Goodbye." I walked out the door to my car before he could start talking again.

Driving down the road, I pulled over to the curb and stopped. "Good grief. That man has no sense of humour. I am not a child that needs to be chastised, and God, it pisses me off." I sat and simmered for a few minutes over our conversation, then with a big sigh put it out of my mind.

Rifling through my diary, I found the address for a secondhand bookstore. "Now, where is it?" I peered through the directory. "Ah, there. Not too far from here." Knowing I couldn't resist a Nancy Drew calling to me to buy it, I went in search of the bookstore. Ten minutes later I found it, parked down the road, and throwing my bag over my shoulder, set off.

The shop was quaint. Tucked neatly between a clothes store and a nail salon, nestled in a nice quiet leafy suburb, with a sign at the front that read 'Ye Olde Time Bookstore'. Pushing open the door, I heard the tinkle of the bell, but as I stepped inside, there was another sound. A noise that sounded like a crash. It wasn't loud, but I heard it.

Turning, and looking up and down the road, I heard two cars gunning their engines. Another bang. I looked to my right, my eyes narrowing in the sunlight that now streamed down. There in the distance, about a block away, were two cars racing down the quiet street. A black SUV, followed by a small van.

The van banged into the SUV again, which then accelerated, though it seemed to be in slow motion to me. Just as the SUV came up to my right, a dog ran across the road in front of it, and with one last smash from the van, the driver swerved along the road and smashed full force into a huge pole. Unfortunately for the van, it rear-ended the SUV.

It was like watching a cop movie or something. I kept expecting the crew and cameramen to come running up, and a director to yell *cut*. But that didn't happen.

Snapping back to reality, I realised this was a serious accident. Quickly grabbing my digital camera from my bag, I took a few shots as I ran to the SUV. The front was crumpled like a toy car, windows broken, the engine smoking and sparking.

Throwing my camera into my bag, I yanked open the driver's door, which took some effort since it was stuck, and saw an unconscious woman strapped behind the wheel.

I knew I had to get her out. Flames were now flicking at the engine, and they looked ready to eat us alive. I tried to undo the woman's belt, but it wouldn't open. Trying not to panic, I looked around for help, then remembered my Swiss Army knife. I pulled it out of my bag and sliced through the seat belt, then grabbed the woman under her arms and tried to pull her out.

She wouldn't move. Her legs were stuck under the dashboard.

Damn it!

I dove down to disentangle her, feeling the heat coming through the front of the car. The smoke was thick and choking. With a final grunting tug the woman's feet came free, and grabbing her under her arms again, I dragged her to where I'd been standing minutes before.

Laying her flat, I checked for a pulse. It was beating. Was she breathing? She was. I quickly examined her. I'd done a first aid course before I left Australia, and except for a problem with her legs, she seemed to be okay.

BOOMMMM.

I fell over her to protect her and covered my head. Debris rained down on us, and peeking out from under my arm, I saw her SUV on fire. It had exploded.

I looked at the van and noticed the driver had escaped, I didn't know where, but it was just as well since it was on fire too. I glanced at the woman. Still unconscious. I pulled out my phone and dialled 911, telling them the address, about the accident, and needing an ambulance.

"Give her to us."

I looked up. Two men were standing over me with guns pointed. They were unsteady on their feet and both bleeding from head wounds.

I tried not to freak out and rolled my eyes. "You have got to be fucking kidding me," I told them. I know I haven't sworn that badly before, but jeez, I was pissed.

"Give her to us," one repeated, waving his gun. He was about five foot ten and had red hair. The blood made it more so.

I tried not to panic and thought quickly. This is what I had taken all of my self-defence classes for; in the event I needed to defend myself or someone else. I knew how to deal with an offender with a gun. But two? I stood slowly, trying to think of a simple but effective martial arts routine that I could pull off with my mediocre butt kicking skills. I faced them, moving between the woman on the ground, and the two idiots in front of me. My heart was pounding so loudly I thought everyone on the other side of the world would hear it.

"Look," I said softly, slowly putting my hands up in front of me. "You've had a nasty accident, and you're hurt. So is she. In fact, she's unconscious." I licked my lips and took a step toward them, hoping the woman wouldn't betray me by waking up. "The ambulance is on its way, and you can all be fixed up." I pointed to one man's head. "You're bleeding really badly. They can wrap it for you." I took another step.

"We don't want no damn ambulance," he spat, "we want her." He waved his gun toward the woman on the ground.

"What do you want with an unconscious woman?" I asked, taking a step. Casting a quick glance around, I saw no one to help me. I was on my own. "You'll have to carry her." I shrugged. "As you can see, she can't walk."

"Why don't you just give us the damn woman," the second man said, before swaying on his feet. I took my chance. With a step and a karate kick, I sent his gun flying and him reeling. The first man lunged at me, and I grabbed his arm, pushing it up. I punched him in the solar plexus, and twisting his arm, flipped him on his back.

The second man came at me again. He was skinny,

about five foot eight, so I knew I could take him. With a swing kick, I knocked him flat, then a roundhouse caught the first man in the jaw, throwing his head back. He fell without a sound. Grabbing my camera again I snapped pics of the two men and, staying aware of them, went back to the woman.

She was still dead to the world. Shielding her and trying to keep her warm, I heard sirens down the block. So did the two men who were now struggling to their feet. I stood again to fight, but they took off running. Well, trying to anyway. A car screeched to a halt down the block, and the men piled in. I snapped a few pics and saw the car take off. After it turned a corner, I attended to the woman again. She was finally groaning and moving her head.

"It's okay," I said soothingly, patting her shoulder. "You're okay, the ambulance is here." It pulled up behind me. "You'll be taken to the hospital."

The paramedics ran up to us and started working on the woman. "What happened?"

"The van smashed her into the pole." I pointed to the car the fire brigade was dousing with water. "I tried to pull her out, but her feet were stuck. I dislodged them and pulled her over here, checked that she was breathing and had a pulse. Called for you guys, and protected her from those thugs." I stood back as they worked on her. They put an oxygen mask over her mouth and wrapped her in a heat blanket.

"You did well," the young male paramedic said. "She might have a concussion, but she'll pull through."

I smiled at him then turned to the scene. Firemen

running all over the place, pumping water through their hoses. Policemen setting up roadblocks and pushing back people that now came out for a look. The fire was being controlled, and I glanced down the road toward my car. It was still there and not affected. I sighed in relief and stepped back to the bookstore to give the officers space to move, and my heart a chance to calm down.

A second ambulance arrived, and the paramedics came over with a stretcher bed. They put a neck brace on the woman and rolled her onto a board to keep her straight. Lifting her, they strapped her to the bed. Wrapping a blanket around her, they adjusted a drip and set up some medical equipment.

She groaned and blinked her eyes. "Where am I?" she asked in a soft, faint voice.

"Ma'am, we're going to get you to the hospital. You were in an accident, but you're going to be okay. A young woman saved your life. You're going to be just fine."

I had a thought and pulled a business card from my bag. "Here." I ran over to the woman the paramedics were wheeling to the ambulance.

"Are you the..." the woman whispered.

I thrust my card into her hand. "That's my number. The ambos will take care of you. I hope you're okay." I watched them strap her into the van and close the door. With a wailing siren, they sped off down the road.

"Miss."

I turned and looked around.

"Miss."

An officer was walking toward me. "Are you the one who pulled the woman out?" He pointed to some people standing on the side of the road. "They said it was you who had the gun and kicked the bad guys. You need to come with me, Miss."

Warily, I followed the man over to a cop car. He spoke to an officer who introduced himself as Sergeant Baker. "Are you the woman who saved the day?" His hands were lodged firmly on his hips, and his stern look and tone worried me.

I sighed. Maybe I should call Sin. "I suppose."

"Okay. I need you to come down to the station and give a statement. The detectives will want to talk to you." He opened the car door.

I knew the rules as I'd grilled Sin on the law. "I'll drive my car down to the station," I said, with more bravado than I felt and gave him a grin. "So, how about I follow you."

His stern expression stayed in place. "Now, Ma'am. I must insist."

"Sergeant." The hardness of my voice made me flinch, so I softened it. "I'm not refusing to come to the station, but I know my rights. You have no need to take me in a cop car so you cannot insist. I'll follow you. I'll even shake on it." I held out my hand and smiled a little.

He knew I was right and slammed the door. "All right," he grumbled. "Grab your car and follow me. Where is it anyway?"

I pointed down the block. "It's the multicoloured star 'Stang. You won't lose me." I strode off down the street, and upon reaching my car, climbed in. Taking a few deep breaths to calm my racing heart, I checked myself in the mirror and had a quick clean up. I started the car and noticed Sergeant Baker had pulled alongside me, making sure I didn't get away, no doubt.

As I drove along, I made a quick call to Sin to let her know I was going to police headquarters to give a statement. "Help!" I cried when she answered, then told her all about it.

"Look, everything should be okay. You're a witness in special circumstances. Call back if there are any problems, although I'm sure there won't be any."

I hoped there wouldn't be either. Legal hassles were *not* what I needed in my new life.

Sin's an entertainment and business lawyer, but has dealt with other issues in the course of her legal career. I knew I could trust her to deal with anything I would need, and to get it sorted in a short amount of time. That's why I trusted her. And why I was paying her well!

Ten minutes later I was escorted into a room in the police station. I waited on a rickety plastic chair till two men walked in.

"I'm Detective Beyer," the good looking brunet said. He was about thirty to forty years old and wrapped in a black suit. He pointed to a man who looked to be in his fifties. "And this is Detective Sold." They sat down opposite me. "You seem to be a hero," Det. Beyer continued, setting a small tape recorder on the table.

"Not really." I shrugged.

They settled in and opened their notepads. "Tell us everything from start to finish."

I recounted every detail that I remembered, and pulled out my camera and showed them the pictures I'd snapped of the offenders and their car.

"That's great," Beyer said. "We'll take this for evidence." He reached for my camera.

I pulled it away from his grasp. "No," I said firmly. "You'll download the photos and give me back my camera." I glared warily at them, hoping they got the point. "You will *not* keep my camera." I raised an eyebrow in tired annoyance.

The detectives looked at each other then back at me.

"All right then," Beyer replied slowly. "We'll just download the photos. I'll take it to the computer tech."

"No," I replied. "You'll take *me* to the computer tech so I can watch him download the photos, then I *know* I'll get it back." I gave him a look of determination and crossed my arms.

Another look between them. "Okay, come on."

Knowing they weren't able to push me around, they walked me to a small room one floor up, and we sat while the tech downloaded and printed my pics.

I tucked the camera back into my bag. "Well, is that it then?"

"Ah, no," Beyer said. It seems he did all the talking and his partner kept his mouth shut. "You'll need to sign your statement and make a note of who those men are." He pointed to the idiots in the photos.

"First, I don't know who they are, so how can I make a note, and second, how much longer will I be?" I looked at my watch and noticed it was well after lunchtime.

"Do you have someplace to be?" Det. Sold asked, sarcasm dripping from his words.

Hallelujah! He speaks! Even if it makes him a pain in the arse.

"*Yes, I do,*" I retorted. "I have classes all afternoon. So, if I'm gonna be stuck here, I need to call and cancel." I was *really* annoyed now, and they were noticing.

"It's going to be some time," Det. Beyer said and led me out to the waiting area.

Two hours later, I signed my statement and walked out to freedom.

After working off my anger in yoga class, I rolled into the hotel car park. Sin met me there, and we talked about it as we went upstairs. I was still talking as I opened my door and threw myself onto the bed. "I really don't want to have to do that again," I said.

"What? Save a life, or deal with the cops."

"Ugh," I sighed. "Both."

"It's all over now," Sin continued. "Do you have any idea who you saved?"

"Nope. I just know it was a woman." I rolled onto my side and stared glassily out the window into the fading light.

"Marnie Wilkins."

"Who's she?" I mumbled. "And how do you know?" I felt myself falling asleep.

"*She* is the wife of Richard Sayer. *And* it's already all over the news."

"What? Wait, what?" My brain struggled to wake. I looked over my shoulder at Sin. "What did you say?"

She lay on her stomach beside me. "The woman whose life you saved is *Marnie Wilkins. The wife* of TNM network's Richard Sayer. You know, *the man you saved last week."*

I blinked a few times and sat up. The thought that my life was coming back to Richard Sayer was unbelievable. Was the universe at work? I shook my head. *No. It couldn't possibly. Could it?* I looked absentmindedly around the room for a few moments before Sin sat up and shook my arm.

"Do you have any idea what this means?" she said, her face animated.

I sighed and flopped back down on the bed, tucking a pillow under my head. "What it means, is that God is trying to tell me that Richard Sayer is supposed to be in my life, and that something is happening." I shrugged and stared at the ceiling. "Whatever happens is meant to happen." I looked at her. "The Universe wants us together for some reason. But right now, I'm bloody tired." I covered a yawn. "God, I'm buggered."

"You don't know how big this is going to be, do you?" Sin asked incredulously then shook her head. "You saved the wife of the CEO of the biggest TV network in America." She looked off into the distance. "The publicity you could get from this! Talk shows, gossip shows, every paper and magazine in the world." She came back from dreamland and looked down at me. "You could get so much publicity from this," she said excitedly. "You could talk about your books and the company." She grabbed my arm and shook it again. "Imagine what kind of reward you could get.

I'm sure he'd give you the world."

"How can he give me the world when he doesn't own the world?" I mumbled.

"You know what I mean." She gazed into the distance again. "Money. What if he gives you a reward? He might want to give you millions of dollars. You could ask to be on one of the shows. *Oh, my God.* You could be on Carmine's show and become a huge star." She flung herself down beside me and threw her arms wide. "Richard Sayer, CEO of TNM network offers the world to Tahlia Cameron for saving his wife's life after crash and attempted kidnapping."

"Oh, please," I said, secretly giddy at the thought of what kind of reward I might be offered. "I don't need his money, I've got plenty. Besides, I don't know if I could accept a reward."

"*What do you mean you won't accept a reward,*" Sin yelled. "You *have* to. It's your duty, as a heroine, to accept all awards and rewards offered to you for your deed. You'd have to be nuts if you don't."

"Well, I'm not nuts," I replied, hauling myself off the bed. "What I am is hungry, dirty, and tired. So order us some food while I take a shower."

I stood under the hot fast spray and let it wash over me. It felt good. Healing. I needed something to calm myself after the day I'd had. The events played through my mind act for act. I shampooed my hair and rinsed. Drying off, I caught a glimpse of myself in the mirror.

"Mmm," I cocked my head, "I don't look like a hero. Brown hair, green eyes, full lips. Nope. Same as I looked yesterday, last week and last month. No, I am not a hero."

After a nice meal, I settled into bed and listened to the peace and quiet. Until it rained. Then I listened to the drops beat on the roof above me. I love the rain. A lot of people don't, they think it's depressing, but I love it. Especially on a cold night when you can snuggle down into a nice comfy bed and listen to it drumming on the roof. It's soothing. It's relaxing. And it was relaxing me into a nice dreamy sleep...

Dreamy all right, but hardly sleep. I tossed and turned as images played in my head over and over. Constantly changing the outcome. First I was the heroine, then I got shot. First I saved the woman, then she died an agonising death. First, the bad guys died, then they jumped up and shot me. The dreams were hell on earth, and I rolled around all over the place.

Kicking out with my legs and thrashing the pillows, I finally came out of la-la land just as the sky was becoming light. I grabbed my travel clock and saw it was only five a.m.

"Ugh," I groaned and rolled away from the window, kicking out at the sheets to straighten them. I punched the pillow under my head, managing to fall into some form of sleep before a ringing noise dragged me out again. My left hand slid to the bedside table and tried to grab the noise, finding it to be my phone.

"Mmm," I groaned again and put it to my ear. "Lo," I sighed. "Hooz callzing?"

"Tahlia? It's Richard Sayer. First, you save *my* life, *then* you save my wife's. We're destined to know each other, Tahlia. It seems God wants us to be together..."

Chapter 8

His words echoed in my ear as I lay there. Destined to know each other...God wants us to be together... My eyes widened then blinked, and I rolled onto my back.

"Tahlia. Are you there?"

"Yeah, I'm here."

"I can't tell you how much I appreciate you being there for my wife. It must have been hell for her trying to get away from those thugs. And then the crash... I thank God you were there to drag her out of the car before it exploded and keep her safe. I hear you're a big hero."

I stared at the ceiling, taking in his words. "Ah, I wouldn't say that."

"What do you mean, you wouldn't say that? Surely it's not every day you save someone from a burning vehicle, or from being kidnapped. You're definitely a hero, and I'm so grateful for what you did."

"Ah, how's your wife?" I asked, sitting up.

"She's doing as well as can be expected. She's got a concussion and fractured legs from being stuck in the car. Some bruises and things, but she's doing well. She woke up this morning, and we spoke for awhile before she fell asleep again. It's best to let her rest."

"I'm glad she's doing okay then. You obviously got the card I put in her hand."

"I did. The paramedics told the nurses, and they found your card clenched in my wife's hand. They said she was hanging on to it for dear life and had to wrench it from her. When they handed it to me, I was shocked. It was the same card you'd given me, and I couldn't believe our good fortune to have you save us both."

"Yeah well," I said, getting up and walking around to the window. "It's no big deal." I flung the curtains aside and blinked rapidly from the light. The sky was as blue as day. "No big deal," I repeated. "The Universe just happened to have me in the place I needed to be at the time I needed to be there." I bounced onto the bed and reached for my clock.

8:30 a.m. Crap!

"Well, it's a big deal to me," Richard said. "I spoke with my wife this morning. We want you to come to the hospital so we can talk, and you two can meet. Can you come today?"

"Ah no." I pulled clothes out of the closet. "I have to be at my factory today. We're going into production on Monday, and then I'll be busy all afternoon." I grabbed my bag. "How 'bout I drop by tomorrow morning, then your wife will be better, and we can chat."

"Sounds good. We're at Hollywood Memorial. It's private, and maybe we can sit in the garden. How does nine a.m. sound?"

"I'll try to make it about ten. How's that?"

"That's fine. Tahlia, we *are* meant to know each other. I guarantee it."

I ran into the shower, his words echoing in my ears.

*****

"I'm going to the hospital tomorrow to meet them," I was telling Sin as I pulled the car into a parking space outside of my warehouse.

"Do you want me to come along?" she asked, getting out of the car. "You might need a lawyer to look over any paperwork."

"You just want to meet them," I said at her smug look as we walked toward the door.

"You're finally here," Richard said, as he, Sonya and Todd came rushing up to me.

"Yep. I had an important phone call to take care of. What's going on?" I looked around at everyone.

"The workers want to know when they can start, and here…" Sonya handed me some papers. "Everything's in order. Supplies are in, machines set up. We can go ahead and open."

I took the papers and read through them carefully with Sin. Everything seemed to be in order. "Todd, show me the supplies."

He led me to a long room at the side of the building. Bolts and bolts of bright coloured material sat in covered racks. My eyes bulged as I slowly walked down the aisle. Rolls of bright denim in a variety of colours lay beside me.

"Oh, my God, I love these colours," I enthused, looking at the shelf. "I have got to get some clothes in this stuff." I turned around and fingered bolts of soft pale pink cotton. "Oh, this is the cotton I wanted. Nice and soft. It'll hang properly and not crease." I looked up and down the room. Racks of material, beads and gemstones in bulk. "I love it. It's perfect." I walked out of the room. "Good going, Todd. Thank you. Guys," I said to my employees. "You will need to keep in contact with Todd about supplies and suppliers. If one wants out, you'll need to keep on top of it and find a new one. Okay, now, do we have enough workers for all three shifts until we can get a good stock up?"

Richard nodded. "We've got temps ready to come in on Monday. Each shift is filled for one month. Then we'll see how the sales go, and if we need the extra workers or not."

"Okay, good. Is everything in order from your ends?" I glanced at each of them.

"Everything's in order, publicity's ready to go. The website's almost finished, and every piece of machinery is in place to start work on Monday," Matthew said.

"Good. Do we have the storage and shipping areas done, and has everyone been fully briefed about their job description?" I asked Todd.

"Absolutely."

"Great. Then let's tell everyone the good news." We walked to the front of the sewing area. "Okay, everyone, listen up." I glanced at my workers, over one hundred of them. God, I employed *that* many people. "Good news. You all start work on Monday at nine a.m." Cheers went up all round. "You see my COs here," I waved a hand at them, "on Monday. They'll let you know what to make and how many, plus for the printers, they'll give you the designs you'll be doing." I looked at the men who would be working the fabric printers. "And then, of course, there's the bling team who'll add jewels." They applauded for themselves. "Until Monday people, have a good weekend."

There were more cheers as they all walked out to their cars. I chatted with my dressmakers about my designs they were doing. They'd found the right materials for most of the clothes, and had drawn up patterns. Seeing my clothes were in good hands, we left.

*****

Saturday dawned bright and warm, and I was awake by seven. I lay there for awhile thinking about everything that had happened in the four weeks I'd been in L.A. They were definitely eventful weeks. Run-ins with bitchy celebs, starting my own business, and getting my book published. Which I'd managed to edit in record time. It was in its final draft, and I'd been told it could be on my website for sale within the month.

I sighed and rolled toward the window, looking at the rich blue curtains that shielded the room from the ascending sun. I had met two stars from one of my fave shows and been asked out by one. I had run into the CEO of a big TV network and then saved his wife.

I frowned. All the papers and tabloids were running

the story. Almost non-stop. How a brave woman had beaten the crap out of the two thugs trying to kidnap a CEO's wife.

Fortunately, no one had a photo, and the witness' descriptions of me weren't accurate. I mean please, in one paper I'm blonde, in another a redhead. First I'm short, then tall. American, then foreign. I didn't want to be hounded by the paps. I wanted my name kept out of it, forever if possible. If there were thugs after Marnie, then what would stop them from coming after me and doing God knows what for God knows how long? Ugh!

My brain started showing the accident again. It played like a movie and I wanted it to stop. I rolled onto my right side and sat up. I had said I'd be at the hospital to talk to Richard and his wife, but my gut was telling me not to go. I wasn't sick or anything, I just had a weird feeling that I couldn't put my finger on. Bugger! I hated it when I couldn't figure things out.

I showered and threw on pants and a top. Being Saturday, we planned on shopping after my visit to the hospital.

Sin and I had breakfast and drove to Hollywood Memorial. "You sure you don't want me to come up?" she asked, pulling her car to a stop in the car park.

I hopped out. "No, it's okay. I don't know how long I'll be so I'll call you." I shut the door and walked inside. Reading some of the signs, I travelled up to the third floor and walked down the hall to my left where I found a nurses' station. It was 9:45 a.m.

"Can I help you," a nurse asked.

I smiled. "Richard Sayer asked me to meet him here. Is he with his wife?"

"He is, but you can't go in as only relatives are allowed."

"Okay, then, can you tell him Tahlia Cameron is here to meet with him?"

Her attitude changed and she became somewhat hostile. "Look, lady. I don't know who you are, or who you think you are, but how do *I* know you're supposed to meet him here?" She stood in defiance of me, even though she was still inches shorter than me and her girth was no match for mine.

Sighing, I was tired and freaked out still over what had happened, and I did not need her getting all troublemaker on me. I tried not to roll my eyes at her macho act. "Look, yourself," I said, trying to control my temper. "You don't know that he asked me here, but he did. Now, either you go and tell him I'm here, or I'll start looking in every room. And if that doesn't work 'cause you try and stop me, I'll just call him and tell him you're not letting me in, or telling him I'm here." I looked her square in the eye. "So, do you *really* want to piss him off to the point he rants and raves to the hospital administration about how slack the staff is?" I cocked my head slightly and narrowed my eyes. "Well? Do ya?"

She looked uneasy for a moment then made the right decision. "He's with his wife in room 228."

228!

My numbers again. That *can't* be a coincidence.

"Thank you," I said softly, and walked down the

hall. I stopped outside room 228 for a moment, took a deep breath, and knocked.

The door opened quickly. There stood Richard Sayer, CEO of America's biggest...

"Yes, we know," you cry. "You've told us enough times. Enough already."

"Tahlia, come here." He moved into the hallway and hugged me.

"Um, that's ah, okay." I pushed him away.

"Come in," he said, and I saw the nurse watching inquisitively as I walked into the room.

"Darling," he told his wife. "This is your hero saviour. The woman who saved your life."

I frowned. "I wouldn't go that far," I said lightly, looking from Richard to his wife.

She looked a little fragile sitting there in bed. A white bandage was around her head, and a wire frame under the covers gave her legs and feet space. Her complexion was pale, but her brown eyes twinkled brightly.

"I am so pleased to meet you," she said, her voice strong. "I'm Marnie. Richard's wife."

"Yeah, I got that," I said with a grin and moved over to her to shake her hand.

"Oh, no dear," she said. "I want to give you a hug. Come here."

We hugged awkwardly, and feeling a little uncomfortable, I pulled back.

"Tahlia, sit here." Richard pulled a chair over.

"Thanks." I settled in for what was to come.

"Tahlia, dear. I want to know everything that

happened after the crash," Marnie said. "I only remember swerving to avoid the dog and heading for the post. I've seen the papers and the news, but no one seems to have an accurate account of the accident. Even the police aren't saying much."

I looked from Marnie to Richard. "What's this about a kidnapping attempt?" My eyes narrowed. "'Cause I had to fight off two gunmen for you. My friend told me about it that night when I got home. It was all over the news." My eyes flicked back and forth again.

Marnie looked down at her hands, and Richard shifted in his seat.

"Well," I demanded. "I move to L.A. and find myself deflecting a kidnapping at the hands of two gunmen. I'd like to know about it." My tone made them both look up.

They looked at each other and then Richard started. "A few months ago my wife received a nasty letter. We don't know who from." He rubbed his hands on his pants. "Then I received a similar letter, telling me they were going to do things to my wife." He glanced at her, then me. "Vicious, vile things."

"So you didn't have bodyguards, an armoured van, a bomb shield around you?" I asked incredulously. "Someone sends you letters like that, and you just go for a drive." I shook my head in stunned amazement.

"It wasn't like that," Marnie said quickly. "I was sick of the guards and tried to lose them." She smirked. "I succeeded...and they struck. Months of letters, sick, vicious letters, and I was stupid enough to lose my guards."

"It's not your fault, my darling," Richard consoled his wife.

"Yes, it is," I burst out, and they looked at me in shock. "It *is* your fault. You just admitted you wanted to lose your guards. They had obviously been watching you for the opportunity to get you alone, and you handed *it*, and *yourself*, to them on a silver platter." I got up and walked around the room. "If the letters were that bad that you had to hire guards, did it *ever* occur to you to keep them *close by*?"

They looked at each other again. "Tahlia, I don't like your tone," Richard said.

"Tough!" I replied harshly. "Your wife knew she was in danger and yet through her own choice acted recklessly. *And* endangered other people's lives. *Mine* especially." I pointed to myself. "Anyone could've been walking down that street and been run over, or a house could've caught on fire, or anyone could've been shot. Mainly me, 'cause I was there. The human race absolutely amazes me with its stupidity." I shook my head and looked around in bewilderment. "Men act like bloody dogs with the way they treat women and children, and women act like brainless idiots." I closed my eyes and rubbed my forehead. The stress was giving me one hell of a headache.

"It's true," Marnie wailed softly. "I knew how bad the situation was, and yet I still chose to do a reckless thing."

With my hands on my hips, I stared her down with a stern look.

"I'm so terribly sorry, Tahlia. That your life and everyone else's life was in danger because of my actions." She wiped some tears away. "I'm so glad you were there to save me and believe me, I've learned a very valuable lesson."

"What's that darling?" Richard asked.

"To do what the police and the FBI tell me."

"The FBI!" I was stunned. "The *FBI* are involved, and you act like a bloody idiot." I waved my hands in despair. "Oh, my God! I don't believe this. I just don't believe this." I stood at the window and looked out over the city.

"Tahlia. I won't tolerate you speaking to my wife that way."

I spun around in anger. "Are you fucking kidding me? I could have been shot, your wife could have been killed." I flung out my arms. "Hell, we all could have been burnt to death when the car exploded, and if it wasn't for me, buddy boy, your wife would be lying in the morgue burnt to a crisp if I hadn't managed to untangle her legs." I thrust my finger at him. "So don't *you* tell *me* you *won't tolerate me.*" I was *so* angry. Angry that her nonchalant attitude towards some maniacal stalker could have cost her *and* me our lives.

"Tahlia." Richard started to get up.

"No," I said viciously. "You just sit there and listen while I tell you *exactly* what happened the other day."

He sat down and held his wife's hand while I replayed every little detail for them. By the end of it, Marnie was crying, and Richard was holding her tightly. I even had tears rolling down my face.

I could have been dead, shot or blown to pieces. God, it was just hitting me. I fell into a chair and burst into tears. I wasn't sure how long I cried, but Richard came over and pulled me into his arms. He patted my back with a soft hand.

"I'm so sorry," he said soothingly. "I didn't realise the full consequences of what happened. Or how it would affect anyone besides my wife. I am so sorry."

I pulled away and sniffed, and he offered his handkerchief so I could pat my face. My breath came in ragged gasps. "Yeah, well. It wasn't pretty." He led me back around beside the bed and sat me down. His wife reached out her hand, and we held onto each other while Richard brought us some water.

We sat there for a few minutes and made small talk. My business, what I'd been doing, how Marnie was. Then Richard brought up the reward.

"We want to pay you for your amazing act of heroism." He shook his head. "I don't even know where to begin. Or what to offer you." Pulling an envelope from his suit pocket, he handed it to me. "I want you to accept this. But don't open it now. It doesn't come anywhere near paying you for what you've done. But we hope it's a start."

I took the envelope. "Why don't you want me to open it now?" I looked at it, trying to see what was inside.

"Because you probably won't accept it if you knew what it was."

I clicked, and my eyes widened. "Oh, no. No, no, no." I tried to hand it back. "I don't need it, please take it back. I don't want it. It isn't necessary."

He rejected the envelope. "Please. Keep it. You

deserve it, plus anything else you want; you only have to ask."

I tried again to give the envelope back.

"No. It's yours to keep."

I sighed and looked from Richard to Marnie, then reluctantly put it in my bag. "I don't need it you know. I've got my business, my books, life's great."

"Put it toward your business then," he said. "Is there anything else you'd like instead?"

I thought for a few moments then blushed.

"Oh, she's thought of something," Marnie said, pushing her long brown hair off her delicate shoulders.

I blushed harder. "Well, I..." I looked at Richard. "Ah, well. You happen to show some programs that I absolutely love and," my eyes glanced away in embarrassment, "and I wouldn't mind being an extra, or having a line in them, maybe." I sneaked a glance.

He laughed a rolling laugh. "That's great," he said, clapping me on the shoulder. "That's just great. You want to be on your favourite show. I could do that. Anything else?"

"Ah, maybe having some of my dresses and fashion labels on your soapies would be nice."

He laughed again. "I can talk to the producers and get your clothes on the shows."

I grinned a big toothy grin. It would be a huge break for me and my labels to have my designs seen around the world on the network's soap operas.

"Anything else?"

"One more thing," I said slowly. "An invite to some of the network's functions would be nice. I've already met Carmine Gionetti and Keith Pritchard, and, of course, I'm out to marry Michael Anthony, so turning up to a couple of parties would be nice."

"You want to marry Michael Anthony?" Marnie asked with a giggle.

"Shhh," I said, putting my finger over my lips. "Don't tell him I said that." We giggled then I turned to Richard. "And don't *you* tell him I said that either." He flashed me a huge smile. "I should go," I added, standing. I hauled my handbag onto my shoulder and faced Richard. "One more thing. Don't tell anyone my name. I want to remain anonymous. If they're out to get Marnie," I glanced at her, "then they may want me for stopping them. So, no press at all. Papers, TV, radio, tabloids. Keep me out of it at all costs. I will not risk my life again just to get shot, kidnapped, or blown up."

He nodded. "Of course. We won't say a word."

I walked toward the door.

"What if the FBI wants to talk to you?" he asked.

I stopped and looked at him. "They know the importance of privacy. Just tell them not to bother with me." I walked out the door and called Sin.

Thirty minutes later we were sitting at a beachside café sipping soft drinks.

"So, what do you think it is?" she asked.

"What do you think," I replied with a glance and a grin. "Anyway, I tucked it away safe and sound for now. We have shopping to do. Especially since I'm getting invites to TNM functions for the rest of my lifetime."

"How did you manage that?" she asked, distracted by the hot guy who walked past, wearing tighter than tight jeans and an even tighter t-shirt.

I shook my head and looked across the street at the funky clothing store I wanted to check out. "Well, he wanted to repay me, so I suggested a job on some of the network's shows, and some party invites."

"God." She shook her head. "That man must love you right now."

We glanced at another hot bronzed body. "Yeah, he does."

We burst out laughing and crossed the road to that little boutique I was still eyeing.

I burst through my door at six p.m. laden down with bags filled with clothes, shoes, jewellery. I dumped the bags on the bed with a sigh of relief.

"Quick, open the envelope," Sin said, locking the door behind us and running over to me.

I pulled it from my bra.

She snorted and crossed her arms. "Is *that* where you stashed it. In your bra?"

"Yes, that's where I stashed it," I replied, annoyed. "At least it was safe."

"Of course it was," she added with a sly wink and a laugh.

I ripped open the envelope and pulled out a piece of paper. My eyebrows hit my hairline in shock, and my eyes bulged out of their sockets.

It was a cheque for twenty million dollars!

My jaw hit the floor, and I collapsed onto the bed just as Sin snatched it from my hands.

"Oh, my, fucking God," she squealed. "Have you ever *seen* a cheque this big?"

I focussed. "Well, yes actually, I have." I looked at her. "The cheque I got when I won lotto. It was bigger than that."

"Oh, well, lucky you," she said, sarcastically, sitting down beside me. "What are you going to do with it?"

I sighed. "I don't know. Personally, I don't need it." I shrugged. "Maybe I could put it into the business."

"Whatever you do decide," she said, handing it back to me, "You should bank it as soon as you can. In the meantime, let's go to dinner."

*****

Monday morning, I found my first invite to a TNM party at the front desk. It was to be held in four weeks and was for two. I tucked the invite into my bag and we drove off to my warehouse, wanting to be there early for the ribbon cutting. We all gathered outside at exactly nine a.m.

"Okay, everybody," I said into a microphone. "I'm here to cut the ribbon on my brand-new company. Today is the start of our future. The rest of our lives. And I am proud that I own a company. Welcome to the family." I cut the pink and blue ribbon with a big pair of scissors.

We all cheered and one by one walked inside. The sewers took their places behind their sewing machines and started sewing. The cutters had been working all weekend to get the first pieces ready for putting together, and the printers were ready to stamp the patterns on.

The designs had been chosen for the first allotment. We'd be putting out ten each for the men and women's line, and five for the kids' line. I wandered around watching everyone work. The feeling that overwhelmed me threatened to make me burst into tears. I chatted with my COs and Todd and watched for a few moments. The sewers were very agile, putting together a t-shirt in ten minutes.

We all had a look and marvelled at how straight and well sewn it was. The fabric was baby soft and hung on the mannequin like a glove. We applauded the workers, and after chatting with my dressmakers, I left.

As I walked toward my car, I shook my head in disbelief, which I'd been doing a lot. Almost five weeks here and I had already started my business. And in another two to four weeks the clothes would be for sale online. Aaron had our campaign running in a hundred different magazines.

The ads teased people. Taunting. Stirring. Telling people they couldn't live without our product. Our website was also online. We didn't have clothes available for sale yet, but we let people know what we were about and what we'd be selling. It was going incredibly well!

Then there was the cheque. Ah yes. The twenty million dollar cheque. I had it tucked safely in my bra again and was now on my way to the bank. I had decided what to do with it and sworn Sin to secrecy. With one last look at my business, I drove off to the bank.

"And what can I do for you today?" the teller asked when I stepped up to the counter.

"I'd like to talk to someone in private, thanks," I replied.

"All right, one moment." She went off to find a manager, and I glanced around the bank. Dark wood, high ceiling, definitely old school.

"What can I do for you, Ma'am?" the manager asked.

"I'd like to do my business in private, please."

"Of course, this way." He led me to an office and closed the door behind me. I sat in a dark wood and green leather chair and he watched me as he sat behind his big wooden desk.

I pulled the cheque from my bra and handed it to him. "I'd like to put this into my account please."

He took it and looked at the signature, his eyes widening as he recognised who it was from.

"I want the utmost privacy on this," I said sternly before he could say anything.

"Of course, Ma'am." He tapped on his computer. "Where would you like it to go?"

"I want it put into this account." I handed him my papers. "Then I want a cheque for ten million."

His eyes bulged again. "Ah, er, oh. Of course." A few more minutes of tapping his keyboard and the money was in my account. "I just need to write out the new cheque," he mumbled, and within a minute I was holding a cheque for ten million dollars.

"May I have a pen please?"

"Of course."

Didn't he say anything else? Apparently not!

I made the cheque out to the American Cancer Foundation then asked for an envelope. "Thank you so much, is that all I need to do?"

"That's all you need to do," he said.

"Fine, thank you so much." I shook his hand and walked out of the bank.

Ten minutes later I found the Cancer Foundation without any hassles and walked into reception. "Who collects donations?" I asked the woman behind the counter.

"I can take the donation here," she said.

"It's a big one. I'd rather speak to someone in charge." I smiled at her. "Is there anyone I can talk to?"

"Um, just let me check." She buzzed someone while eyeing me suspiciously. "There'll be someone here in a moment," she told me.

"Thank you." I stood admiring the paintings until a woman walked up to me.

"I'm Sandra Cabott, the manager of this branch of the Foundation. I hear you have a donation for us."

"Yes," I said in a low voice. "It's a sizeable one and would rather hand it over to someone in charge."

"Of course. Do you have it on you?"

Nosy, and so quick to get it!

"Here." I handed the envelope over. "I want the Foundation to have this." I watched her face whiten with surprise at the amount.

"Oh, my God! Thank you, thank you." She pumped my hand up and down.

I laughed. "Well, I'm not God, but you're welcome."

"Michelle, Michelle, get this lady a receipt for her donation please," Sandra called to the receptionist.

Her eyes bugged out too when she saw the amount.

Needless to say, I was feeling very good as I walked out of the foundation.

*****

After opening my company for business, and donating half of the money Richard had given me, I was floating on an adrenaline high. So, imagine how I felt when I stood with my editor and watched my book's cover being printed out. All just for me. I got the very first copy to frame and hang on the wall. So bright, so colourful, *so me*!

Goddamn, it was a fine day. A new business, a new book, a donation. I knew God, and the Universe at large was smiling down on me. Especially after that whole crash kidnap thing which was itching to make me remember. I had also managed to get two tickets for the Debbie Gibson show on Friday night.

Sin didn't want to come. She'd gotten two tickets to see Carmine and his band for Friday and begged me to go with her. I told her to get some of our blogger friends together and go, but to hang on to my ticket just in case I wanted somewhere to go after Debbie's show.

My life was so sweet. So freakin' sweet. And believe me, I thank you God for it. My life was going so great I had no idea what was about to hit me that coming week.

Chapter 9

Okay, so I need to talk about Wednesday first. I went to my factory to see how the clothes were coming. They were going great. The t-shirts were being printed, and I wanted two of everything in my size. One to wear, and one to keep.

We all stood back while the workers loaded the paint into the machines, then pulled the shirts onto the holders. With one twist of a handle and a ten second wait, the first t-shirts were printed.

We checked them over and they were fabulous. I handed my COs theirs. As heads of the lines, they needed to advertise our company too. The clothes were perfect, and I particularly loved the hot pink tee with a blue eighties theme on the front. Since I was going to the Debbie Gibson show on Friday, it would come in handy.

I watched my gem ladies glue on the stones. Each design had a specific gem placement which the women worked on from a pattern. Half an hour later we saw the finished pieces.

Bellisima! I was so proud!

The clothes were hung on racks and wheeled into the storage area where photos and measurements were taken. For the website pics, I wanted the clothes to have measurements so buyers would know what size to buy. Once the pics were taken, the clothes were folded neatly and sealed in clear bags for safe keeping. A printed picture was placed on the clear container the bags were put in, along with the sizes of the t-shirts. Each size went in a different box. Everything was so efficient.

I turned to my chief officers with a big grin. "And now we have stock," I said proudly.

"Yay," Sonya squealed. "I can't wait to show off my shirts. My family will go nuts."

Matthew nodded in agreement. "I'm gonna change into the blue men's shirt before I leave. Might as well wear to work what we make."

"Absolutely," I agreed. "I'm wearing the pink eighties tee on Friday night. Then everyone will be asking about the company."

To make it easier for people to recognise my company I had each label's name in small print at the bottom of the designs, plus the company name. We were ahead on t-shirts, so I wandered back into the sewing room and spoke to the cutters about starting jeans and jackets.

"Do jeans and jackets in every size and every colour. We've got designs for the denim, plus the different styles I want. I want these clothes to fit all women of all body shapes." We went over the designs and started with the pink denim.

As I left that day, I was even happier than I had been on Monday. I was floating on cloud nine, and things were about to get so much better.

*****

Friday morning was warm and wonderful. I sprang out of bed and flung the curtains back, then bounced into the bathroom for a shower. After throwing on the usual clothes, I had breakfast then picked out my outfit for the show that night. Since Debbie was a huge eighties poppet, I wanted to go a little wild.

I had my very own shirt from my line and just needed my new jeans that I would tuck into my three quarter length hot pink and turquoise leather boots with their three inch heels – yes, I know I'd said I wouldn't wear heels, but a girl can change her mind. Right? – They also had a few studs and chains. I had a wide silver belt to wear on my hips which had small zip up pockets for my things, plus the pièce de résistance, a blue wig with pink highlights!

"What? A blue wig with pink highlights?" you ask.

Yes, a blue wig. And not just any blue, turquoise blue. A long fluffy blue wig with big fairy floss – that's cotton candy to some – pink streaks. I was also going to have my make-up done by an artist 'cause I wanted blue and pink eyeshadow zanily streaked across my eyes. Basically, I wanted to go overboard.

"That sounds awful," you cry in disgust. "How could you?"

What do you mean awful? And what do you mean

how could I? I could and I would and I will. I'll wear what I want to wear and if you don't like it, tough! Go screw yourselves!

"Excuse me?" you stutter.

No, I won't! My outfit is ready, there's no need to wait, so I'm going to my factory.

The first jeans rolled off the production line and headed for the printers. Not only were we doing pink, but turquoise and royal blue as well. The assistant pulled them onto a board, and the pattern was set. Thirty seconds later I was taking my jeans to the gem ladies. Thirty minutes after that I had my turquoise jeans to wear to the concert. They felt like a dream, and I was a very happy gal. I may not have mentioned my vitals, but even after slimming down I still have wide hips. It's just my bone structure.

I told the cutters to start more colours and matching jackets, then went off to speak to Todd. After chatting, I left, but was stopped before I got to my car by my ringing phone.

"Ms Cameron? It's Rachel Wilson. I own the house you put an offer on." I stopped dead in my tracks. Yes I know it's a cliché, but it's my book. And I didn't *actually* die.

"Ah, yes, how are you?" I cocked my head knowingly. "You're ringing to tell me you're accepting my offer and want me to come around. Aren't you?"

She gasped. "How…how did you know?"

"The power of positive thinking and some simple deduction," I said matter-of-factly.

"Oh, my God, you're so right. We've decided to

accept your offer and was wondering if we could meet today. Now, in fact. Can you come to the house?"

I looked at my watch. Ten thirty, I had time. Especially for this house. "I'm on my way." Needless to say, I was quick as a flash, and ten minutes later pulled in to my driveway, er, make that, *their* driveway as I didn't own it yet.

Rachel met me at the door. "Come in." She opened the door wider, and I stepped inside.

I felt like I was home. The feeling was so overwhelming.

I shook hands with her husband Michael – coincidence? I think not – who was a lawyer with a study I wanted, and he offered me a seat.

"Now," he said, as Rachel sat beside him. "We've considered your offer, which is very generous, and realising it comes at exactly the right time, we've decided to take you up on it. The house is yours."

I know!

My heart stopped dead, again, *not literally*, and I sat staring at the two of them, my mouth working up and down. I must have looked like an idiot.

"Well," Rachel prompted.

"Absolutely," I gushed, finding my voice again. "I'm definitely taking the house. Thank you both so much." I was on my feet and shaking both their hands at the same time.

"Great. Well, how about we show you around," Rachel suggested with a laugh.

"Lead the way," I replied.

They took me into each room, telling me how the

house was fire-proof, wind-proof, rain-proof, quake-proof, everything-proof. The materials were as natural as possible, and the safety standards were updated each year.

Michael showed me his book-lined study. "Since I'm a lawyer I need a lot of books, so I had the wall-to-wall shelves put in."

"Fantastic," I said. "They'll come in handy for all my book collections. Can the shelves be moved for bigger or smaller books?"

"They can. I used a company that will come and do it for you. I'll give you their details."

"Great."

I saw Rachel's studio. She's an artist, and it was perfect for designing and creating. They walked me to the other side of the house and showed me four bedrooms which their kids and guests had occupied, and then took me into the walk-in closet.

It was freakin' huge!

In fact, Rachel had had it built down one side of the house. There was hanging space everywhere and an island down the middle. It was exactly how I wanted it.

"The company that did Michael's shelving also did the closet if you want to change it," she told me.

"Oh, no," I interrupted. "This is exactly what I want. I won't be changing it."

We walked into the bedroom, and I stopped. *No, not dead this time.*

"And this is the master bedroom," Rachel said. Michael had gone off to answer the phone. "You know, you'll be living in good company."

I frowned. "What do you mean?"

"Well. The hot actor, Matthew MacGyver, lives over the road."

"Really?" I wasn't interested in him.

"And hot stud Michael Anthony lives next door."

"Rea-ll-yy?" I was interested now, but tried not to show it.

"Absolutely. He's such a nice guy, and great with our kids. He's got a son you know."

"Mmm, I think I've read that somewhere," I said, following her out to the living room.

"So," Michael said. "Are you ready to buy?"

"Of course. I'd like my lawyer here as a witness. Should we call the real estate agent?"

"The realtor? Good idea," Rachel said, and made the call.

We wandered around the backyard while waiting for Sin and the agent to show, and when they did; I signed the papers and offered to put the money directly into their account by going to the bank. They agreed and off we went.

The bank manager was surprised to see me back, and even more surprised that I had the money to transfer so easily. Which is surprising in itself since he'd deposited the other cheque for me. More papers were signed, then Rachel and Michael asked when I wanted them out.

"How about next weekend?" I surprised them with. Again, what's with being surprised?

After some talking, it was agreed, and Rachel

invited me to the house the next day for a goodbye barbecue. "Everyone we know will be there, even your hot actor neighbours."

Well, how could I say no to that? Michael Anthony, here I come!

Faster than expected actually…

I was cruising the car park of the local shopping centre, or malls as some call them, and going along five kilometres an hour when a black car reversed so fast it smashed into my Mustang.

My head wrenched sideways, even though I was going five kms an hour, and I angrily yanked the keys from the ignition and slammed out of the car. The black car had gone back in to the park, and the driver alighted, but being too angry I didn't notice. Staring at the right side of my bumper, I saw the dent that had been stamped into my poor car. Leaning down, I ran my hand over it and only vaguely heard a voice profusely apologising.

"You stupid bloody bastard," I stuttered. "How could you?" I stared. I couldn't help it. Because standing in front of me was the man I had moved halfway around the world for. Moved continents for. Waited for, for five weeks…

There in front of me, not five feet from me, was the most gorgeous, amazing, wonderful, incredible, and any other word you could use, man I had ever seen. I had ever wanted. All six foot two, spiky brown hair, amazing blue eyes, and luscious lips that moved in animation as he spoke. Cheeks I wanted to caress, chest hair poking out above his t-shirt that I wanted to run my fingers through. A body I wanted to wrap my arms and legs around, hold on tight and never let go of.

His dark blue tee brought out the blue in his eyes, and his old blue jeans clung to his very manly frame. His sneakers ensconced his feet that were quite sizeable, and you know what they say about the size of a man's feet?

My eyes roamed upward and landed on his crotch. A sizeable crotch! My gaze continued and saw his lips moving, but I didn't hear a word he was saying. He was the man I loved. The man I wanted to love for the rest of my natural days. I wanted to love, honour, and cherish him. Treasure and adore him. Stand by his side forever as his wife and lover. Be the mother of his two gorgeous little girls that I would give him, and be stepmother to his son. Stand by him through thick and thin, for better or worse, in sickness and in health, till death do us part.

Don't even think about that last part!

The man I wanted, ached for, longed for during long and lonely nights. I wanted his arms around me, his lips on mine, his furry chest to ignite my breasts. I wanted to lay my head upon his chest each night and hear his heart beat with love for me. His strong muscular arms wrapped tightly around me, his lips murmuring 'goodnight sweetheart, I love you' against my forehead. I wanted to wake up with him in the same position and thank God for our time together. For the long and joyous life we'd have.

I wanted to be at home waiting for him with a hot

meal to warm his stomach. A steamy hot shower to relax him, and a long slow massage to get him in the mood. Then, we'd make long, lazy love before falling into a contented tangle of arms and legs. And in the mornings, I'd prepare his breakfast while he showered, then kiss him goodbye and wave him off to work. I loved this man more than anything in the world, and finally, he was standing in front of me.

Staring at me with a strange expression…

"Are you…all right?" he asked.

What the! Are you kidding? I'm standing in front of Michael Anthony. Of course I'm not all right. Oh, wait…it was him asking.

Oops. Did I say that out loud? No? Oh, thank God!

I realised my jaw was working up and down and I was staring. *Of course* I was staring. Again, Michael Anthony was standing right in front of me. I got a hold of the situation and blushed. "Sorry. I, ah, was surprised to see it was a celebrity who bumped into me."

He grinned. "Oh, I guess that's understandable." Pointing to my bumper, he added, "I'm so sorry. I didn't look where I was going. I'll have my insurance pick it up. Do you have your details?"

I looked from my bumper to his bumper to his gorgeous face. He wanted my details! I was staring again, but hell, who cares!

"Ah, I have a business card I can give you." I wanted to give him so much more.

"Okay." He stood waiting.

"Okay." I got a card and my notebook from my

bag. He took the card and glanced at it. Then wrote his details down in my book.

I have his details! Yay me!

"Your accent; you're Australian, aren't you? I love Australia. I was down there a few years ago, you know." He looked at me with his gorgeous blue eyes and I wanted to drown in them.

I felt myself turn into a puddle of goo. "Oh, I know," I said. I looked left and right then leaned toward him conspiratorially. "I know a lot, 'cause there was a lot of rumours and gossip about you for months afterwards."

A huge grin crossed his lushy lips. "Was there? That's so cool."

I laughed. "Apparently."

"So are you visiting?"

"No, I moved here, ah five weeks ago now. Set up a clothing and jewellery company, publishing a book. Even bought a house today."

His grin was still on his lips. "Really? That's great. Good for you."

"Yup. My clothes rolled off the production line this week, and I'm going to wear some to the Debbie Gibson show tonight."

A strange expression came over his gorgeous face. "The Debbie Gibson show?"

"Yeah," I said, a bit worried. "It's in town…tonight."

"Yeah, I know. I'm taking my brother to the show for his birthday. He was a huge fan when he was younger."

That knocked me for a six. "Well, ah, that's great. I'll see you there then."

"Ah. Yeah. Maybe you can tell me more about those rumours."

I smiled my pearly whites at him. He was so amazing. His skin so soft and clean shaven.

"How do you know his skin is so soft? Did you feel him?" you ask.

I just know. I wanted to cup his cheeks and plant a kiss on his lips. "Yeah," I said softly. "Maybe I will."

"Okay, then," he said, backing away to his car. "I'll see you tonight, maybe. And I'm sorry about your car. Really, I am. It's amazing by the way."

"Thanks, that's okay." I shrugged. "The insurance company will take care of it."

"Okay, see you tonight."

I watched him jump into his black BMW and roar away.

Oh, my, holy, fucking, God. And there was no wedding ring. He was still mine!

I jumped into my car and raced back to the hotel. There was no way I was going to waste any spare time I had.

Within the hour I had told Sin everything, had lunch, and roared off for my singing and dance classes. Forgetting the gym, I raced back and showered, and was ready for the make-up artist when she arrived. Two hours later I pulled on my hot pink and blue leather boots and admired myself in the mirror.

I. LOOKED. HOT!

My blue and pink wig looked fantastic and matched the wild make-up the artist had applied. My brand-new, never before seen or worn, clothes were nice and snug, and my boots, belt, and jewellery all matched to perfection.

"Good fucking grief," Sin said when she saw me. "Who and what the fuck do you think you are?"

"Don't insult me," I snapped. "I look freakin' fantastic. *And* I'm meeting Michael there."

"Ah, no," she shot back. "*He* said, he'd see you tonight, *maybe*."

I looked in the mirror and adjusted my earring with a shrug. "Same diff."

"Are you sure you don't want to come to Carmine's show? I'm sure he'd love to see you." She smiled smugly, leaning against the bathroom door frame.

"Nope. Not unless Michael and his brother want to come."

"Carmine wouldn't like that," she said with a frown, tucking a strand of hair behind her ear.

"Like I give a crap what he won't like. I'm not dating him," I said bluntly, walking into the bedroom and grabbing my room card from the bed. We left to meet our blogger friends for dinner. They had a long time to wait for Carmine's show, but Debbie's started at eight, so Sin dropped me off at the theatre at seven-thirty.

The huge crowd was piling through the doors, and as I waited for my turn, I looked around for Michael. I didn't know if he'd stand in line or come in at the last minute. The problem was, he wouldn't recognise me dressed the way I was.

I gave the attendant my ticket and walked inside. The club held about one thousand people and was decorated with all sorts of things; eighties themed stuff and current memorabilia as well. I stood near the exit to see if Michael would come in, waiting until the announcer came on and the doors were closed.

The show was about to begin.

I moved through the crowd and stood near the stage. The lights dimmed, and the first notes of music started. Debbie bounced out in a flash of light, and the show went on.

Forty-five minutes and ten songs later, I found myself dancing next to a guy. I glanced at him and saw he was enjoying himself and full of energy. He glanced at me and smiled, and we found ourselves singing and dancing along, doing the hand movements and dance steps. We had a great time and were out of breath when we broke for intermission.

"Whew, what a show," I said, eyeing him suspiciously. He looked very familiar.

"She's great, isn't she? I've been a fan forever." His big toothy grin was one I knew well. His height, brown hair and blue eyes were definitely genetic.

He saw me staring. "Is something wrong? You're staring."

"Sorry," I said, blushing, my brow furrowed. "You just look a lot like Michael Anthony."

He rolled his eyes and laughed. "I should. He *is* my big brother."

My jaw hit the floor. Which it shouldn't have since I'd been suspicious. "You're kidding," I said. "Is he here? He said he would be." I looked around the club.

Now, it was his turn to look confused. "You're

meeting my brother here?"

I looked at him. "No, ah sorry. He hit my car today, and when I mentioned I was coming here tonight, he said he was bringing you for your birthday."

"Wow," he said, realising who I was. "So *you're* the one with the multicoloured Mustang. Michael told me all about it on the way here. He said you just stood there staring at him, your mouth moving up and down but nothing coming out."

I blushed harder. "Well, you know," I mumbled. "He's gorgeous."

"Then wouldn't that make me gorgeous?" He stuck out his hand. "I'm Charles by the way. Call me Charlie."

I shook his hand. "I'm Tahlia. Nice to meet you." My eyes wandered over the thousand strong crowd again.

"He said he'd be standing at the back."

"What?" I said, blushing again.

"He's this way." Charlie led me through the crowd to the back of the club. Standing in the corner near a doorway was Michael. So damn deliciously wrapped in black.

"Hey," Michael and Charlie said at the same time.

"Who's your friend?" Michael asked his brother.

"Uh uh. Not my friend." Charlie laughed. "The woman whose 'Stang you pranged into this afternoon."

Michael frowned and looked at me closely. "No..."

"Yes," I said, raising my brows in amusement. "You wanted to know more about the gossip and rumours from when you were in Aus."

"Oh." Recognition dawned in his eyes, then they took me in and brightened. "Wow, you look great."

I blushed. "Thanks, so do you." I couldn't help myself. He did. I was rewarded with a huge grin.

"So, are you enjoying yourselves?" he asked.

"Absolutely," Charlie and I replied together and laughed.

"I'm going to freshen up before the show starts again," Charlie said, walking off and leaving us alone with each other. As alone as you can be in a crowd of a thousand plus.

"You do look great," he said, leaning in close. "Those yours?" He pointed to my clothes.

"Yep, fresh off the printer this week. Actually, the jeans are fresh today. First pair ever!"

"Fantastic."

"Thanks."

We were rudely interrupted by a stream of people asking about my outfit, and I mentioned they were from a brand-new label due for release in a few weeks.

Cool was the general consensus, and I knew my label was going to be a big hit.

I thought I heard the sound of a train above the beating music, and leaned in to ask Michael, but the ground started shaking, and the room started spinning.

"Get in the doorway," Michael yelled. He grabbed me and pulled me under the arch of the doorway, holding me tightly. I ended up nuzzling his neck.

The earthquake forgotten, I breathed in his scent. Spicy, manly, edible. Nuzzable!

"Nuzzable? What the hell's that?" I vaguely hear you ask.

It's when someone is so yummy you just want to nuzzle them. They're nuzzable.

So, anyway, my nose was in his neck, and I wanted to lay my fangs in. Damn, he was hot. His aftershave wafted around me and I didn't notice the quake was over. I just knew I wanted to stay wrapped in his strong muscular arms forever. I felt so safe, so warm, so loved. I didn't want to leave. I didn't want him to let go.

But he pushed me away gently and gazed deep into my eyes. "Are you okay?"

Oh, hellooo!!!!! Nooooo!!!!!

I was still so close to him. My eyes came up to his nose. Such a cute nose. I looked into his eyes. So close. So were his lips. "I'm fine," I mumbled softly, drinking him in.

We stared into each other's eyes until Charlie butted in. "Are you guys all right? That was some quake."

"Huh," Michael and I said together as we looked at him.

"Apparently you are," he said, with a knowing grin.

The announcer came over the sound system. "Ladies and gentlemen. Since everyone and everything is all right, we'll get back to the show in five minutes."

"All right," Charlie said. "I'm going back to get my spot." He moved off toward the stage.

"Are you okay?" Michael asked again.

"Yeah," I said. "A little shaken, ha, ha. But it's still gonna take some getting used to."

"I bet." His eyes gazed into mine, his lips so kissable. The lights dimmed. "Better go catch up with Charlie," he said, leading me over to his brother.

After an hour of singing and dancing, which Michael joined in on, Debbie said goodnight and left the stage. One by one we all filed out of the club.

"Where are you off to now?" Charlie asked while we waited to get out.

"I'm not sure." I glanced at my watch. "My friend Sin wants me to go to see Carmine Gionetti and his band at some club. But right now, I'm starving." I looked at the boys. "Is there somewhere to eat nearby? If I meet up with Sin, I'll have to take a taxi 'cause she dropped me off."

Charlie nudged Michael. "We can take you," he piped up. "I'm hungry too. How about a burger?"

"Is there a burger place nearby?" I asked.

"That depends on where Carmine is playing," Charlie said, again nudging his brother.

"Over on Sexton Street," I volunteered. Was that name appropriate or what!

"There's a Burger King on the way. We can eat there and catch the show," Charlie went on. "Besides, Michael owes you for smashing your car."

"I didn't / He doesn't," Michael and I said at the same time, then grinned.

"I don't want to intrude upon your birthday. This was Michael's gift to you."

Charlie waved his hands. "I don't mind. I want to keep dancing, but need some sustenance. Michael will shout us to burgers and another show."

Michael tried to look angry, but failed. His gaze roamed over me and I shivered.

"I don't want to intrude," I repeated.

"You're not," he said with a soft smile. "Let's go grab a burger."

Half an hour later we were munching away in Burger King. Charlie had politely sat opposite his brother so he'd have to sit next to me. It was *so* embarrassing. I loved Michael so much, but felt so high schoolish.

"You know, Michael's about to break up with his girlfriend," Charlie said. "Their relationship is pretty much over."

"Charles," Michael said sharply.

"What? It's true." Charlie took a sip of cola, and I sat quietly, ears pricked. "The two of you haven't seen each other in what, a month? And you haven't mentioned her to me. When was the last time you talked to her in person? Or on the phone?" He picked up a fry and waved it around as he spoke. "All of that says to me, that you're over." He glanced at me slyly. "You know, big brother, you shouldn't be with a woman who's shy and timid. Afraid of whether pictures will turn up online. Doesn't like to say much."

"Charles, stop it. Now is not the time or place to discuss this, besides which, it is none of your business." Michael was not happy, and neither was I for that matter, to find out he *still* had a girlfriend. Although they did seem to be falling apart. I said nothing.

"Michael, come on," Charlie said, eating the fry

and casting another glance at me. "You need a woman who's a woman. Someone who's not shy and timid. Not afraid of speaking her mind or wearing bright colours and wigs." I knew he meant me. "You need a woman who's like you. Will get on the dance floor and party, or sit in front of the TV and watch a movie."

"Charles—" Michael tried to butt in.

"No, Michael," Charlie went on. "You need a woman who wants to be with you and not someone else. I give her the fact that her profession is noble and she's helping people, but that means she doesn't have the time to spend with you. What sort of future does that mean for the two of you? Her beeper will go off, and she'll go running, leaving you behind. And you won't be having kids anytime soon 'cause she won't have the time to have them." He sighed and looked at his brother. "Michael, you're my brother, and I love you. I just want you to be happy."

I finished my burger and fries.

"And you don't seem to be happy with Gina."

Gina! So that was the bitch's name.

"Charles, I told you this is not the time or place, enough already," Michael said through gritted teeth as he finished off the last of his soda.

Charlie shook his head. "No. It's obvious to me. Especially tonight. Your relationship with Gina is over. All afternoon you talked about another woman. And now I see that the other woman is perfect for you. Michael, look around you." He leaned in. "The perfect woman for you is right next to you."

I pricked up my ears.

"She's bright and bubbly. She's fun. She clearly adores you, and on top of that, she drives an amazing car. Michael. The perfect woman for you is sitting right next to you."

He looked at me, so did Michael. I looked at Michael, and as our eyes met, the electricity flowed.

Chapter 10

The world fell away, and there was no sound, no people, no nothing. Just me and Michael. I gazed lovingly at him, and he seemed interested too. A small smile crossed my lips, and he smiled back. The world was ours.

His thick luscious pink lips parted as they made their way toward mine.

My breasts quivered with wild anticipation of what was to come. My heart pounded like a jackhammer in my chest.

They were closer now. Only inches of space between us.

My eyes couldn't tear themselves away. My breath came orgasmically in quick, uneven rasps as I struggled for air.

The lips were only centimetres away now, coming closer and closer.

My body was so ready and ripe for him and all he could do to it.

My tongue snaked out to wet my lips, ready to mate, as his found their way home.

They were so hot, so sure, as they planted themselves and hungrily devoured mine…

…Until a car beeped its goddamn horn and we jumped apart. Bloody driver! Bloody dream! Damn it! He hadn't been kissing me at all. Or had he?

I blinked and realised I was still in Burger King, with not only Michael, who was blushing and settling back into his seat, but his highly amused brother and quite a group of people looking and cheering us on.

"Ah," I breathed, "I, oh." I glanced around in embarrassment. Damn that dream. Or was it? Now I was really confused as to what had just happened. Had we kissed or not? Or did we almost? Or had it been a figment of my overactive very fertile imagination? "Oh, is that the time." I glanced at my watch. "I'd, ah, better call Sin and see if the show's still on then. I'll just go freshen up as well. Back in a mo." I escaped to the ladies' and saw my face in the mirror. Beet red and boiling!

"Oh, God, did that really just happen or not?" I asked my reflection. "Oh, God, oh, God, oh, God." I berated myself for a good five minutes over my stupidity, then sighing, freshened up and called Sin. The phone rang and rang.

"Hello."

I barely heard her over the noise in the background. "Sin, is the show still on?"

"What, I can't hear you, hang on." She was drowned out by the music. "What did you say?" She was a bit clearer.

"I take it the show is still on."

"Yeah, a few more songs and they'll take a break. Where are you?"

"I'm at the Burger King nearby with Michael and his brother. We're going to head over there shortly."

"Oh, okay. I don't know if Carmine will like seeing you with another man, though, he might get jealous. And damn, does our stallion look hot tonight."

I remembered my last phone call with Carmine. We hadn't spoken, and I hadn't seen him since Big Willy's. I wasn't interested. No point getting involved with the guy. "All right. We'll try and get there soon."

"Okay. I don't think the place is full, so you should be able to get in. See you soon."

"Bye." Taking one last look in the mirror, I walked out to the boys.

"Ready to go?" Michael asked softly, his eyes examining my face.

I shyly glanced back. "Ah, yeah. Sin said they're about to take a break, so we should be there in time for the second set."

"Great, let's go." Charlie clapped his hands in glee.

Trying to ignore, or forget what had just happened since it was *so* embarrassing, we piled into Michael's BMW with Charlie taking the back seat 'cause it's a two door. We drove off to find the club Carmine was playing at, located in downtown L.A. and managed to get a car park nearby. There was a small crowd outside waiting to get inside, but upon seeing Michael, the bouncers let us straight in.

Walking down a small hallway which led to the dance floor, I strode in like I owned the place. I stood and watched, hands on hips, straight and tall, striking a pose.

People noticed.

Of course they did.

How could you not notice a chick in hot pink and turquoise blue with two gorgeous men standing behind her? One of them being Michael Anthony.

The band wasn't onstage, so I assumed they were on their break. I perused the crowd and saw Sin running up to us on my right.

"Oh, my God, you made it," she gushed. "They were freakin' hot I gotta tell ya." She noticed my companions. "Oh, my God." She looked from me to Michael to me with a knowing look. "Hi, I'm Sin." She thrust out her hand.

"I'm Charlie," Charlie butted in with a laugh. "And this is my big bro, Michael. You might have seen him around."

"I have, I have. Listen, we managed to get a table near the band." She leaned toward me. "You will not believe who else is here. His castmates came to support him, and we've been chatting with them all night." She brushed her hair back over her shoulder. "Of course, it helped that Keith is here and recognised me from our date, so the girls and I have been with them. It's been great."

"Of course it has," I said with a grin.

Sin waved her hand toward the tables, and I saw Carmine staring at me from across the room. A sexy smile and a warm welcome on his face. He was dressed in tight blue jeans, and a tight white singlet and biker boots. Damn, he looked hot.

His fingers waved hello.

"Looks like you've got some competition," Charlie said to Michael, who gave him a dirty look in return.

Even though there was music playing, I still overheard the conversation. And what he'd said was not good.

"I told him you were coming tonight and it made him *very happy*," Sin said slyly.

"Synergy!" I chastised angrily through gritted teeth, shoving my hands onto my hips.

She *hated* being called that, and knew by my using it I was pissed off. She also hated people knowing it. Her parents were free loving hippies of the sixties and had named her that because she was the result of their "synergy" when she was conceived. So, she changed the 'y' to an 'i' and shortened it to Sin, thinking it made her sound sexy, exotic and sinful.

"You should *not* have told him that." I looked around me at the crowd. "Besides, I feel like dancing. Say hello to the girls for me." I grabbed Michael's and Charlie's hands and pulled them into the crowd. I didn't look at Sin or Carmine, so I had no idea if they were simmering.

Who cares!

Exactly!

I found myself in the middle of an Anthony sandwich, which was a very nice place to be, thank you very much, until the announcer told us it was time for Karaoke.

"Come on, guys and girls, if you've got a beat in

your feet and a rhythm in your livin'" – What? That did not make sense – "Then get up on the stage and sing your heart out. Anyone? Do we have any takers?"

I looked at Michael and Charlie. "Why not," I said excitedly. "Should I? I love singing."

They looked at each other then back at me.

"Go for it," Michael said, with a huge smile of encouragement.

"All right." I bounded over to the DJ who was laying down the tracks and gave him a list of songs. Taking the microphone he handed me, I walked to the edge of the stage and waited till I was introduced.

"Okay, guys and gals we have a taker. A hot little hottie who's going to belt out some songs you all know. Put your feet on the floor and your hands together for...Tahlia."

I walked onto the stage to a round of applause and stood front and centre. Michael and Charlie moved a little closer so I could see them, and my friends hit the floor as well.

The first beats of Pink's *U + Ur Hand* came on, and I started singing. After all my lessons I knew I was good, and the crowd knew it too. I strutted around the stage like I owned it, making hand movements and playing up to the crowd. I bounced around and got the crowd going for the chorus, and then walked off stage into the throng.

They cheered and sang along with me, and as I sang, I danced with Michael and Charlie. Making risqué movements and gestures to go with the song, we all bounced along to it. I followed up with Pink's

So What and *Leave Me Alone I'm Lonely*. Three Kelly Clarkson songs later, I was not only on an adrenaline high, but so was everyone else.

The announcer told us the band would be on soon and if anyone else wanted a go, do it now. But the crowd cheered for me, and I gave the DJ one more song to play.

"Okay, everyone, listen. I'm gonna do one more song. Now, some of you may know it. I'm sure most of you won't. But it was made famous a long time ago by Barry Manilow. Then famous in Europe by Brit boy band Take That. And in the second verse, there's something about a stallion." My friends cheered. They knew what that was about. "So enjoy the song."

The strains of *Could It Be Magic* came over the sound system and because the DJ had the Take That version, I was able to keep up with singer's vocals. Leading into the first verse, I ran into the crowd and bopped along. The chorus got everyone going again, and come the second verse, I strutted over to Carmine while singing something about a stallion meeting the sun high on a hillside. I grabbed his singlet, pulled him toward me, and planted a big kiss on his lips. Letting go, I turned, singing the next line as I walked away, and finished off the verse. Belting into the chorus again, I stepped onto an empty chair, then onto a table to dance on it.

The crowd screamed and went wild as I shook my booty and sang my heart out. Charlie came over and carried me into the crowd, and for the rest of the song, I gyrated with Michael.

The man I love. And he felt so damn good.

I threw every ounce of energy into it, and he seemed to as well.

When the song was over, we all went nuts, and the DJ thanked me for the show.

The girls corralled me into telling them what it was like kissing Carmine, then went back to their seats. I turned to Michael and Charlie. "Wasn't that fantastic." I clapped my hands like a giddy schoolgirl.

"I don't think fantastic's the word for it," Michael said. He gathered me into his arms and spun me around. "You were amazing." He obviously wasn't affected by me kissing Carmine.

I squealed with glee and slowly slid down Michael's body. Our eyes met. Our lips nearly met, and we had a moment.

"Ladies and gentlemen, I don't know how we're goin' to follow that show, but we'll give it a red hot go." Carmine and his band were back on stage.

Michael let me down, but kept his yummy arms around me.

"Thank you to Tahlia, my hot woman for a great show, and here's our song."

His what?

"Excuse me, I am not your..." My annoyance at his ownership was drowned out by the song, and I felt Michael's arms slip away. I looked at him and the confused expression in his eyes. "I'm not his woman," I repeated with emotional force.

Michael backed off and walked toward the entrance.

"Michael," I yelled, running after him, grabbing his

arm, spinning him around. "I *am not, not* with Carmine. I've met the guy twice, and he wants to date me. I *don't* want to date him."

Michael looked unconvinced. Staring at me with a betrayed look in his eyes that killed me deep down inside.

I love this man more than anything, and some poncy little foreigner was not going to ruin my life with him. "I don't want him," I repeated firmly. "I want *you*." That made him perk up. God, this was killing me. "Look, if I have to get Sin to tell you how many times I've met the guy, I will. She told him I was coming when she shouldn't have. She got his hopes up after I turned him down time and time again. And yes," I sighed and rubbed my forehead, "I know I went over and kissed him tonight, but it was more for the girls than him. Or me. It was stupid, all right." I closed my eyes, shaking my head in regret and disbelief. *This will not fall apart. This will not fall apart.* "I really shouldn't have done that." Gazing into his eyes, I saw him coming around. "Obviously he didn't like me turning up with you, or dancing with you, and when I kissed him, he probably thought there was hope." I hoped my love for Michael was radiating from my eyes. "But there's *no* hope. I don't love *him*. I don't want *him*. I want you." It sank in, and I saw him soften. "I think Carmine said it to make you jealous or something, hoping you'd storm off and leave me here for him. It almost worked."

We stood looking at each other while the last strains of music died down.

"Let's go," I said, taking his hand in mine. "Let's go home."

Charlie had followed, staying at a discreet distance. Now, he came up. "I can find my own way home. You two go and do...whatever." He glanced at the stage. "Besides, I want to see what Mr Italian Stallion does when he sees you two leave together."

I was still holding Michael's hand and saw his eyes sparkle.

"How about it? Would you like me to take you home?" he asked.

"Yes," I said with a soft smile.

A huge grin appeared on his face.

"Okay, you two lovebirds. Off you go." Charlie waved us off, and we left.

Slipping out of the club into the cool night air, we walked arm in arm towards his car. Before getting in, we looked up at the big new moon, hanging lazily in the black velvet sky.

"God I love new moons," I said quietly. No one else was around, and the quiet made the moment even better.

"They are beautiful," Michael agreed, gazing from the moon to me.

I had my eyes closed letting the moon's rays wash over me. Breathing deeply, I didn't notice Michael studying me.

"Time to go," he whispered.

I opened my eyes to see him watching, and smiled as he opened the door. "Ah, so chivalry is not dead," I joked, getting in.

He jumped in himself. "No, it isn't," he said with a grin, starting the car.

I gave him directions, and we drove along the highway, watching the moon slowly move higher into the sky. It was quiet. Cool. So peaceful sitting there with the man I love driving me home. I shivered a little and noticed the hairs on my arms standing up.

"Are you cold?"

"A little."

"I'll change the temp then." He fiddled with a knob, and the air became warmer. "Better?"

I smiled. "Better." I settled into the seat and noticed how comfy it was. "This is a nice car. A bit low," I stuck out my lips, "But otherwise a nice car."

"Thank you. I wanted to splurge a little. I saw this car and knew I had to have it." He watched the road.

"Why not? You work hard for your money, why shouldn't you buy what you want," I said. "Look at everything I've done in the last five weeks. Bought a car, an office block, two factories, a warehouse, machinery, got my book into production, and bought a house today." I caught a glimpse of the car's clock. "No, make that yesterday. And, I got run into by Michael Anthony. I'd say that's a pretty good five weeks. Wouldn't you?"

He laughed. It was a light musical sound since he was a singer himself, and he flashed me a huge grin. "So, what would you say was the highlight?"

"Ah, let me see." I thought for a moment, looking up, my finger touching my pouting lips, pretending not to have a highlight, knowing it was making him nuts. "Mmm...don't have one," I said, teasing him.

He rolled his eyes and pretended to be hurt. "You mean *I'm* not the highlight of your last five weeks here in the good old U.S of A?"

"Um, nup."

He grumbled. "Well, that's not very nice then, is it? And here I was going to ask if you were doing anything over the weekend."

"I'm going to a barbecue tomorrow," I volunteered, eager to see what would happen.

He perked up. "Really? So am I. My next door neighbours are leaving in a week or two and are having a goodbye barbecue. They've invited the new owner to introduce us all." He cast a glance my way. "Maybe you could come to that? I'll have my son tomorrow, but it won't be a problem, will it?"

"Your son? Of course not. I'd love to meet him. But what's he going to think when his dad introduces him to a new lady who's not the girlfriend?"

He blanched, having forgotten his relationship. "Yeah. You're right. But you and I are friends, so that's okay. Where's your barbecue?" We pulled to a stop at a red light.

I gave him the address, and he stared at me until the car behind us honked.

"Wait, are you telling me you're going to be my new neighbour?" he asked, unbelieving.

"Yup." I watched his reactions.

He shook his head. "Of all the things and all the places. I didn't even know they were selling until this week."

"Rachel only called me yesterday and said they'd sell. They had an agent offer the house to prospective buyers, and after seeing the photos of the inside, I put in an offer. The place is perfect for what I want. The bookcase-lined study, her studio, and walk-in closet. It's exactly what I wanted."

"Wow. That *is* a surprise." He drove through my hotel's car park and stopped beside a lush green lawn. "Well," he said, leaning back in his seat. "We're going to be neighbours."

"Seems so," I replied, undoing my belt.

He looked at me and shrugged. "I guess I'll see you tomorrow then."

"Yeah."

"Do you, ah, want to come a little early? You can park in my drive, and we can go together. And you can meet my son. He will *love* your car."

I smiled softly at him. "Sure."

"Okay," he smiled back. "I guess I'd better let you go then."

Neither of us moved. We just sat there smiling at each other.

"Yeah. I'll go," I said finally, throwing glances from Michael to the door and pointing.

"Oh, right, right." He got out and ran around to my side. Opening my door with a flourish, he bent down and waved his arm. "M'lady."

I snorted with laughter and he helped me out, pulling me into his arms. We stood for a moment, gazing at each other. The moon popped into our line of vision and we looked up.

"It really is beautiful," I said.

"Oh, I don't know. There *are* more beautiful things in the world."

I looked back into his eyes, and he lowered his head. Our lips met. Soft. Lingering. We smiled, and he pulled away slightly.

"I'll see you tomorrow," he said.

"Tomorrow." My lips were touched by his again, and they stayed a little longer.

He moved. "Tomorrow," he repeated, before pressing his lips onto mine.

It was everything I'd thought it would be. Amazing. Electric. Fantastic. Incredible.

His lips moved with finesse, and I responded in turn.

For several minutes we stood there, lips locked. Soft, lingering, beautiful.

A car came screeching into the car park, disturbing our intimate moment. We jumped apart and laughed nervously.

"I'll see you tomorrow," he said. "Come early, about eleven thirty, and you can meet my son." He held my hands and kissed them.

"Okay. I'll be there," I gushed.

"Okay." He didn't move.

"Okay." Neither did I.

Reluctantly we let go, my hands sliding between his big strong manly ones.

"Bye." I walked backwards toward the hotel so I could still see him.

"Bye." He walked around his car.

I waved.

He waved back and got in.

I waved as he gunned the engine and flicked on his lights.

He waved as he drove out of the car park.

Then he was gone. But I knew our life was just beginning.

*****

Bang. Bang. Bang.

What the bloody!?

Bang. Bang. Bang.

'"Ugh!" An eye popped open.

Bang. Bang. Bang.

I realised someone was banging on my door and reluctantly rolled out of bed to stumble towards it, banging into a chair with my foot, causing pain to arc up through my leg.

Bang. Bang. Bang.

"All right, already," I yelled, opening it and rubbing my leg at the same time.

There was Sin, standing in her robe, hair all a muss, make-up smudged under her eyes, looking absolutely furious. "What the hell did you do last night?" She stormed into my room. "Do you have *any* idea what happened after you left?" She stood facing me, hands on her hips, and a look of pure anger on her face.

I shut the door. "Well, how *could I* know what happened after I left when I haven't seen you to tell me all the details." I grabbed my robe and threw it on. "God, what time is it?" I threw open the curtains and blinked at the sun already high up in the sky.

"It's ten o'clock, but that's not the point," she said.

"Ten o'clock," I screeched. "I have to be at Michael's at eleven thirty." I ran into the bathroom and washed up, then started pulling clothes out of my wardrobe.

"Who cares about Michael after what you did to poor Carmine." She jumped onto my bed and crossed her arms and legs.

"Puh-leeze, what do you mean *poor* Carmine. He had all of you to console him, and believe me, I am highly annoyed at what he called me." I pulled out a pair of pink summer pants.

"What he called you?" She looked puzzled. "Oh, right, "my hot woman"." She made quote marks. "After you kissed him it's no wonder the poor guy thought he had a chance. When they finished the second set he was all over me, asking about why you'd left and what was going on, why you were there with Michael but kissed him? Were you serious about him, or leading him on?"

"What?" I turned to Sin. "I have *never* led Carmine on. *At all!*" I waved my arms in anger. "And *how dare* he even think so let alone say it. He's the one that kissed me in the diner." I ticked off the points on my fingers. "He's the one that called me, and I told him I was interested in someone else and just wanted to be friends. He's the one who still invited me out even though we went, and he's the one who called me a second time, and I rejected him then too." I stormed around the bedroom. "So, who the hell does *he think he is* crapping on about how I led him on?" I shoved my hands onto my hips. "When I *so clearly* didn't."

"He called you a second time?" Sin asked, frowning. "You didn't tell me."

I waved a hand. "Who cares, I'm not interested. But I *am* hungry, and I have a barbecue to get ready for, so unless you want to have breakfast with me, get out." I pulled a soft pink and gold flowing top from the closet. Yep, that would go nicely with the pants.

At eleven fifteen I was ready. My top did go nicely with the pants, my sandals were colour co-ordinated, and my bling was well placed. I put my hair into a bun and pinned some flowers in it, then brushed on some simple make-up. I strapped on a gold belt with pouches, like the silver one I'd worn the night before, and shoved my cell, lipstick, purse, driver's licence, and a small bottle of perfume into it. I glanced in the mirror and smiled. I was going to knock Michael's socks off.

I grabbed my keys, went downstairs and drove to Michael's house. I knew where he was, as it was next door to my new house, so I found it easily. Rolling into his driveway, I saw Michael and his son Dylan sitting on the front step waiting.

"Hi," I called out my open window as I stopped the car.

"Hi," Michael called back.

"Wow," his son said, sauntering up to the car. "This is so cool."

"Glad you think so," I said, getting out.

"Can I sit in it?" he asked, so eager and so young,

but trying to act cool and mature.

"Sure, hop in." I held the door open, and he climbed in. So cute for a twelve year old burgeoning on teenhood.

"Can we put the roof down?"

"Sure." I turned the ignition switch and hit the button. The roof lifted back, and in thirty seconds had popped itself away. I turned the car off.

"That is *so* cool," he gushed. "Can we go for a drive in it? Please, Dad?" He looked imploringly at his father.

"That will be up to Tahlia," Michael said, glancing at me.

"Please?"

I looked at Dylan. He was so cute, sitting there looking up at me with his big blue-green eyes. A child, yet growing up so quickly. "How about after the barbecue?" I asked.

"All right," he crowed.

I looked at Michael with a big grin on my face. "Hi."

He grinned back. "Hi."

"Hi."

Surprised, I turned around.

"I'm Dylan." He held out his hand.

I shook it. "Well, hello Dylan. I'm Tahlia. It's so very nice to meet you."

"Okay," Michael said with a small laugh. "Now that the introductions are out of the way, Dylan, why don't you go inside and get ready for the barbecue, and we'll lock up and go."

"Okay." He sauntered inside while I put the roof back up and locked the car.

"Hi," Michael said again.

"Hi." We smiled softly at each other.

His eyes roamed my body with fierce hunger. "You look great."

"Thanks," I managed, a hot shiver racing up my spine under his gaze.

He took a step toward me, and his lips found their way onto mine.

Heaven!

"Hi."

"Hi."

God, I was floating on cloud nine.

"Ready," Dylan yelled, running out of the house.

"All right. We'll lock up and go." Michael went into the house and set the alarm, shut the door behind him, and held out his arms for us to take. So, arm in arm, me on his left, Dylan on his right, we happily walked next door.

The barbecue was very nice. Rachel and Michael – hers, not mine – had set up the backyard with tables and chairs, a barbecue, and containers of icy cold drinks. There were a lot of people already there, and glancing at my watch I saw it was a quarter past twelve.

"Oh, you're here!" Rachel exclaimed, rushing up to us. "Together?" She looked confused. "I didn't know you knew each other."

"Actually, we met yesterday after I bought the house," I replied, watching Dylan run over to play with the other kids.

"Oh, okay. That's great. You've met one neighbour, but there's a few more to go." She clapped her hands and faced the crowd. "Okay, everybody, listen up." She pointed to me. "This is Tahlia. She's bought our house, so that makes her your new neighbour. As you can see, she's already met Michael, now she can meet all of you. She's an Australian who's not only about to make her mark in the publishing industry with her book, but also with her fashion and jewellery company. She's going to take on the world. So, please welcome her to the neighbourhood."

There was applause all around and I noticed the men eyeing me off while the women shot daggers at me. I was embarrassed and uncomfortable but laughed at Rachel's words. "Wow, that was some introduction. Maybe I should hire you as my publicist." We laughed some more, and she took us around to introduce me to the neighbours.

They seemed like a nice bunch of people, but since I'm a private person, I knew I wouldn't be inviting any of them around. I don't particularly care for neighbours, as in the past I'd been used, abused, and screwed over by them. If they can't be helpful, why have them?

Michael led me through the crowd and we chatted with people he knew. We munched on burgers and fruit, and I told him some of my plans for the house and garden.

"I'd like to put a pool here," I said, sweeping my arm over a space at the back of the yard. "I'd love a waterfall, waterslide and fountain." I looked at him. "What do you think?"

He seemed impressed by my ideas, even though they may have been a little grandiose. "If you want a pool, have one. I've got one. I don't know if the council will let you have the waterslide, though."

I shrugged nonchalantly. "What I want I get," I said with light-heartedness. "If a good company can do it within the week, I'll be very happy. I'd like to move in next weekend. Then there's the TNM network function—"

"Why are you going to that?" he inquired, a little curious.

Bugger!

"Ah, yeah." I tried to find a reasonable excuse. "I managed to get a double invite for something I did for the network." I didn't want *anyone* knowing for the sake of my own safety. If the kidnappers found me, then I was a goner! So I had to keep myself out of it.

"Oh," he said, accepting my answer. "Did you hear about the crash and attempted kidnapping of Marnie Wilkins? She's the CEO's wife you know."

"I, ah, vaguely heard something, somewhere," I mumbled.

Someone from nearby joined the conversation. "I heard it was a gang trying to kidnap her to get money from her husband."

"I heard it was a group of people who saved her," a woman said.

"I heard it was a black chick that did karate," another said.

I'm a black chick now!? For God's sake.

The whole conversation was making me very

nervous, but I swallowed it down. Before long, everyone was talking about it and it made me want to leave.

"Dad, can we leave now?" Dylan asked, appearing behind his father.

My thoughts exactly!

Michael looked at his son affectionately, ruffling his curly brown hair. "Sure we can." He turned to me. "You don't mind, do you?"

"No, no, I want to leave too. I have things to do."

"Okay, great. Let's say goodbye and go."

We said goodbye to everyone, and Rachel told us they would be out the following weekend so I could get the keys then. Heading down the drive, we walked arm in arm back to Michael's, where Dylan asked for the ride in my car.

With a laugh we piled in, and putting the top down, we drove up and down the street a few times before I pulled back into the drive.

"I don't want to take up your father-son time together," I said. "So, I'll let you get back to it."

They got out of the car, and after Dylan thanked me, he said goodbye and went inside. Michael leaned on my door. "I want to see you again."

I smiled softly. He always makes me do that. "I want to see you, too. But according to Charlie, you have a girlfriend in a waning relationship. You really need to decide if you want to stay with her or date me. In which case you need to say goodbye to her 'cause I *will not* be the other woman." I gazed expectantly into his eyes and saw the truth dawn.

"You're right," he said, glancing down and rubbing

his hands through his hair. "Ah, I need to make some decisions, don't I?"

"Yes." I touched his cheek. "It shouldn't be too hard. You just need to understand your feelings for both of us." I smiled again. "Personally, I believe there's two kinds of feelings. On one hand, you can meet someone and really like them, think they're great, and you want to see them again. Then love grows from that. Or, on the other hand, you can meet someone for the first time, and your hands don't want to let go when you shake. You stare into each other's eyes and have such an overwhelming sense of knowing radiate through every pore of your heart, body, soul, that this person is so right for you. That you want to be with them, just from meeting them and looking into their eyes. You just know, instantly, that they are for you, to be with, to love, honour, and cherish, for the rest of your life."

His smile said it all, and I think he knew. "I want to keep seeing you."

"Then you know what to do."

"I know what to do." He leaned in and kissed me.

So sweet, so beautiful, so perfect.

"Bye."

"Bye."

Chapter 11

Monday morning Richard Sayer called. "Tahlia, my dear. How are you?"

"I'm fine, thanks. Everything's going along swimmingly."

"That's great. Did you get the invitation I sent you last week?"

"I did. It was at the front desk. Only three weeks to go." I was so excited.

"That's right. Do you have an outfit picked out?"

I stared at my overflowing closet. "Well, I'm not sure what to wear, since I haven't been to anything like this before. So I may just wear what I feel comfortable in."

"As long as it's dressy. You don't need a ball gown, but I know you will look good in whatever you wear."

What a charmer!

"I also rang to tell you my wife is out of the hospital."

"That's good."

"Yes, it is. Her legs are healing nicely. She's in a wheelchair while she gets her strength back, but she's as feisty as ever. She'd like to talk with you again. Can you come over to our place this week?"

Wow! Hellooo, I was being invited to the house of America's biggest network CEO.

I sighed. "I don't know, Richard. I kinda want to get on with my life now. I have a company to run and a house to decorate."

"I understand. I do. But we'd both like to talk to you, see how you're doing. We can talk about some of the things you mentioned at the hospital."

Well, how could I resist that?

"When is this supposed to be happening exactly?"

"How about tonight?"

Well, I didn't have anything on. "Okay. Tonight would be fine." I wrote down his address. "You haven't mentioned me to anyone have you?"

"No. Neither of us has mentioned your name to anyone. Not even the FBI."

"They haven't called me yet, so maybe they don't need me."

"I hope that's the case. They've told us they doubt these thugs will be trying another kidnapping attempt. Especially after the crash and explosion. Not to mention having the holy crap kicked out of them by a woman. The FBI thinks they're running scared."

"I hope so. What time tonight?"

"Is seven okay?"

"Seven's fine."

"All right, see you then."

I spent the morning at my office, where for the first time I was *in my* office. I hadn't even begun to make jewellery and needed to get to it as soon as possible. Fortunately Tina, as head of the accessory line, had found a supplier, and we now had a room full of beads and jewellery bits filed neatly on the shelves.

We also met with our designers and found we had hundreds of designs to choose from. We wouldn't be caught empty-handed. The website and publicity were going well, with our site getting at least a hundred thousand hits a day. People were intrigued. We had ads in worldwide magazines, and more details online to let everyone know what we'd be selling. We also decided to start putting the pics of the clothes up as we had enough to show.

After our meeting, my COs and I drove to the warehouse and checked in on the clothes. All clothing lines were nearing completion; the t-shirts were fantastic, and the jeans blinged out. Supplies were stocked up, and the storage area was filling in next to no time.

"A couple more weeks and we'll debut," I told everyone. "I can't wait." I consulted with Tina before we left. "Are the sunglasses coming along?"

"God yes. The Cancer Foundation is all in, considering your donation," she said. "I found that out when I spoke to the manager of the branch."

I blushed and remembered her carrying on when I handed her the cheque. "Well, the sunnies should happen very quickly then. Have you seen any designs?"

"I have, and they are fantastic."

"Good. What about bags? Can we do them, or is it better to do them with a company?"

"At this stage, we can do it ourselves, so the leather is on its way, and the stones can be professionally done here at the factory."

"Can our sewers put together a bag?"

"As far as I know."

"Well then, once the clothes are done, we can have the bags made up. I also need to get some designs made up for the shows. Can you get some jewellery designers into the office on Wednesday and we'll get some jewellery made?"

"Sure thing, see you then."

I consulted with my dressmakers for awhile. The clothes I'd had made up for me were nearly ready, so they were able to start on some of my designs.

"I want a rich royal blue for this dress and hot pink for this one. I also need the emerald green and fire engine red. Can you have these done this week?"

"On Friday."

"Fantastic. I'll see you then."

*****

That night, I promptly arrived outside the gates of Richard Sayer's house at seven and buzzed the intercom. The gate opened, and I drove up to the front of the expansive mansion, stopping at the door. Richard walked out to meet me with a kiss and a hug.

"Tahlia, it's so good to see you, my dear. How are you?"

"Fine thanks," I said, and followed him into the house.

It was luxurious to the extreme. Chandeliers, marble floors, and two impressively wide wood staircases greeted me, along with tables of statues, art, and massive gold framed mirrors on the walls. He led me into an ornate living room to the right of the entrance. It too was furnished with everything riches could buy.

"Tahlia, how nice to see you again. And in much better surroundings." Marnie Wilkins held out her hands to me. I took them, and we hugged. She was sitting on a plush sofa of gold velvet with a blanket over her. "Sit beside me so we can catch up."

"Dinner is served at seven thirty, sir," a butler said.

"Thank you, Stewart. Tahlia, is there something you'd like to drink?"

"No, thanks, not right now." I felt a little underdressed for my surroundings. Sure, I wore a hundred dollar pair of black slacks, and a silk blouse the colour of wine, but still.

Richard sat in a chair to the left of Marnie. "So tell us, what's been happening? How's the business going?"

"Ah, the business is fine. Great actually. Into our second week of production. We're getting a good supply for when we open in three weeks, and we're going to do varied accessories as well."

"That's fabulous," Marnie murmured. "You'll have to design me something for the network function coming up. And didn't you want your designs on some of the soaps?"

"I did. In fact, I brought my designs with me. Four so far, but there will be more if they're a hit." I pulled my pad from my bag and showed them. "My dressmakers are doing them this week, so they'll be ready soon."

"Oooh, I love this emerald colour," Marnie said, fingering the swatch of material I had attached to the design. "I'd love a gown made from this."

"I can have my dressmakers come over to take your measurements, and I'll design a little something for you before I go."

"That would be wonderful." Marnie smiled.

"These designs really are first class, Tahlia," Richard said, handing me my sketch pad. "I'll let the producers know tomorrow to show your designs."

"Thank you. That would be so incredible. You have absolutely no idea what that would mean to my company and me," I gushed.

"You have no idea that what you did means more to me than anything else in this world." He took his wife's hand and gazed at her with love.

"Dinner is served," the butler said.

"Thank you, Stewart." Richard helped his wife into the wheelchair while the butler held it still. It took some doing, as Marnie was still somewhat fragile and couldn't really help herself.

Dinner was amazing. The best food, drink and dessert. Well, it would have been had Richard not brought up that day I wanted to forget. We discussed it every which way, and I was relieved to know that guards were stationed all around the house.

Then it hit me. If they were watching the house, would they have recognised me? Oh, crap! "Do you think I could have a couple of guards follow me home to be on the safe side?" I saw their questioning looks. "If they're watching the house, they'll know what I look like."

None of us had thought of that until now.

"Of course, Tahlia, anything you need. You know all you have to do is ask."

After dinner, we sat in the living room again and chatted as I drew a design for Marnie.

"Strapless?"

"Yes, please. A fitted bodice."

"Snug at the waist?"

"Yes. And I want a huge skirt down to the ground. Gathered a little around the dress."

I finished the sketch and showed her.

"Oh, I love it. It's perfect."

"Are you home tomorrow?"

"While I still recover, of course."

"I'll have my dressmakers come around and take your measurements."

"Can't you?"

I smiled. "It's better for them to get a good look at you and take your details themselves. Would you like the gemstone bling my label will be known for? I know we have some amazing beads at the factory that will match this perfectly."

"That would be wonderful. Surprise me with the design," she said. She was happy to have a one of a kind gown from a not yet released label.

"You're going to have the first evening dress from my design label." I put my pad away. "I'm only doing the tees and jeans so I can spend time designing gowns. That's what I really love. All the girly, fluffy, feminine clothes, skirts, gowns, blouses, all evening wear."

"Oooh, that sounds wonderful. I'll have to tell all my friends about you," Marnie said.

"Ah, but not until you've worn the dress and made them all green with envy," I replied, and we burst into a fit of giggles.

Richard shook his head in amusement. "Women!"

The mantel clock struck ten.

"God, is that the time? I need to go." I picked up my bag and stood.

So did Richard. "I'm so glad you came, my dear. You don't know how much it meant to both of us." He reached out and took Marnie's hand.

"Yeah, I think I do," I said, and bade them goodnight. A guard met me outside and told me he'd follow me home. "Thank you," I said, and drove off with him close behind. I checked my rear-view every few seconds. I didn't want to put myself in harm's way and needed to know if anyone was out there following me. As I drove into the hotel's car park, he flashed his lights and drove off. Safely tucked away in my room, I allowed myself to relax.

*****

Wednesday morning, I was at my office at eight-thirty. I wanted time to have a look around before everyone arrived. I stood outside the front door and looked over the building. All pink and blue with a bright red roof.

Our name hadn't gone up on the front yet, as I wanted to wait for the day we officially opened. The gardens on either side of the dark glass door had bright flowers and ran the length of the walls. An arch framed the door with an overhang which glistened proudly with Swarovski gems.

"Of course it did," you mutter.

Of course it would. I love bling!

I unlocked the door and walked in, relocking it behind me. Wandering slowly through the ground floor, I took it all in. Bright coloured walls, funky prints and carpets. I made my way to the office for jewellery making, and found tables set up and ready.

Walking past the shelves, I pulled a few jars and containers out and then sat down. By the time my staff arrived, and Tina had found me, I had completed the basics for ten pairs of earrings.

"Hi," she said, surprised to see me.

"Hi. Are my j.makers here yet?"

"Your? Oh, right, jewellery makers. Waiting in reception."

"Bring them in."

Tina left and brought back ten young women.

"Please, sit down," I said, waving a hand over the table. Once they were settled, I started. "Now, I know that you're all students of jewellery and design. So, would you like a job here?"

"Yes," was said in unison.

"Okay." I wandered around the room. "I expect you to be on time, ready to go with good work ethics, and willing to put in overtime. Are you up for that?"

Another yes.

"However, if you have the intention of working here just to get a kick start into having your own business, leave now." I stopped and looked at them. "Because I won't tolerate someone using me as a stepping stone to their own business. Is that understood?"

They nodded.

"Right. You'll start work today." I showed them what I had done so far. "We'll do designs just like these. All with charms and stones hanging off them. We'll do a variety, a lot of stones, a few stones. No earrings will be the same colour or design. I'll get you what you need." I pulled a box of silver hoops and hooks from the shelf, followed by gold ones. "These are the basics for the earrings. It's proper silver and gold. Not junk." I placed the boxes on the table. "Grab yourselves a handful, and I'll get some beads."

Pulling out box after box, I placed them on the tables then grabbed the chain that we'd be threading onto the hoops. "I'll show you how to thread the chain on...like this." I demonstrated. "And then you need to hang smaller pieces across. You'll need tools, so while you gals do that, I'll come up with some colour combinations."

On velvet trays, I laid out beads in size and colour for each design and chatted with Tina about our accessories. "I want hats. Fedoras, newsboy, caps, and sailor kind of hats. Should we have the bling put onto the bands directly, or onto a band then stitch the band on?"

"It depends on what bling you want on. Just the band or the whole hat?"

"All of it. Like with the clothes. I want to offer a little or a lot. Some will have the bands, some the brims, some the whole lot. Then there are the different sizes. Or can we do one size fits all?"

"Not sure," Tina said. "I think we'd have to do it separately, then stitch it together."

"Yeah." I placed some more beads out. "What about the belts and scarves?"

"The belts can be done two ways. Either glue the beads on or do a tray kind of thing."

I frowned. "What do you mean?"

"Set the beads into a setting, like on jewellery, how the stone is put into the silver or gold."

"Oh, okay." I think I got her.

"Then attach it to the belt."

"Why don't we do a few of each in prototypes and see how they go."

"Okay." She made some notes.

"All done, ladies?" I asked.

"Yes."

I started handing out the trays. "This is the position the beads will go on. Smaller ones hanging from the top chains, bigger ones on the bottoms. Like this." I showed the girls how to attach the beads then let them get on with it as I laid out another set of beads.

"What about the scarves?" I asked Tina.

"We can either get in plain scarves and do them up, or make our own—"

"Make our own, so it's completely ours," I interrupted.

"Okay. I'll get in a range of material perfect for

them. Anything you want in particular?"

"Velvets, silks, cotton," I shrugged. "We'll try everything and see how they go. Do we have a good supply of beads and stones at the factory?"

"Up to the eyeballs." Tina grinned.

"Good. Now, what about shoes. We've got everything else. Could we do shoes?" I laid out some more beads.

Tina raised her brow as she thought. "The problem could be sizing."

"Yeah, I know. American sizes are different to Australian sizes, and I've already had to have shoes and boots made to fit and accommodate my flat feet."

"So, you see the problem?"

"Yeah. How about we do a survey on the site." I looked at her. "See if anyone would be interested in boots or studded heels. Not every shoe designer and maker makes a good shoe you know. Maybe we could offer personally made shoes?"

"Maybe," she said. "Set up a questionnaire to see what people want that's one of a kind."

"Great." I picked up some trays. "You do that, and we'll finish off these earrings."

"Okay." Tina left us alone, and by midday, we'd managed one hundred pairs of earrings.

*****

Friday it was back in jewellery making mode, and we accomplished bracelets and necklaces to match the earrings. Simple designs, like long chains with gemstone pendant, and bracelets with jumbles of stones. The line was coming along well, and photos were being taken of each set to put up on the website ready for sale. We were really going well, and I was very happy.

I'd been in America for six weeks, and everything was fantastic. I was picking up the keys to my new house on Sunday, and I'd met the love of my life.

Michael Anthony.

Who just happened to call me that night.

"Hello."

"Hey." His voice melted through the phone.

So did I. "Hey," I said, turning into a puddle of goo.

"Are you doing anything tomorrow?"

"Probably watching your neighbours move out of my house," I joked. I hadn't seen or heard from Michael since the barbecue last Saturday.

"Can you come over tomorrow? I'd like to talk to you."

That sounded ominous.

"Okay. What time?"

"About ten."

"Okay. I'll see you then."

"Okay, bye."

"Bye." I tapped my phone on my chin while I thought. There could be only two things he wanted to talk about. Either he was staying with his girlfriend and couldn't see me, or, he'd dumped her and wanted me. I prayed for the latter.

*****

I pulled into Michael's driveway at precisely ten on the dot. He ran out to greet me and open my door.

"Thank you, kind sir." I grinned brightly as I got out.

"You're very welcome, lovely lady," he replied with a bow.

Okay, so he seemed happy. This could be good.

He took my hands in his. "How are you?" His grin grew bigger.

"Better now." I smiled back nervously.

He nodded toward the house. "Let's go inside."

I shyly followed him in, and we settled onto the sofa in the living room. My eyes took everything in. Wow! I was in Michael Anthony's house. Staring at all of his stuff, sitting on his sofa, taking it all in. Wow!

"So, uh," he faced me, "I, uh, wanted to see you to talk to you." He touched my knee. "How are you?"

I gazed at his face with a big smile on mine. "I'm fine."

"Great." He kept grinning. "I, uh, guess I should explain."

"That'd be good," I laughed.

"Okay, ah." He wiped his hands on his jeans. "All weekend I thought about you." He looked down shyly. "Even though I was with Dylan, I thought about you." He looked up. "And then after taking him home, I came home and did a lot of thinking. And I mean *a lot*." His expression emphasised his words.

"Good thoughts I hope."

"Ah, yeah." His grin was still there. "I did a lot of thinking on Sunday night, and I realised that you and

Charlie were right." He glanced away in awkwardness. "My relationship was waning, and I didn't notice. So, I went through every step of it, and realised that there was no point being with someone I didn't see or hear from." He looked back at me. "And I had met you, and you were great, and I wanted to see you again." He took my hands in his. "I want to see you. So, Monday night after work, I saw my girlfriend and we... we broke up."

"Technically," I said. "You broke up with her." So *not* a moment for me to get technical.

"Ah, yeah. I broke up with her." He shrugged. "I told her that our relationship was ending, and while it's not her, I just no longer felt that it was going the way I wanted it to go."

"How did she take it?" I asked softly.

"Not well, as was expected. But when I pointed out we were hardly together, she finally understood it was over."

"It must have been hard for her. Having you break up with her."

He smiled softly then looked at me. "It was time for her and me to be over, so I could be with you and explore what we are about to have."

I felt like crying. In fact, tears overflowed, and I started laughing. As much as I'd hoped and dreamed of having the man that I love fall in love with me, the fact that it was happening was completely overwhelming.

Michael gently wiped them away. "Tahlia. I want to be with you. *You.* So...do you want to be with me?"

I cried harder. "Yes, yes, I want to be with you."

"Okay, then," he said, and taking my face in his hands, he kissed me.

It was bloody amazing!!!!!

And yes, it requires five exclamation marks to celebrate.

We spent the rest of the day talking and laughing. Michael took me on a tour of his house and made me lunch, then showed me photos of his family.

Which is huge you know. So, I won't go into details as it's too confusing.

We lay on the sofa all evening until the clock chimed eleven. I sighed in contentment. I didn't want to leave, but I needed to come back tomorrow to collect the keys to my new house. I reluctantly pulled myself from Michael's arms. "I should go."

"Do you have to?" He swept a strand of hair from my eyes. "You can stay here."

Oh, God, you don't know how much I wanted that.

I smiled at him, and resting my chin on his manly chest, gazed into his big blue eyes. "I'd love to. But you only broke up with your girlfriend this week. You haven't had time to grieve the end of the relationship." I sat up. "Besides, I'm assuming she slept in your bed."

He looked surprised at that. "Ah, yeah. She stayed."

"Well, Mr Anthony, when we're together for the first time, I want it to be in a new bed. Preferably, the one I buy and put in my house next door."

He raised his brows in amusement. "Really?"

I became serious. "Look, Michael. I think we should be upfront about what we want. I want a relationship. I'm thirty-five, and I want a relationship with the man I love. That would be you. And I want kids, a family, a wonderful loving marriage. Can you give me that?"

He thought for a few moments. "I think I can give you that."

"Really?" I think my grin split my lips.

"Well, you know, we're just starting out, but we want the same things, so yeah, I think I can give you that."

"There's something else I want." I took a deep breath. "I want us to live together." I waited for his reaction then raced on. "I'd love it if you moved in with me when my house is finished. I know you love this house, which is why you bought it, but if we live together, it won't accommodate everything I want. So, you could bring a load of stuff over and set it up in my house. Our house. Because I want to christen my bed, *our* new bed, the first night we move in."

Michael sat there looking at me in amazement, a smile playing on his lips. "Wow. That's a lot to take in. Moving in and all." He gazed around the room. "Leaving the house I've lived in for years. Leaving most of my stuff behind." His eyes flicked back to me. "But I want to be with you."

"I want to be with you," I said, my eyes watering. "But you need to get over your ex and decide if you want to move into my house permanently. I'm not saying sell this one. I would never ask you to do that. I know you love it. But maybe it could be a guest house, or entertainment hub or something." I kissed his cheek softly. "I want to spend the rest of my life with you, Michael Anthony. And I want you to move in with me and live as a happy family in our house next door. But the decision is up to you. I won't push you or force you into anything you don't want to do. You've got one week to decide."

"Gee, thanks," he said dryly.

"The day I move into that house I want you to move in with me." My hand stroked his cheek. "I have very special plans for the bedroom you know. And I *know* when you see it you'll never want to leave."

Now that intrigued him. "Really," he said in a low sultry tone, eyes ablaze with passion and curiosity.

"Really," I replied. "But if you don't want to move in, then you won't get to experience the adult playroom either."

And that turned him on. "Adult playroom? I really should decide shouldn't I?"

"Well, you have one week." I looked around for my bag. "Oh, one more thing I just realised."

"What's that?"

"*Technically* we're not a couple yet." I pushed my hair behind my ears. "I mean, you haven't asked me to be your girlfriend. I'm kinda old fashioned you know. You need to ask."

"No, I didn't know," he said. "Well, it looks like there's a lot I have to learn about you. I guess I'd better do the right thing then." He cleared his throat and sat up straight. "Tahlia, would you do me the honour of being my girlfriend."

"Only from the day you decide to move in with me."

That stunned him. "What?"

"Michael, you just broke up with someone. You

need time. So, for the next week, we'll just get to know each other, and you'll deal with the end of your past relationship, then on the day I move in next door, you ask me again." I stood. "But you know what the answer will be anyway. Of course, that's on the expectation you move in."

He stood and enveloped me in his arms. "Well, then, I guess you know what *my* answer will be then."

I radiated happiness. "Of course, how could you say no?"

Chapter 12

Sunday afternoon at two p.m., I was standing in the driveway of my new home. Sin and Michael were with me, and along with Rachel and Michael, we watched the moving van full of their belongings drive away.

My Michael was behind me, his hands on my shoulders. "It's yours," he whispered.

I glanced at him with a very excited grin.

"So here you are then."

I turned and saw Rachel handing me the keys. "Thank you very much." I took them and held on for grim death.

"Michael, it's been great knowing you, but it's time for us to move on." She hugged him.

"It's been nice having you guys as neighbours," he replied, hugging back.

"Tahlia, enjoy your new home."

"Oh, I definitely will."

They climbed into their stuffed-to-the-ceiling car and with a wave goodbye, were gone.

For a few moments, we stood there in the quiet until Sin pulled out her cell phone and spoke to the locksmith company. "Can you come straight away? Good. We need our locks changed. Yes. Thank you."

I had already decided to change the locks and security system for my own safety purposes. She called the security company while Michael and I wandered inside. It was quiet, peaceful, empty. And so much to do.

Hand in hand, we walked through the house, and I gave Michael a few details about what I'd be doing. Of course, I didn't mention the plans for the bedroom or adult playroom. We met up with Sin in the living room.

"Security and locksmith on their way," she said.

"Great," I replied. "We can get that done today, and then the painters will be here first thing in the morning."

I had prepared as much as possible the previous week. In between classes and work, Sin and I had found a company that not only paints your house but lays the carpet and hangs the curtains. Their showroom had been full of swatches, and I'd chosen all the colours I wanted in paint, carpet and curtains. It all matched. Plus, they put me in contact with a paint company that does murals. I wanted a few rooms with murals and wanted it all done in one week, so I made sure to hire enough people. On top of that, Sin and I had done a lot of shopping. Most of my furniture was ready to be delivered in the coming week. I'd fill each room as it was finished. See, it wasn't all about business, you know.

"We'll get this done today, and then this week the

house will be set up the way I want, and I'll move in next weekend." I looked up into Michael's big blue eyes. "*We'll* move in next week?" I asked with raised eyebrows hoping the answer was a definite yes.

"It looks like it might be going that way." He grinned.

"There's a room opposite my study you could use as an office. I can buy some bookcases, a huge desk and a big comfy chair for you. You can fill it up with all the things you bring over." He hadn't given me an *actual* yes, but I was very hopeful.

He smiled and kissed me with those lush lips. I love it when he does that. "Let's say I'm feeling very eager," he said, his arms wrapping around me.

Yay me!

The locksmith arrived and changed the locks on the front door and the back sliding doors. While he was doing that, the security company arrived and showed me how to work the system. A new number, some instructions, a checking of the safety of the system to make sure it was all in place, and they left us to it.

I set the alarm, closed the door, and stood on the front porch. My eyes wandered over the lush green lawn, a fountain with koi fish, and circular driveway. Flower filled gardens blazed around the edges, and the stone walls were tall enough to keep people and their prying eyes out.

My eyes closed against the late afternoon sun, and I relished in the warmth and happiness of having my own home and the man I loved. A shadow blocked out the rays, and opening my eyes, I saw Michael standing in front of me. His yummy strong arms slid around me and held me close. His lips found mine and softly kissed me.

I sighed. Damn it was good to be alive! I wrapped my arms around his neck and held him tightly. "I love you." Crap! Was it too soon to be saying that? I was about to find out.

He pulled his head back to look in my eyes. "I love you too."

I felt a bubbling ripple of joy flow through my body. I finally had the man of my dreams, in my arms, telling me he loved me. It was unbelievably amazing and incredibly quick. But as much as I had gone after him once I'd met him, I was still freaked out as to how fast it had actually happened. And how he'd fallen for me almost instantly...if he really...did...love me...

My insecurities perked up and started threatening to erode my joy. *You're not thin enough, not gorgeous enough, not good enough, not truthful enough for such a huge megastar...*

Don't! I snapped at them. *Go away! You will not get in the way of my happiness with the man I love! And damn it, I* am *good enough! I...Am...GOOD ENOUGH!* I pushed them away into the recess of darkness at the back of my mind and smiled up at Michael.

We kissed. It deepened. And we stood there like a couple of teenagers making out.

"Ewww, do you mind?" Sin mumbled. "I'll wait in the car."

We pulled apart reluctantly and giggled.

"Will I see you this week?" he asked.

"In the evenings," I said. "I'll take the week off my classes to get the house done and furnished. So, once you get home I can be there waiting."

"Mmm." He kissed me. "I'll give you a spare key, and then you can be waiting when I walk through the door."

I kissed him back. "Mmm, okay. I'm having my stuff sent over from Australia this week, so when it comes, you can help me unpack my study." Our lips met again. "And I bought a load of furniture and stuff last week, so that will be piling in as well." Another kiss. "So I'll see you every night."

"Mmm, I can't wait," he mumbled against my lips.

"How about in the meantime we spend the rest of the afternoon together?"

"Sounds good."

*****

So, it was Monday again – there are just too many of them – and I'd rung in to the office and told the girls to make what they wanted, so I didn't have to run in myself. I was standing in my new house with a huge crowd of people. Painters were bringing in paint and sprayers, curtain makers were taking measurements, and I was conferring with the muralists about which rooms to do. It was bedlam!

"Okay, people," I called. "Listen up." They quietened down. "I want this house done by Friday at five p.m. Do you understand?" They nodded. "I am paying for you to do the work quickly, but professionally. Most of the bedrooms and hallways can be done first as they'll be plain. But the murals will take the most time" – luckily I had hired several companies, so I had the people – "I'll lead you through the house. You've got the plans in front of you, so let's go."

I started with the studio that I wanted to be splashed in bright colours. Another company was making a huge sign of my business name in Swarovskis to stick on the wall. Very sparkly! My study was shelf-lined, so the ceiling and one spare wall were being painted bright blue.

The lounge room was to have a mural of a Greek seaside village and be mostly blue, with the alcoves either side of the front door done up differently. One was for a baby grand piano and would be a music corner. The other for two lip shaped couches and some funky prints.

The kitchen was to be bright yellow, the floor black and white check, as I was having the dining room set up to look like a fifties diner, with a booth and jukebox, pinball machine and a mural of fifties teenagers on the wall.

The four bedrooms would be painted in colour themes. A rose pink coloured room would have a darker shade on the boards. The carpet and curtains would match. The theme would be continued in the other rooms. One would be a nice shade of purple, one, a soft white, and the fourth, a turquoise shaded room that I had decided would be for Dylan.

As for my bedroom, well it was going to be very

special, and the bathroom was going to match. My walk-in closet was perfect thanks to Rachel and just needed a vacuum.

"Okay, everyone. I know the four bedrooms will be done first, and fastest, so start there now. Muralists, please get to work on drawing up the pictures, and the rest of you, you know what to do."

"The pool people are here," Sin called.

"Okay, everyone, get to work." I walked out to the backyard and started discussing what I wanted with the pool guys.

The hole would be easy to dig up, and the pool easy to put in. A waterfall from fake stones and recycled water and a fountain were simple. It was the waterslide that would be the problem.

After half an hour of to-ing and fro-ing, with legal advice from Sin, it was decided to go ahead with the waterfall at the same time. The diggers were brought in, which completely wrecked my lawn, and started the hole. I had picked the pool and design the week before, so they knew how big a hole to dig.

Sin and I left them to it then ran around checking everything. I vacuumed my closet, but decided to change a few things around, so I called the company who came right over.

"I want a small section at the end cornered off," I said, demonstrating. I wanted the end to have a walk-in feel with two hanging spaces facing the back wall so it would be like a closet within a closet.

They told me they could do that and took some measurements. "We'll get it all cut out and be back tomorrow."

"Fantastic," I said, showing them out.

One and a half hours later, the bedrooms were painted with two layers of quick dry paint, then it was just the skirting boards to do, curtains to hang, and the carpet could be put down. Two hours later, they were dry, and at three p.m. the carpet layers came in. With all four bedrooms being done at once, the underlay and carpet were done within the hour. The curtain hangers came with my curtains, and the four bedrooms were complete for decorating.

At five p.m. I called a stop for work. So much had been done. The bedrooms, the murals pencilled on, the hole in the backyard; even my study and studio were done, along with the office for my darling Michael, which had been done in bright, cheery yellow shades. I'd asked, he'd suggested.

"Okay, everyone. Good work today. Be back at nine sharp to continue. I'll see you then."

Everyone was gone in ten minutes, and after locking up, I wandered next door to my baby's. Letting myself in, I walked around, casting an eye over his memories until exhaustion overtook me and I plopped down on the sofa to wait…

Something as trying to wake me. "Go, way," I mumbled, then slowly realised where I was. My eyes flew open, and I saw Michael kneeling beside me. He had been nibbling me awake.

"God, what time is it?" I shot up into a sitting position and wiped my face.

"Seven."

"Oh, my God," I groaned. "I fell asleep waiting for you. How long have you been home?"

"Just got here," he said, sitting beside me and putting his strong arms around me. "And believe me, it was quite a nice sight, seeing you lying on my sofa."

I grinned softly. "Well, it's been a long day, running back and forth around the house all day. And there's more to do."

"Why don't you tell me all about it over dinner," he said with a kiss.

We walked into the kitchen and set about making something to eat, chatting about our days and lounging on the sofa afterwards.

"The four bedrooms were done today, so I'll be decorating tomorrow. I want to do a theme in the blue room for Dylan since it will be his room when he stays." I looked up at Michael. "What's he into? I thought of getting those slap on picture things so you can change them around. Maybe a planet and star theme, like a solar system."

"That sounds good. He'd like that. Especially if it glows in the dark at night."

"Oh, I think I could do that." I laid my head on his manly chest that was covered in a soft woolly jumper, and he tightened his arms around me. "I had your office painted yellow today. I can put the furniture in tomorrow." I waited with bated breath.

"That sounds nice. Make sure you get pine furniture to match the colour."

I smiled. I knew what that meant.

*****

Tuesday morning, I had some furniture delivered. For the blue bedroom, I had a double bed, big desk, and lots of shelving. A TV and DVD, plus cd system were put in place. I rang a store that sold stick-on decorations and ordered a load of solar system pictures. Sin went to pick them up, and by lunchtime, Dylan's room looked like it was floating in the sky.

Sin had also picked up a planetary quilt cover with matching cases and some throw pillows in the shape of stars and planets. A huge comfy chair and a nameplate on the blue door with his name, Dylan, and the room was complete.

"He'll love it," Sin enthused.

"Yes, he will," I agreed, and walked into the rose room. I had the decorators put a rose themed border around the top of the room, and had similar themes in the others.

I stood for a moment in the doorway. I'd considered buying a cot and stroller because I wanted the room to be for our first child. But if it were a boy, pink would not be appropriate. I wanted to give Michael two gorgeous little girls, with golden-brown curls. I wanted them desperately. So desperately, I was on the brink of bursting into tears. It was gut-wrenching.

Quickly closing the door, I wandered down the hall, which was done, past the lounge room and into Michael's office. Sin had instructed the delivery guys where to put the furniture, and I gazed at the pine desk and shelves, plus the big comfy chair.

"It looks great," I said, having gotten control of myself. It was all set against the walls, so Michael had space to move around. "I know he'll love it."

One of the delivery guys checked his clipboard. "Another huge desk, sofa, chair, TV, cabinet and desk chair?"

"They're for my office," I said.

"And some design tables, desks, and computers?"

"They're for the studio."

"Okay, we'll bring them in, and you tell us where they go."

Which I did, 'cause I love telling people where to go!

My studio was set up perfectly. I had the design tables put under the front window so I'd get plenty of light to draw. There was a small room at the end which was for storage and taking photos of jewellery I'd make. I had desks put against the wall, and the computers set up for business purposes. I just needed the sign of my business name and the dressing area done.

Outside, the hole had been finished, the piping system laid, and the pool put in.

The murals were getting their paint outlines, and since at least five people were working on each one, they looked to be done by the end of the week. All in all, everything was on track.

I told Michael about it that night. "It's great. Everything's zipping along, and Dylan's room and your office are done. You should see them. I know he'll love his room."

"Since you decorated it, I'm sure he will." Michael gently stroked my hair as we lay on the sofa. I didn't want to go anywhere near his bed, so we stayed in the living room.

"And my study and studio are almost complete. My stuff should be coming in the next day or two. You can help me set it all up."

"Sure."

He wasn't saying much, and that worried me. Lifting my head from his chest, I gazed into his eyes. "Are you okay?"

He smiled softly. "I'm fine. Just enjoying being with you. Holding you. Loving you."

"Well, you know, you can love me more when you move in on Friday night."

His smile grew bigger. "Yeah, I guess I can." His lips found mine.

Ohhh, heaven.

"You going to the TNM function in a couple of weeks?" I nestled into his hairy chest that was showing itself through his unbuttoned shirt.

"Yeah, well I have to don't I."

"Since I managed to get an invite, do you want to go together?"

"We could."

I looked at him again with a raised brow and questioning expression. "We could?"

He grinned. "I guess I should have said, it's a date."

"Damn straight!"

*****

Wednesday I spent a couple of hours at the office to

keep up with the jewellery and goings on at the factory, then it was back to see what was being finished.

The kitchen was done, as was the diner's booth, stools, and counters I had a company make up for me, and they were ready to be installed. The mural just needed to be finished.

The closets were finished, and so was my personal bathroom, along with the two bathrooms shared by the four bedrooms.

The pool was sealed and secured, and now they were working on the waterfall and slide.

The murals were taking on lives of their own, my decorator had a few things made up for me that would be put in the master bedroom, and I had sound systems and lighting put in.

Since the alcoves to the sides of the front door were done, I had the baby grand, lip couches and prints moved in.

They looked freakin' fantastic.

And the good thing was my stuff arrived from Australia, so I stored the boxes in my study. They sat side by side with some of the things we'd transported from the hotel. Talk about boxes galore. We were waist high in stacks of them.

I saw Michael that night. "Are you doing anything tomorrow night? 'Cause while you unpack my boxes, you can learn all about my childish tendencies." My foot tickled his.

His expression showed mock surprise. "Surely they can't be any more childish than mine?"

"Oh, I don't know." I laughed. "Do you have a huge

collection of dolls and kids' books?"

He realised I'd beaten him. "Ah, no. No, I don't."

"Well, then. You gonna help me unpack?" My fingers stroked his cheek.

"Well…" His expression fell. "I had planned on doing other things tomorrow night." He looked around the room while my curiosity boiled over. "I was kind of hoping to get some packing done so I could move in over the weekend."

Wait! What?

I squealed. "Oh, you beautiful man, you." I jumped him and we madly made out for awhile before I pulled him to his feet and helped him start packing.

*****

Thursday was an even better day. The lounge room was completed, so I had the furniture and electricals delivered. A huge black leather sofa that had recliners at each end, two comfy chairs for guests, side tables and lamps, a large TV, DVR, Teevo etc. A coffee table that you can pull a drawer out of and display your collections. Then you can see them through the perspex top. I put my eraser collection in there and popped my snow globes around the room. A huge funky rug went on the newly polished floor and it was complete.

Sin and I sat on the sofa and looked at the view. Opposite us was the TV. The mural made it look like a window was above it, and we could see down to the bay. A Greek style village sat to the left, and little sailboats bobbed on the water to the right. I'd also had white windowpanes put on the wall, so it looked like we were actually looking out of a window.

It was very relaxing, and I felt myself melting into the couch.

"God, that's nice," Sin said, putting her feet up.

"Yes...it is," I agreed, slowly drifting off along the Greek coast.

The murals were almost done in the other rooms, and I just needed the furniture.

"I'm gonna pack up the rest of my stuff tonight. Can I borrow your suitcases for all of my clothes?"

"Sure. You got enough boxes and bags as well?"

"I hope so. God knows how I'll get it all over here. Might have to make several trips."

The decorators arrived with the bling sign for my studio, and we watched them put it up. The stones, Swarovski stones in all sizes and colours, had been applied to a mesh netting which was durable and had its own adhesive. Each letter was stuck up individually and when completed looked fabulous.

"Girls, you made one for my office, now you've done one for my house. Thanks so much."

"You're very welcome. We also have the section for the piano and smaller pieces for wherever you want to stick them."

"That will be pretty much everywhere," Sin said, and we all laughed.

Going back into the living room, I watched them wrap a piece of bling all the way around the piano. Then they laid a huge piece on the top, and one on the keyboard cover.

"This stuff will stick on forever," the woman said. "But if you need to take it off, it won't wreck anything. No paint, no varnish, no lacquer."

"Fantastic." I watched them do my piano stool, which had a bright blue leather seat. We stood back and admired the handiwork. Damn, that looked good!

Sin shook her head. "God knows why you want it that way. It's certainly not my taste."

"Just as well ya not livin' here then in'it?" I quipped.

After lunch, I got a call from Michael. "Hey."

"Hey, yourself beautiful. Listen, there's a problem at work, and we can't film today, so I'm heading home now to finish packing. You wanna meet me there?"

"Absolutely."

"Great, I'm on my way. I love you."

I tingled all over. "Love you too."

I met Michael at his house ten minutes later when he rolled into his drive. "Hey."

"Hey, beautiful." We threw our arms around each other and kissed. "Let's get packing then we can take it all over and spend the night *un*packing."

"Okay, let's go."

We spent the next two hours packing Michael's most prized possessions. Photos, knick-knacks, memorabilia. Prints came down from the walls, guitars went into their cases, photos were neatly placed into boxes.

"How do we get all of this over there?" he asked, eyeing the piles of cartons as we took a well-earned break.

I shrugged a shoulder. "Easier to pack it all in the

car and drive next door."

So we did. Of course, not everything fitted the first time, so we had to make several trips.

As I led Michael through the house, he gaped at everything he saw. Especially the piano. "You didn't," he grinned, "First the car, now the piano."

"Yeah, well, Debbie Gibson has Liberace's mirrored piano, so I made up my own. Plus, I have stands for your guitars."

"Aw, how sweet," he said with a kiss. He loved the living room, my studio and study, where he eyed the number of boxes to unpack. His office was perfect, and he adored the room I'd set up for Dylan. "Oh, he will *love this.*"

"I hope so," I said, as we stood in the room looking around at all the blue and star covered walls. "I put a lot into it so he'd be happy to come here."

Michael's grin was infectious. "Oh, he'll love coming here." He looked at me, and his grin softened. "Thank you." His finger traced lines along my jaw.

"For what?" I stared up into those big gorgeous eyes, all tingly from his touch.

"For considering my son, and showing such love and adoration, even though you've only met him once."

I shrugged, embarrassed. "He's a part of you. And I love you, so I love him too."

He kissed me. "Thank you."

After making sure everything was inside, setting up his office took no time at all, and since we still had some time, we went for some of his clothes. Two huge suitcases and five bags later, we stood on the lush blue carpet in his new walk-in closet.

"Wow. This is great." He looked around and ran his hand over the lacquered wood cabinet for his personals. "This is so nice."

"Well, this is how the other Michael had it," we grinned, "so I didn't change it. I thought I'd let you decide." I watched him explore his new surroundings.

He circled the closet and all the hanging space. "No, it's great. I love it the way it is."

"Great, let's unpack." By the time we collapsed onto the sofa, Sin had sent the workers home and left herself. "God, what time is it?" I looked at my watch. "God, six o'clock. Guess we'd better get something to eat." We sat side by side, arms around each other.

"Yeah," he sighed.

We didn't move.

Six-thirty came.

"Guess we should order. How 'bout pizza?"

"Sounds good. I know the guy at the local pizza place. I'll call," Michael said.

While waiting for the pizza, we went into my study and stared at all the boxes.

"That's a lot," Michael said, crossing his arms.

"Well," I sighed. "It always seems to take less time unpacking than it does packing, so it shouldn't take long. And I've placed the boxes in front of the shelves they're going on." I glanced at him. "It should only take a couple of hours."

He frowned in fake disgust. "A couple of hours! We could be doing other things."

"Oh, no," I said, wrapping my arms around him and tickling him under his shirt. "That's for when you move in tomorrow night."

Michael's lips pursed together before forming a grin. "I can't wait."

We managed to unpack five boxes before the pizza came, so we didn't spend much time eating. And I won't bore you with the details of my collections, so I'll just breeze over them.

The door to my study opens, and on the left are five bookcases which house my Jem and the Holograms doll collection. Straight ahead of the door is a wall that runs to the front of the house. The wall opposite is also shelf-lined, and they are the ones into which we unloaded my book collections, Connie Blair, Penny Parker, Beverly Gray, Susan Sand, and Trixie Belden all in one bookcase. The next six shelf units were for Nancy Drew books and collectables, then after those, there are two full of Hardy Boys and Dana Girls. After two hours we sat back and had a look. From left to right I perused my collections.

Bright colours, boxes, books. Jem and my Barbies sat side by side. My books all lined up like coloured soldiers in order. Two shelves set aside for my Madame Alexander and Tonner Nancy Drew dolls. U.S. and U.K. versions of the books, every series standing proudly. My Hardy Boys collectables showed Shaun Cassidy and Parker Stevenson – I had a crush on Parker – on board games, a lunch box and thermos. Activity books sat next to puzzles and lookalike dolls from the seventies. And they were next to the updated

Tonner versions.

I had collected Nancy for over twenty-six years of my life. And thanks to getting the internet connected back in late 2004, I had bought most of the collection since. And I mean most. I had a few books, but nowhere near what I had managed to acquire in six years. Along with the other book series, not to mention all the dolls, I had bought thousands of books, collectables, and ephemera for my collections. I'd even *started* book collections.

I looked around the rest of the room. Bright, colourful curtains, big comfy sofa chair, TV and cd system. Big wood desk. I had some shelving to the right and left of the desk against the wall so I could store my stationery and collectables.

There were five boxes left. "Just the knick-knacks left," I said. "Then the carpenter will hang my posters tomorrow. Along with yours."

"This was certainly a big undertaking." Michael ran his hands through his soft brown hair and let out a soft sigh.

"Aw, don't worry baby," I crooned. "You can go home as soon as we unpack these boxes." I stroked his cheek, my fingers feeling the roughness of his whiskers.

"Who said I want to go home?" His eyes fired on all cylinders.

"Oooh, down boy," I murmured, feeling sexual tension race around my body. "You get to move in tomorrow night. 'Cause tomorrow I'll be hauling my clothes in and finishing off the bedroom and adult playroom."

"I can't wait," he growled, grabbing for me.

"Well, you're just gonna have to." I playfully slapped him. "'Cause once we send everyone home and lock the door tomorrow night, that will be it for the weekend." I wrapped myself around him. "Just you and me and... wait…don't you have Dylan this weekend?"

"I was supposed to, but my ex has some family thing to take him to, so I'll get him for some extra time in a few weeks."

My fingers wound through his hair. "Oh, okay. So it's just you and me and our brand-new playground." I squeezed him. "So get ready for one hell of an adventure."

Chapter 13

A strange sound was going off somewhere. I didn't know if it was in my head or out in the distance. It persisted, and I was moved slightly.

"What, what?" I mumbled, squinting my eyes and looking around. Wait, where am I? "Oh, my God." I shot up from where I was lying and saw I was on top of Michael. Which wasn't a bad thing, I just hoped I hadn't squashed him. We'd fallen asleep on the sofa. "What time is it? Oh, God what time is it?" I turned a lamp on since it was still dark outside and looked at my watch. "Five a.m. What the hell is an alarm going off at five a.m. for?"

"Because I set my watch alarm last night in case we fell asleep," Michael said, rubbing his weary eyes and yawning.

"You get up at five a.m.?" I asked incredulously. "Why?"

He laughed. "Because I'm an actor, darling," he said dramatically. "I need to be on set early." He wiped his face. "So it looks like I'd better get going."

I looked at his dishevelled appearance. "You're

going like that?”

"No. I intend on showering and changing first." He pulled his shoes on.

"You'll need to go home to your soon-to-be old place to do that. We won't be moving in till tonight. And besides." I pulled on my own shoes. "We both still need to move some stuff in. Let's go," I said with a yawn and grabbed my bag.

After turning the light off and setting the alarm, I shut the door and watched Michael jump into his car. "See you tonight."

"Bye, love you."

"Love you too."

I made it back to my hotel and informed the manager, who was unbelievably early, that I would be moving out that day and to get the paperwork ready for my departure. Since I'd gotten in early, but needed to be at the office at nine, I had three and a half hours, so I got a lot done. I showered, went over my schedule, packed cases, bags, boxes, my computer, portable printer and whatever else I could before leaving.

"Can you go to the house and make sure everything is being finished?" I asked Sin as we cruised down in the lift. "I need to go into the office then the factory, so I'll be a couple of hours. And I'll pack my car before I come."

"Sure," she said. "Not much needs to be done anyway. Have you got the linen for your bed that you want in your bedroom?"

"Yup, and I have the stuff ready for the adult playroom too."

"Oooh, Michael's going to love that."

"He's not going to see that till tomorrow. In the meantime, I'll see you later."

I was at the office for an hour, making new jewellery, going over business, checking on publicity and the website. "Great," I said. "Let's go check out the factory."

We spent an hour there too. Supplies were in, clothes were made and printed then all blinged out. Photographed and packed away neatly. Even all of my outfits copied for the Jem range were finished and fitted to perfection. Plus, the four dresses ready for the soapies, and Marnie Wilkins' dress were done as well.

"God, that's gorgeous," I breathed. The emerald taffeta hung with grace and looked like a cake with all its layers. The beads had been placed on the top section of the skirt in bulk, then they seemed to drip down to the bottom, like an umbrella with rain falling from it. The effect was stunning and I decided she should have it now. "Take this to her today, please. And thank you so much for my outfits, they're fabulous." We went over a few more designs for dresses I wanted for myself then I hurried back to the hotel to pack.

Suitcases, bags, boxes. I packed my car to the top, more so since I had put the roof down. Every little space was crammed with something, and when a box wouldn't fit, I pulled out what was in it and shoved it into a space.

The boot was loaded, and I had to tie it shut. Even the front seat and floor was filled. Unfortunately, it still wasn't everything I had, so I took it to the house.

Sin helped me unload, and I got to see my bedroom complete for the first time. I was amazed at how great it looked, but it just needed the bed and a few bits and pieces.

We quickly hung my clothes, stacked my shoes, put my wigs on heads in a glass cabinet, and slid my lingerie into drawers.

"I'm going back for the next load. Can you see to the furniture when it arrives?"

"It's on its way now," Sin said.

"Great. Just have them put it in the rooms, and I'll help set it up when I get back." Back to the hotel I went and loaded up my car again. Thankfully, that was it, and I checked the room one last time. Had to double check and make sure I had everything I owned, or I'd freak if I lost something. I signed the papers at the front desk and left the hotel.

Driving into my yard, I was dismayed to see the lawn out the back not yet laid. Due to the diggers on Monday, I needed it fixed and replaced. And it wasn't finished yet.

I walked through the front door rolling two cases behind me. "Sin...can you check what's taking so long with the backyard and see if the pool's finished?"

"Okay." Sin knew how to crack the whip and break the balls.

I wheeled my cases into the bedroom, and saw the bed already set up, but not yet in place. Two bedside tables were waiting along with a chest. I decided to put my clothes away first, then get the room ready for tonight.

Half an hour later, and after emptying my car, Sin was helping me push the bed into place. "There." I brushed off my hands. "Bed and bedhead in place." I set up the table and placed a lamp on it. "And tables. Just need to make the bed."

Since Michael was moving in that night, I wasn't bothering with too much linen. It would just end up on the floor anyway. A few pillows and a couple of blue silk sheets. I moved the chest to the end of the bed, and we stood back and surveyed the room.

"Now *this* is a room I could have for myself," Sin said.

I sighed happily. The curtains blended in with the mural, the paint was dry, the palm trees up. It was bloody perfect! "Now for the adult playroom."

We walked in to see a carpenter screwing the last of the nuts and bolts into the wall.

"Have you done my study, office, and the hallways? We need to hang everything now."

The man stepped down from his ladder which the decorator climbed up. "Ma'am. All the screws are in place, and the pictures are on the floor underneath the screws they're supposed the hang on. The size and weight dictated what size screw I used."

Useful information I'm sure, I just didn't need to hear it or know it.

"Great," I said, watching the decorator hang the white netting from a ring she connected to the wall. "Can you help us hang them before you go?"

"Sure thing."

He helped hang my Jem and Nancy Drew posters –

which I'd had framed the day before and had arrived that morning while I was at the office – in my study. Some of Michael's pictures went up in his office and his movie prints in the hallway.

My fifties diner dining room was completed. We set up the jukebox and pinball machine and turned them on. The black and white floor had been laid, and the company that had done my booth had bolted it to the floor, and the counter to the kitchen bench. The stools were done in chrome and hot pink leather. The booth seats were turquoise leather, while the table was pink Formica and the counter was blue. Chrome was everywhere and polished to within an inch of its life. We set up fifties salt and pepper shakers and serviette holders on the table and counter. An Elvis clock, with him swinging his legs, sat on the wall, and I saw Marilyn Monroe, James Dean, Elvis, and a cast of other celebs poking out from the mural watching the fifties teenagers dancing in their poodle skirts and bobby socks. I also placed a few knick-knacks around the kitchen and had repro appliances that looked like they fitted right in. All in all, it was a hell of a bright kitchen.

I thanked the guys from the companies – so many companies – and as Sin showed them out, I turned to my decorator. "It's two o'clock, can you get everything mopped and vacuumed while Sin and I do the other room?" While she and her team did that, Sin and I put the adult playroom into place, then going from room to room, I inspected and made sure everything was clean, tidy and brand new.

The man from the pool company came in at four. "Ma'am. We've got everything in place. The pool is sealed, the suction works, the waterfall and slide are ready. We just need to come back tomorrow to fill it with water and put in the fountain."

I frowned in dismay. "Can't you do that now?"

"No Ma'am. It could take a couple of hours, and it's four now."

God sent me a message.

My phone rang.

"Sweetheart. I won't be home till seven. Will that be a problem?"

It was Michael. Right on cue, he solved my problem. "No, not at all, it will give the pool company time to finish."

"Cool! Then we can go skinny dipping later."

I snorted with laughter. "You wish. I'll meet you at your place at seven to pick up the rest of your stuff. Then I can show you around."

"Oooh, that sounds good. I'll see you then."

"Okay."

"Bye. I love you."

"Love you, too."

I turned to the pool guy. "Since it's only four, you still have an hour before knock-off time. You told me you would have it filled by five today. So, please do so, and finish my lawn as you stated you would in your contract." I kept my temper in check and tried not to let it blow. I don't like companies that state one thing and then go back on it or run overtime and expect extra money for dragging out a job. And I also don't like people thinking they can take advantage of me just because I have money. That's why I don't talk about myself. When people know you've got money, they try and take you for all your worth.

He didn't look happy. And neither was I. I wanted the pool done tonight. "And make sure everything works before you go. Thank you," I called after him as he walked away.

"Well, girls." I turned back to the decorator's team. "Let's finish the house."

I moved a few things here and there as I went. I wanted it to be perfect for when Michael moved in. Raiding my lingerie drawer, I pulled out something special, then realised it would be more appropriate for our night in the adult playroom than the bedroom, so I pulled out something else. "Perfect." Walking into the bathroom, I made sure my toiletries were nice and neat on the counter and towels were piled on the wicker shelving. "More perfect."

Going into the living room, I thanked everyone who was still there and paid them handsomely. They were happy with the bonuses I gave them and asked if they could feature their work in magazines.

"I'd prefer it to be original and personal," I said. They understood. Once they left, Sin and I sat on the outdoor lounges and watched the pool fill up. "Thanks for filling the fridge for me," I told her.

"That's all right. The store I ordered from home delivered. They couldn't believe we bought so much."

"I love my food and needed a variety of stuff. It's just as well I made a list of what Michael had in his cupboards and fridge so I could stock up on those."

Sin sighed and put her hands behind her head. Stretching out on the poolside lounge she closed her eyes. "I'm just glad this is nearly over, and I can go home."

"Haven't you gone home during the weeks? I didn't see much of you."

"I managed a couple of days here and there," she said.

"You can go home tomorrow and come back next weekend for the party."

"Mmm, I might do that. Do you know what you're wearing?"

"Black jeans, red top and leather boots, a hat and lots of bling."

"What?" Her eyes flew open. "You can't be serious." She sat up and looked at me. "You can't be attending a huge network function in jeans and a top."

"Why not? Richard asked me what I'd be wearing, and I told him I didn't know what to wear to such a function. That I might choose to be comfortable. He said he didn't care."

She calmed down a little. "Have you spoken to Richard since the dinner at his house?"

"No. But my dressmakers have seen Marnie for fittings, and they took her dress over to her yesterday."

"Wonder if she liked it?"

"She bloody well should. It cost thousands." I frowned then smiled. "My first sale, yay."

The lawn was finished, the gardeners went home, and now we just needed the pool to be done.

My phone rang. "Hello."

"Hello, Tahlia. It's Marnie Wilkins. I got my dress yesterday, and it's absolutely beautiful. Thank you so much."

"You're welcome. Glad you like it. Now, remember, you have to brag like crazy about it to all your friends and make them greener than the dress with envy."

She laughed. "Of course. I'll tell everyone about this amazing new designer I've found to make me fabulous new clothes. I'll keep your name a secret until I burst and blurt it out. They'll all be so envious."

"So they should be, it's an amazing dress."

"It is. I'll be wearing it to the network function next weekend to show it off. You are still coming aren't you?"

"I am. I'm coming with Michael Anthony."

There were a few seconds of silence. "So you found him?"

"Oh, I certainly did." A huge grin lit up my face.

"I'm happy for you and can't wait to see you next Friday. Thank you for my dress, dear, I'll see you then. Bye."

"Bye." I snapped my phone shut. "She liked it."

"And so she should."

"Pool's done," the guy called out.

"About time. Is it clear?" I asked, getting up from the lounge and walking over.

"Just cleaning it now."

"Can you turn on everything? I want to see how it works." The fountain and waterfall flowed smoothly, and the slide was ready to slide down. "All right. Thank you so much." We shook hands.

"Our pleasure." They packed up their belongings and left.

"That just leaves you," I said to Sin with a pointed look.

At seven sharp I met Michael in his driveway.

"What else do I need?" he asked, getting out of the car.

I kissed him hello. "Well, unless you want mouldy food, then your food for a start."

"Oh, yeah." He laughed, and we went inside.

Boxes of food and more knick-knacks later, we loaded up his car, made sure the house was solidly locked and secured, and for the first time, we drove up to our house together.

Since I had a four car garage down the side of the yard, he pulled in next to my 'Stang. "Wow. I have a new garage to park my car in," he said excitedly.

I laughed lightly and waved my hand at the other places. "I plan on sharing this spot with a thirties roadster when I get one."

"Don't tell me," he deadpanned. "Nancy Drew's."

"Of course, darling," I replied with a grin. We got out and piled up the boxes, locked the garage and walked around to the front door.

"Why are we at the front door?" He frowned.

"Because," I dangled the keys with relish, "we are officially moving into our house tonight, so we need to walk through the front door together." I watched his facial expressions run the gamut of emotion.

He leaned down and kissed me. "I love you."

I flashed him a huge grin. "I love you too. Shall

we?" I shook the keys.

"We shall," he agreed.

I inserted the key, opened the door, and disconnected the alarm. Standing aside for Michael, I closed the door behind him.

"I'm still amazed by this place and what you've done with it." He dropped the boxes on the sofa. "God I love it."

"Let me show you some of the finished product then." I took his hand and led him around my studio. The dressing room was up, the model stand was down, and the curtains gleamed like a rainbow.

"Nice," he said, looking at the sign on the wall. "Very you. Next."

In my study, he examined the prints on the wall closely since he's a movie buff. His office was next, and he smiled at the photos and prints on the wall as he gently touched a photo of him and Dylan that was on his new desk.

I led him back to the living room and stopped in front of the sliding doors. "I had these doors muraled in rainbows and pots of gold because I rode my own rainbow all the way here and found my pot of gold in you."

"Aw." His face crumpled up with happiness.

"Close your eyes." He did, and sliding the doors open I flicked the light switch. "Open them."

He gasped in shock. "Oh, my God." He stepped into the kitchen/dining area and stared at every little detail. "This is freakin' fantastic."

I smiled in pleasure. "Thank you, thank you."

We stood for a few more minutes before I opened the sliding doors and showed him the pool. At the flick of some more switches, the waterfall started, and the fountain spurted to life.

"Oh," he laughed. "We have *got* to go swimming in that." He put his hands over his mouth in shock. "This…is…wow. So much better than my pool."

"Well, you know," I smiled slyly at him, "I wanted what I wanted, and I got it."

"It certainly looks like you did." Michael pulled me into his arms and kissed me.

I kissed him back.

"Of course you did," you mutter.

Of course I did!

"We have *got* to go for a swim," he repeated.

"A little later." I reluctantly pulled out of his arms, and we walked toward the house. "We need to finish unpacking." I turned to look at him while walking backwards. "Then we may want something to eat, *then* we can go swimming."

"Ohhh." His face fell.

"It won't take long." I picked up a box, and ten minutes later the food was put away, and we were changing into bathers.

"Whoo," he called when he saw me in my bright blue bikini.

"Calm down," I said, eyeing his sexy hairy body that I couldn't wait to get my hands on. "Do we want to eat some fruit or something, so we don't starve to death?"

"How about I eat you, and you can eat the fruit?"

He playfully grabbed at me.

I gave him a dirty look, and after an apple, we walked out to the pool and stood on the side looking in. "Don't even think of doing a bomb," I warned. "It's only six feet in the deep end."

"Why six?"

"I, ah, have some fears about deep water. If I can't touch the bottom, I start to freak out."

"Why?" His look was of love and concern.

I shrugged. "Don't know. Shall we walk down the stairs together?" I held out my hand.

He took it. "M'lady, we shall."

Step by step, we walked in to my brand-new blue tinted pool. I wanted it to look like a tropical hideaway. With the green plants hiding us, and the waterfall, it looked great.

It was heavenly. The wind blew gently for late spring, casting off the water nicely. We paddled for awhile, and at one stage I flung my arms around Michael's neck and let him piggyback me around. We ended up under the waterfall overhang.

"Oooh, private." Michael wiped his face.

"I wanted a little hideaway in the pool so no one would or could see us," I said, hugging him close. I felt his chest hair against my body and melted all over. Being this close to him was heaven, as I've said before, and something I'd wanted for a hell of a long time.

His lips touched mine. His tongue probed delicately, trying to find its way inside. I responded, and we held onto each other for dear life. Like we were each other's lifeboat on a very stormy sea.

Finally coming up for air we smiled at each other and giggled.

"Our very first swim together," I said.

"Our very first swim together with a kiss," he replied.

Smiling, we left the pool, and grabbing a couple of towels, walked hand in hand into the kitchen. I threw a meal into the micro, and five minutes later we were feeding each other pasta carbonara, garlic bread, and chocolate mousse for dessert.

"I'm going to shower first," I said afterwards. "Then I can get ready for our first night together while you have yours. I'll show you our lovely bathroom then you can wander around till your shower."

"Okay, lead the way."

I remembered something and stopped. "This whole couple thing. You haven't asked me yet." My expression reminded him of what the question was.

He tightened his towel, then took my hand and kissed it. "Will you, Tahlia, be my girlfriend? My lover. My partner. The woman I live with, the woman I love with?" He leaned in with a huge grin. "The woman I *make love* with?"

I nearly burst into tears. "Of course I will be." I threw myself into his arms and kissed him passionately then pulled back. "I love you so much that I moved halfway around the world for you." That shocked him, and I blushed. "I'm not a stalker," I rushed on. "I could have set up my business at home, bought a house, two cats, two dogs, which I know I haven't done yet, and published my books." I shook my head. "But you weren't there. And I wanted you so much, so I moved." My face crinkled with emotion. "Please don't be alarmed. I didn't stalk you. I didn't meet you till you ran into me. But I knew when I saw you, with all of the feelings that rushed through me, that I had made the right decision to move here." I kissed him. "I love you so much. I want to be with you so much. Please, please believe that."

He obviously did and stopped looking freaked out. Staring into my eyes, he would've recognised the love and happiness that radiated from my heart. "I love you too." He laughed.

"What's so funny?"

"I am so glad you decided to move here, 'cause otherwise, I wouldn't have met you."

"So am I." We kissed again. 'Let's go see the bathroom." I led him into the hallway that connected the bedroom, bathroom, and our closets. Opening the door, I turned on the light.

"Oh, my God," he laughed raggedly, even more surprised by what he saw. "It's amazing."

The floor tiles were sandy yellow, and the shower door had a bamboo screen stuck over it to look like an island shower. The wall tiles in the shower were dark green. There was an overhang with palm trees, and a bamboo screen was to the side so you could undress behind it before stepping into the shower. The walls were painted with the same mural as the bedroom, so the theme was continued, and there was a huge black marble Jacuzzi bath with the same bamboo around it as the shower.

"Oh, my God." He wiped his face. "This is amazing."

"You ain't seen nothing, yet," I said, pleased that he was happy. "So how 'bout you go potter around and I'll take a shower. I'll let you know when I'm done."

He still stared in amazement. "Uh...okay."

"Okay." I pushed him out the door. "See you in a minute."

Ten minutes later, I called him. "Your turn." I kissed him as we passed.

"Mmm, you smell good."

"I know, and I know the bathroom is amazing, but don't take too long. We have things to do you know."

"Oh, we certainly do," he said in a sultry tone that sent shivers down my spine.

I ran into my closet, and quick as lightning, dressed in a silky white negligee. I'd smeared citrus scented moisturiser on in the bathroom after using a similar body wash, which is what Michael had smelled, so I smelt as good as I felt. I wrapped a matching robe around myself and brushed out my hair. I heard the bathroom door open and close, and Michael walk into his closet. A few moments later, I followed.

He was standing with his back to me pulling on navy shorts.

"Yum," I growled, as I drooled and perved.

He turned with a laugh, then stopped as his eyes widened. "Hey...wow."

"You like?" I spread my dressing gown out so he could see better.

He nodded vigorously. "I love."

"Let's go then." Feeling very shy, I took his hand, and we walked to the bedroom door. "Close your eyes," I said, unlocking the door.

"You locked it?" he asked, feigning surprise.

"Of course I did." I slid a sly look his way. "Which you'd know since I have no doubt you tried to look while I was in the shower."

He blushed deeply with an embarrassed laugh.

"Close your eyes." I opened the door and led him through, closing it behind us. We walked over to the bed. "Turn around and keep your eyes closed. Step back against the bed. Now, sit and swing around and put your legs up." I slowly climbed over the top of him, making sure to wiggle a little and get his juices flowing, and got comfortable beside him. "Open your eyes."

"Oh, my fucking, God," he stuttered in more surprise. He blinked a few times to see whether what he was seeing was real or not.

"It's real," I said. "And all ours. Our very own tropical island paradise."

I wanted our bedroom to look like a tropical island. A real one. Like we were living on it and looking at the ocean every day. The carpet was sandy yellow, the walls covered in the mural of blue ocean, and blue sky with big fluffy clouds, palm trees with coconuts and bright coloured birds. In the corner of the room, I had a handmade palm tree bolted to the wall. Hanging green leaves and a rope finished it off.

"A rope?" you ask.

Eh, never mind, moving on. Behind us were three palm trees with large green branches hanging over the bed like a cover.

"This is unbelievable," he gasped, eyeing everything

he could take in, even the treasure chest at the end of the bed. He cocked his head. "We have a treasure chest...mmm...now what's that for?"

I blushed. "Well, that's filled with our treasure booty...and a few...pirate costumes."

He laughed in a low sexy tone. "Pirate costumes? Argh, me mateys, looks like we'll be playing the Pirate and his Island Wench." He jokingly grabbed me and laid his teeth in.

I giggled. "Well, what do you think the tree with the rope in the corner is for?"

He stopped and looked at the tree. "Mmm, a rope." Dirty ideas formed in his eyes.

Changing the subject. "And listen," I said, leaning seductively over him and pressing a button on a small machine. The sound of ocean waves crashing on the beach came over the built-in sound system.

His expression became animated. "Oh, wow. It's like we're actually there."

I was still draped over his hairy torso. Very much to my liking, it was too, and he certainly didn't mind. "Yup." I pointed to the corner ceiling. "You see the sun?" – yes, there was a sun painted on the roof – "When I turn the light off, it will show as the moon thanks to the glow in the dark paint, and there'll be little stars in the sky." I looked up. "Wanna see?"

He looked so gobsmacked it was endearing. "Sure."

I grabbed a remote from the bedside table and turned down the lighting. After our eyes adjusted, we could see the moon glow brilliant beams.

"This is absolutely amazing." Yes, he was still

gobsmacked, and I was really glad he liked it. It was our bedroom, and we needed something just for us.

"I wanted something special for us to sleep in. Wanted it to be a personal private getaway. Where we could go at the end of a long day and relax."

Michael looked at me with his trademark big goofy grin. "I definitely want to come home to this."

"That's good to know," I said with a grin, nodding my head with knowledge. "I told you once you saw it you wouldn't want to leave."

"You were right," he said, leaning in with a gentle kiss. "I don't want to leave. Ever." His finger traced along my jawline onto my lips. "I love you, Tahlia. And I never want to leave." He kissed me, his lips pressing firm, his tongue delving into the deep cavern.

This was the moment I had waited for forever. The moment I came together with the man I love with every fibre of my being.

He took my face in his hands and leaned against me, his right leg gently sliding between mine. I moved down underneath him, wrapping my arms around him as he slowly pushed off my robe. His hands roamed my body burning my flesh as his fingers seared along.

I groaned, I couldn't help it. I mean, hellooo!!!!!

He lay on top of me, and my legs wound with his. Our kiss deepened further and my breasts caught on fire, ignited by the furry nest of hair on his manly chest.

Needless to say, that night was bloody amazing!

Chapter 14

And like I was gonna tell you about it!!!!!

I mean, please. I will *not* divulge any of the secrets from last night. Not if you begged, screamed, or cried. Except to say, we woke up about ten in a contented tangle of arms, legs, and other body parts…

My eyes slowly opened, I breathed deeply, then nestled my face into the mass of soft silky hair I wanted to bury myself in. Ahh, heaven!

Michael's arms tightened around me, his lips pressing against my forehead. "Good morning," he murmured.

I sighed with happiness and pressed myself against him. "It is, isn't it?"

His laugh was light. "It certainly is."

We lay like that for awhile. Arms around each other, bodies pressed against the other, legs entwined, a sheet barely covering our naked selves. The sound system was still on, so the waves crashing against the shore made it seem like we actually were waking up on a tropical island paradise.

Again, heaven!

Deciding, after an hour, to get up for brunch, we had a long lazy shower. Which took an hour since we were naked, soapy, hot and steamy, and well, you know the rest, so I don't need to tell you that either. We strolled into the kitchen in time for lunch, and after a casual meal, we planted ourselves by the pool. With a sunshade over us, we lay wrapped in each other for some time.

I moved my head back a little, so I could see Michael's face. His eyes were closed and a small smile playing delicately on his thick lushy lips. "Michael," I whispered.

"Mmm?"

"There's something you need to know." That caught his attention.

"What?" He opened his sleepy eyes and stared into mine, full of curiosity.

I took a deep breath and squeezed my eyes shut for a moment before looking back at him. "It's about the TNM function and why I was invited." I was starting to feel scared.

He moved his head a little to get a better look at me. "You said you were invited for something you'd done."

"I said that because I didn't want to talk about it." I sat up and glanced away. "But it will more than likely be announced at the function anyway, so I should tell you myself." My eyes found Michael's. "Since we're now a couple."

He pulled himself up and adjusted the back of the lounge then settled in. "Okay. Tell me. What is it?"

"I know who saved Marnie Wilkins from the crash and attempted kidnapping." My nerves were on edge now.

"What?" He was disbelieving. "Who? How do you know? What are you—?"

"It was me. I'm the one who saved Marnie. I'm the one who was there."

Shock thundered over his face and his head shook. "What? What are you saying? You're the one who saved her?" He turned his body toward me. "It was you? The woman we've all heard and talked about?" He looked at me, full of questions. "You?"

"Yep." My emotions were fiery knots in my stomach, and I started feeling sick. "Look, just sit back, and I'll tell you everything," I said, proceeding to tell the whole story from go to whoa. The visit to the hospital, dinner at Richard Sayer's house, and the fact the men might still be out there. I shook a little with fear at the thought of those men being after me, but Michael pulled me close and held me for a long time. I wiped away some tears. "I've just been getting on with my life, my business, my factory. I pick up my books on Monday, and they're ready for sale. My life is taking off, and I don't want to be involved." I gazed at him imploringly. "Please don't tell anyone. The only other person to know is Sin since she's my lawyer. I want no one to know. I don't want anyone, especially you, to be hurt in any way."

A mass of emotion flitted back and forth across Michael's gorgeous face as he took it all in. Shaking his head slightly, sighing, and stroking my hair. "Good

God," he finally said. "Everything you've gone through. It must have been terrifying."

I gave a little shrug. "It was, but it's over now. Please don't tell anyone."

He shook his head and kissed me. "I love you. I'll keep your secret."

"Thank you." I kissed him back.

I felt so emotional. Here was a huge secret I'd kept from him for his safety as well as mine, and it was so great to finally get it off my chest. And he'd understood and forgiven me so quickly and easily. Dear God, thank you for making him so incredibly wonderful.

We lay there for awhile longer, going over small details, talking about the future. *Our* future. The sun slowly descended, and we swam and played until that evening when I donned my sexy animal print negligee with matching robe and seductively led Michael to the wall outside of the adult playroom.

"Open it."

He looked perturbed. "How? It's a wall."

Smiling sweetly, I kissed his cheek. "Push the wall."

"Push the wall?" Now he was really confused.

"Push the wall," I repeated, my eyes flicking back and forth from him to the wall.

"Okay." He pushed the wall with both hands and a section moved back. "Oh," he said, laughing. "A secret door."

"A secret door. Of course." My smile said it all. "Slide it to the right."

He did and stood stock still. Jaw hanging, eyes bulging.

"Go in." I pushed him into the room and slid the door closed behind me.

I had wanted the adult playroom to look like a retreat in the Amazon jungle. The walls were painted in a mural of rainforests with animals poking their heads out. A huge waterfall was painted on the wall to our right, so it sat opposite the huge bed covered in a fake animal fur cover with matching cushions. A white net hung over it, and the ceiling looked like a thatched roof hut with ceiling fan. The curtains were dark green netting, and a comfy chair sat in front of the window with a fake bear rug. A small bench and fridge were to the left of the door, and the floor was dark stained wood. All in all, it looked very rainforesty. Like a romantic jungle getaway.

I climbed onto the fur covered bed. It was like a sofa bed, the kind you pull the bed out of, but the bed was a proper bed with the sofa attached around it if you know what I mean. Michael stood staring at everything while I arranged myself on the cushions and pulled the netting around a little more. "I take it you like it."

"Yeah! I love it. It's like the bedroom." He laughed and noticed me on the bed. "Oh," he grunted lightly. "It's a second bedroom."

I wiggled my brows seductively. "It's the adult playroom. I couldn't decide between the two, so I have both."

"Ohhh." He dropped onto all fours and crawled toward the bed. Climbing up he pounced on me. "And now Tarzan gets to hunt his prey and make her do the things he wants her to."

"Is that so?"

We didn't emerge until eleven a.m. Sunday morning.

"Oh," you cry. "No fair."

Well, it's not like I was gonna tell you about that night either!!!!!

We spent a lazy day together, inspecting each other's study, my studio, Dylan's room. Learning things about each other that we didn't know yet. It was really the only time we would have for the coming week was going to be hectic. My last week before opening, the network function, my book, making more jewellery. Not to mention Michael up at five every morning for work. And it was our first week in our new house as a happy, loving couple.

We tumbled into bed that night, in the bedroom, after a long hot steamy shower full of sex and soap. A relaxing massage, and more hot insatiable sex later and we fell into a contented deep sleep.

*****

The alarm went off at five, and we dragged ourselves out of bed, thanking God that is was the last week before hiatus. A shower and some breakfast later, which I got to serve my man for the first time as a live-in couple, and I was kissing him goodbye and waving him off to work.

Aw, how sweet!

Yes, it was. I was waving the man I love off to work.

I was living with him, sleeping with him – yum – making a life with him. And all in not quite eight weeks since flying into L.A.

God, that seems like so long ago, and so much has happened. I dressed for the day and sat in the lounge room going over my schedule with *The Morning Show* playing softly in the background.

"News just in, it seems that Marnie Wilkins, the wife of TNM network CEO Richard Sayer, is going to talk about her accident and kidnapping attempt," the woman said.

"What?" My head shot up with a frown. "Since when?"

"That's right," the male co-anchor said. *"Marnie Wilkins is going to talk about her ordeal in an exclusive on her husband's network. No plans yet though on when it will be. Apparently, the police and FBI are telling her not to do it as it could jeopardise their case. But she's adamant that she wants to talk. In other news..."*

I turned off the TV then jumped as my phone rang.

"Can you believe she's going to do that?" Sin asked, a hardness to her tone.

I sighed in frustration. "No, I can't. I hope she damn well keeps my name out of it. I don't want the press and paps hounding me for a story. And God knows what the kidnappers would do to me. I want to stay as far away from it as possible."

"You'd better call her and tell her then. Otherwise, you could sue her for disclosing your name without permission."

"I don't want to do that." I grimaced. "That could make things even worse."

"It might, it might not. So, how was your weekend?"

I found myself grinning like the Cheshire cat. "Amazing, incredible, fantastic, beautiful, mind-blowing, incredible—"

"You said incredible. That good huh? Wait, don't repeat yourself."

"I told Michael," blurted from my mouth.

"Told Michael what?"

"About the kidnapping, my part in it, that I don't want him telling anyone."

"What! How did he take it?"

"Okay, actually. At first, he thought I was joking or lying or something. Then after I told him every morbid detail, he believed me."

"That's good."

"Yeah, it is. So, that was Saturday, and Saturday night we spent in the playroom, so things were *great*." I expressed the last word very enthusiastically.

"It sounds like you had a great time, and Michael's the love of your life."

I smiled dreamily. "Yeah."

"You pick up your books today don't you?"

"Yep. A box of my very own books. Yay me!"

"Don't forget to save me one. I'll be down Friday morning so we can go to the hairdresser's together." A pause. "We *are* still getting our hair and make-up done aren't we?"

"Of course. I made the appointment last week," I stopped, "Or was that you..." With everything that had gone on I couldn't remember.

"That was me. I'll see you Friday."

"Okay, bye."

Now *I* had to make a call.

"Hello."

"Marnie?"

"Yes."

"It's Tahlia. I heard on *The Morning Show* you're planning on telling your story." I paused a moment. "You weren't going to give me away were you?"

"Oh, no dear, not at all. Richard and I talked about it and decided if we took it public, they'd back off and stay away. After all, the world would know about it. Why would they continue to try and grab me?"

"Money, notoriety, they hate you, Richard, or were treated badly and want to get at him."

"We've seen the photos of the kidnappers, and neither one of us recognised them. We have no idea who they are, or why they would want to hurt either one of us."

"Doesn't mean they're not working for someone you do know, or was fired by Richard."

"That's true. But we just can't think of anyone. Regardless of how far back we go."

"Just keep my name out if it, thanks, for my own safety. And look, I hope it goes well for you. When are you planning it for?"

"Next week, after the function."

"So, what will happen at this do I'm going to? I hope you're not going to gush over me?"

"Not if you don't want us to."

"No, I don't."

"All right, then. We'll keep your name out of our speeches."

"Don't mention I'm there either."

"If that's the way you want it."

"It is."

"All right then, dear. I'll see you Friday night."

"See you then." I studied my schedule again. God, I hope this week goes well.

*****

I stood with my editor at the publishing company and opened my box of books. Pulling the top one out, I drooled over it. It was beautiful. Las Vegas in the background, hot looking guy hitchhiking on the road in the foreground. The colours bright and cheery. It was a decent size, fitting into my hands neatly, and you could read it in an hour or two.

I flicked through the pages, smelling that new book smell. My eyes devoured the back cover blurb along with the dedications and acknowledgements inside. "Wait, where are my dedications?"

"What?" my editor asked, a blank look on her face.

I grabbed another book, and another, pulling them open, looking for my dedications page. "There are no dedication pages in any of these books," I cried.

"No, there can't be," she said, flipping through them. Her face drained of colour when she realised I was right. "I...we...are so terribly sorry," gushed out of her like a waterfall.

I tried desperately not to laugh and cry at the same time. "I...want...these books...redone by Friday. And make sure...that the dedication page...is put in *ALL* of the books you've published so far. *And*," I emphasised with a point of my finger, "this company will be picking up the tab and working overtime to do it. Do you understand me?"

The poor girl was shaking and stone cold white. "Yes, yes, we will...we will."

"ALL OF THEM. BY FRIDAY." I left her standing in the middle of her office with everyone staring after me.

When I told Ben about the books later, I was on the edge of a teary emotional breakdown.

"That's not good," he said. "They're needed for next week."

"I know," I cried, leaning back in my chair. We were in the conference room at the office going over the opening for next week. "I told my editor they had better be redone for pick up on Friday."

"They'd better be. We need photos and a price to put up on the website."

"I know, I know." I spun around in my chair. "But everything else is going okay and on track isn't it?" I calmed down a little and got myself together.

"Right on track," Richard said. "Clothes are ready to go, publicity's set up. Phone network ready for calls. We're all prepared for the bombardment to come next week."

"Great," I said. "I want the sign up this week outside, but leave it covered till Monday, and we'll have a little opening celebration. Now, I'm off to check on the jewellery. Tina, how's it going?" We walked into the design room. All ten girls were working full steam.

"Great," Tina replied. "Photos are being taken with the measurements. Hats and belts are in, and we have the first five prototypes of the bags."

"Great, let me see. Good work, girls." I checked over the belts. Thick leather, lots of bling. "Nice." The hats were in all colours and had varying stages of stones. I tried some on. "Mmm, I'll take these, so get some more made."

"Okay."

We inspected every inch of the bags. Pockets, zips, the handles were strong, stitching firm, the colours shone nice and bright in patent leather. Each bag had bling, a little or a lot. God, I wanted them bags. "I'm taking these too," I told Tina. "Have them made up, extras for yourself to help advertise the company. We agreed on ten of each, but make it twenty-five, and we'll see how we go."

"All right." She leaned in to whisper. "I love the black one."

"Then have one made for yourself," I said with a grin.

*****

"So," Michael said, clapping his hands together. "Where's my copy of the book?"

"You'll have to wait till Friday," I said miserably, almost collapsing into tears. We were standing in the middle of our kitchen as I told him about the missing dedication pages.

"That's not good," he said, pulling me into his arms. "I'm sorry."

I sighed. The world seemed better when I was in his arms. "I'm trying to be positive, *I am*. The books will be done on Friday, and they will all be fine."

"They will *all* be fine," he repeated with a kiss.

"Yes, they will be," I agreed, going back for seconds.

*****

"Owww, that hurts," I cried Tuesday morning after my chiro cracked, yanked and moved something inside my body. I was face down and flat out on the table in utter pain, I tells ya.

"You're tense," she said, moving my left arm.

I sighed. "Yeah, well, it's been a hectic eight weeks. Last week I was decorating and moving into my new house, and I have the opening of my company next week."

"Had you have been here last week and done your exercise classes you'd be better off. But now you're all stressed out."

I smiled half-heartedly. "Like I said, I've been busy. But I'm here now, so fix me up."

"Okay, you asked for it."

"Owww, that hurts!"

With my poor bones cracking, and my poor muscles aching, I drove to my weapons training class. I didn't have a gun of my own, so I logged one out every week. I'd been shooting with different types of guns to become used to the feel and power of each. Pulling them apart, learning how to clean, and putting them back together was also a part of training.

Taking my goggles, earmuffs, and gun to the range, I pulled on my leather gloves, which I had always chosen to wear while shooting, and lined up my target.

The day was sunny and warm, I was surrounded by likewise people, and I had a clear field of vision. Donning my protective headgear, I picked up my gun, loaded the cartridge, and aimed at the target. Standing for a moment, legs shoulder width apart, right arm straight out with my left hand cupping my right, back straight and locked, I bent my knees slightly and narrowed my emerald green eyes.

1...2...3...

I pulled the trigger and found myself flying backwards onto the ground with a thud.

Owww!!!!!

People came running. "Are you all right?" the day instructor asked, rushing up.

I sat up in a daze and full on body pain. What the hell happened?!

"Ms Cameron? Are you all right?"

His voice was vague as I turned my head slowly to look at the face filled with concern. "What?" I didn't even hear myself speak I was so deaf.

"Are you all right?" The instructor checked me over as an attendant ran over with a first aid kit. They did a quick examination of my arms and face, and I sat there as if I was watching a movie in slow motion.

"It's a good thing you were wearing gloves." I heard.

My ears were still ringing but my vision cleared.

"I'm okay?" I asked.

"You seem to be," the instructor said. "No burns, just some ringing in your ears, and a sore butt." He helped me up, but I swayed around in a circle before he grabbed me with both hands. "We'll take you to the office where you can sit before going home." He looked concerned again. "You're not driving are you?"

Considering what I'd been through with Marnie, this was nothing. I shook my head and grimaced. "No, look, I'm fine." I bashed my ear. "Just need to get rid of this damn ringing." I glanced around for my gun. "What happened anyway?"

The assistant picked up the gun. It was a twisted mess. "Could be dirty inside. That would have caused it to backfire."

"Didn't you check the gun after the last person?" the instructor demanded.

"I don't know," the assistant mumbled. "I'll have to check it out back in the office." He scurried off with the gun while the instructor, whose name tag read Mike, helped me up and walked me to the office.

"It's a good thing you had gloves on," he repeated, sitting me into a chair. "Otherwise, your hands would be sore and burned."

I studied my hands. The leather gloves were covered in something slimy, and my arms had red spots above the cuffs. "I've always worn them," I said. "Even in Australia. I just thought it was better if something happened." I shrugged lightly. "Can I have some water?"

"Of course."

I sat sipping the water, waiting for the ringing in my ears to die down. I felt like crap and called all of my classes to cancel. I did not feel like dancing and Pilates after being thrown ten feet onto the ground. Thanking the instructor for his help, I headed for my car and drove home. All I wanted to do was sleep.

"Tah-li-a...Tah-li-a..." Michael's soft sing-song voice called.

I opened my eyes and stretched, taking in his manly frame on the bed beside me. "Hey," I yawned. "What time is it?"

"Five-thirty, we got off early." He kissed me gently, bringing a smile to my lips. "How come you're home sleeping and not at some class?" He lay beside me, and we spooned.

"I haven't been sleeping all afternoon. Only on and off. After what happened at the gun range, I was too buggered to dance and exercise." I pulled his right hand up and under my chin while I snuggled my head into the pillow.

"What do you mean, *what happened at the gun range*?" He brushed my hair aside and nibbled on my ear. "What happened?"

Since Michael works on a crime drama he gets to use guns and rubber bullets, so he knew enough about them. I told him about my gun backfiring, and he carefully examined my arms.

"You have no spots or burns now," he said, kissing both my arms.

I smiled and took his face in my hands. "I love you."

I kissed him. "So much. You take great care of me."

"Of course I do," he said, pulling me into his arms and we snuggled. "I love you, too."

*****

Wednesday morning, I was at my office making jewellery when I received a call.

"Ms Cameron. I'm Ed Wood, the manager of the *North Hollywood Gun Range*. I've been told about what happened to you and am ringing to apologise for the unfortunate mistake. How are you today?"

"Thankfully, no harm was done," I replied, suspicious of his tone.

"Good, that's good. As you may know, we have cameras around the place, so I was also able to see what happened. The assistant has been warned about not checking the weapons after each session. He's very sorry as well."

"Yeah, well, sorry doesn't make up for the fact that one, that shouldn't have happened, and two, it won't make my body stop aching."

"Yes, of course. I understand completely." He paused for a few moments. "Ms Cameron, did *you* check the gun before firing?"

That made me angry. I knew the rules of the firing range inside and out, and I had followed them to a T. The hairs on the back of my neck bristled, and I slammed my way into the conference room so no one else could hear me.

"*Mr Woods.* I am perfectly clear on the procedures

of the shooting range and follow them with proficiency. I *did* check my gun, and it was fine, so obviously there was dirt in a place I couldn't see with the naked eye, or, there was another problem with it. Either way, as you stated, it was up to *your* assistant and instructor to ensure all the guns are in working order. They *obviously* aren't!" My hackles were up, and I was pacing back and forth madly. "So I suggest you get in contact with my lawyer and send a copy of that video to her at once. God help you, Mr Woods, if you end up with a court case on your hands because my lawyer will eat you alive. And so will I!" I snapped my phone shut and stormed around the room.

"Who the bloody hell does he think he is blaming me for my bloody gun backfiring? Who the bloody hell?" Slamming the door back against the wall, I made my way into the design room. "Can you girls continue on your own?"

"Yes." They looked at me with curious eyes, having heard some of the conversation.

"Good, I need to leave, so I'll see you Friday when we will go over the jewellery before the big opening next week. Okay?"

"Okay."

I needed to get the hell out of there and thought maybe a spot of shopping would help calm down my raging temper.

Driving down a city road, I glanced at my watch and noted it was twelve on the dot. I decided to head for the posh home accessory store I'd heard about before grabbing some lunch. I found a park down the block and walked under the gold arch over the door. The store was huge, with all manner of household goods; linen, crockery, cutlery, lamps, vases, chairs, most things you could, or would, need for your house.

I browsed for awhile, admiring a vase here, a lamp there, and a silk sheet set that Michael and I could slide all over. I saw that the store was busy, then noticed it was because a teen actress was shopping with some friends.

The store assistants ran after her, offering goods, shooing away customers who might've wanted an autograph. It was all rather amusing really.

I moved on and looked at some artwork, but my focus was distracted again by the teen actress. This time she was demanding, quite loudly, that she must have the fur couch for free since she was a huge celebrity. The manager refused her request with dignity, but then quickly became angered when the actress knocked over a crystal vase.

Bet that cost a bit! Keeping an eye on the crowd that was now fighting, I kept my distance as I walked around. Finally, the actress and her posse were thrown out of the store after her manager promised the vase would be paid for.

For a few minutes, all was quiet, and I was enjoying the store.

Until *she* walked in!!!!!

Margaret Daly-Tomes!!!!!

The *bane* of my existence!!!!!

Or should that be...*BITCH* of my existence!!!!!

And yes, the situation requires so many exclamation

marks!!!!!

I stood stock still, glad to be hidden by shelving, as she walked down the front aisle, laughing with her *lady friends*. I quickly turned around and walked down another aisle. I did *not* want another fight with that English bitch, especially after the one at The Ivy.

But I was too late.

Damn!!!!!

"Oh, look," a voice dripping in acid said. "There's that vile Australian girl who dumped my drink all over me."

That stopped me. After the argument with the gun range manager, my hackles rose again. I slowly turned to face the English queen bitch. "If I recall, *sweetheart*, you spilt it all over yourself." My own voice dripped acid. "Did you ever get that stain out of that pristine white dress?" I chuckled. "Although, it wouldn't have been pristine after the wine."

Her eyes narrowed. You know, every time she did that she reminded me of a cat about to strike. Her lips thinned, her nails came out, her friends stood silently by. "My dress *was* pristine until you, thank you very much. I should make *you pay* for the damage. The dress was *ruined. RUINED. And,* it was one of a kind. I can't get another one *anywhere,* and that one can't be cleaned." She took a step closer to me. "I should make you pay," she spat.

I rolled my eyes. "Well, gee, you'd think with all the dry cleaning techniques there are these days they could at least get red wine out of a white dress. Oh, well." I moved aside to pass her. "Your problem, not mine." I managed to get a few paces between us. I did *not* want a showdown.

"*My problem?* How dare you tell me it's *my problem?*"

I kept on walking, but could hear the tapping of heels behind me.

"*You viciously threw that drink all over me and ruined my dress. I should sue you for assault.*"

I spun around to face her, my anger boiling over. "You stupid bitch," I sneered. "If I had assaulted you, you would've sued me by now, but you haven't because you can't, and you know it. There were too many paparazzi there that day, so there's way too much proof showing *I didn't touch you.*" I stepped back and took a breath. "So, you know damn well there's nothing you can do."

The expression on her face said it all. She knew I was right. And she hated it!

Ha, ha, ha!!!!!

"How *dare you* speak to me that way?" Her icy tone could've chilled a drink. "Do you have any idea *who I am*, who *I'm married to*, and the *power* I hold in the palm of my hand?"

"What power?" I spat. "No one gives a crap who you are, or who you're married to, and as far as I'm concerned, you can go to hell." I turned and headed for the door, seeing the staff and manager watching everything with wide eyes. I heard the tap of her heels behind me, and then someone yell out, "No, not the china!"

After months of martial arts training, I knew what

to do. Spinning on my heel, I ducked down and threw up my arms to protect my head and face.

Crash!

The huge china vase came down on me. Half of it hit my head, and the other half was deflected by my arm. I knelt for a few moments in shock until the pieces finished falling.

The store was stone cold dead silent.

I glanced to my left and saw shapely legs in navy heels. My gaze moved up over a classic cut navy dress, gold jewellery, and a sly smile. Our eyes met, and I stood. I'd had enough. Pretending to turn I put my right arm up and swung hard, landing that loud, pompous bitch, Margaret Daly-Tomes, with the belting of a lifetime.

She flew backwards, landed on her delicate English arse and slid along the floor. "Oh," she cried. "You bitch."

"You got what you deserved," I said. "And about time." I turned to the manager who was just standing there. "Get me a copy of the security tape," I demanded. "I'm going to need it as proof." He just stared at me like a struck dumb fish. "Get it," I yelled.

"What do you want a copy for?" he asked blankly.

He could seriously not be this stupid????

"In case," I pointed to the English bitch being helped up by her friends, "I need to prove she started it. Now get it. Unless you want to be sued?" Being threatened with a lawsuit made him move.

"Sue me?" Margaret snorted. "What on earth makes you think you can sue me. I'll sue you first."

She waved her arms around, flicking people off her.

The manager handed me the tape.

"I want one too," she demanded, furious. "Why should she get one and not me?"

"It doesn't matter if you have a tape or not," I retorted. "Because it will show you hitting me over the head with a Chinese vase."

"*I did not,*" she stuttered.

"Oh, yes, you did. How else would you have been right in front of me when I hit you?" I was boiling over again.

"Yes. That's right. *You* hit *me*. Everyone saw it." She looked around at her friends.

So did I, and no one said anything. "If these people are dumb enough to take your side, then I'll sue them too." I took a step toward her, waving my finger in her face for emphasis. "You're an evil cunning bitch who thinks the world should love you, but *I don't*, and you've proved yourself to be a hostile, angry cow," I yelled.

"I hate you," she yelled back. "You've done nothing but ruin my life."

"You've made the problem far bigger than it needed to be, instead of ignoring it, you had to make a big deal of it, so go to hell!"

"I will not go to hell!" she screamed.

"Oh, yes, you will, you bitch." My voice rose to a hysterical pitch as I waved the tape in her face. "You *will* go to hell, and I will put you there myself."

Chapter 15

"*My God*, you did *not* say that," Sin said over the phone the next morning.

"Yeah, I did. I couldn't help myself; it just flew out of my mouth. I have the tape, and I watched it to make sure it's the right one. It's definitely her smashing that vase over my head."

"Make a couple of copies and keep them safe. I'll start the lawsuit straight away, and we'll sort it out when I get there."

"Also, the firing range," I added. "They're accusing me of being at fault." When I'd called, I told her about the gun range and subsequent call from the manager, and then my run in with Ms Daly-Tomes.

"God...anyone else you want to sue?" She laughed.

"Well...there *is* the publishing house, but they said they'll pay to reprint the books."

"Oh, God." She laughed again. "What are you doing to me?"

"Don't worry, I pay you well."

She sighed. "Yeah, you do. Did you go to the hospital?"

"Nah. Went to my doctor and had an x-ray there. No problems, just a bloody headache and some blood. I don't think I'll be making it to martial arts class tomorrow."

"Will they put up with you skipping classes?"

"So what if they don't. Who cares? I had a house to do up. And after gun training, and that English bitch, I've had enough." I sighed deeply. "I gotta tell you, this week has been bad. For weeks everything's been smooth sailing, and now, it's like all the bad shit is hittin' me in one go. Maybe I should stay home till you get here. Rest up before the party."

"Maybe it's Karma. Or maybe God's trying to tell you something."

Chills cascaded through my body and I shivered despite the warm day, *and* being inside with the doors and windows closed. "Like what?"

"Like maybe you're not supposed to go to that party? After what happened and all."

I sighed again. I didn't know *what* it was, but I had a bad feeling in the pit of my stomach. "Something's wrong," I said. "I don't know what it is, but I have a bad, bad feeling."

"Why don't you take tomorrow off like you suggested, do some meditation, and see if you can come up with an answer."

"I don't meditate."

"Maybe you should. You might find the answer. I gotta go sue some people for you, so I'll see you on Friday. Bye."

"Bye." Settling into the sofa, I contemplated the

events of the past three days. Were they omens? Warnings? Signs from God, trying to tell me something? Or Karma telling me to pull my socks up? I didn't know, but I was determined to stay home until Sin got here.

*****

But staying home didn't stop the bad things from happening. Like Thursday morning when I got a call.

"Hello."

"Tahlia."

Carmine!

Once again, chills flowed through my body like a frozen mountain waterfall. "What do you want?" I asked tartly.

"I was wonderin' if you were still comin' to the network function this Friday. Sin, ah, mentioned it at the gig the other week."

That's not good! "I am, but I'll be coming with Sin and someone else."

There was silence. "Who?"

"None of your business." I heard him steaming in the background.

"What do ya mean none of my business?" he spat. "I thought we could at least be friends—"

"So did I, but you've made it extremely difficult to do that. Or hadn't you noticed my disinterest? I told you there would be nothing between us, but you kept pushing and pushing. I thought you would've gotten the message at the gig."

For a few moments there was silence, and then his anger flowed. "Who the fuck do you think you are doin' that to me? Leadin' me on then showin' up with another man—"

"Excuse me!" I cried indignantly. *"Who the fuck am I?* Who the fuck are *you* ringing me and talking to me this way? You don't have the right to have a go at me, Carmine Gionetti, not when you wouldn't back off when *I kept telling you* I was interested in someone else. I kept telling you, and still, you kept coming—"

"'Cause I thought I was in with a chance when ya said ya wasn't with 'im, but looks like ya are now. Michael Anthony, huh. What the hell's he got that I don't?"

"Manners and respect for a start," I spat. "I knew I shouldn't have gone to your gig, but I figured I'd told you enough for you to stay away—"

"After the way ya strutted over an' kissed me, I figured that maybe Michael wasn't the one an' you had come back to me—"

"Come back to you! Are you fucking nuts? I was never yours to be gone, let alone come back to you. My stand-offish feelings should have told you I WAS NOT INTERESTED—"

"Well, maybe ya should'na bothered givin' me ya number in the diner then—"

"Well, that's my mistake. So was kissing you, so was taking your number in the first place and giving you mine, believe me, I regret that and my head was telling me at the time to not give it to you, but no, I did, and now I regret it big time. So was thinking that we could AT LEAST BE FRIENDS. Obviously, I was wrong to think—"

"Yeah, ya were. Looks like I was too. An' ya right, *you're* to blame in the first place for givin' me ya number, hell, ya even wrong to wear a shirt with my face on it. Ya might as well burn that shirt 'cause I don't want ya wearin' me on ya chest—"

"Fine, I'll burn it, 'cause I sure as hell don't need you or your crap after the week I've had. I've been assaulted by a bitch who thought she could smash a vase over my head and give me a split head, and my gun backfired and sent me flying on my arse. So ya know what, arsehole, I've got enough pain in my body that I don't need *you* giving me anymore for my heart to deal with. So piss off." I started to hang up.

"Tahlia, wait."

"What," I snapped, ready to bite off more.

"What do you mean you were assaulted? Are you all right?" His voice was softer now.

I sighed and tried to calm my anger. "She smashed a vase over my head, but I deflected most of it. Sin's suing her for me."

"An' what about the gun, what happened?"

"It was dirty in a place I couldn't see, and it backfired on me. I'm okay, flew back on my arse and got some burn spots on my arms, but they're gone now."

There was silence, then, "I'm glad you're okay. You are goin' to be okay, aren't you?"

"Physically, I'll heal." I'd had enough of this and needed to hang up. "Look, if you can't deal with things, then that's your problem. But I don't want to be involved with you, and I told you that. So...get over it."

His anger rose again. "Yeah, I'll get over it, tell me ya not with him an' I'll get over it—"

"Who I'm with is *none of your business*," I yelled. God, we were just going round in circles.

"At least you coulda told me who it was. Then I woulda known who the hell my competition was—"

"Carmine, there never was any competition, so you sure as hell were never in the running." I snapped my phone shut then turned it off.

I did not need this shit today!

*****

Friday morning, I was sitting in the design room at the office when Sin breezed in.

"Thanks for the limo from the airport. Very nice."

"You're welcome. Come look at what we've got." I waved my hand over the wall. The jewellery hung on a rack, and we were checking them over before packing them for sale.

"Ohhh, fantastic." She studied a pair of black and gold gemstone earrings. "You know," she said, holding them up to her ears. "These would go perfectly with the little black dress I'm wearing tonight."

I rolled my eyes. "Would they now," I muttered, seeing the look on her face. "Have them. Tina, cross them off the list."

"So, you ready to go?" Sin picked up a necklace.

"Earrings are all you get," I said. "We have to go check the factory, pick up my newly printed books,

314

then go to the hairdresser this afternoon." I watched her try on the necklace with her new earrings. I sighed and knew I was defeated. "Tina, cross the necklace off too."

"Yay," Sin squealed.

"How are the lawsuits coming?"

"As expected, Ms Daly-Tomes denies she did anything wrong, and the gun range won't be blaming you for anything."

"That was quick," I said, putting another pair of earrings in a bag.

"Yes, well, I'm the bitch with the whip who knows how to break the boys' balls."

"Why do you think I hired you!"

She pouted and flung her hair over her shoulder. "And here I thought it was for my sparkling personality."

An hour later, we checked in at my warehouse. Everything was going great and was all set for the opening on Monday. "Make sure there's enough packaging for shipping the goods," I told Todd. "Especially now we have bags."

"Ooooh, bags?" Sin asked, looking intrigued.

"Yes, bags," I said, showing her.

"You know, the black and gold would go perfectly—"

"With your outfit for tonight," I replied in mock anger. "Well then, I guess you'd better have it then."

She flung it over her shoulder, already in love. "A girl needs to match her accessories. And I can be a walking advertisement at the same time."

Now, how the hell could I argue with that?

Twenty minutes later, I was holding my book in my hand. I scanned it carefully, opening the cover, turning each page...and there it was. My dedications page. I relaxed and smiled. My eyes looked up to see my editor and the manager of the publishing company standing in front of me waiting for a reply. "Do they *all* have the dedication pages?" I asked.

"Yes, they certainly do," the manager said, his hands nervously fumbling with each other.

I quickly looked through the rest of my personal batch. "They better have. They go on sale Monday, and I want them ready."

"Oh, they are, believe me," the manager went on, his voice quivering. "We are so *very* sorry for the mistake we made. At our expense, we've printed the book and pulped and recycled the old ones." He glanced at Sin, who for some reason was putting him on edge.

Must have been the *Eau de Ball Breaker* perfume she was wearing.

I sneaked a look at her. "That's very environmentally friendly of you," I said, shaking the manager's hand. "There's something I want to add."

Since my week of crisis was continuing, I had been having major conversations with myself about Karma, and the way I had been treating people since my new found wealth had moved me to L.A. I wasn't normally rude to people, but I had made a choice to stand up for myself and not take crap from anybody. Unfortunately, when people know you're nice, they take advantage, and that can wear on a person's emotions and soul. Continually being used by people that didn't give a damn about me, made me a bit too tough and ready to fight back. Even with people that weren't fighting me in the first place.

When I had left the publishers last time, I had felt that twinge in my chest and flinched. I knew what it was like to be put down and yelled at, and yet there I was, reaming that poor girl out when the missing dedications page wasn't even her fault. I knew, for my own sake, I had to make things right.

"I wanted to apologise for my behaviour the other day," I said, looking at Amy. Her hands were clenched, wringing themselves together. "I fully understand that my anger has nothing to do with you, and the way you have conducted yourself with me over the weeks we've been working together has been nothing *but* professional." I felt my stomach slowly start to unclench itself. "I am sorry for the way I spoke to you, and in no way do I blame you for what happened. I was angry, that after all the trouble I went to, that a simple page was missing from my books. And I understand that was a printing error, which I see has been sorted out." I looked at the manager, who nodded. I noticed some of the other workers watching the scene unfold. I looked back at Amy, who now had a small smile on her face.

"I think pulping and recycling the old books is a good idea, and I'm glad to see that my books are printed using recycled paper." I glanced at Sin. "I think we should take them and be on our way." I turned back to the manager. "Thank you for reprinting. I know it would've been quite a cost to you."

"That's perfectly fine," he muttered, shaking the hand I offered. "It was our mistake, and our policy is that we fix our mistakes at our cost."

"Well, thank you for that," I said, trying to get my hand back. "We'll take the books now and go."

"Of course, of course. They're right here." He pointed to a stack of boxes.

I spoke to Ben, who'd met us there. "Can you see to it that these get back to the office and get everything set up for Monday?"

"Sure thing."

I picked up my box of books and turned to my editor. "I'll go then. Thank you so much."

"Absolutely. You're welcome."

We walked out to my car and sat looking at the box of books on my lap.

"So...*what* was that?" Sin asked in complete disbelief.

"Karma," I replied simply, worn out from what had just happened. "How do you want it?"

"I want mine signed," Sin said, digging around in her bag for a pen.

"To Sin," I wrote with a flourish. "Thanks for being a great lawyer, and for drooling over the stallion that was the inspiration for this book. Love Tahlia. How's that?"

"Nice. Speaking of stallions," she glanced at me, "have you heard from Carmine since the night of his band's gig?"

I wished I could say no, but told her about his call. "How *dare he* bother calling me especially after trying to ruin my night with Michael. Bloody bastard!" I felt myself getting angry again.

Sin was surprised by our interaction. "He'll be there tonight you know since his show's on the network." She stuffed her book into her oversized bag.

I looked at her and sighed. "Yeah, I know." A slight shrug came from my shoulders. "I know we talk about all sorts of things concerning him at my blog, but after meeting him, yes, he's a great guy, but I clearly told him we would *not* be getting involved. And he *still* didn't listen, and *still* thought he could convince me to see him, even after all the times I told him, he didn't listen. And now I'm screwing up my Karma even more." I sighed again. "I just won't talk to him then. Ignore him, and he will go away."

"You can't do that. Are you really going to do that?" she asked incredulously.

"I'll be with Michael, the man I love. Why would I bother talking to Carmine after what he did to me? Pretty much pissed me off."

"Because it would be rude to ignore him if he spoke to you." Shock rolled over her face.

I shrugged again. "Like I give a crap. He tried to screw up my life, so I have the choice to ignore the bastard or not. I'm an adult. I *do not* have to play nice!"

There goes my Karma!!!!!

After lunching at a local restaurant, we went home. Sin was staying in Michael's old house, and after having a shower and dropping her outfit off at my place, we drove to the local hairdresser's where we had our hair washed, then read magazines while we waited.

"So, how are you having yours?" Sin asked.

"Pulled back into a small bun. I'm wearing a hat, so I want my hair back."

She looked aghast. "You're *still* wearing a hat. Why?" she cried.

I shrugged. You may have noticed I do that a lot, 'cause it's non-committal. "'Cause I decided on an outfit that would look good with a hat."

"Good grief, girl." She shook her head. *"A hat!"*

"And how are you having yours?" I asked.

"Hanging neat and curly down my back."

"So...like you wear it every other day then?"

"Hey, I don't..." she started, then realised she did.

"And what are you ladies having today," the stylists asked as they walked up to us.

"Side part on the right and pulled back into a neat bun about here." I pointed to a spot on the back of my head.

"That's simple enough."

"Yes, it is," I agreed, with a nod of my head.

"And you, Ma'am?" Sin was asked.

"Um." You could tell she was changing her mind. "Straightened, with a bit of a wave through the back and some flicks on the side. Oh, and I'll have a side part too."

I shook my head in mild amusement.

Half an hour later, I was in the make-up chair and ready for my wild look.

"Hey, how are you?" asked Rhiana, the girl who'd done my make-up for the Debbie Gibson show. She was all decked out with wild hair and make-up of her own.

"Great, thanks."

"So, where are you going tonight?"

"Some function," I replied. "I'm wearing red, black and gold, so I want something that will not only make my eyes stand out, but make *me* stand out in general."

"Okay, that I can do."

When she was done, I looked in the mirror. Fan, freakin', tastic!

Thick black kohl pencil lined my eyes, and bright red shadow curled up and around to my eyebrows. Gold glitter was laid over the top. Fire engine red lipstick, a touch of blush, and thick black mascara finished the look.

"Fucking hell! You're not going to a freak show," Sin said, outraged that I could choose such a face for such a party.

"You don't have to come with me," I replied coolly, getting out of the chair. "You done?" I glanced at the clock on the wall. Four p.m. "We should get home soon."

"She has a few more minutes," her make-up artist said.

I paid for everything plus a lipstick so I could retouch, and chatted with the girls while Sin was finished off. "You look great," I said when she was done. "Let's go."

We made it home at four-thirty and headed for the kitchen. We had to eat as it would be hours before the function started, and we didn't know when we'd be eating next.

"This will ruin our make-up," Sin mumbled around a mouthful of food.

The phone rang.

"Hey, sweetheart. I won't be home before the network do, so you'll have to go without me."

"That's not fair." I frowned. "I wanted to walk in with you."

"Think of it this way. You'll be there," his voice softened, "I'll walk in, no one knows we know each other. We'll be two strangers in a crowd of many...kinda kinky."

I laughed. "Yeah, kinda kinky. Okay then." My lips pouted. "If you have to come later I'll be there with Sin. You should be able to recognise me. I'll be the one with the wild red eyeshadow."

"Mmm, red eyeshadow. I take that to mean you're wearing red?"

"Red and black with gold bling."

"Okay. It starts at eight, and I think we're working till seven-thirty or so, so I'll see you there. I'll call when I'm on my way."

"Okay. I love you."

"Love you, too. Bye."

I almost slammed the phone down onto the counter. "That sucks."

"Michael can't come?" Sin asked, slurping cola through a straw.

"Not till after seven-thirty. He'll meet us there." I pouted my disappointment.

"So, we're going on our own?"

"We're going on our own."

"Just as well we'll have the limo," she said, a mischievous twinkle in her eyes.

"Is that all you want to go for? The limo?" I glanced at her, half amused, half annoyed.

She blushed. "Not *just* the limo. The free function, gorgeous men, mingling with celebs."

I rolled my eyes and felt like choking her.

We watched the news for awhile before wandering into the bedroom. Sin was changing in my room, I changed in my closet. Hot red lacy underwear, skin-tight black jeans, a red top with the shoulders cut out and long sleeves, with a gold design on the front. A black waistcoat, and three-quarter high red leather boots with gold studs and three inch heels – yes, again, I know I didn't like heels and I still don't, but I am getting used to them for vanity's sake – I buckled up my gold belt with the zip up pouches, and loaded myself with gold jewellery. Bangles on my arms, chains around my neck, long dangly chains in my ears. Picking up a black fedora with its red bling band, I placed it at a jaunty angle, then gave myself the once over in the mirror.

Nice!

Walking into the bedroom, I saw Sin adjusting the skirt of her dress. Short, black, tight and sleeveless. She slipped into five inch black stilettos and put her new jewellery on. "See," she said, hearing me come in. "It does go with my dress." She turned and saw me, staring at my outfit in angry disbelief.

I shook my head in dry amusement at the look on her face. "Ready?"

She shrugged her defeat as her expression fell. "Ready."

We went through the house locking up then waited for the limo. Richard had made sure we had one since we were so far out of town. Ten minutes later the driver buzzed the gate.

"Nice," Sin murmured, watching the limo pull up to the house.

As I set the alarm and locked the door, the driver stepped out and held the door open.

"Oh, really nice," she added, climbing in.

The car was black, the inside comfy. Do you really need to know more? We chatted about the function and who we might meet, finally arriving just after seven-thirty.

"Oh, my God, there's a red carpet," Sin squealed, grabbing my arm in excitement.

"God, and look at all the photographers," I groaned in reply. "God help me."

An attendant opened our door, and Sin stepped out first. Giving her a chance to be snapped, I followed thirty seconds later, and we both stood on the path.

The paps had absolutely no idea who we were, but must have figured since we were at a huge network party we had to be somebodies.

Right?

Not yet!

We walked the red carpet as the other network celebs stopped to be interviewed. I saw E.T., T.M.Z., Richard Reid, and Richard Wilkins from Australia.

"Who are you girls?" one person called.

"Is he talking to us?" I muttered to Sin under my breath, bright lights going off in my face.

"We're new to the network," Sin called, pulling me to her side. "But *believe me*, you'll know who we are soon enough."

I flashed her a deadly look as more flashes went off, blinding me. I didn't particularly want to stop for a photo, but it was starting to make me excited. We posed for a moment, me doing a rock star stance of putting my weight on one leg and sticking the other one in front of me, knee bent, hands on hips. I narrowed my eyes and pouted. I had to put on a show after all.

"Okay, that's enough," I said and pulled Sin along. She was enjoying this *way too much*. Reaching the doorway, we went through a metal detector and were frisked by guards.

"Cute," she said, flirting with one of the guards.

"Do you mind?" I gave her a dirty look. "Let's go."

We walked into the plush lobby with its marble floor and velvet lined walls. Red sofas were against the walls, and pot plants sat in between. Chandeliers with their gleaming crystals hung delicately from the white ceiling.

"Wow, this is great," Sin said, as I gazed around. There were a couple of actors from a crime show, some from a comedy, and the host of a reality show. Since partners were invited, I assumed the people they were with were wives/girlfriends/husbands/boyfriends.

I glanced at my big gold bling watch. Just after eight. "I wonder if everyone else is here?" I muttered and heard the doors shut behind us. We spun around to see guards packing up the stations inside, and shooing away the paparazzi outside. And Michael *still* hadn't called.

"That answer your question?" Sin asked as we looked at each other.

"Let's go," I repeated, and we followed the celebs down a short hallway on our right and through a huge double door on our left. "Wow," I breathed.

We were standing on a landing made of marble, and down two steps was a cavernous room filled with the celebs we drooled over. More chandeliers were placed through the room. A bar sat on the far left wall. Exit doors to the left and right. A huge stage was at the back – or in front of us if you know what I mean – and a band was playing something loud and melodic.

My eyes roamed the room from left to right. I didn't see Michael, but I did see Carmine and Keith Pritchard talking to their fellow hunky co-stars. "Uh oh," I muttered when Carmine noticed me.

"What?" Sin asked, flicking her Farrah Fawcett hair back. "Oh, my God," she squealed.

Carmine and Keith were making their way through the sea of people, and I mean a sea, as the place was filled with every actor, host, and CEO from the network, not to mention their partners. I wanted to run, to get away as fast as I could and find Michael. I pulled away, but Sin pulled me back.

"Hey," Carmine said, taking the two steps in one move.

I stared at him coolly with a cocked left eyebrow and pursed lips, having not forgiven him for what he'd said at the club. Or his call.

"Hi," Sin gushed and gave them kisses on their cheeks. "Hey, Keith. How are you?"

"Great, how are you. I haven't seen you since Carmine's gig," he said to Sin.

"Oh, my God, I've been so busy. Working with Tahlia, and then home this week with my family. Lawsuits, contracts, clients, you name it, I did it."

I raised another brow in amusement at that last remark and gave her a sly glance.

"Oh," she blushed, "I didn't mean it that way."

Carmine and I perused each other.

Andy Garrick, the boys' co-star, came up to join us. "Hey, Sin, how ya doin'?" He'd been at the club too, but I hadn't met him.

"Fine thanks, Andy, and you?"

"Great, great. So how come you ladies are here tonight? And I don't believe I've had the pleasure of meeting your hot lady friend. Hi, I'm Andy." He stuck his hand out, and I coolly looked from it to him.

The mention of being hot made my skin crawl as that was what Carmine had called me that night. I surveyed his tall, dark and handsome good looks and piercing blue eyes.

"I'm Tahlia, nice to meet you." We shook.

"So, what are you girls doing here?" Keith asked again. "You both look great by the way."

"Thanks. Well, Tahlia got an invite, so here we are."

I had gone back to searching through the crowd for Michael, but found Carmine still standing there staring. "For Christ's sake, why don't you take a picture; it'll last longer." I was pissed at him and had had enough.

There goes what little Karma I had left!!!!

"We did, remember?" his thick New York accent

drawled. "In the diner when we met. Since ya didn't gimme any copies, I had to track 'em down on your website to get 'em."

"You have photos of us?" I asked tartly.

He riled a little and licked his lips. "Yeah, I do. Considerin' an' all."

"Considering what?" I spat. "You stalked me, rang me, asked me out, even though you knew I was interested in someone else. Get rid of them. I don't want you having any photos of me. Let alone photos *of me, with you!*" My anger shocked everyone, and they took a step back. Like I cared!

Anyone notice a big fat seething lack of Karma?

I spied Michael over Carmine's shoulder, standing in the crowd watching the scene with amusement. My face and anger softened, my head tilted to the left so I could see him better, and a smile crossed my lips. God, I love him.

Carmine noticed my expression change and glanced over his shoulder to see Michael making his way through the crowd toward us. He looked back at me and realised he'd lost.

Michael stepped onto the landing. "Hey, sweetheart, you made it."

I dove into his arms, literally, and clung to him like a life raft. We hugged and kissed passionately. God, it felt so good.

"Ready to party," he asked. "You, look *fucking* fantastic," he added. For Carmine's benefit I was sure. Because it brought a deep red glow to Carmine's face.

"Ready," I replied, gazing into his gorgeous blue

eyes. He started leading me through the throng, and I called back to Sin. "You go mingle, I'm sure you won't have any trouble." I then chastised Michael for not calling.

He introduced me to other celebs he knew, some of his fellow cast members, directors, producers. We had discussed how he was going to tell people about me since we'd only met two weeks ago and we'd lived together for a week. So, I was introduced as his *lovely lady*.

Awww, how sweet!

The band finally took a break, and we found ourselves on the other side of the room as Richard Sayer walked onto the stage. Michael and I continued to the back of the room, or front, depending on what you want to call it, and stood on the landing.

This was it. At least *I* thought so. The moment he was going to mention everything Marnie had gone through.

I felt sick, but Michael, standing behind me, slid his arms around my waist and whispered in my ear. "I'm here, I love you."

I glanced up at him with a grin. "I love you, too."

Richard cleared his throat, and we turned to watch. "Ladies and gentlemen. I'm glad you could make it tonight, as this network function is about unity, and bringing us all together."

Cheers went up.

"Now, as some of you may already know, my wife Marnie and I have gone through some particularly bad events recently. Which we will be discussing in an upcoming interview on this very network."

A few more cheers.

"Tonight is very special in more ways than one. After the accident, Marnie had a severe concussion and fractured legs and feet." He glanced around the huge room, the light reflecting off his silver coloured suit and grey hair. "My wife has been resting at home and having extensive physiotherapy every day, plus she's been following doctor's orders for tonight's event. Having been in a wheelchair for weeks, I am now pleased to say, that my wife can walk freely, without the help of an aid."

The crowd applauded. So did we.

"Thank you, thank you." Richard put his hands up to stop us. "Without further ado, I will present my wife, Marnie Wilkins." He held out his arm to welcome her as she gracefully glided across the stage, despite her newly-healed legs, in the glowing emerald green evening gown I'd made her. It sparkled like there were millions of emeralds on it, and made all of the women ooh and ahh.

It looked freakin' fantastic!

"That's my dress," I squealed to Michael.

"Yours?" he asked in my ear.

"I designed it for her for tonight. When I was at their house for dinner," I said in his ear so no one could hear me.

"Oh, right." His face showed his approval. "It's beautiful."

Richard clasped his wife's hand and led her to the microphone.

"Thank you, thank you. Thank you so much, ladies and gentlemen. First, for coming here tonight, and for all of your support and well wishes." More applause. "I may not be here tonight," she touched her cheek, "if it weren't for a brave young woman, who just happened to be there that day."

I tensed, and Michael held me closer.

"She was an absolute God-send to me in my time of need. Pulling me out of a burning car, protecting me from kidnappers and being shot. She was a true heroine that day. I am ever so grateful to God, for putting her there to save and protect me, and to her for having the knowledge and wherewithal to do so. I thank you, so much. My heart is full of appreciation, and you will never know how grateful I am. Thank you, so much."

The crowd applauded and looked around the room, wondering if the heroine was in the crowd for Marnie to be talking in such a way. Michael and I applauded too, to remain inconspicuous, and then Richard stepped up to the mic again.

"Ladies and gentlemen, the band is back with some tunes, so dance, eat, drink, be merry."

The crowd went wild as they walked off the stage, and the first strings of music came pounding out of the speakers.

I turned to Michael. "Well…that was okay…I think."

He looked tenderly at me. "You don't want people to know anything, and they didn't mention your name, so it should be great."

I had to agree. "Yeah, you're right. Let's dance." I

grabbed his hand, and we started gyrating there on the landing. We were so raunchy that we drew the attention of the band and they thanked us for rockin' out to their songs. Then, of course, half the crowd stared before going back to their own dancing.

How embarrassing!

Later, when Michael and I were slow dancing to a love song, and God it felt so good to be in his arms, I felt a tap on my shoulder. Rudely dragged out of our romantic moment, I turned to see Richard and Marnie standing there smiling.

"Tahlia dear, you made it," she said, ready to hug me.

"Nice to meet you, how are you?" I stuck out my hand which shocked them, and they didn't know what to do. I raised my brow. "It was nice of you to invite me after the work I did."

They caught on, and we shook.

"So nice of you to come," Richard said, shaking my hand. "Michael, how are you?" He slapped him on the back. "Taking care of her, we hope."

"Yes, sir, I'm taking very good care of her," he replied, as I radiated happiness at him.

I turned and studied Marnie. Her brown hair was piled into a high bun, and gorgeous emerald earrings decorated her delicate white earlobes. Skin like ivory and a dress made to fit. "Mmm," I said. "My, that *is* a gorgeous dress, wherever did you get it?" I grinned slyly.

She laughed lightly, covering her mouth with her hand. "I had it made by an up-and-coming Australian designer who's setting up her new business here. It's one of a kind and making *everyone* green with envy, so I can't possibly say no when they ask for the name of the designer. My friends all want dresses now too."

"Well then." I grinned. "The designer will be mighty pleased to hear that. It was lovely meeting you," I repeated. "Thank you for inviting me."

"You're welcome, dear, thank you for coming." They moved on, and Michael and I were alone again. As alone as you can be in a crowd of people.

"You didn't want people thinking it was you?" he said in my ear.

"Nope," I replied. "Let's just dance." We danced for a few more minutes before grabbing some drinks at the bar.

I downed my juice in one gulp I was that dry and thirsty, and had just put my glass on the counter when Sin showed up.

"Hey, Michael," she said cheerfully.

"Sin."

"Tahlia," she said coolly, adding a dirty look.

"Sin," I said with a small smirk at her attitude.

"You know, you were rude to Carmine before. Keith and Andy too. They didn't deserve that. As much as you have problems with Carmine, the others didn't deserve your hostility." She ordered a mineral water with lemon.

"You're right," I said, putting an arm around Michael. "I was meeting Andy for the first time, and he didn't deserve for me to be rude to him."

She sipped her drink. "Maybe you should tell him that. Apologise too. Keith as well. As for Carmine, he's been mopey since. All dark and moody, just frowning away." She laughed. "Damn it, it just makes him even sexier."

I snorted and shook my head. Even Michael rolled his eyes.

Sin finished her drink. "Look, we'll go freshen up in the ladies', and on the way, you can apologise to the boys." Grabbing my hand, she looked at Michael. "Back soon."

"Don't be long," he called.

We found our way through the crowd and came across Keith and Andy to whom I sincerely apologised. We shook hands again and smoothed things over. Carmine was nowhere to be seen.

Well, who cares!

Is it just me, or should I really stop saying that?!

Making our way to the ladies', which was out the door, down the hall to our left, then down a second hall on the left, we barrelled our way into a room on our right and into the group of celebs waiting to go.

Little did we know that going to the ladies' room was going to save our lives.

Chapter 16

"I wonder where Carmine went," Sin said, as we found our way into some form of line for the ladies'. The place was crowded with actresses, and we stood goggle-eyed at all before us.

"You mean Carmine Gionetti?" a girly voice asked from behind us. We turned and saw Carmine's co-star, Amy Bellamy, a petite actress whose character was Carmine's character's love interest on the show. She was also his fellow co-worker, and so the play between them bantered back and forth. She was also the one none of us liked at my blog. Her character, anyway. Although sometimes, people got personal.

"Yeah, we mean Carmine Gionetti," Sin answered, wary of who she was talking to. "He seems to have disappeared."

"I think I saw him having a cigarette with one of the waiters somewhere," Amy said. "Oh, do you mind if I cut in front of you? I'm busting."

"No, go ahead." I waved my hand. We watched her scurry into a cubicle then gazed around while we waited.

Maria Conchita Consuelos, star of a huge Latina-turned-American show, was checking her make-up and hot green dress in the mirror.

Michelle Moreau was chatting to her fellow co-star, Beth Everway. Both women were stars of a hot new cop show about female cops.

Delia Smythe was smearing lipstick, the shade of blood, onto her full, collagen injected lips, on her expressionless Botox injected face.

Yes, I know they were because I read it in the tabloids!

"Oh, please, like you can believe the tabloids," you *cry.*

Yeah, well. I gotta say, her lips did look pretty full.

By the time Sin and I came out, we seemed to be alone. Well, the cubicles were empty, and no one else was there, so yeah, we were alone.

The ladies' was pretty nice. Ten cubicles, a lit up vanity down the middle of the room, which was double sided. Marble floor, nice wallpaper.

I washed my hands and checked my make-up. Pulling out my new lippie from one of the pouches on my belt, I smeared it on.

"Oooh, can I have some?" Sin asked.

"Where's yours?" I looked at her. "Obviously in your new bag, *at home.*" I smirked.

"Gimme." She snatched it from my hand. "My bag was too big to bring tonight for just a lipstick, so I figured I'd use yours."

"An' give me cold sores," I piped up. "God knows what germs you've got." I snatched it back, wiped it off with some tissue, and popped it into its pouch.

The door flung open, and we were silent. The vanity hiding us from whoever was on the other side.

No one came in.

That was weird!

Sin and I glanced at each other, both holding our breath until the door closed.

Who was that? she mouthed.

I shrugged and spread my hands, mouthing back, I don't know!

We waited a few more seconds before we moved, but then a sound shook us to our cores.

It was loud.

It was long.

It sounded like a machine gun firing.

And it was now coming into the bathroom.

We turned to each other in a desperate rushing panic as bullets flew through the doorway, smashing apart the cubicle doors and into the vanity mirrors, spinning us onto the floor in a puddle of glass and spraying blood.

Shit!!!!!

"Oh, my God," Sin desperately whispered in my ear. She was clinging to me for dear life, and we hung onto each other in horror. "What do we do, what do we do, what do we do?"

There was silence.

"We have to do something," I whispered back. "Call the cops, find out what's going on. We need to do something."

"What? We can't leave the bathroom, they might

kill us. We have to stay here."

"What we need to do is get my arm bandaged and then figure out what we do." I winced in pain, and I looked at my left arm. I wasn't sure if it was a bullet or flying glass that had cut me, but it looked bad. I glanced around at what was left of the bathroom. "Crap, there's nothing here." I shoved my right hand on top of the cut and squeezed tight. "Mmmahhhh." I grimaced in mind-altering pain before looking at Sin. My instincts kicked in. I knew I had to do something. Michael was in that room.

"I *can* do something," I said quietly. "I know how to use guns, and if we can make it to the manager's office there might be cameras there, and we can see what's going on. Michael's in there. I need to do something."

She was crying without a sound, staring at me with grim death.

"Do I need to slap you to knock some sense into you," I whispered furiously. "Where've your balls of steel gone?"

That stopped her. "Okay," she breathed, then nodded. "Lead the way."

"First we need to clear a path," I said, digging around in the cupboard under the vanity for something to use. I came up with several toilet paper rolls and handed two to Sin. "Here, use these." We slowly crawled across the floor to the door, carefully brushing aside the smashed glass and debris. My arm ached like hell and bled everywhere as I moved. Sin was right behind me, following the exact path I took, so there was less damage from the stray glass.

Pressing my ear to the door, I heard nothing. I reached up and touched the door handle. Cold. Good, no fire. I stood and turned the knob, but my fingers slipped from the blood. I wiped my hand on my jeans and grabbed it again, opening the door a crack. No one there.

Silently opening the door, I stuck my head out. No one in the hallway. I swung the door open wider and grabbed Sin's hand, pulling her out of the ladies'. Making sure the door didn't slam shut so the noise wouldn't attract attention, we ran quietly down the hallway to the manager's office. There were two guards on the floor.

"Oh, my God. Are they dead?" Sin whispered, shaking in terror.

I felt for their pulses. "Knocked out, I think," I replied, and we quickly made our way into the room, locking the door behind us.

"Quick," I said. "Let's look for a first aid kit or something." We searched through cupboards and filing cabinets until we came across a kit of creams and bandages. Sin quickly, but shakily, wrapped my arm while I gritted my teeth in pain.

Crap!!!!!

Karma!!!!!

"Oh, my God," she whispered.

"What?"

"You...you have blood on your back."

"What? What do you mean? I don't feel anything?"

She grabbed something in my back and pulled.

"Uggghhh..." I grimaced again, clenching my teeth,

so I didn't cry out and alert anyone. I twisted around. "What the hell was that?"

She showed me the ten centimetre long shard of glass in her hand.

"Shit!!!! Is there any more? Quick, pull them out." I tried looking over my shoulder at my back then glanced around for a mirror, but didn't see one.

"I don't think there's any more...wait...there." She yanked another shard out.

"Argh" My voice shook from the pain, and I sucked in a deep breath. "Quick, shove a bandage or something on it. Stop the bleeding. Quick, quick."

She raided the first aid kit and smothered my cuts in gauze and big square Band-Aids.

"Crap, crap, crap, crap, crap!" I grabbed the packet of painkillers. "Get me some water please." I pointed to the tray of bottled water on the side cabinet. Sin cracked one open, and I downed five pills in one gulp. I breathed deeply a few times trying to get myself in control. Once I was good, we turned around to see what was happening.

On the wall there were ten TV screens all showing the function room. Ten more showed the surrounding hallways and doors. We saw guards on the floor. Some had dark pools of something around them. No doubt it was blood.

We zeroed in on the screen from the camera above the door in the function room. Three men were on the landing, backs to the camera. We could see the crowd of celebs kneeling on the floor, their hands on their heads.

They looked sick. The women were crying, the men wanting to do something, but unable to, all for the fact the three men had guns.

Two of the thugs had what looked to be rifles in their hands. But considering the sound we had heard, they were more than likely machine guns. They were wearing coats, so I couldn't see what else they had, and they seemed to be nervous, moving from one foot to the other, constantly looking around.

The other man had long light hair, and a long overcoat or trench coat on. He seemed to be the calmest of the three, and was waving his arms around in small motions, as if emphasising what he was saying. The man moved, and I saw Richard Sayer and Marnie Wilkins standing in front of him.

"Oh, no," I said, stepping back in shock. *"Do, not, tell me. Do not* tell me.*"* I looked up to the ceiling. "God, do *not* tell me they're the men after Marnie. I swear to God." I sighed and rubbed my temple. "This can't be happening, this can't be happening." I stared at the monitor in a daze. "I knew when she told me on Monday that her interview would be the Monday after the party that this week wouldn't be good. Then there were the missing dedication pages in my books. The backfiring of my gun at the range. My run-in with the bitch queen. Carmine's phone call. This week just hasn't been good. Omens, warnings, signs, whatever the fuck you want to call them, you were right when you said God was trying to tell me something. Or maybe it's just my pissin' bad Karma!"

"You mean the men who tried to kidnap her that

day are those men there?" Sin pointed to the screen. She looked so sick. "Oh, my God...he's *definitely told you*."

"I don't know if they're the same men or not, but since Richard is clinging to Marnie, and they're standing right in front of them, I'd say it's a safe bet." I thumped my head with my hand and walked around the small room. "What do I do, what do I do?"

"Fight them," a voice said.

What? I frowned.

"Fight them. You can do it. I am with you."

Where the hell did that come from?!

I glanced at Sin, but she was glued to the monitors. I sighed. "God, why me? Why me?" I rubbed the bridge of my nose and made the decision. "I'm going in."

She spun around. "What?" she shrieked.

"Shhh," I hushed her quickly. "Call the cops and watch the monitors. I'm going in."

"You can't," she wailed quietly.

"I can. After all, I'm the only one left who knows how to use a gun. All the guards are dead or knocked out cold. I'm the only one left."

"Oh, my God, you can't," she begged in a whimper.

"I have to." I shook her firmly. "Michael's in there and I will do what I need to save the man I love. Keep watch of the screens. I'm gonna grab the guns from the guards outside."

"No, Tahlia, please don't."

"Shhhh," I silenced her. "Watch." I motioned to the screens and opened the door, looking left and right. I ran the few feet to the prone men. Yanking the guns from their holsters, I ran back into the room and checked them over. "Full cartridge, nice and clean." I looked at Sin. "Call the cops. I'm going in."

"But they have machine guns," she wailed in a whisper.

I saw something happen on the screen. The men moved, and we heard more gunfire. The main man flung his coat open and slowly turned for all to see.

"Oh, my, God," we said, staring open-mouthed.

"I have to go now," I said, and was out the door in seconds. Tiptoeing at a run down the first hallway, I glanced around the corner. More prone guards. But these were dead. Making my way up to them, I grabbed their guns, and checking them, shoved them into the back of my jeans. Time was of the essence.

Standing to one side of the closed double wood doors that led to the function room, I took a deep breath, counted to three, and banged on the door with the butt of my gun. "It's the police, open up," I shouted loud and firm.

Machine gun fire erupted through the wood, and I dove to my left. I knew this would happen and had been prepared. If they emptied out a round of bullets, they wouldn't have time to reload. I flicked a quick glance at a camera in the hallway knowing Sin would see I was alive and okay.

The firing stopped, and I sneaked to the door. There wasn't much left of it, but I still had some cover. I peered through a missing section. The men had turned their backs to the door obviously believing they had eliminated the problem.

Dickheads!!!!!

With a gun in each hand, I pushed the doors aside, aimed my guns at the two men, as much as my bleeding arm would allow, and took a few steps into the room. "Did ya really think I was dumb enough to fall for that?" I spat.

The two men spun around in shock, everyone else looked up in shock, but the main man just cocked his head slightly to the side and didn't turn around.

"How the hell?" the two men blubbered, fumbling for their guns.

"Oh, my God." My brow furrowed in recognition. "I, don't, fucking, believe it," I said, shaking my head. "*You two*, bloody idiots. Didn't you get enough of an arse kicking last time we met?"

They looked at me in more shock. "Wait, aren't you," the man on my right stuttered.

"The bitch that tried to stop us from getting the broad," the one on my left said, flicking his thumb over his shoulder at Marnie.

Damn! *That* cat was out of the bag!

"No. *I am* the bitch that stopped you from getting the broad, *and* I kicked your arses to kingdom come because you were too useless to fight a woman. *And* it looks like I'll have to kick your arses again, 'cause you just don't seem to learn. *Do you?*"

The men laughed between themselves. "It ain't us that will be learning bitch. It's gonna be you," the one on my left said. With a glance at each other, they pulled guns from under their jackets.

But I was too fast for them.

I fired three bullets from both guns.

Bang. Bang. Bang.

I scored a hit in both foreheads, and the men fell with a thud.

"God that felt good," I gushed energetically, noticing the celebs on the floor staring at me in horror. "What? Like you wouldn't've enjoyed it." I levelled my guns at the man who was left, pain searing through my arm. "Well, mister whoever you are. Either you leave, or I'll kill you."

He laughed. A deep and guttural sound. And kept on laughing as he slowly extended his arms and turned around to face me.

I kept my eyes on his face, but saw it anyway. It was kinda hard not to. Being right there in front of me and all. I tried not to show how panicked I was by rolling my eyes. "Pfft, like that's gonna scare me," I said with more bravado than I felt.

"Oh, it will. I'm sure it does," he said in a gravel filled tone. "You won't do anything. You may have stopped my boys last time—"

"And I killed them this time," I defiantly butted in, noticing how ugly he was.

"And you may have killed them now," he continued slowly. "But I will take Marnie Wilkins with me tonight. Because if I don't, I will take *all* of you with me."

Shit! There wasn't much time.

My eyes narrowed in anger, and my blood rushed through my veins. I desperately needed to see Michael, to know he was all right, but I couldn't risk looking for him. So I kept my eyes on the man in front of me. It was just him and me in that room, no one else.

"Don't fool yourself," I told him, keeping my guns level. "You're not taking anyone. Because it's far easier to take *you* out of the room than three thousand people."

"Little girl," he droned patronisingly. "You're not taking me anywhere." His attitude fuelled me even more.

Did I mention he was ugly? More like fugly!

"No, you're right. I'm taking that," I nodded at the thing strapped to his chest, "out of the room. 'Cause *you* are goin' to hell."

I fired both guns. The bullets blasting through his head, blowing bits of his fugly brain all over the place. I clicked the switch that disconnected the cartridges then threw the guns to the ground. This all happened in slo-mo, so I had no real idea of the time. I ran to him and grabbed his coat by the lapels.

"A little help here," I yelled, pushing his coat over his shoulders and down his arms in one quick movement. He was still standing. "Michael, where are you?" I screamed, grabbing the bulletproof vest the man was wearing. My hands searched for wires and devices, but I found none. I did get his blood on me, however, and my face was mooshed into his foul smelling body. Yuck! I did mention he was fugly, right?

"I'm here, I'm here." Michael ran up behind the man.

"Grab his arms and hold them above his head and *don't* let go."

Michael did as he was told, standing there, holding the man up while fugly blood and brain dripped everywhere. He was deathly white, and looked ready to throw up, but was being strong, as he knew he was needed. And for me I was sure.

Searching his shoulders I unpulled the Velcro straps. "Okay, careful. I'm going to slide it up his body and over his head. Hold tight, careful." I slid the jacket up slowly, reaching his head, his arms, moving it up. It was just a matter of Michael letting him go.

"Let him down slowly," I told him.

Still holding on tight he let the man's body weight sink him to the floor as he lowered him, then once he saw me free the jacket, he let go. The gunman fell to the floor with a thud. We stood there staring at each other. Dead silence all around.

Sin came tearing into the room. "I saw everything. The cops are on the way, oh, my God." She skidded to a halt before tripping over one of the gunmen and saw me. "You're...holding...a..." Her hands flew to her mouth.

"Bomb," I remarked dryly, glancing at Michael. His eyes were full of pure panic. I looked at the thing in my hand.

2:30

All the time we had left.

The realisation hit me. "Oh, my God, a bomb," I said unbelievingly. "I'm, holding, a fucking, bomb." I looked from the bomb to Michael. "What do I do?" I whispered. "What do I do? Where do I go, where can we take it?"

"Across the road," a voice said in my ear.

Across the road?

"What's across the road?" I asked.

"A lake," Sin said, her eyes bulging. Everyone else was silent, staring in horror.

"A lake?" I stared at the bomb.

"A lake," Michael repeated, staring at the bomb.

"What's in it?"

"Just fish, nothing else," he said quietly.

Seconds passed, but it seemed like forever. Considering there was a bomb in my hands.

"There's only one thing to do," I told Michael, gazing into his eyes. Eyes that I may never see again. Tears rolled from my own and down over my cheeks. "I love you."

He seemed confused. "I love you, too." Then his expression changed. "We run."

"What?" I wasn't sure I'd heard what I just heard.

"We run," he repeated, grabbing my right arm.

"Sin, get the gas off, shut the doors, and get everybody on the floor," I yelled as Michael and I ran out the door.

"No, Tahlia, wait," she yelled.

"Tahlia, nooo..." another voice yelled. It was somewhat familiar, but I didn't have the time to stop and see who it was.

Michael and I ran for our lives. Through the bloody lobby and over three dead guards. Out the glass doors that were fortunately easy to open. Down the pathway and across the main road. Over the small hills in the park until we stopped at the water's edge.

:30

"We need to get it in the middle," I gasped, then looked at Michael. "Have you seen what they do in discus? You know, the sport?"

"Swing it around and throw," he said, taking off his coat. He grabbed the vest by a shoulder strap.

"I love you," I said, stepping back.

"I love you, too." He swung around three times and threw it with all of his might into the middle of the lake. "Run," he yelled, grabbing me by the hand.

KABOOMMM…

Chapter 17

The force sent us flying about fifteen feet in front of us onto the ground. Water, dead fish, dirt and debris rained down on us as we lay where we'd landed. I was face down on the cold hard soggy grass.

Michael lay on top of me.

"Oh...God..." I groaned. "Get off me. You're bloody heavy. And I'm in pain."

He rolled aside. "Oh...are you okay?" Crawling to his knees, he pulled me to him. "Oh, my God, Tahlia. What happened? Are you all right? Oh, my God."

"Ouch, watch my arm," I said, brushing my clothes off after seeing the mess we both were. "I'm dirty. God, I'm dirty. And wet. Bloody from getting shot or glassed or something. But I guess it will come out in the wash."

He grabbed me in a bear hug. "God, I love you. When they came in shooting the place up, I was scared to death. I didn't know where you were. If you were back from the ladies' or still there. I didn't know, and it scared me because I couldn't protect you." I could feel his heart racing through his shirt, as was mine. He pulled back and held my face in his hands. "I love you, so much. I'm so glad you're okay." We kissed, our lips mingling with the tears rolling down our faces.

"I love you, too, oh, God, I love you, too," I mumbled against his lips. "Marry me?"

His head moved back and forth in shock. "What?"

"Marry me?" I repeated in desperation.

He didn't seem to be registering what I was saying.

"I moved halfway around the world to be with you, Michael Anthony, and I am not letting you go. Especially after tonight. I love you, and I want you to marry me."

He cried and laughed at the same time. "Yes, yes." He kissed me again. "Yes, yes, yes, I'll marry you. God yes." We held onto each other for dear life.

"Let's go to Vegas tonight, so we don't have to wait," I said.

"You...want...to elope?" he asked, a strange look on his face.

"Let's just see it as getting married as quick as possible so we can be wife and husband."

"Don't you mean husband and wife," he corrected with a huge grin.

"No," I said slyly, "I got it right the first time." I glanced toward the function centre. "We should go in. Get everybody out." I climbed to my feet.

"Okay," he said, helping me. "Let's go."

"Don't mention getting married to anyone except Sin," I said. "I want to keep it private."

"That's fine." His lips met mine. "Let's go in."

We ran hand in hand across the street and back

into the building. Sidestepping the dead guards, we made our way through what was left of the function room doors. The sight that met our eyes was extreme and unbelievable, to say the least. Women were screaming or crying in shock. The men were sitting there in a daze shaking their heads.

Sin was holding herself tightly, but the one thing that shocked me most was Andy Garrick lying on Carmine Gionetti's back. That looked highly...um... inappropriate for two men in public. Carmine was crying, his arms outstretched. Andy was stroking his hair gently, speaking soothingly into his ear. *Sooo*, it was Carmine's voice I'd heard yell out 'Tahlia, no'.

I gazed from left to right and saw Richard and Marnie huddling on the ground in front of me. Celebs that were normally so rowdy and full on were sitting in heaps of patheticness.

And it pissed me off!

I walked forward a few steps and slammed my hands onto my hips. "I find it hysterically ironic that most of you play cops on TV shows and know how to handle a gun." I stared angrily at the faces that turned up to me. "Yet here you all are, cowering on the floor in fear." My face expressed my distaste. "And it takes some Aussie chick to come in and save the day by blowing away the bad guys. How pathetically piss weak." I glanced around. "And Richard—" I turned to him and Marnie sitting on the floor, arms around each other. "This is *absolutely the last time I ever* save either of your lives. 'Cause quite frankly," I adjusted my hat, "I'm sick of it. The next time you need someone to help save you," I shook my head, "don't call me."

Everyone was still looking at me in stunned silence, and it was annoying, so I took the opportunity to add one more thing. "And you know, you two," I said to Carmine and Andy. "Lying there the way you are is highly inappropriate considering what Sin and I talk about online. Doing what you're doing is just adding fuel to the fire."

Sin, Richard and Marnie ran at us together, and we nearly fell over as they hugged us. "Hey, get off, that's enough," I yelled, pushing everyone off me. "Now, Richard." I became serious. "We need to evacuate the building. God knows if there's any more bombs around, so now is the time to get everyone out. There's dead guards out front, so use the side exits. Get everyone out into the street and the park. Who cares if we block the road off? Can you arrange that?"

"Absolutely."

"Sin." I turned to her. "Split the crowd into two, and get this side of the room out of the exit past the ladies', and did you call the cops?"

"I did. When they didn't believe me, I told them I was a lawyer and I'd break their balls if they didn't come." She was shaking like crazy, but her voice was getting stronger.

"Well, they're still not here, so we have to do it ourselves." I noticed the dead men on the ground and saw the matter splattered all around. "Ewww, is that what real brain looks like?" I crouched down and peered at the open skull of the fugly bomber. It was gross, to say the least.

"All right, people, we're going to evacuate the building through the side exits. Move onto the street out front. Do it quickly. Go," Richard commanded.

I had a good look at the dead men while everyone filed out. I hadn't seen real brain before, only the fake stuff on the TV crime shows.

Five minutes later, miraculously, everyone was out, and it was just Michael and me.

"Let's go sweetheart." He pulled me up into his arms.

An overwhelming sense of some feeling came over me like a tonne of bricks. I looked around the room and saw emptiness when an hour before it had been so full of music and life. Stone cold empty. Except for Michael and myself. And the three dead gunmen.

DEAD.

DEAD as doornails.

DEAD on the floor.

And I had shot them!

It hit me hard.

I had shot and killed three human beings.

Michael half pulled, half carried me out of the room. "Come on, let's go. You don't look so good." We walked back through the lobby. Back over the dead guards. Back out the door. It was all happening in a daze. I didn't know where I was, but I knew I didn't want to be there. We ended up on the road with everyone else just as the cops came screeching to a halt.

"Okay, people, what's going on here?" a detective asked, arrogantly stepping from the car.

"What's going on," Richard barged up to him, "is

that we had three gunmen with a bomb threaten to blow us all sky high and where the hell were you?"

The cheap suit clad detective was highly annoyed. "Now just a minute—"

"No. Don't you even dare stand there and tell me just a minute," Richard shot back.

"Oh, God, I can't deal with this," I said. "I'm gonna be sick. I'm gonna be sick." Michael led me over to the bushes on the side of the path. It was a small space away from everyone else, but I still heard Richard and the detective argue while I threw my guts up.

Michael rubbed my back gently, noticing the bandages. "You'll be okay. You should be checked over by the paramedics," he said, as we watched them rush past us into the building, knowing they were after any surviving guards.

"No." I stood and wiped my mouth. "I'm okay...do it later." I was *not* in my right mind. We walked back onto the street with Sin to stay out of the way.

The lights on the building shone, the headlights of the cop cars glared in our faces, and they had set up huge searchlights so they could see. Night was turning into day.

We were all in a daze. Standing around, doing nothing, huddling in small groups. Women comforting each other, men slapping other men on the back because they were too macho to hug. Some sitting on the curb, others on the rocks in the park.

"Okay, everyone," someone said. "Get into small groups, and an officer will take your statements. You can come down to the station at a later date. Let's get this moving."

The paramedics wheeled out five guards and loaded them into the ambulances. Cops were rounding people up and moving them around like cattle, or running into the building to take photos and see the dead men. We just stood there in the middle of the road watching. Not really having any idea of what the hell was going on.

Richard came up to us. "Tahlia, we're going to set up the news cameras so we can get the news first. I want you to—"

"No! *I am not* doing an interview. No cameras, no interviews, no nothing. Keep your people away from me. Keep everyone away from me. I will *not* talk." I gave him my angriest, sternest look. *"Do you understand me?"*

He looked confused for a second, but then understood as he inspected my dead expression. I think I scared him. "Of course, dear. We won't do anything." He strode off with a steely, determined look in his eyes.

I leaned my head against Michael's chest. "Oh, God, I want to go home. I just wanna go home." I started crying and could feel my body collapse into him. I just wanted to let go and be taken home.

"We all do," Michael replied, his voice soft, his arms tightening around me.

I could feel his stress seep through to me, and it made me more anxious. I had nearly lost the man I love. God, it was really hitting home. I closed my eyes to the crowd around me and tried to shut my brain off.

"Let's get out of here when this is over," I said. "We'll go to Vegas tonight and then go somewhere else by the sea." I lifted my head. "I want to go away to the sea. Just you and me. Get away from this."

He stroked my face. "We'll go anywhere you want."

I nodded and turned to Sin. "Come here." I pulled her into our hug. "Michael and I are flying to Vegas tonight to get married tomorrow. Tell no one. Then we'll fly off somewhere for a holiday."

She stood wide-eyed. "Okay," she said in a daze. "Where will you go?" Her arm slid around me. She didn't look good either, and I thought she might be sick as well.

I sighed. "I don't know, beachside, seaside, somewhere," I rambled. "So far away from here. Private. Alone." I didn't know where so I shrugged. "Hawaii?"

Michael's eyes lit up. "Hawaii sounds nice."

"Yeah...Hawaii. Is that all right?"

"It's fine. We'll go there," he said, kissing my head.

"Okay," I said, nodding and feeling better. "We'll go to Vegas tonight then fly to Hawaii tomorrow." I looked at Sin. "Can you handle things this week? The business, the book. My COs know what to do. I just feel..." My head fell against Michael's chest. "So worn out."

"I'll fix everything," she mumbled, her eyes glassy and unmoving.

I heard people shouting, crying, screaming. The atmosphere was weird. It was like I was stuck in some bad disaster movie, and I just wanted to go home.

"Michael, Michael." His brunette ex-wife came running up to us. "Oh, my God, you're all right." She dragged my man out of my arms. Something I *did not* appreciate! Her show just happened to be on the same network, and she was married to her tall, hunky blond co-star who was with her.

"I'm fine," Michael said, disentangling himself from her and putting his arms back around me. "We're both fine."

"Oh, right," she rambled, looking from Michael to me. "You're the woman that saved us."

I shrugged. "Yeah...whatever." I *did not* want to be recognised.

"I'm just glad, thank you so much," she continued. "You saved our lives." She grabbed her husband's arm. "And Jake's, and Michael's, so Dylan doesn't have to be an orphan."

"Yeah, that's great," I said, meaning it. "I just happened to be there."

"Hey, listen," Michael said. "Tahlia and I are taking a holiday after this, and we'd like to take Dylan with us."

"Oh, no, no," she said. "I need to spend time with him too. We could've died. I need my son, Michael."

He sighed and tried to remain calm. "I get that, Marilee. We're going to Hawaii for the week. Can you send him over for part of the time?"

Oh, for God's sake. I inconspicuously rolled my eyes.

"Hawaii, oh, that sounds good." She looked at her blond hunky husband. "Can we go too? Surely they can't expect us to work after this?"

"If we can get time off, sure," Jake, the hunky husband, said to his gorgeous brunette wife.

God, it *was* like watching a soap opera.

She turned to Michael. "Okay, how about we all fly

over with Dylan and he can spend half the week with us and half with you."

Michael and I exchanged a glance. "We're going tomorrow," I said. "Not sure when, but we could leave a note to let you know we made it." I didn't want anyone knowing we were heading to Vegas first.

"Oh, that's fine," she said. "We don't know when we'll go either. We'll see you there."

"Fine," I said, and she flew at me with a hug. "Uh, that's okay." I pushed her away.

"I'll call you," she told Michael, before walking away.

"Oh, God." I fell into Michael's arms. I was so tired, so sick. I just wanted to go home.

"Uh, oh," Sin said.

"What now?"

"The cameras are out and pointing in this direction." We turned to the sidelines where the camera crews had set up just outside the yellow police tape.

"Oh, God, get me out of here," I panicked, looking for an escape route. Everyone was talking to an officer. They had been cornered off into their shows' casts. Some were standing or comforting each other. Some were sitting on the grass or side of the road, staring into space.

I saw Carmine staring at me with a blank expression. He was sitting on the curb with Andy on one side and Keith on the other.

I did *not* need this.

I glanced around frantically. "Where? Where can I go? Get away, no cameras, get away. I can't do this."

"Tahlia, it's all right," Michael said. "Let's go over here and sit down. It's away from the lights and the people." He led Sin and me over to the curb outside of the function centre. The cop cars had parked in such a way that it covered us from prying eyes.

"You sit," I mumbled, feeling freaked. "I need you to hold me. Hold me." I was so out of it, having no real idea of what was happening.

"Okay, okay," he said, sitting down on the curb.

I sat between his legs and turned my body to his left. I put my legs over his left one, and he wrapped his arms around me tightly. I sat there all curled up like a mummy. Not thinking, not talking, just rocking back and forth. *I do not want this. I do not want this. I do not need this.* My mind turned to jello.

"Tahlia...Tahlia...Tahlia. Can you hear me?"

I looked up slowly, my eyes focussing.

"Tahlia," Richard said. "After what you've done there must be something I can do for you." His face showed concern. "You don't look well. Why don't I send you on a holiday?"

"We've already decided on that," Michael said. "We leave tomorrow."

"That's good," Richard replied. "Are you flying? You can take my private jet anywhere you want."

Blankly, I snuggled back into Michael's arms.

"That would be nice, thank you," Michael said. "Can we use it tonight?"

That surprised him. "I'll tell the pilots to get it ready and standby. Where are you going?"

"Vegas."

Richard's brows went up. "Vegas," he said, understanding. "I'll have it waiting for you, and you can take it anywhere else you want."

"Thank you," Michael said, holding me close. "How much longer will it be?"

"Hours, considering the cops are so stupid." Richard sighed. He studied me wrapped up in my man's arms. "I'll get the detective to take your statements now, so you can leave. Tahlia needs to get out of here."

"Who doesn't?" Sin mumbled. She was curled up next to Michael, clinging to his right arm, her head resting on his shoulder. Tears streamed down her face, and she tried to choke back the sobs that were starting to rack her body.

Michael reached up with his right hand and patted her gently. It seemed to calm her some.

Richard went over to speak to the cop that had mouthed off when he'd arrived. They had what seemed to be a very heated discussion, then the smart arse detective strode over to us.

"So *you're* the killer?" The power of his angry, hostile arrogance defied belief.

My head shot up and my eyes coldly penetrated his. "How dare you?" I hissed.

"Dare," he shot back, sitting beside me on the curb and flicking open his spiral bound notepad, enclosed in its worn, black leather pouch. He clicked open his pen. "Why don't you tell me what happened so you can leave. You don't look so good."

I angrily gave my statement in a barrage of forced

words, throwing in a few 'fuck yous' as he spat dig after dig at me. He obviously had no idea what killing someone was like and the strain it puts you under. Or the shit it makes you feel. Or the sickness it fills your body with. Rotting away at your soul as you realise that you've taken a human life. Or in my case, three human lives. Three human beings. Three living souls of their own. As bad as they were.

Michael and Sin gave their statements when I was done. It felt like hours had gone by since the shooting, but surprisingly, it was only one.

"All right, Ms Cameron." Det. Wanker closed his notepad, shoved it into his inside jacket pocket and stood. "You're free to go. Go be a hero."

"Don't call me that," I spat viciously. "I am no hero."

Chapter 18

As it turns out, we didn't get to Vegas after all. Sitting in Michael's arms, I had completely forgotten about my injuries, thanks to the five very strong painkillers I'd swallowed. We ended up in the local hospital with me being x-rayed, scanned and stitched. Thankfully, nothing was broken, but my arm had been severely sliced and diced by either a bullet or a flying piece of glass. Then there was my back. Only two glass shards had stabbed me, but had done no major damage. All of my wounds were tightly stitched and bandaged.

Wow! That bitch called Karma had stabbed me in the back!!!!!

We headed home after the hospital, showered, quickly packed a bag or two, then drove off to Burbank Airport, since it's closest to our home. After a quick call to Michael's ex about flying to Hawaii, we were on our way.

I picked up one of the newspapers Sin had given me. The story was all over the place. Every tabloid, paper, TV news, current affairs shows. Every one of them talked about the party, the gunmen, the bomber, and the woman who saved TNM. The Mystery Woman.

Not too many people at the function knew my name, as Michael had introduced me to everyone as his lovely lady. I don't think he used my name. Which seemed odd now, but not at the time. So really, not too many people knew who I was. Thank God!

"Oh, my God, look at this," I cried in dismay, showing Michael the paper. The story had a zoomed in picture of me standing in Michael's arms, but I was turned away from the camera. Sin was beside me, other celebs around us. The caption read: *Is one of these women the woman who saved TNM?*

I screwed the paper up and threw it on the floor. A stabbing pain went through my arm. "Ugh, like I need that." Sighing, I looked out the window at Hawaii in the distance. "God, look at it." My hand touched the glass, and I smooshed my face to the window to see it better. "It's so green. And the water's so blue." I stared at the ocean far below us then remembered I had a fear of drowning.

I also had a fear of flying, which technically, you could put down to a fear of dying. As in, you fly, you crash, you drown, you die. Anyhoo, enough about my fears. "You ever been to Hawaii?" I asked.

"No, I haven't." Michael leaned into me and looked out the window. "It does look nice. Ohhh," his face lit up, and he became animated, "they did Magnum PI here. Oh, we could go to the place they filmed it." His grin said it all as he daydreamed about being Tom Selleck.

I'm old enough to remember the show, and I gotta tell ya, Tom looked damn fine in his short shorts, moustache, and hairy body. In fact, my Mikey would make a *damn fine* Magnum PI. Ah, Mr Bellisario, sir, when you film the Magnum movie, how about putting my Mikey in the lead role. He's gorgeous and has great legs. And he's hairy too!

I giggled at the thought of Mikey being Thomas Magnum and wound my arm through his. Laying my head on his shoulder, I breathed in deep. A part of me began relaxing, muscles slowly unwinding, aches slowly dissipating. We were on our way to Hawaii!

*****

"Welcome to The Belmont Hotel, Hawaii," the clerk said brightly when we rocked up to the front desk. "We hope you enjoy your stay here. We will have you and your luggage driven to your private bungalow, and anything you need is only a phone call away." He looked strangely at Michael. "Weren't you at that... um... network function...last night...Mr Anthony?"

"I was," Michael replied shortly, not wanting to talk about it as much as I didn't. He wrote out a note for his ex-wife. "Can you tell me if Marilee and Jake Johnson have booked in yet, please?"

The clerk checked the log in book. "No, sir, they're to arrive shortly."

"Good. Can you give her this note please?"

"Of course, sir." He must have been wondering about the women in Michael's life since he was in the paper with one, there in the hotel with me – who was the woman in the picture, but the clerk didn't know that – and now he was leaving a note for another.

"Thank you, for everything," Michael added, picking up his bag.

"That's what we're here for. Your buggy awaits." He motioned to the golf cart outside.

Our luggage was loaded onto the back, and we were driven down to the beach. The hotel had several buildings; the main hotel with smaller wings in offshoots, and the private bungalows down along the beach. The cove was cut off from the beach for the hotel guests. They had their own, they didn't need ours. We drove along a wide rainforest soaked pathway before shooting off onto a smaller one.

"This is the road to your ocean address," the driver said, coming to a stop and unloading our bags. After he left, we unlocked the door and went in.

It was beautiful!

"Oh, this is gorgeous," I cried, running through the tropically decorated living room. Flinging the big French doors open, I stepped out to the landing where a small private pool was in front of us with a tree-lined path to the beach and gorgeous ocean views beyond that.

"Richard certainly knows how to thank you," Michael said, shutting the front door and dropping the keys on the kitchen counter to the left of the entrance. Richard Sayer had not only given us his private jet to fly to Hawaii and back, but had also organised our accommodation as well.

I stood on the wide pebbled terrace and gazed at my surroundings. Beautiful, quiet, peaceful. Perfect!

Michael came up behind me and wrapped his arms around my waist. I sighed and leaned on his chest, breathing in the warm tropical sea breeze floating up from the beach. "This is perfect," I murmured, feeling all aches and pain slowly float away thanks to great painkillers.

He nibbled on my ear. "Mmm, it is," he whispered.

I snorted and laughed. "Stop it. We have things to do before tonight." I glanced at my watch. "What time is it?"

"Don't know, better check the clock on the wall."

It was four-thirty.

"That gives us awhile." I rolled my case into the bedroom. Rose petals and scented candles decorated the tropical paradise of a bedroom. "Did you do this?" I called to Michael.

He shook his head as he stopped behind me. "Sorry, no. Must have been Richard."

"Well, we have some phone calls to make," I said and got to work.

Half an hour later, I placed the phone in its cradle. It rang, making me jump.

"Hello?"

"Ah, hello? Tahlia, is that you? It's Marilee. Is Michael there?"

"Sure." I covered the phone. "Your ex," I said to my soon-to-be husband as he took the phone.

"Hello...hey...right...okay...half an hour...all right, see you then." He hung up.

"They're here, I take it?"

"They're here," he said, turning to me. "They just booked in and will unpack, then she'll bring Dylan over."

There was a knock at the door.

Michael answered it. "Hello," he said to the man standing there.

"Sir, your suit is ready."

"Already? Bring it in."

The man walked in with a formal suit for a teen boy.

"Is it the right size?" Michael asked, looking over it.

"Yes sir, but if it needs altering, just call, and I'll be right over."

"All right, thank you." Michael showed the man out.

"That was fast," I said. "Now we need a shower."

"Oooh, I'll join you," he said, eagerly moving over to me.

"Oh, no, you won't, buster," I warned. "You can wait till later." His face fell and he pouted. Tough, he could wait till tonight when he'd get to see me in my lingerie. *Then* he'd be happy. I was in and out and in my underwear and a robe when Michael's ex arrived with Dylan.

"Dad," he cried, diving into his father's arms.

"Hey." Michael held on for dear life.

That I completely understood and didn't interrupt.

"So," Marilee said. "How long will you be keeping him for?"

"Two or three hours," Michael said, kissing his son's head. "Then I'll bring him back."

"Oh, okay." She pushed her hair behind her ears.

"Ah, since we're all here, and you want to spend time with him too, I thought we'd split the week. We'll have him Sunday through half of Wednesday, then you can have him Wednesday through Sunday morning. Then we'll meet up for brunch before going home."

"That sounds all right," he said and looked at Dylan. "You wanna spend half your week with Tahlia and me? We'll have fun, go surfing, swimming, snorkelling."

"Yeah, cool," he said, his face lighting up.

"Okay, then." Michael looked at Marilee. "I'll bring him back in a few hours."

"All right." She kissed Dylan. "See you later, sweetie, be good for your dad."

"I will."

Michael led Dylan to his room, which was opposite ours, to try on his suit, and five minutes later there was another knock on the door.

"I'll get it," I yelled, walking to the door in my robe. The hairstylist and make-up artist I'd called were there. "Hey, come on in."

They'd started doing me up when Michael came for his suit. "I've told Dylan, and he's kind of excited. But since he's only met you once it's kinda fast for him."

"Yeah, I get that," I said while having foundation smeared on.

Forty-five minutes later, I thanked the women, who'd also helped me dress, and saw them out.

Michael and Dylan came in from outside. "Wow...you look beautiful," Michael said softly, unable to tear his eyes away.

"Thank you." I looked at Dylan. "And *you* young

man, look very mature in your black suit and blue shirt. You match your dad."

He blushed. So cute for a twelve year old on the cusp of teenage years. "Thanks."

"I take it you're ready," Michael said.

"I am." I kissed him. "Let's do this. Dylan, are you ready to be best man?"

"Yeah." He pulled the ring box from his pocket. "Dad gave me the rings to look after."

"Well, that's what a best man does. Looks after the rings." I was quite surprised by the fact there were rings as I hadn't picked any out. But unbeknownst to me, Michael had bought them so he could propose. I just happened to get in first. I touched Dylan's cheek. "Are you okay with this? Us? Your dad and me? I know we only met two weeks ago, so it's happened pretty fast, but I want you to be okay with this too."

He looked from me to his dad back to me. His eyes were exactly like his mother's, and I thought I was looking at her. "Dad told me he loves you a lot, especially after last night. And if you make him happy, then I'm happy. I'm glad you're going to be my stepmom, 'cause you make Dad happy."

Awww. My face screwed up in happiness. "Oh, Dylan, that is so sweet." I kissed his cheek. "I love your dad *so much*. And I love you too, even though we've only met once, because you're a part of him, and I love him, so I love you too." I stepped back and wiped away my tears of complete joy. "Did you tell him you've moved in?" I asked Michael.

"I did. And I told him you did up a room just for

him when he stays over."

"Dad said it's all planets and stars," Dylan said, trying to be cool and not over-excited.

"Yes, it is. You've got a double bed, TV and DVD, cd system and a huge desk. And, glow in the dark planets and stars on the walls."

"Cool." A huge grin spread across his face.

There was a knock at the door. It was the celebrant, photographer, and hotel manager. "If you'll follow us down to the beach, we'll get started with the ceremony."

"Of course," I said, and we followed them down. Stepping onto the sand, I lifted my pink and blue chiffon dress, and we walked to the water's edge.

"Are we ready?" the celebrant asked.

"We are." Michael and I faced each other, and feeling overwhelmed, I wrapped my arms around him under his jacket.

The blue of his shirt brought out the blue of his eyes which were twinkling brightly. His arms slid around me, and we held on tight.

"We are gathered here today to see these two people come together in love and happiness for the rest of their lives," the celebrant said.

A huge grin lit up my face.

"Do you Michael, take Tahlia, to be your lawfully wedded wife. In sickness and in health, for richer or poorer, for better, for worse, till death do you part?"

"I do." Michael's grin mirrored mine, and we kissed.

"Do you Tahlia—"

"I do!" I jumped in because I couldn't wait and we all laughed.

"Take Michael, to be your lawfully wedded husband. In sickness and in health, for richer or poorer, for better, for worse, till death do you part?" the celebrant went on.

"I do. I do so much." My heart was bursting with happiness.

"We will now exchange rings."

We turned to Dylan who'd been standing next to his dad silently, watching the proceeding. He pulled the box from his pocket and opened it, before handing it to the celebrant.

Michael picked up a shiny gold ring and I gasped. It was gorgeous. A huge ruby heart sat in the middle, an emerald heart was to the left, a moonstone heart to the right. Tiny diamonds filled in the gaps. The emerald and moonstone were our birthstones.

"This," he said, holding my left hand. "Is your engagement ring. I managed to buy it when you weren't looking," he said with a big grin. "So...will you, Tahlia, marry me?"

I cried and laughed at the same time. "Yes, yes, I'll marry you. You know I will." He slid it on.

My God, it was gorgeous!

He picked up the wedding ring, a band with matching stones embedded in the gold, and slid it onto my finger.

My right hand was over my mouth since I was blubbering like an idiot. I reached for Michael's ring and pushed it onto his ring finger. His own tears were dripping down his face. We kissed and wrapped our arms around each other again.

"I understand that you both have vows," the celebrant said.

"Well, not really. None planned anyway," Michael said. "We just thought we'd say whatever came into our heads."

"All right then. Tahlia, why don't you start?"

Oh, God!!!!

I laughed, almost hysterically, through my tears. "Oh, God," I sniffed. "I don't even know where to start. Ah, I." Taking a deep breath, and staring into my husband's face, I started again. "I remember sitting in my bedroom wanting *so desperately* to be with you. To be your wife. The mother of your future children. The woman you would spend the rest of your life with. I wanted it so much." I sniffed again. "When I won lotto, I knew, that all of my dreams, had or would, come true. I love you so much." I gazed into his teary eyes. "I love you so much that I packed up my belongings and moved halfway around the world just to be with you."

I gasped a jagged breath. "It took seven weeks to meet you." We laughed at the memories. "But it seems that God planned for you to meet me instead, by having you back into my car." I slid my hands up to his face and wiped away his tears. "I love you, so much. I want to be the woman you spend the rest of your life with. The woman that gives you children, a happy home life, a future filled with happiness, and joy, love, passion and desire. Everything you could possibly want. I will love you, honour you, cherish you, treasure and adore you, the way you want, and need, and should be loved."

I kissed him. "There is no one else for you. There will never be anyone else for you. Only me. I will be, and am, the only woman who will love you, for the rest of your life. The wife you've always wanted. The wife who will always be there when you get home from a long day at work with a hot meal on the table. The wife who'll scrub your back in the shower, and give you a relaxing massage. The wife who will fall asleep in your arms and wake up the same way in the morning. I'm the wife who will fix you breakfast, kiss you goodbye, wave you off to work, then thank God for another day with you. A day filled with happiness, and joy, another day in a long list of many."

I stroked his cheek. "I will love you for the rest of my life, Michael Anthony. No ifs, buts, or maybes. I am the woman for you." I glanced at Dylan. "I love your son like he's my own because he is a part of you. And I love you, so I love him too." I stared deeply into Michael's eyes. "I am giving myself to you, body, mind, soul, and will love you with my heart of hearts, and my soul of souls, and with every fibre of the being God made me. I *will* love you for the rest of my life, and the rest of yours. I *am, so proud,* to be your wife. The woman you love and have chosen to spend the rest of your life with. I am proud to be Dylan's stepmother and to call him my stepson. I am so proud, and so happy that you have taken me into your family and accepted me as part of your lives. And I promise that I will do *everything* in my power to make you both happy. To make this family a united one, and to be the woman, and the wife, the life partner, mother and stepmother, that *you* will be proud and happy to call your own."

I wiped away his tears. "I love you, Michael," I whispered. "And I am *so* happy and proud to be your wife." I planted my lips on his, and we kissed with fire and passion.

Everyone was crying, and we laughed, wiping our tears away.

"Michael," the celebrant managed, wiping her tears. "Do you have anything to say?"

"What she said," he laughed. "I have no idea how I'm going to follow that."

"You don't have to," I replied. "Just say what you feel."

"Okay." He licked his lips. "I, ah, I had no idea, that when I went shopping that day, that I would be meeting the woman I was going to marry. Especially within two weeks." He laughed lightly. "When I saw you and your car, I had no idea what was about to come, and how my life would change, and that everything would happen in such a short amount of time." He shrugged. "I didn't know I was going to spend the rest of my day thinking about you. After I saw you that night, I wanted to keep seeing you. Then I saw you on Saturday, and I knew I had to. That I had to change my life so I could."

He nodded and swallowed the lump in his throat. "So I did. And I'm so glad I did because it has led me here to you, standing on a beautiful beach in Hawaii, with my son, and the woman I want to spend the rest of my life with. The woman I'm marrying, making my wife. About to make a new life, a new future, a new family with. I am proud to marry you. I am proud and grateful that you are my wife. The woman that I love, the woman that will stand by my side as my partner, my lover, the mother of my children, and stepmother of my son. The woman that will be there for me when I need her, and when she wants me. The woman that will have the utmost faith in me as a husband, a partner, a lover and father of her children. And I will be. I am proud to call myself your husband, and I will be there when you need and want me. I will stand by your side through thick and thin, for better or worse, till death do us part. And I will do it proudly, with confidence, that I am the man you want as your husband. The man that you will love for the rest of your life." He kissed me. "Because Tahlia, *you* are the woman that I will love, for the rest of mine."

"Aw," I cried, my face crumpling as I threw my arms around his neck and kissed him hard.

"With the power vested in me, I now pronounce you, husband, and wife."

Everyone applauded madly then the manager announced he had a surprise for us. Hula girls came down the path onto the beach. Men carrying torches and drums followed.

We stood mesmerised for a few moments at the special treat they had organised and then posed for our pictures. The hotel photographer ran around snapping photos. Pics of Michael and me, then of us with Dylan. Then all of us with the hula girls.

After awhile, Michael and I found ourselves slow dancing at the water's edge, the sun just setting over the ocean, the colours lighting up the sky in all shades of the rainbow.

It was magical.

"I love you," I whispered, gazing into his eyes.

"I love you, too," he whispered back.

We danced with Dylan till it was dark, then made our way back to our bungalow.

"I'm going to take Dylan to his mom then I'll be right back."

"Okay," I said, as his lips touched mine, and after they'd left, I quickly changed into a silk negligee and lit the candles in the bedroom. Downing some more painkillers, I threw back the bed covers, got a bottle of champagne ready, along with choc covered strawberries, and managed to display myself before Michael burst through the door. "Don't forget to lock it," I called.

He came running into the bedroom and skidded to a halt when he saw me. "Oh, oh, oh," he grunted, yanking off his suit jacket. "You sexy woman you." His pants and shorts slid down. "You look amazing." His shirt flew off. "And guess what?"

"What?" I looked at him expectantly, laid out on the bed in next to nothing.

"You're my wife, I'm your husband, and I'm going to ravage you." He dived onto the bed, and I burst into a fit of giggles.

It was our first official night as husband and wife, and, of course, we didn't get any sleep!

Chapter 19

"The ceremony sounded beautiful," Sin said over the phone Sunday morning.

"It was," I gushed. "Especially when the hula girls came out. Lots of photos were taken, so we've got plenty to give you. The hotel made up this beautiful album and DVD package." I was lounging by the pool listening to the waves crash on the beach. "God it's so beautiful here, you should see it."

"Stop, you're making me jealous." She paused. "So, everything's great then?"

I heard the tone she used. "Everything's fine so far. I haven't slept in what, forty-eight hours, since Friday morning." I glanced around. "And quite frankly, I don't want to sleep." A yawn overcame me, betraying me. "God, I'm so tired, but I don't want to sleep 'cause of what I might see. Then there's all the bloody pain, but the pain pills are good. And last night we went at it like rabbits. Every time I found myself falling asleep, I'd wake up and start on Michael. Poor boy." I looked at him sleeping on the lounge beside me. "At least *he* can sleep. I wore him out." The sun was making his chest hair glow red, and he was already tanning. I'd rubbed sunscreen on him before he fell asleep because I didn't want to spend the week with a lobster. "Listen, I called 'cause I need you to handle any police or legal matters that may come up."

"I can do that," she said. "Do you still want your business to open tomorrow?"

I sighed deeply and watched two brightly coloured birds play around in a tree. "Tell Richard to open for business. Start selling online, clothes, accessories, books, but *don't* uncover the sign on the building, or give my name in conjunction with the business. I'll do something when I get home."

"When will that be?"

"I don't know. Probably next Sunday. It'll depend on how I am."

"And how are you?"

"Coping. In pain. How 'bout you?"

"Glad I'm with my husband. Nightmares come and go. I'm getting on with things and working through it." A long pause. "Everyone thinks you're a hero."

"Don't call me that," I said angrily. "I *am not* a hero. I'm a murderer." I drew a breath and glanced at Michael to see if he'd heard me. "Look, just, take care of everything, and only call if something happens that I need to know about. Okay?"

"All right. I'll take care of the legals." She paused. "By the way. There are more stories about the woman who saved TNM. They want to know who you are, what you did, and how you did it. I'll collect the papers and tabloids so you can see them when you get back."

"Ugh," I groaned. "Like I need to keep being reminded of it. I'll see you next week. Bye." I had to keep my mind off last Friday night 'cause I just didn't want to think about it. Deciding on a swim, I slipped into the water and paddled back and forth wanting someone to play with. Swimming to the side where Michael was, I threw a handful of water at his sexy hairy body.

"Hey...what?" Michael mumbled as the water splashed over him. "Hey." He jumped up, wide awake as I continued splashing cold water over his hot body – hot in more ways than one – and the effect was obvious. "What are you doing?"

"I wanna have some fun," I said, throwing my bikini at him.

He caught it in one hand, and realising what it meant, yanked his shorts off and jumped into the pool. He grabbed me, and with a kiss, I showed him exactly how I wanted to play.

Hours later we lay on the lounge with just a towel over our privates. The warm summer breeze was amazing as it floated off the ocean, up the pathway, and over the pool. It caressed our naked bodies as we lay facing each other, stroking, caressing, canoodling. It was such a perfect day. The second day of us being husband and wife. Or just over twenty-four hours depending on how you want to see it.

My lips traced kisses along Michael's jaw to his ear, I nibbled, then kissed down his collarbone to his shoulder. My fingers played in the nest of fur on his chest, squeezing his nipples.

"Ow. Oh, no, no, you don't," he gasped, catching my hand in his and kissing my fingers. He kissed my hand, up my arm to my neck, my ear, and my jaw. Then his lips led the way back down to my right breast where they enveloped it.

I gasped at the warmth I felt pulsate through my body as he sucked. Knowing I wanted him more than anything, I sat on top of his sexy hairy body and made my own way down.

I'm not sure why, or what it is about Michael's body, I just know that I'm addicted to it. That's right. Addicted! My body needs and wants to feel his against mine. My hot naked skin wants to rub against his hot naked hairy skin. My hands need and want to slide their way through the nests of sexy hair on his sexy body. And his body *is* sexy. To me anyway. I always find myself wanting to rip his clothes off and have my wicked way. My breasts want to rub themselves in the furry nest on his chest and feel the fire ignite within them. My body craves Michael's. I want to eat him, taste him, rub myself all over him. I need to wrap my arms around him and never let go. And once my hands find their way into his furry nests, they don't want to let go either. It's weird, I know, but that's just the way it is. *I* am totally addicted to Michael's body. Physically, emotionally, mentally and *definitely sexually.* My hands, my breasts, my body, are all addicted to, and crave, Michael Anthony.

Needless to say, Hawaii was not the only heaven that day.

Dinner was a platter of delicious seafood brought

in by the hotel restaurant, as I still wanted to hide away in our own piece of paradise and be together. Drinking chilled soft drink by the pool, and eating chunky chocolate ice cream for dessert out of the cartons, we were happy. Sex was amazing, as usual, then we fell asleep. And that's when they began.

"No! No, get away, don't you dare. Leave him alone. Don't you dare shoot him. No. No. Leave him alone."

BANG!

I looked down at my chest. There was a gaping hole and thick red stuff oozing out.

I fell to the floor.

I sat bolt upright.

Kicking out my legs that were entangled in the sheet, frantically flicking the stuff on my face away. I realised it was my hair. I gasped for air, looking around the darkened room.

"Sweetheart?" Michael turned the bedside light on. "Hey, what's wrong?" He saw my dishevelled appearance and kissed my shoulder.

I flinched, twisted away with a gasp, then turned to him. I saw the shock on his face as he saw my frenzied look. "I'm sorry," I rasped, reaching up and touching his cheek. "I'm sorry. My arm hurts...my back hurts and I just...had..." I burst into tears.

"A nightmare? It's okay, sweetheart. It's okay." He pulled me into his arms and I sobbed, almost hysterically. "Shh, baby, everything's okay. A nightmare is perfectly understandable. Shh, it's okay." He stroked my hair, pushing it away from my face. We sat there rocking, me howling, Michael holding me tight as he soothed me. I don't know how long we were like that for, but eventually, I pulled away and sat up.

"I'm sorry." I wiped my face and drew a jagged breath. "It's my first nightmare." He gave me a tissue, and I blew my nose. "I haven't slept properly, if at all, since Friday morning when we woke up. And now," my bottom lip quivered as I stared mournfully at him, "I don't want any nightmares." Bursting into tears again, I fell into his lap and curled into a ball.

"Shh, it's okay, Tahlia. I'm here. It's all over, and we're here in Hawaii for a break." He went into the kitchen for pills and a glass of juice for me, and when I was done, he pulled me to his side, and we spooned. "It's okay. It will all be okay. Shh, I'm here. I'm not going to let anything happen to you. Shh, sweetheart, get some rest...get some rest..."

I don't know how long I was asleep for, or if I'd even been sleeping, but I woke to see the sun pouring in through the doorway along with a warm, soft breeze. The curtains billowed gently, and the doors to the living room were closed. I was also alone.

Stretching lazily, I lay there enjoying the moment, wondering where Michael was and trying not to ruin it by thinking about last night. Finally, and reluctantly, I rolled out of bed and showered, then walked out onto the porch to see Michael sipping juice and reading a paper.

"Morning." I kissed his hairy head and poured myself a glass of juice.

"Hey, sweetheart, good morning. How are you

today? Did you end up sleeping okay? You were out of it when I woke." He tried to hide the paper, but I spied the cover.

"And how come you weren't there when I woke? You said last night you weren't going anywhere?" I raised a brow at him.

He looked guilty. "I thought I'd let you sleep some more, so I crept out without disturbing you." He kept the paper out of reach.

"Gimme," I said, holding out my hand.

He looked reluctant. "After last night do you really want to see?"

I sat down heavily and sighed. "Probably not. But gimme anyway."

"Are you sure?" He didn't want to give me the paper.

"Michael," I said sternly, and he slowly handed me the paper.

"I'll get you some breakfast while you read it," he said.

"And some painkillers, thanks," I added.

Being Monday morning, the papers were all over it. Interviews with Richard Sayer and Marnie Wilkins, actors and actresses, expressing their horror of the events that had unfolded, and their gratitude for the woman who'd saved their lives.

"Have you read all of this?" I asked Michael when he sat down with my food.

"I have. Do *you* want to?"

"No." I frowned. "But for the life of me, there's that macabre black part of me that wants to read every detail." My eyes wandered back to the celeb interviews. "Listen to this. *'We managed to score several brief interviews with some of the actors and actresses who were at the ill-fated TNM network function last Friday night. Here's what they had to say.*

Amy Eckhart – I just thought I was going to a normal party for the network. I never dreamed I would end up on my knees begging to God to let me live. Praying that he kept me alive while those mad gunmen shot the place up. I do thank God for the woman who shot them, though. She saved our lives and got the bomb out of there, so we weren't killed. She's a true hero in my eyes.

Peter Barry – I work all day on a soap, where we can get weird storylines. I've been shot, held hostage, and survived bombs on the show, but at the end of the day, I go home with the knowledge I was acting. But that *night. That night was real. If it hadn't been for a true hero that God sent to save us, I wouldn't be here now. Neither would the three thousand other people in that room.*

Michelle Ferrerra – Whoever the woman was that saved our lives, we, I, owe her a deep debt of gratitude. I have two small children at home, and working on a crime drama, you do ask yourself, what would I do if this situation happened to me in real life. The answer is nothing. I did nothing. But one brave woman did, and now we're all here to tell the story. I thank our hero, my children thank our hero. She is, a true hero.

Mitchell Casablanca – I was held up once when I was a teenager. I didn't do anything, and my friend was killed. That's something I've had to live with all my life since. And I vowed that if it ever happened again, I would be prepared. But no matter how many karate classes, or learning to shoot a gun, you are never prepared for something like this. So I thank the woman who saved us from the bottom of my heart. She's a hero.'

"*I am not, a hero,*" I spat. "I wish everyone would stop calling me that. I am not a hero. I'm a murderer, a killer. A gun wielding maniac who slayed three men."

Michael watched me in horror from across the table. "Don't you *ever* say that again."

"Well, it's true." I threw down the paper, sighed and rubbed my arm. "It's true," I repeated softly. Glancing at Michael, I waved a hand at the newspaper. "I'm surprised they didn't get a blurb from you." I grinned wryly. "Thank God no one knows my name."

Michael reached for my hand and squeezed it. "Sweetie, this will all be over soon. In the meantime, you need to deal with this."

"I know," I said, squeezing back. "It's just so hard."

"I know, sweetheart. But I'm here for you. We'll get through this together."

I gazed into his gorgeous blue eyes and saw the love and concern. "Together."

*****

I called Richard Manning later that evening to see how my company was going. I wasn't going to stop now that I had worked so hard to get it ready to open. "So, how was our first day of business?"

"Fantastic. Sales started early, t-shirts have sold

well, several hundred in fact. The jeans and jackets are very popular. The jewellery is half gone, and we've had interest in the scarves, bags and hats."

"What about the book?"

"For sale today. There's interest because we mentioned the actors it was dedicated to, and that they inspired the characters. So the book has been picked up by quite a few people who bought the clothes."

"Great. Did Sin call you?"

"She did. She's dealing with publicity, and we're keeping your name out of it. It's the brand name all the way. And the sign's still covered." He paused. "Was that really you Friday night?"

"Say nothing," I said with more force than I intended. "Keep my name out of everything."

"O-kayyy. When will you be back?"

I sighed. "Next week. So if there's a problem, call Sin, and I'll see you then."

"All right, Boss, have a nice holiday."

That night, Michael and I had needy insatiable sex. Yes! Again!

I had a deep need to be close to him after nearly losing him, and had to show in every way that I loved him. So, yes, it was very fast and needy. I was addicted to him after all. It just didn't stop the nightmares.

"Don't you dare," I spat, clenching my jaw, and aiming my gun at his head. *"Put it down, or I'll blow your brains out."*

He laughed. Deep and guttural. "You won't kill me, little girl. You don't have the balls."

I fired three shots into his head. But the fugly

bastard stood there smiling while his fugly blood poured down his fugly face.

He laughed like a maniac and fell toward me. Falling on top of me as we flew backwards and landed on the ground.

KABOOMMM…

The bomb went off.

I was dead anyway.

"No, no," I cried, lunging out of bed.

"What's wrong," Michael mumbled, jumping up in a sleepy panic.

"No, no." I clawed at myself, thinking the gunman was on me and wanting him off.

"Tahlia, it's okay." He snapped the light on to see me standing naked in the middle of the bedroom, trying to get imaginary blood and guts off me. "Tahlia." He came toward me.

"No. Don't touch me," I cried, flinging the doors open and running down the pool stairs, allowing myself to sink, hoping to cleanse my body, my soul. I was lifted up through the water and gasped for air as I reached the surface.

"Tahlia, it's all right," Michael crooned, slipping his arms around me. "It's all right."

"No, no it's not." My body was racked with the most agonising pain, and sobs of fear and tears. I shook my head. "It's not, it's not, it's not," I wailed into the Hawaiian night.

"It is all right, Tahlia. Everything will be okay." He smoothed my hair back and held me tight while I fell apart.

*****

"Sorry about last night," I told him the next morning. We'd finished breakfast and were deciding if we'd do anything that day.

"Sweetie," he said, stroking my face. "It's all right. What we went through, what you did, it was hell. But we'll get through this together. I love you."

My lips rose at their corners into a soft smile. "I love you, too." We kissed. "So, what do you want to do today?"

"Well," he said with a smile of his own. "I thought we could go swimming. A little surfing. A picnic on the beach."

"A picnic sounds nice. We can set it up with the hotel."

Half an hour later, we were in the beautiful blue water splashing and having fun. We body surfed and paddled, ate amazing food the hotel set up on the beach for us under an umbrella and spent the rest of the day making love on the blankets until the sun set and the stars came out. After all, it was our honeymoon.

We wandered inside and headed for the shower. Soaping each other slowly, kissing, touching, washing bad memories away. Or so I thought. Gently, Michael dried me off and carried me to the bed. He lit the candles, opened the French doors, and brought in chilled soft drink and a carton of chunky mint chocolate ice cream.

I snuggled under the silk sheet against the pillows piled behind me as Michael climbed onto the bed.

"You spoil me."

His grin was huge. "Yes, I do," he said in a sing-song voice. "Look what I've got for you. Ice cream and cola."

"Mmm, gimme," I said, ready for the ice cream.

"Uh, ah," he said, pulling it away. "Not so fast. I have plans for this deliciously cold and chocolatey delight."

"Ohhh." My eyes widened in surprise and wonder. I cocked a brow. "Plans?"

"Plans." He wiggled his brows and lay beside me, pulling the sheet from my body. Taking a handful of ice cream, he smeared it all over my left breast.

"Oh, my God, that's cold," I gasped, my nipple hardening under the cold delight.

Michael laughed wickedly. "And all mine." His tongue licked around my breast greedily, his mouth taking it all in one go.

I groaned, my left hand grasping his hair and holding on like never before. My legs squeezed themselves together and moved up toward my chest, my back arched, and my head pushed into the pillow. "Uhhh," I gasped, feeling myself become ready for the man I loved.

We smeared ice cream all over each other, licking it off, rubbing against the other, smooshing it with body heat till it melted. The sex was incredible. Covered in cold minty chocolate ice cream melting between us, we ignited the room with passion.

"Oh, so you want to save him do you?" the man asked, levelling a gun at Michael.

"I won't let you shoot him. You will not kill him.

Because I will kill you first." I aimed my gun at the man's head.

He laughed then turned to Michael

"No," I screamed, diving in front of the man I love and firing my gun. We fell to the floor.

The gunman was dead. My bullet was in his forehead.

I lay bleeding, gasping for breath, the bullet having punctured my lungs.

"You will not die," Michael cried, pulling me into his arms and rocking back and forth. *"You will not die. I will not let you die."*

I saw black.

I felt something sticky all over me.

"Ugh, what is that," I cried, rolling out of bed. "What is it? Get it off me, get it off me."

"What's happening," Michael said groggily, struggling to sit up.

I dived into the bathroom and under the shower, frantically scrubbing away the blood.

Blood? What blood?

The substance on me wasn't red. It was faint brown with dark bits.

I was confused. What was it?

"It must be the ice cream," Michael said, stepping in behind me. "We fell asleep in it." He gently washed me all over.

"Ice cream? Oh, God." My laugh was ragged. I'd forgotten about the ice cream. "I thought it was the gunman's blood."

"It's not blood, sweetie." He kissed me. "Just choc

mint ice cream."

I started crying in relief and happiness. "Oh, God... oh, God." I collapsed against him as he encased me in his strong arms.

"It's okay, sweetie. I'm here...I'm here."

*****

"What time are you picking Dylan up today?" I asked Michael. We were lying out by the pool, and it was heading for lunchtime.

"About one or two this afternoon. I thought we could go on an adventure." His grin showed how enthusiastic he was about spending time with his son.

"What sort of adventure? A boy's own adventure," I teased, my fingers dipping into his belly button before winding their way through the furry nest on his lower abdomen, then sliding under the band of his shorts to secure the coveted possession they sought.

He grinned, grabbed my hand and kissed it. "No, no, no, you don't. Not necessarily. We could all do something." He waited for my reaction, knowing full well I'd wanted to stay away from prying eyes.

"How about you guys go swimming and stuff. Explore the rainforest here." I pointed to the green foliage around us. "You could find all sorts of things in there."

"Maybe we could get one of those sea ducky things and go for a ride." His tongue tickled my earlobe.

I giggled. "If we can get it out here in the cove, so it's just for us." I don't like deep water, so I wasn't keen on going out.

"I'll make the call," he said with a kiss before running off to call the manager.

At one-thirty Michael's ex knocked on our door.

"Dad," Dylan cried, flying into his father's arms.

"Hey, kiddo." He hugged him back tightly. "You get to stay with us now. Got your bag?"

"Yeah." Dylan pulled his suitcase into the room.

"Good, let's get you settled before going swimming." Michael turned to Marilee. "Thanks for bringing him. We'll see you Sunday."

"Okay. Bye, sweetie. I love you. See you Sunday."

"Love you, too, Mom, bye. Tahlia." He ran into my arms and squeezed.

"Hey, Dylan." I squeezed back. "How's my new stepson?"

"Good," he replied, looking at me. "Where are we going today?"

"Well, your dad and I decided that we'd head down to the beach, and you guys could snorkel and surf and stuff. Why don't you get changed and we'll go."

"Cool, okay."

Ten minutes later we were sitting under a beach umbrella on our towels.

"Okay, we just have to wait for the rubber ducky to get here, and then we'll go have some fun," Michael said. "Let's swim till it comes." He and Dylan ran down to the tropical blue water and dived into the crashing waves.

I watched them splash around for awhile before a boat came into the cove with the rubber ducky trailing behind it. It was a long raft of rubber tubes. Two on the bottom, and one on top for sitting on.

"It's here," I called, and we all stood by for the instructor. She showed us how to don our life vest, how to act when we fell off, and how to float while waiting to be picked up. I climbed into the boat while Michael sat behind Dylan on the ducky.

"You're not coming?" he asked.

"You guys have some fun first," I called. "I'll just sit here and watch."

"You sure?" He looked concerned.

I smiled at the love that radiated from his eyes. "I'm fine," I assured him. "Have fun." I waved as we took off. I really had a fear of deep water. If I can't see the bottom, I don't want to know. It just freaks me out, and so did being on that boat, sitting there hanging on for grim death to the rail as we zoomed back and forth across the cove. But, after an hour, I loaded myself up on pills and joined them. I was determined to put my fears aside for my new husband and stepson. So, sitting between them, I hung on for dear life. And I was so glad I did. Laughing like maniacs, falling into the water where Michael would fall in with me, to hold me and keep me calm till we were picked up. I was safe with him. And it was the best fun.

The boys snorkelled for the rest of the afternoon while I watched from the beach. And after a delicious dinner, we tucked a very worn out Dylan into bed.

"He's so adorable," I whispered in Michael's ear as he sat on the bed smoothing the blanket out.

"Yeah, he is." He grinned at me. We left without making a sound and plopped down on the sofa, catching the soft breeze as it floated in through the doors.

"Oh, God, what a day," I said in a hushed tone. "I feel like going to bed."

"Mmm," he growled sexily into my ear. "Now that's an idea."

"You cheeky shit," I said, slapping his arm.

"Oh, you wanna get physical." He grabbed at me, and I slapped him again before he chased me into the bedroom…

"No. No, you will not kill him. I will not let you kill anyone in this room."

"Like you have a choice," he said, laughing maniacally.

I fired my guns, the bullets penetrating his body. Unfortunately, they also penetrated the bomb strapped to his chest.

KABOOMMM…

I flew backwards, seeing my body melt off my bones into a million pieces.

"Nooooo," someone screamed.

I landed with a thud on the floor.

"Oh, my God, what the hell?" Michael flicked the lamp on and saw me lying on the floor grabbing at myself. "It's okay, baby, it's okay." He reached for me.

"No, no." I pushed his hands away and ran out to the pool, washing the sweat that poured from my body. I was so hot, I thought I was on fire, considering the dream and all.

Michael glided up behind me. "It's okay, baby, it's okay. I'm here."

I was racked with sobs, but cried silently, so I didn't

wake Dylan up and freak him out.

Michael turned me around and locked me in his arms.

I wound my arms around his neck, feeling his around my body. The strength that I felt was powerful, seeping into my soul. Calming me. Soothing me. I buried my face in his neck as I stopped sobbing. "I'm sorry. I'm sorry. They just won't go away."

"I know. It's okay." He rubbed my back in slow calming circles.

An urge overwhelmed me, and I needed my husband. "Michael," I whispered urgently, gazing into his eyes. "I want to, I need to. Now. I need you, please," I pleaded.

He looked toward the bungalow. "We can't in case Dylan sees."

"Well…" I looked around. "We'll grab a towel and go down to the beach."

Seeing the expression on my face and the need in my eyes, he nodded.

Silently stepping out of the pool, we grabbed a couple of towels that were lying over the lounge and ran down the path to the beach. We barely managed to lay them down before falling onto them in a frantic act of mating. Arms grabbing, legs entwining. We were like wild animals in need of each other. In need of our fix. We were like each other's drug, and we couldn't get enough. When we were done, we quietly slipped back into the bedroom and fell into a tangled sleep.

Chapter 20

Thursday was spent driving around the island. We hired a jeep through the hotel and saw the sights all day. I kept a big hat and huge sunnies on since I didn't want to be recognised. The papers and the news broadcasts were showing the story all over the place. But I just wanted to get away from it all.

Michael got around in a baseball cap and black glasses, and thankfully no one noticed him either. He was just another tourist visiting with his wife and son.

We spent time shopping, eating, buying Hawaiian shirts – á la Magnum PI – Michael making sure Dylan's matched his. I snapped photos of them pretending they were on the show, and even though I felt a bit crappy, I laughed.

We gorged on ice cream sundaes and watched the sunset before heading back to the hotel.

"That was nice," Dylan said, as he tucked himself into bed.

"What was?" Michael asked, ruffling his son's hair.

"Today. Shopping, hanging out. Stuff." He shrugged nonchalantly.

"Yeah, it was," Michael agreed, kissing him. "Get some sleep, and we'll do it all again tomorrow."

"Okay." He shifted down in the bed.

"Night, sweetie," I said, kissing his cheek.

"Night, Tahlia." He hugged me then slid back under the covers.

Michael turned off the light, and we closed the door behind us.

I sighed and walked out onto the porch, looking up at the moon so brilliantly shining down. I wondered why. *Why did it have to happen to me? Why was it me? Why did I have to be suffering the way I was?*

"You okay?" Michael asked, coming up behind me and resting his chin on my head.

"Physically, in pain. Emotionally, holding up. Mentally...definitely not. I'm losing my bloody marbles."

He turned me around to face him. "No, you're not. You just aren't dealing with what happened, and what you did. When the light bulb goes off in your head, and you finally get what you need to do, everything will fall into place."

I leaned against him, feeling his strength, hearing his heartbeat. "God, I hope so."

Bang. Bang. Bang.

Bang. Bang. Bang.

I fired my guns and kept firing, even when I fell to the ground. "Die, you bastards," I screamed. "Die and stay dead."

I sat bolt upright, dripping in sweat, throwing the sheet back.

"Tahlia, what's wrong now?" Michael mumbled.

"Shh," I said, rubbing his arm. "Go back to sleep. It's okay, you sleep." I watched him settle back in. I tied my hair up, threw on a summer robe, and wandered outside. Laying on a lounge, I gazed up at the moon. *I have got to get this out of my head. I have to. I can't let it control my life. My future. My life with my husband and his son. My stepson. Michael, my husband. The man waking up each night to support me after a nightmare.*

I scratched my arm where a mozzie had just bitten me. "You little shit." I slathered on some saliva then rubbed my arm, which was emitting a dull ache. I looked out at the ocean. The moonlight bounced off the waves as they rolled toward the shore. It reminded me of our bedroom at home. The bedroom Michael and I had christened our very first night together. I smiled at the memory. Together as a couple. Together in a new house. I listened to the sound of the waves. They were so calming, so soothing, so...peace...ful...

"Tahlia, Tahlia, wake up."

Something was poking me, and I turned my head to see what was annoyingly waking me.

"Tahlia, Tahlia. Are you awake?"

My eyes slowly opened and I saw two faces peering at me. "Hey...oh." My mind registered who they were. Michael and Dylan were leaning over me, waking me up. I blinked and looked around, seeing it was already broad daylight. "God, what time is it?" I sat up, rubbed my eyes, and yawned.

"Nine o'clock," Dylan said. "You want some juice?"

"Yes, please, sweetie," I said, swinging my legs around.

"Did you sleep here all night?" Michael helped me to my feet.

"I must've," I replied, accepting the glass of juice from Dylan.

We sat around the outdoor table and munched on some fruit.

"What do you want to do today?" I asked, popping a piece of apple into my mouth.

"Swimming," Dylan said

"Snorkelling," Michael said.

I rolled my eyes and shook my head. "How about you have the rubber ducky this morning, and then we'll take the tour boat out with the glass bottom so we can see the fish?"

"Cool," they both cried. Like father, like son.

So all morning I sat on the beach and watched them go back and forth on the duck. They fell off, got back on, and laughed like maniacs. After a nice lunch, we boarded the tour boat which took us up and down the coast. Through the glass bottom, we saw bright coloured fish, eels, coral and turtles. It was great. We got back to the bungalow about five and found Marilee waiting for us.

"Mom," Dylan cried, running into her arms.

"What does she want?" I muttered under my breath, exchanging a glance with Michael as we unlocked the front door.

"Hey, sweetie, how's my boy?" She hugged him fiercely.

"Good," he said. "We just came back from the boat with the glass bottom. We could see under the water. It was *sooo* cool."

"I'm glad you're having fun with your dad and Tahlia." She swept a strand of hair behind her ear.

We stood in the doorway, and I still wondered what she wanted.

"Ah, listen. Since you guys just got married, I thought maybe we could get together for a meal. So you and I can talk, and get to know each other," she said to me.

"Where?" I asked.

"How about the Aloha Dining Room up in the hotel. We've eaten there a few times, and it's great. Not too crowded and has some privacy."

I glanced at Michael, and he knew what I was thinking.

"I kinda wanted to stay out of the public eye after last week," I said.

"Oh, believe me, I get that, really, I do," she replied.

"After the gunmen with the bomb, you mean," Dylan piped up.

We looked at him in surprise.

"How do you know?" Michael asked, frowning.

"I told him," Marilee interrupted, stroking Dylan's head. "I figured he'd hear it soon enough, so I just told him the basics."

"Oh," Michael replied, still surprised. "I guess he needed to know then." He looked at Dylan and grasped his shoulders. "All you need to know is, that everyone is okay. Your mom and Jake, Tahlia and me, we are all okay. You still have all of us."

"Tahlia was there too." Dylan's eyes grew wide as he looked at me.

I smiled grimly. "Yeah, I was sweetie, and as your

dad said, we're all okay. Except for my arm." I glanced at it and rubbed it lightly.

"Whoa." His eyes grew wider still. "Then you know who saved you then. Do you know? Can you get her phone number 'cause I want to thank her for saving my mom and dad, and you and Jake?"

Now that shook me.

Michael, Marilee and I looked at each other. "Um," I mumbled. "I'm sure she knows how grateful everyone is. She must be dealing with a lot herself though, it might be tough on her."

"Why would it be?" Dylan continued. "She's a hero. She saved all those people's lives, and all of yours, and I want her to know how grateful I am that I still have my family."

Tears poured from my eyes, and my heart ached. I grabbed him and held on tightly. "She knows, sweetie, she knows."

"She's not the only one dealing with this, you know," Marilee said, and I looked at her. "We're all dealing with it," she went on. "That we could have died. Left our children as orphans. Was held up at gunpoint and almost bombed to death."

So much for telling Dylan the basics. I think he just learned a whole lot more than she had originally told him.

She brushed her tears away. "We're all dealing with each aspect of it. But we don't know what the woman who saved us is going through. She is a heroine, whether she wants to be or not. It's up to her to come to terms with what she did." Wiping her face, she laughed. "How about we meet at seven?"

I nodded. "That's fine."

"Okay. Bye, sweetie. I'll see you later," she said, shutting the door.

"Bye, Mom."

"Why don't we take a nap before dinner?" I asked. "We've been busy all day having fun, so let's rest before we go out again. Okay?"

"Okay." He started for his own bedroom.

"Uh, uh," I said. "This way." We went into the bedroom Michael and I had, and all piled onto the bed with Dylan in the middle. I set my alarm clock for six-thirty and we all snuggled up together.

A happy little family.

*****

We strode into the hotel's rich green, tropically decorated restaurant just before seven and looked around for Marilee and Jake.

"There." Dylan raced off, and we followed him over to the table.

"Hi," we all said at once and laughed.

"Dylan, come sit between your dad and me," Marilee said.

Michael was next to him, I was next to Michael, and Jake was on my left. His and Marilee's son sat in a high chair between them.

We chatted amongst ourselves while ordering, talking about what we'd been doing that week and how we were.

"That glass bottom boat and rubber ducky are *soooo* cool," Dylan enthused. "We've been out on it twice."

"I'm glad you've been having fun with your dad and Tahlia," Marilee said, running her hand through his hair.

I sighed and leaned over to Jake. "I'm starting to feel left out."

"Why's that?" he asked, a smile on his fair face.

"Well, I'm married to a man who has a son with his ex, who has a son with her new husband. We're all sitting together, and I'm the only one without a kid." I glanced from him to his son back to him. "So either we need to get married, have a kid, and get divorced, or," I turned to Michael, "my darling husband and I need to have a baby, 'cause I'm feeling very left out in this moment."

Michael snorted as he laughed and his hand squeezed mine.

"That would be cool," Dylan said. "Being a big brother again."

We all smiled at his enthusiastic face.

"Yeah, that would be cool," Michael agreed, looking from Dylan to me with a mushy look.

My hand squeezed back with my own mushy look. "Yeah, it would."

Our meals arrived and we dug in, enjoying the sumptuous seafood and salad. We were halfway through when I reached for my glass and noticed people here and there in the room were watching us.

"Uh, oh, we've been spotted," I muttered behind my glass.

Everyone looked up from their meals and glanced around.

"Oh, God," Marilee sighed. "That's what happens when you're on TV."

"Like now," I said, motioning to the huge screens around the room. "God knows why they've got those in here." We sat transfixed as the story was played over. Actors came on and had a say, even though we couldn't hear, the detective from the night, footage from all of us standing out on the road. Richard Sayer talking.

"I hope he didn't say anything," I mumbled.

There were pictures of the casts of TV shows, Michael's and Marilee's, plus a few others.

"That'll help people recognise us," Michael said, turning back to the table.

I sighed and closed my eyes. "Why are they still going over it?" I complained.

"Because it's still news," Jake said, scratching his blond head. "The woman who saved TNM is huge news. They want interviews, stories, photos, to talk to anyone who might know who she is." He looked at me. "They want to know the full story."

I rolled my eyes in disgust and picked up my fork.

We were just finishing when an older woman and her friend came over to our table.

"Oh, my, God," I barely mumbled.

"Oh...hello," she said. "We saw the news on TV and thought we recognised you." The four of us looked at each other. "We saw you were nearly finished and wondered if we could maybe get some autographs and photos?"

"I'll be happy to sign something for you," Michael said. "But no photos."

Disappointment rained down over her seventy-ish face. "Oh...okay."

While they were signing things, I sat drinking my cola. After all, *I* wasn't on TV, no need for me to sign anything.

"We've seen the papers all week and read every detail. Saw it on the news too." She patted her grey hairdo. "It must have been horrifying to go through that with a mad bomber—"

"Dylan, sweetie, why don't you go check out dessert," Marilee quickly cut in.

"Okay." He headed for the dessert bar.

"Please don't mention it in front of my son," she went on with a deadly look.

"Oh, dear no, I'm so sorry. I didn't realise. My mistake. It's just that it's so awful what happened. All of you on your knees, begging for mercy from the mad bomber."

"Begging for mercy," I repeated in amazement, looking from her to Michael. "Were you begging for mercy?"

He shook his head. "No, I wasn't. I was worried about getting out alive, so I could see my son and be with the woman I love."

"Same here," Jake added.

"Well, from what you can see, *no one* was begging for mercy." I wanted this woman to go away and take her polyester-clad friend with her.

"And what did *you* see, dear," she said coldly. "*You*

weren't there, so why would *you* know anything? *Who are you* anyway? *You're* not on any of the shows, so why would *you* have a say in this conversation. *You* weren't involved. *You're* a nobody."

Michael looked from the woman to me and saw the fire raging in my eyes. It was also raging around in my body. *A nobody?* Who the fuck did this old bag think she was, calling *ME* a nobody. The interruptive old hag had no idea what she was talking about, and yet here she was intruding on our dinner. My eyes narrowed, and I went in for the kill.

"*A nobody,*" I spat viciously in a low tone. "Who the hell do you think you are calling *me* a nobody?" She took a step back in shock at my demeanour. "I saw *everything* you rude old cow. *I* was there too, and *I, saw, it all.* Every little detail of what happened. I saw everyone on their knees with their hands on their heads praying to God for someone to save them. I saw the guards dead or unconscious on the floor. I saw the gunmen fall with bullets in their heads." I leaned forward in my seat and my voice got lower. "So don't bother to stand there and judge me when you have absolutely no freakin' idea who I am." I thrust a finger at her. "Because *I am not a nobody! I* am a woman. *I* am a human being. *And I* am married to Michael Anthony." That really shook her. Michael squeezed my hand as he glanced from her to me to her with an angry glare. She looked sick at the thought she'd just insulted his wife. *A big star's wife.* "So if you want to be a sour old cow, go somewhere else," I said icily. "You're not welcome here."

"Oh," she gasped, as everyone looked at me, small smiles trying to be hidden. She looked so frazzled she could've collapsed.

Like I cared!!!!!

"Oh." She patted her chest like she was having a heart attack, gasping for air, her friend rubbing her back trying to soothe her.

Still didn't care!!!!!

"No one has ever spoken to me that way before." She fanned herself with a hanky.

"First time for everything," I butted in, crossing my arms in defiance.

"Oh…you rude little girl," she hissed. "You obviously have no respect for your elders."

"Not if my elders are like you I don't!"

"Oh…oh…come on, Sylvia, we don't need to tolerate this." She started walking away.

"Neither do we," I called after her, then leaned back in my seat and took a long gulp of drink. "Rude old cow," I muttered.

So much for trying to get back good Karma.

Damn it!

Michael shook his head in amazement, shock, denial, and a few other things I couldn't read as he looked at me. "I haven't seen that fire in you since last week."

"What?" I asked, my eyes still narrowed from the visit with the old bag.

"That fire. The passion. Is it back? Is the old Tahlia back?"

I thought for a moment. "Yeah, maybe she is, in a new sense." A few things popped into my head as

Dylan sat down with a huge bowl of ice cream topped with all sorts of things.

"That lady didn't seem very happy when she left. She looked sick," he said, picking up his spoon.

"Well, she was kinda rude, and Tahlia put her in her place," his mum said.

"You know what?" I said. "I've just come up with a few things, so you guys go ahead and have dessert." I stood and kissed Michael. "I'll be back soon."

"Where are you going?" Michael asked with a smile, grabbing my hand as it slid between his.

"Oh, somewhere," I replied with a touch of mystery and walked out the door. I was on my way to our bungalow when I stopped and back-tracked to the manager's office. I knocked.

"Come in."

Opening the door, I walked in. "Do you have a minute? I want to organise something."

"Of course, come in."

I sat down at his desk and told him what I wanted to do for the next day.

He spent a few minutes on his computer and then gave me a card. "All done."

"Really? That was quick."

"Really. Enjoy your tour tomorrow, Mrs Anthony."

"Thank you, so much," I said, and walked down to my bungalow. Finding my phone, I called Sin. "Where are you?"

"Home."

"Get down to L.A. tomorrow. I'll need you next week. Get every paper you can, I'll need to read what they've been saying about me. Get Richard Manning to my house on Sunday about twelve. I'll also need to know what's going on with the case. Am I being arrested?"

"Are you kidding? Richard spoke to the Governor of California, *and* the President of the United States. *The President* for Christ's sake. There is *no way* you'll be arrested for what happened. You're the woman who saved America's biggest network."

I sighed. "Yeah, whatever. Look, just have Richard there on Sunday. I'll call before we fly home. See you then."

My next call was to Richard Sayer. "*What the hell has everyone been in the media for?*" I asked angrily. "In the papers, the news. Even you, I saw tonight. You'd better not have mentioned my name."

"Tahlia, no I haven't. I've completely kept you out of it. But everyone wants to know who you are. What you did, everything about you."

"That's what Sin just said."

"Well, she's right. Everyone's fighting for the first interview with the woman—"

"Don't say it," I warned.

"Who saved the world."

"Oh, dear God," I yelled, fed up to the eyeballs. "*I hardly saved the world.*" I sighed in despair then rushed on. "Look. I'll do a speech, but I will *not* do any interviews. How many reporters and cameramen can you fit into one room?"

"Hundreds, if not thousands."

"We'll be home Sunday. I'll do the speech in the

afternoon. That gives you time to let everyone know that the woman who saved TNM will be ready for the cameras. *Do not* mention my name. Be at my house at twelve on Sunday. We'll go over it then."

"All right, see you then."

I raced back to the restaurant and kissed Michael's head. "Have I got plans for you."

His face lit up and he kissed me back. "Ohhh, really."

"Really." I flashed a grin and looked around the table and noticed someone had gone. "Where's Dylan?"

"He's playing with some kids outside," Marilee said, pointing out the window behind me. I turned and saw Dylan running around playing chasy.

"Oh, good, listen." I turned back to them. "I've decided on something." I reached for Michael's hand. "And it will, *might* affect us. But I hope it doesn't."

He frowned his thick brows in worry. "What did you do?"

I sighed and licked my lips. "I phoned Richard Sayer and told him to set up a news conference. I'm going to admit what I did."

"What!" all three of them exclaimed, astounded, shocked and dismayed.

I put my hand up to stop the barrage of questions that followed. "Look. I won't be doing an interview, even though every Jay, Dave and Conan, and Ellen, Oprah and Barbara wants me apparently. I'm just going to give a speech and answer the questions they all want to know. I won't be taking questions from them either but answering the ones in the papers. I'm hoping it won't take long, and I won't be giving any more afterwards. Which means since it will be on every news bulletin, we should tell Dylan. So he's prepared when he sees his friends. Otherwise, they'll tell him all sorts of things."

"But...we..." Marilee stumbled, confusion in her green eyes.

"I wondered what the fire in your eyes was about," Michael said, his thumb stroking my hand as he held it. He was leaning on the table, his head in his other hand. "That old broad got you going."

"Oh, she certainly did, and I *am not* a nobody!"

"No, you aren't. *You* are my wife." He smiled brightly for the world to see.

I smiled back. I always felt good when he smiled and felt happy just looking at him. "We need to tell Dylan."

Marilee sighed. "I don't know, I suppose we should, I've already mentioned some stuff..." With a look between her and Michael, they agreed.

We collected Dylan and walked back to our bungalow. Going into the lounge room, I told him to sit. "We need to talk to you."

"Okay." He flopped onto the sofa. Marilee sat to his left, Michael and I to his right. Jake sat on the chair opposite with his son.

I started. "Remember what you said to your mum, dad and me about wanting to thank the woman who saved us? That you're grateful, she did?"

"Yeah." His eyes were identical to Marilee's, and it was a bit weird seeing them side by side. They were also full of something that resembled fear and unknowing.

"Well...you did," I said.

He frowned, now confused. "What do you mean?"

"Well," Michael said. "You know how all of us were there that night?"

"Yeah." He looked at his father.

"Well, we know who saved us. And so do you," Michael went on.

Surprise fell over his face, and he looked even more confused. Poor bugger! "I know her?" His brow furrowed.

"Yes, sweetie," his mum said, brushing aside his hair. "The ah, woman who saved us...was...is, Tahlia."

Dylan's head swivelled around to look at me. "What?" Now he was really confused.

"It's Tahlia who saved us, by killing the bad men," Michael said, squeezing his son's hand.

"But there was a bomb too," Dylan said slowly, his wide eyes taking me in.

"Yeah, there was," Michael continued and licked his lips, "Ah, Tahlia and I got that out of the building."

"You?" He looked at his father. "You're a hero too?" He dove into his arms and hugged him tightly.

"Ah," Michael laughed and hugged him back. "No, Tahlia's the hero."

"No, don't say that," I mumbled. "Really!"

"But you are," Dylan cried, flying into my lap. "You saved my mom and dad." I held him for a few minutes, rocking back and forth before he sat up. "You're my hero. 'Cause you saved my family."

My face crumpled up, and tears started rolling down my face. "You're making me cry," I sniffled, kissing him before he sat back. "Now, look," I went on. "I'm ah, gonna do a little speech for TV on Sunday afternoon when we get home, so you need to know all of this before, in case all your friends start saying things. Okay?"

"Okay," he said, staring me in the eye.

"Okay." I ruffled his brown hair and pinched his cheek. "You're such a great kid, Dylan. I am *so proud* to be your stepmother."

"I'm glad you're my stepmother too," he said, throwing his arms around my neck and hugging me. I hugged back and held him as close as possible.

Awww!

"Are you okay with this, sweetie?" Marilee asked.

He pulled back and settled into his seat again. "Yeah," he said, looking at her.

"Okay, then. We'll go and let you spend the last day with your dad and Tahlia. And we'll see you on Sunday when we go home."

"Okay."

"Have you got your tickets for your flight?" I asked, having an idea.

"Yeah, they were return," Jake said, standing with his son.

"Why don't you chuck 'em in and fly home with us on the network's private jet?"

"What?" they all said.

I looked at Michael. "That's all right, isn't it? You'll get to spend more time with Dylan."

"Oh, yeah." He caught on, and a huge grin spread over his face. "That's fine with me."

Marilee and Jake conferred for a moment. "Okay, then, it's fine by us. Thanks for inviting us to come along."

"Great then. See you Sunday." I shooed them out.

Dylan hugged me. "I'm glad you're my stepmom. Thank you for saving my mom and dad."

I kissed his head and held on tightly. "You're welcome, sweetie. It's late, how about we head to bed 'cause I got plans for you and your dad tomorrow."

"Ohhh, really?" Michael said, getting excited.

"Yep," I replied, then looked at Dylan. "Time for bed."

After tucking him in and changing, Michael and I snuggled in our own bed, enjoying the cool summer breeze floating through the open doors.

"So, your attitude has changed then," Michael said, his lips on my forehead, his fingers tracing lines on my shoulder.

"Which attitude? Changed how?"

"You've been calling yourself a killer all week. Wanting to forget. Having bad dreams. Now, suddenly, after the old woman has a go at you, you come alive again." He moved his head to look into my eyes. "Have you really changed?"

"No," I said with a sigh. My head was lying on his hairy chest and I heard his heart beat slowly in my ear. "I'm still a killer and don't see myself as a hero. But...maybe I need to say something." I rubbed my cheek around in his furry nest.

"What?" He caressed my back.

"I've been selfish."

"What?" He moved me so he could look into my eyes. "How have you been selfish?"

I sat up against him and pulled the sheet around me. "Just worrying about myself all week. *My* feelings, *my* nightmares. Then Marilee said what she said this afternoon, and Dylan, then that woman. It's just all been about me." I stroked his face and kissed him. "I haven't even thought about what it might be doing to you. You were in that room, wondering where I was and if you'd ever see Dylan again." I pushed my hair back and glanced around. "*I get* that everyone went through hell and that they see me as a hero. But I'm a killer. And *they* don't *get that.*"

"I get it." His finger gently turned my face to his. "*I* get that *you're* going through hell because you've killed three men. We all go on about how you saved the lives of three thousand people, but all you see is that you killed three men. You're not dealing with that, and I've seen it every night when you jolt awake from your nightmares. I see it when we make love, that it's fast and needy. I get that 'cause I need it too. I need to know that *I'm* alive, and you're alive, and we're actually here together as husband and wife. I need you. I know you need me." He brushed my hair aside. "And I need to be with you, close to you, as far inside you as I can be, making love to you, loving you, needing you, wanting you."

I kissed him hard. "I need all of that, too."

So with all of that need and want, we joined. And

when I jolted out of my nightmares hours later, I saw my surroundings and knew I was okay. They hadn't been as bad as previous nights because in Michael's arms I was safe.

*****

"Okay, you two," I said over breakfast the next morning. "Get your matching Hawaiian shirts and shorts on, we're going on a day trip."

"Oooh," Michael cooed while Dylan clapped. "A day trip."

"Yup, so get changed 'cause we're about to leave." I gathered my things while they changed. Big bag full of sunscreen, camera, bits and pieces. My big floppy hat and sunnies to hide behind. I was wearing a blue sundress over my bathers and had sandals on. "Okay, let's go."

Michael barged into the room and out the front door.

"Aren't you forgetting something?" I called.

"I'm coming," Dylan yelled, running out of his own room and after his father.

I laughed and locked the door, then we walked up the path to the hotel, meeting the manager at the entrance.

"Here's your key, Mr Anthony," he said, dropping it into Michael's hand.

"My key for what?" Michael asked, curiosity flaring as he looked back and forth between us.

"Your Ferrari, sir." The manager pointed behind us, and we turned.

"Oh, my, God!" Michael exclaimed. "Thomas Magnum's

Ferrari! Oh, my, God." He and Dylan stood drooling over the shiny red car before them.

"Do you have all the details, Mrs Anthony?"

Shaking my head in amusement, I glanced at the manager. "Yes, I do, thank you."

"Then enjoy your day."

"Oh, we will," I said, shaking my head again. Michael was stroking the car's hood, talking to it like it was his baby. "All right, you two, get in. We are going out for the day."

"All right." They high-fived each other and climbed in.

Michael gunned the car, and we sped off into the distance. We toured the places Magnum had been filmed and sped along the same highway he did, had a picnic lunch at the beach, and swam with some dolphins late into the afternoon.

It was a great day. So perfect.

Michael, Dylan, me. A happy little family enjoying their Hawaiian holiday. Finally, I was relaxed and happy. Contented with myself and my lot in life, and working on getting my extremely bad Karma back into good shape again. I had Michael for my husband and Dylan for my stepson. Damn, I was one lucky gal.

When my nightmare started that night and jolted me awake, I knew I was safe. I was happy, and I was with the man I love.

Chapter 21

After an uneventful flight, we arrived back at home to find Sin, Richard Manning, and Richard Sayer in the house.

"Okay, Richard," I said to my CO. "How's the sales been going this week?"

"Great," he said. "Almost half of everything has sold. Some designs more than others. Everything has been going fantastically."

"Well, it won't be fantastic tomorrow," I told him. "Sin, where's the papers and tabloids? I need to know what's been written." I led everyone into my studio so we could use the design tables for space.

"Spread out on the tables."

I saw the mile-high piles then turned to Richard. "I do not want the cover on the sign to come down till eight-thirty tomorrow morning. Prepare *everyone* for the onslaught to come, and have Thandie set up an automated reply recording for the phone calls. I don't expect her to answer all of them, and that way I can listen to them later and decide who to call back, if any."

"I'll get on that today," he said, making notes in a

small notepad.

"Also, get press kits printed up in bulk. Once they know who I am, they'll track down the office. Be prepared. Get everyone in today to help," I told him.

"We'll do that for the morning," he replied.

"One more thing," I said, looking at him. "*Do not*, I repeat, *do not* speak on behalf of me, or my company. If you have to say anything, tell them who you are and what you do, but it's not your place to be giving statements about your boss and her company. Get on that now, and be at the office at eight to unveil the sign at eight-thirty."

"I'm on my way." He nodded and left to do his job.

I flicked through the paper on top of the pile in front of me. Sin had stacked another ten or so piles on the table. "Are we in *all* of them?" I glanced from Sin to Richard Sayer.

"We are, I am, you are," Richard said. "The story will not go away."

"It's only been a week," Michael said. "The story's still very fresh in everyone's minds, not to mention the fact that everyone who's anyone on TNM, plus the CEO and heads of departments were there. This," he flourished a paper whose headline read, *Hero of the Century,* "is a huge story. *You're* a huge story," he said to me. "Everyone believes you're a hero."

I shook my head and rubbed my forehead. "I'm not, and I still don't see it that way."

"How *do* you see it?" Richard asked, looking concerned. He'd been having a hard time himself and looked a little older.

"Probably worse than you," I said. "You don't look too good."

He shook his head. "With Marnie and me it's been hell. Standing there in front of a gunman with a bomb, believing we were about to die. You're a hero, you really are." He put up his hand to stop my protest. "Deny it all you like, but you saved *thousands* of people who got to go home to their families."

"You don't get it, do you," I butted in. "*I get,* that everyone thinks I'm a hero, and I saved their lives from the big bad bomber." My shoulder sagged. "But *I* killed three men. Plain and simple. The only other person in that room was Michael. It was him I was saving. *I* killed three men." Michael slid his arm around me. "That is something I will have to live with for the rest of my life." I looked at Richard and Sin. "I'll have to live with being a *killer* for the rest of my life. Regardless of how many people it saved."

"Will you see someone?" Richard asked, finally realising how hard it was for me.

I shrugged, and a sigh escaped me. "Maybe, if I can keep it out of the public eye." I remembered I didn't have the answer to the one question that needed an ending. I zeroed in on Richard. "Exactly *why* did they come for Marnie, and exactly *how* did they get in to shoot all those guards and hold everyone up?" I wanted to know why everyone had to go through hell because of something that hadn't been answered.

He shook his head and spread his hands. "I'm still not exactly sure. The bomber mentioned something that was supposed to have happened a long time ago, or I did something to him. He rambled on and on without really saying anything. The only reason I can come up with is that I did something to him that he didn't like, and he decided to pay me back by kidnapping my wife and making me pay. When that didn't work, because you stopped it, he got insanely angry and decided payback was going to be a bitch."

"What about shooting the place up and the bomb? He *got serious*." I still had the memory of being shot, and it was one I didn't want. I rubbed my arm at the thought.

He sat down and let out a deep sigh. "I don't know. He said I needed to take it seriously, so he brought out the big guns. He must have thought that a bomb would scare me quick enough to hand over my wife, so all those people didn't die. He was almost right." He rubbed his forehead and looked up at me with a sad expression. "I almost handed her over just so we didn't. Is that selfish of me?"

"No," I replied. "It was a matter of keeping the majority alive." I rubbed my arm and stretched my back. "As much as that sucks, and God knows what would have happened to Marnie." My gaze flicked back and forth between their sad faces. "At least we're alive." I picked up a paper. "Sin, you call the hairdresser and make-up artist, and I'll get into these."

"Sure."

"Oh, and Richard, is the car ready to take us and bring us back without anyone seeing us?"

"Ready to go, and I even have decoy cars waiting to block the paparazzi."

I raised a brow in amusement. "Now, that's very James Bond of you."

A smile lit up his face. "What can I say? I owe you for the rest of my life. Anytime you need anything, just call. How was Hawaii?"

"Fantastic," Michael and I said together with huge grins on our faces.

It was twelve-thirty, and for the next two hours, I read every column, story, and tidbit in every paper. I made notes of the questions they were asking, and what they wanted to know, and got annoyed at the idiotic things they claimed. The hair and make-up artists made me presentable. Pink pants, a pink and gold blouse, some appropriate bling, and I was ready.

Michael had changed into a nice black suit and pink shirt, and Sin styled herself as well.

Cruising along in the limo toward town, we chatted while I worked on a speech. Well, it wasn't really a speech, I just wanted notes to play off of. "How's Marnie?" I asked Richard. "I didn't ask before."

"Holding up," he said, as we pulled into an underground car park to stay out of the paps' eyes. "She's just glad it was you who saved us."

We stepped out of the car, and I noticed guards placed around the place. "For our protection?" I asked dryly. "Didn't do much good last week."

Ouch!

Travelling up in the lift, I told Richard to keep my name out of his speech.

"I haven't put it in. Here, take a look." He slid the paper from his blazer pocket and handed it to me.

I quickly read it before handing it back. "No mention of my name, my business. Good job."

The doors opened to a carpet lined hallway with five more guards waiting to meet us. "This way," one said and led us around a corner, then through a door into a backstage area.

"Richard." A woman I didn't recognise came over to us. "You go on in ten minutes. All the world's press is here and chomping at the bit." She noticed Sin, Michael and me. "Ah, which one of you is the hero?"

"For God's sake! Could people stop saying that," I demanded. "I'm sick of hearing it."

Everyone looked at me and saw a woman in a bad mood with a deep frown on her face who was adjusting her clothes. "Seriously people." I looked at them. "Can you just stop. I don't want to be known as the woman who saved the world. I just want to get on with my life the way I want to get on with it, with a decent amount of privacy."

"Tahlia still needs time to adapt," Richard said.

"Don't speak for me," I spat at him with an angry glare. "I'm an adult. I don't need to damn well do anything if I don't want to." I crossed my arms in defiance.

Still need to work on my delightful personality, I see!

Did someone say...Karma?

Talk about having lessons to learn. I had loads!!!

I know, I suck!!! Especially bad at the moment. Yes, I know I need to pull my head out and re-evaluate my life. The world was not out to get me, even though I thought it was. Although getting sliced, diced and almost blown up definitely made me *think it was*. And I needed to work not only on my personality, but my self-respect, self-dignity and my Karma. 'Cause the bank was runnin' *real low* on that. In fact, I was wondering if it was scraping the bottom of the Karmic barrel. There seemed to be none there, and I *really* needed to get some back.

Obviously wanting to calm the situation down, Michael kissed my cheek gently. "I'm here for you if you want me to come on stage with you."

I softened; how could I not. "Maybe at the end. You'll know when. And we'll give them a photo shoot."

His grin was huge. "Glad I wore this suit then."

I brushed it down. "Mmm, so am I. Is that the one you wore at our wedding?"

"Certainly is."

"Mmm," I muttered again. "Then I can't wait to get you out of it again."

"All right, you two. Richard, one minute, take your place." The woman stepped out onto the stage to address the audience.

He stood at the top of the stairs at the back of the stage. Huge black curtains meant no one could see us. We walked over to the stairs and waited.

"Everyone. Please welcome TNM CEO, Richard Sayer."

We heard what sounded like a million flashes going off as Richard stepped onto the stage and up to the podium.

"Ladies and gentlemen of the world's press. You are here today to hear an important speech. Last week, as you all know, the TNM network party was held up by three gunmen. One of them had a bomb. Just when we had all lost hope, believing we were going to die, a young woman came barrelling into the room and killed them. She got the bomb off the bomber, and with God on her side, ran it out of there, saving us all." More flashing.

I rolled my eyes backstage. "I noticed he forgot to mention you ran out with me and threw the bomb into the lake," I said to Michael just as my nerves kicked into full gear.

"This woman is someone I know personally. As this was not the first time she had saved my, or my wife's, life. This young woman rescued me from the side of the road when my car and cell had died. This young woman then saved my wife from her deadly car explosion and attempted kidnapping. And now, she has saved us again, from the deadly bombers and kidnappers who wanted to take my precious wife away from me. This young woman saved three thousand people. She saved TNM. She saved the lives of people whose families are thankful and grateful. So, what she did, affects more lives than the three thousand people in that room. Basically, this young woman saved the world."

"Oh, for God's sake," I said, backstage. "What the hell does he think he's doing?"

"Today, I stand before you, incredibly thankful and grateful to the young woman I am blessed to introduce.

She moved here from Australia less than ten weeks ago to start a new adventure. A new life. A new business which is doing very well. To publish her first novel. To meet and marry the man of her dreams." Michael and I kissed. "And yet, this young woman has done so much more. Please, welcome this young woman to the stage."

With a comforting squeeze from Michael, I walked up the stairs and onto the stage to applause and snapping cameras. Richard kissed my cheek and left me to face the sea of people alone. Several started calling out questions, and I put my hand up to stop them.

"I won't be answering any questions today. You have already asked them in the papers and tabloids, on the news and radio. So, I'll answer those instead." My eyes roamed the people before me. They were from everywhere. And I *mean* everywhere. I blinked at the brightness of the flashes, took a deep breath, and tried not to throw up.

"All week you have covered this story, and I have seen what you've written, asking a million questions. Wanting to know who I am? What I do? Where I'm from? Well, Richard already covered that one. I'm from Australia, and I moved here to start up my business and publish my first novel. Now, some of you may then think, well she only did it for the publicity so her business would do better. You'd be wrong. Richard didn't mention my company name. *I* haven't. Because what I did was not for publicity." I looked around. "It was to save the man I love." Flashes went off in my face, blinding me once again.

"I was at the party as a thank you from Richard for saving his wife, now you know that. So, I just happened to be there at the time they needed me. It wasn't the right time or place. I just believed God, the Universe, or whatever you want to call it, had me in the position when he needed me to help. And for those wondering, no, I'm not a religious person. I'm also not a cop, detective or guard, for those with that question. When I knew I would be moving here to L.A., I started martial arts and weapons training classes. I wanted and needed to be prepared for living in California. I've continued those classes since being here, and I'm glad I did. They held me in good stead for saving Marnie's life, and then everyone else's. So, I knew how to handle a gun, and I knew how to handle someone *with* a gun. Lucky me," I said sarcastically. "I got to kill three men. Because *that's* what I did. Some of you have said, 'but you're a hero now, what does it feel like to be a hero.' And the answer is, I don't know. Because I am not a hero. Which is ironic considering the type of people I consider to be heroes. They're the kind who run into burning buildings to save a woman or child. Would dive into the ocean to save a drowning man, or jump into a raging river to pull someone out. To me, cops, fireys and ambos, you call them paramedics, aren't heroes because they're trained to do those things." I put my hand up at the tittering in the crowd. "Don't bother having a go at me because you disagree. It's my right to think what I want."

My eyes took it all in. "But I am not a hero, by my own definition. 'You are,' you say, but I don't believe it. I saved three thousand people, and you're carrying on about that. But how many guards died that night? *Their* families are affected. The families of the gunmen are affected. But you don't care." I shrugged. "Nope, none of you give a damn because you still see me as the woman who saved TNM, and all the actors on the network. So, that automatically makes me a hero. Well, I'm not. I am not a hero. *I am* a killer. A murderer. A woman who killed three men. Put bullets into their skulls and saw their brains splatter everywhere. I am a killer. And I have to live with what I did for the rest of my life. I don't know if I'll ever accept it, or deal with it. How does one accept killing three men, even if it's for the greater good? I'll leave that up to the politicians."

That drew oohs and ahhs from the crowd. "I will *never* see myself as a hero. I get, that all of you will, and do, see me as a hero and that you're all thankful and grateful. That I saved you and you're alive. But have any of you, even thought, for *one* moment, how *I* feel? No. I highly doubt it. So, I don't know what it feels like to be a hero. But I do know what it feels like to be a killer. And to the families of the guards, I am sorry you have lost your sons, brothers, husbands, fathers. They did not deserve what happened to them."

My head moved from left to right, my eyes scanning the crowd. "There are more important things in this world, and stories to cover, than you sitting here looking at me. I just want to go about my life, waking up in the morning, kissing and waving my husband off to work. Thanking God that we have another day together. Go off to my office to write and design, then welcome my husband home. I don't want to talk about it at this time. And don't know if I ever will. That's why you're all here. To get the story together. So, don't expect to see me on Sixty Minutes, or with Barbara Walters, 'cause it won't be happening. If it comes up in conversations, that's one thing. But I won't be sitting down specifically to talk about it in detail. So, don't expect the scoop. And don't think you can throw all the money in the world at me because that won't work either. 'But everyone has their price,' you say."

I shook my head in disgust at the people before me. "Nope, not this girl. You can't buy me. You can't buy my story. Because it, and I, ain't for sale. But then in which case, you'll probably make up something like you all do." I glanced around. "Oh, please, don't be so shocked. We all know the tabloids, magazines, and gossip shows make everything up. If a celeb is friends with another celeb, or they've just met, and there's a photo of them, you've got them having it off, getting engaged, getting married, having a baby, getting divorced, cheating on each other. Not to mention whenever an actress or singer actually *eats* something, you've got her fat, or pregnant, with twins no less, but then the week after that you tell us about the hot new diet she went on to become anorexic."

I looked at them, still disgusted. "I mean *seriously*

people, I hate you so much for that. Lying week after week about celebrities just to make a story for that night's news, or that week's rag. You people make me sick. So, I'd better not find *any of you* writing *anything* other than the truth. I do not want to see you climbing over my fence. I do not want to read about how I'm having an affair. *I will not*, and I will repeat it, *will not* tolerate you people bullshitting about me. I will sue your arse off if you do." That shocked them. "As for hounding me to write a book about this, forget it. I don't know if I ever would. And if I did, I'd publish it myself."

I took a deep breath and glanced around. Time to start winding this up. "You all came here today to find out who I am and what I do." I paused. "I'm a designer of fashion, jewellery and accessories. In fact, I designed the gown Marnie Wilkins was wearing that night. I run my own office and factory, making the clothes from American made material, sewn by American people. One hundred percent American. Even though I'm one hundred percent Australian." That made them laugh. "I'm the author of an erotic romantic suspense thriller which is available now from my company." More laughs. "I am a woman. I am a wife and partner to the most incredibly gorgeous man and stepmother to his incredibly adorable son. I am a resident of The United States of America but am still very much Australian. I am proud to be living here and am proud to be a wife and stepmother. I am grateful and thankful to God, that I was able to do something useful, and that I have another day, every day, to live, and run my company, and be with my husband and family.”

I breathed deeply again, glancing around the room. Definitely time to finish. “I've had enough now. It's time to go home, and I don't want to be hounded or chased down the street. So, please, please, just let me get on with my life.” I took a step away from the podium then moved back. “But I will leave you with one more tidbit of information that you're all dying to know, so shh,” I put my finger over my lips that were smiling slyly, “don't tell anyone.” They laughed and leaned toward me eagerly with their microphones, waiting to hear what I was going to tell them.

Breathing calmly and evenly, I slowly gazed at everyone. Standing straight and proud, I spoke. “I...am Tahlia Cameron. I...am Jem Stars, and I...am Mrs Michael Anthony.”

Epilogue

5 months later

Wow, so much has happened since that press conference. It was absolutely unbelievable. They all went wild, like a pack of frenzied animals. Especially when Michael walked onto the stage after I said, "I am Mrs Michael Anthony." He strode out oozing with confidence and took me lovingly into his arms with a kiss. We stood there smiling like two in-love idiots while they snapped away. Then I told him I wanted to go home and we left via the backstage area with Sin. We took Richard's limo back home, and Sin went to Michael's old house to spend the night. We've done it up in the last five months, with more theme rooms for entertaining. And we've had a couple of parties there as well. It's been great.

The story was all over the news that night, and the next morning the press besieged my poor staff at the office. They unveiled the sign, and the press went nuts. We had to keep the doors locked for weeks. It did help our sales though. We kept three shifts going and made thousands more t-shirts and jeans. Plus, the bags and hats were redone a hundred times. We've done more designs since, deciding to change them over every two months to something new, so there have been three sets of designs so far, and about to be a fourth.

Sin settled my lawsuit with Margaret Daly-Tomes. The English bitch was suing me, but when a judge saw what she did, and then realised who I was, he made her pay me five hundred thousand dollars. Plus, one hundred thousand to the store for the china vase she broke. Sin also managed to get ten thousand dollars from the gun range for me, since they were in the wrong. I donated both cheques to a women's foundation.

Then came Michael's forty-third birthday in July. Yes, that's right, my old man is old. I surprised him by setting up a movie-themed party for him, since he loves movies, and he went as Steve McQueen, as he loves Steve McQueen. I went as Scarlet O'Hara in her robe – from the scene where she goes downstairs in the middle of the night to find a drunken Rhett wallowing in his crap. She teases and torments him then walks off to go upstairs, but he runs after her and carries her up to bed. The next morning she's smiling and humming away. Well, we ALL know what happened *that* night – and after Michael's party, we went off and recreated that scene for ourselves. Many times over!!!!!

I also talked to Mr Bellisario about the remake of Magnum. Since Michael's already on a well-established TV show, he said he'd put serious thought into it. I was behind Mikey all the way, and am still pushing for him to be the new hairy Magnum.

My erotic romantic suspense thriller has sold well, needing several reprints. And to date, we've sold one and a half million copies, and I'm working on the prequel and sequel. It was on the bestsellers list for two months before it was knocked off. But with a resurgence, it came back and is still in the top ten. I'm also still writing that Nancy Drew book, so we'll see how I go with that. Publishers have been hounding me to write a book about what happened to me, and I keep turning them down. I don't know if I want to write one yet, as I'm still dealing with it all. But I'll tell you this, that night after the press conference when my nightmares came along, I didn't even wake up. Because I knew I was safe and sound with the man I love. And, I had won!

My gowns have appeared on several TNM soaps, and the world is in love with them. I'm designing for many women who want an original to wear to the latest function or fundraiser. It was all thanks to me mentioning during the press conference that Marnie wore my dress that night. Considering there were millions of pictures of it, the whole world got to see it.

Of course, now that my gowns are famous, Margaret Daly-Tomes keeps harassing me to design one for her. She *can't bear* the thought of not having an original gown to call her very own. Never mind the fact that she smashed a vase over my head and had to pay me half a million dollars for it. And she's completely forgotten that it even happened, or that she hates my guts, or that she has been nothing but a complete and utter bitch to me, or that I may hate *her* guts with an absolute passion. But she seems to think that I'm her new best friend, and the *bloody gall* of that woman completely and utterly astounds me and blows my mind!

And yes, I've been working on that amazingly bad Karma of mine. Realising I need to get back to the way I was *before* striking it rich. Being nice, but keeping an assertive edge, and *not* ripping into everyone every time they speak to me. Or thinking they were out to get me.

Summer was hot, but now autumn, that's fall to some, has been nice. Michael and Dylan took me on my first Halloween trick-or-treat, and do I need to say, we got sick on all the candy. But it was nice for our first family Halloween. Now, it's November, the air is getting chilly, the new designs are about to roll out, and Thanksgiving is on its way. Michael and I have *a lot* to be thankful for. We're both alive and are parents to Dylan. And I just have a little something special to tell the man I love...

Many interviewers have been hounding me for a scoop, and I've said no. One show even offered to preview my new designs, have a chat about life, love, and being the most successful fashion designer with the hottest, hippest, fastest rising label and company of all time. I would be crazy to say no to publicity like that. Especially the worldwide publicity *that* show would give me. All because I received a call. *The call.* The call that would change my life. *Again.* So...how could I refuse?

"Hello...Tahlia. This is Oprah Winfrey."

About the Author

L.J. has been writing since 2006, when her first of many novels, ***The Road To Vegas,*** was born. In 2016 she created the ***Porn Star Brothers*** series about three sizzlingly hot Australian born Greek Island raised brothers who became the hottest porn stars in '70s America.

L.J. lives in Australia, loves '80s music, disaster movies, and collecting Jackie Collins books as Jackie is her inspiration and mentor.

*L.J. **Diva*** is the adult pen name for author Tiara King. You can find more about Tiara on her website; follow her on social media, or visit her publishing house, Royal Star Publishing.

Socials

tiaraking.com.au/ljdiva

royalstarpublishing.com.au

Sign up for *Tiara's* Newsletter…

Make sure you're always in the know and never miss free exclusives, the latest news, book updates, and so much more with newsletters from…

tiaraking.com.au

Have you read these?

THE PORN STAR BROTHERS SERIES

Porn Star Brothers
Forever
Love Never Dies
Stefan: The New Generation
DeLuca
Spiros & Jenny
And Always

THE ILLICIT THINGS SERIES

Her
Him
Madam X

A NOVEL INVESTIGATION SERIES

Deigns in Crime
A Killer Plot
Murder on the Set
A Novel Investigation (omnibus)

Or these?

NOVELS

Burning Desires
Anything for You
Falling for London
The Road to Vegas
Hollywood Dreams
The Billionaire's Dirty Little Secret

SHORT STORIES

The Body
The Perfect Plot
The Star of Your Own Crime Scene